Unseen Wrath

Also by Morgan Spring-Glace:

The War of the Mountains

       The Witches of Serna

       Unseen Wrath

       Winter Fever (Autumn 2026)

       The All-Consuming Flame (Autumn 2027)

www.morganspringglace.com

https://www.instagram.com/morgan_springglace/

https://linktr.ee/morgan.springglace

Unseen Wrath
Book II of the
War of the Mountains

Morgan Spring-Glace

ISBN 979-8-9914481-3-0 (paperback)
ISBN 979-8-9914481-2-3 (e-book)

Cover Design: Sam Kipp and Morgan Spring-Glace
Formatting: Morgan Spring-Glace
Editing: Sam Kipp and Morgan Spring-Glace
Maps by: Luke Bauer and Morgan Spring-Glace
Illustrations: Morgan Spring-Glace
Calligraphy by Esther Wong

www.morganspringglace.com

Acknowledgements

To Jade and Tom, my two test readers that have been with me from the beginning.

Likewise, to Amanda and Dale, who took the plunge with me on book one.

To my Mother, Sandra Spring, who has coached me through this and been a champion for me.

To Luke Bauer, who continues to turn my crude drawings of land into such depictions as you shall see herein. He is every bit as much of an explorer of unreal lands as he is a mapmaker.

To Samantha Kipp, my editor, who has been pivotal in getting things on track, being timely, and overall a source of stability in this tumultuous process.

To my guys in 2007. I'm here.

To Brandon, who saved my life in 2009.

To Evelyn, who saved my life in 2024.

To Melissa, who showed me life is worth living.

As before, to gamer developers, writers, story-tellers, musicians, historians, re-enactors, and the internet at large for making such a breadth of information available. I can never seem to get enough weird videos of people bludgeoning each other with blunt weapons in plate armor or shooting a bow while also holding a sword, a buckler, and sipping a latte.

And to you, the reader. The road behind you is book one. The road ahead has many stops and things from which you will not be able to look away.

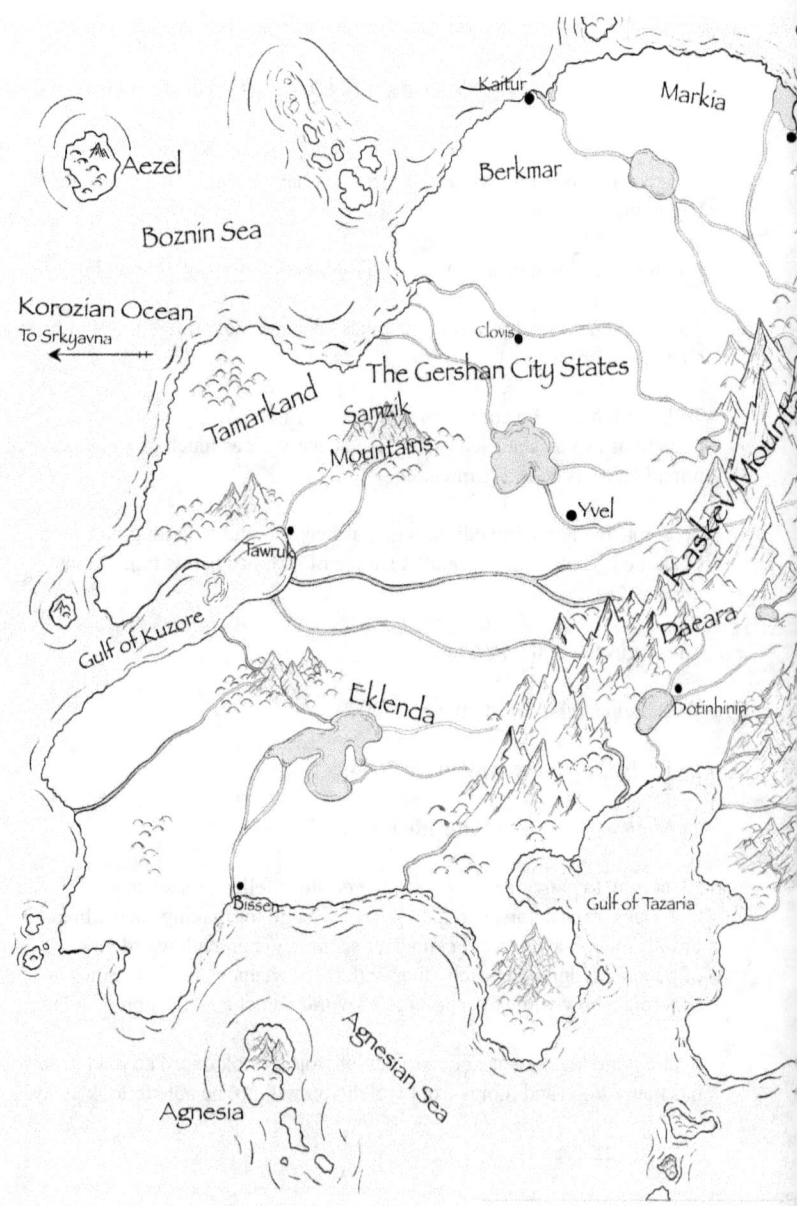

Figure 1: Map of the continent of Paeta

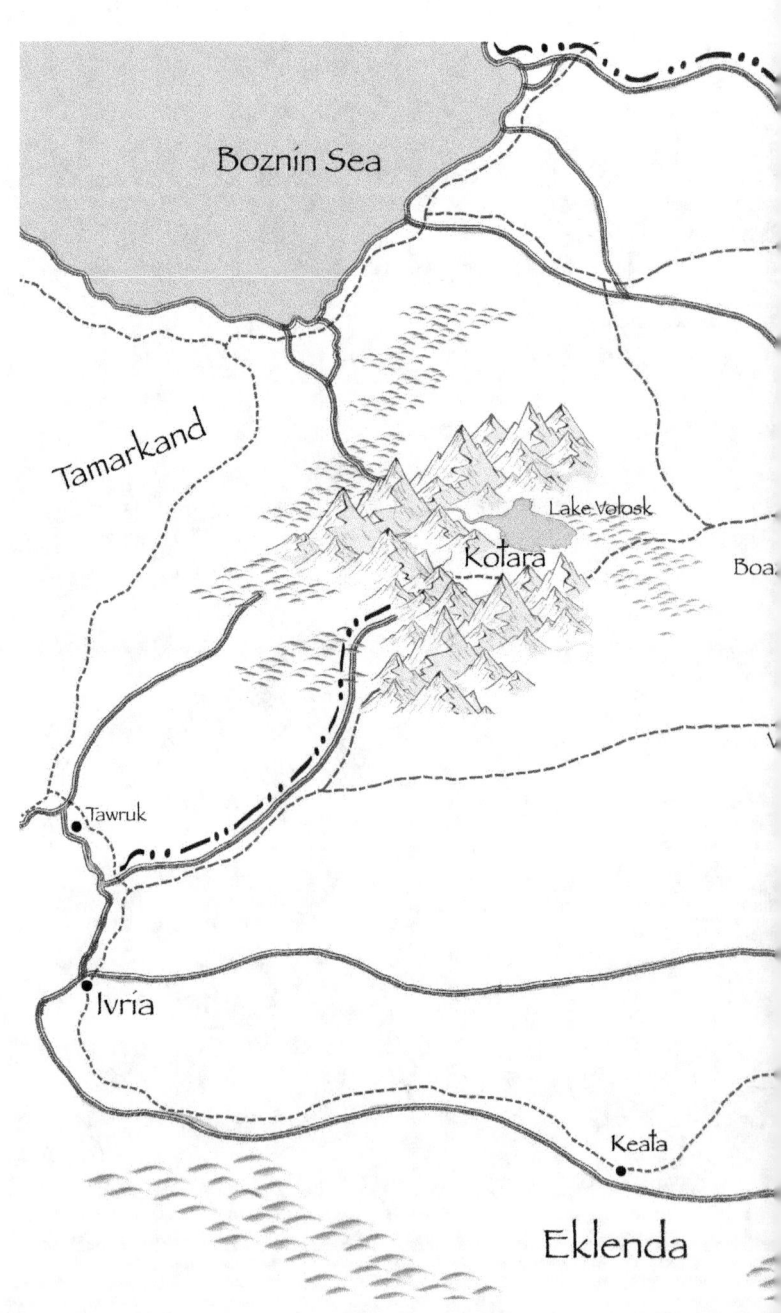

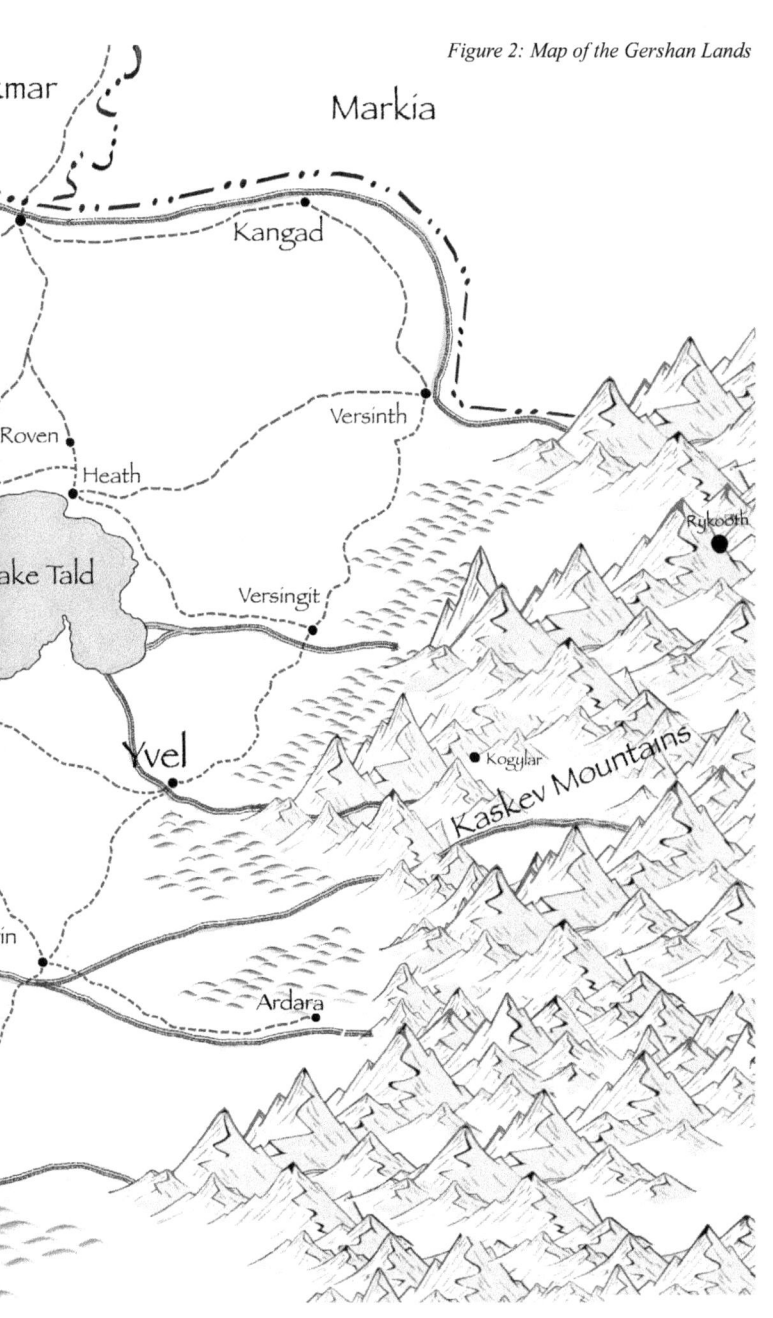

Figure 2: Map of the Gershan Lands

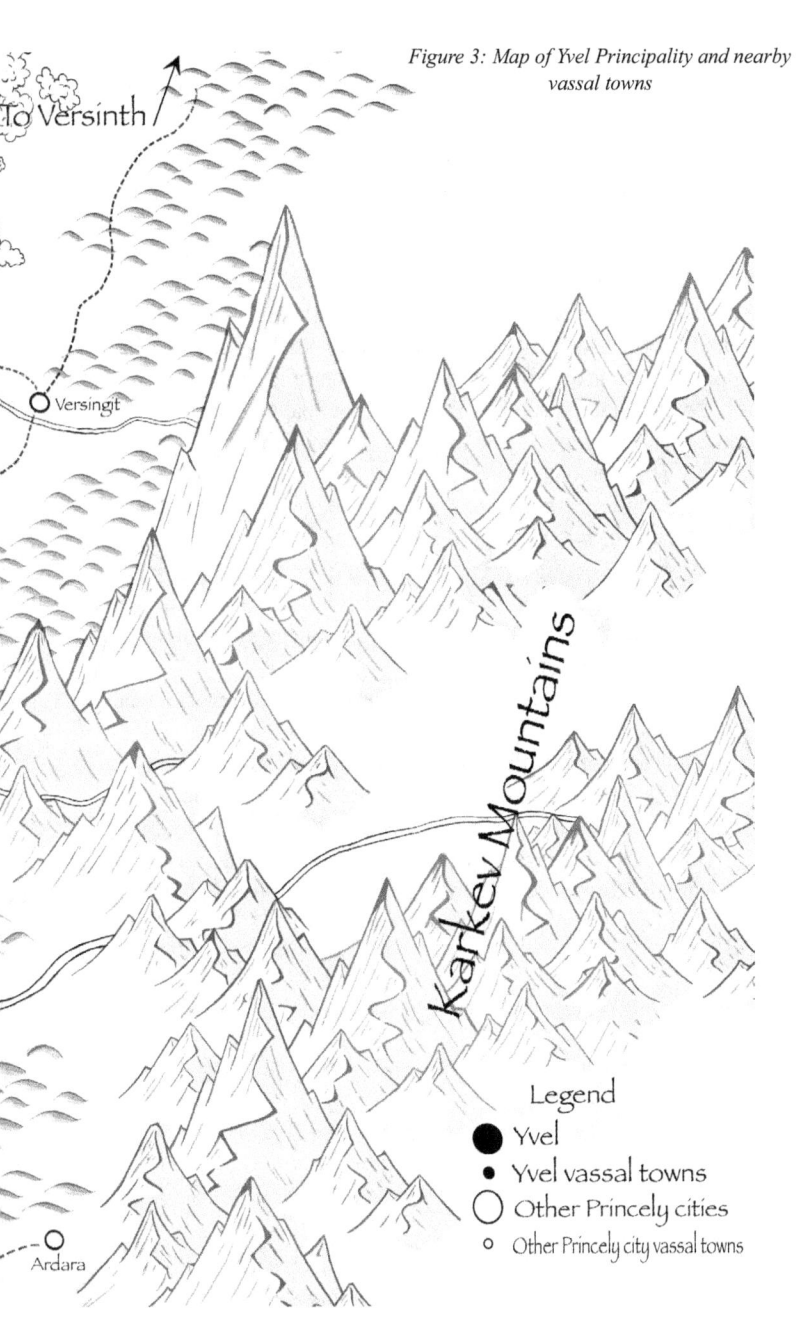

Figure 3: Map of Yvel Principality and nearby vassal towns

To Versinth

Versingt

Karkev Mountains

Ardara

Legend
● Yvel
• Yvel vassal towns
○ Other Princely cities
○ Other Princely city vassal towns

War rushes down the mountains in a great flood. For some, it has only been a few months. Others have already been at war for years. In the east, Daeara holds, but the orcs and gnolls threaten, plunder, and conquer parts of Vostind. Gilliam begins to crumble. Thabia hides behind its rivers and Mardalon watches from the far side of the Atlayan wall.

In the west, the burden of the war rests on Markia, Eklenda, and the Gershan City States. Berkmar and Tamarkand have yet to provide any assistance to their neighbors. Markia has space and depth in its territory, safe haven for its people, ports for its supply, land to grow crops and sustain its armies in the field. Yet lands of Markia are dwarfed by those of Eklenda, who seem content to contain the incursions of the orcs and the hobgoblins of the mountains. The Gershan City States have it the hardest for they are not united. Each city stands alone with limited lands and people.

A view of the whole of the Gershan Lands is necessary to see that Versinth, Versingit, Yvel, Soorin, and Ardara are the most at-risk of not only the Gershan lands, but all human lands, for these cities stand alone. Not even their fellow Gershans come to their aid. Some may even side against them...

With the recovery of Dariyet's maps in the aftermath of the Battle of Serna Hills, the approximate location of the Place-called-Kogylar and the Stone of Rykooth add some context.

The eastern Gershan cities bear the worst of the burden. Ardara has already fallen. Soorin and Versingit shall soon follow. Heath, Vidara, Boaz, and the other Gershan cities, much like the Tamarks and the Berks, seem content to watch and wait... much to the dismay of those looking for hope in Yvel.

Contents

Acknowledgements..v
Prologue..1
Chapter 1..33
Chapter 2..38
Chapter 3..58
Chapter 4..69
Chapter 5..83
Chapter 6..105
Chapter 7..121
Chapter 8..129
Chapter 9..151
Chapter 10..169
Chapter 11..175
Chapter 12..193
Chapter 13..207
Chapter 14..217
Chapter 15..231
Chapter 16..245
Chapter 17..261
Chapter 18..276
Chapter 19..300
Chapter 20..315
Epilogue..335
Appendix I: Glossary of Terms...352
Appendix II: Index of Characters..359
Appendix III: Index of Tribes and Peoples....................................377
Appendix IV: Gazetteer..381
Appendix V: Index of Figures, Artifacts, and Events of Lore and
History..389
Appendix VI: Calendar Systems of Paeta, Revised.....................393
Appendix VII: The Western Reformed Church of Orneth............397
Appendix VIII: Dwarves..401
Appendix IX: Ratfolk, Gnolls, Bugbears, and Ogres..................405
About the Author..407

List of Figures

Figure 1: Map of the continent of Paeta..vi

Figure 2: Map of the Gershan Lands..viii

Figure 3: Map of Yvel Principality and nearby vassal towns....................x

Figure 4: Side-view map of the Dwarven city of Adyrnaarn....................0

Figure 5: Map of the City of Versingit...68

Figure 6: Map of the Battle of Versingit, first assault..............................74

Figure 7: Map of the Battle of Versingit, second assault, phase one.......86

Figure 8: Map of the Battle of Versingit, second assault,
phase two..90

Figure 9: The Avart Massacre...96

Figure 10: Map of the Battle of Versingit, second assault,
phase three...104

Figure 11: Map of the town of Keppa..244

Figure 12: Clerical and militant clergy of the Western Reformed Church
of Orneth..396

Figure 13: Dwarves and gnomes meeting humans and elves................400

List of Tables

Table 1: Comparison of Yearly Calendars Between the Races of
Paeta...394

Table 2: Formulae for Calculating Year Differentials by
Calendar..394

Table 3: Saints and Values of the Western Reformed Church of
Orneth..398

Table 4: Rankings within the Religious Orders of the Church of
Orneth..399

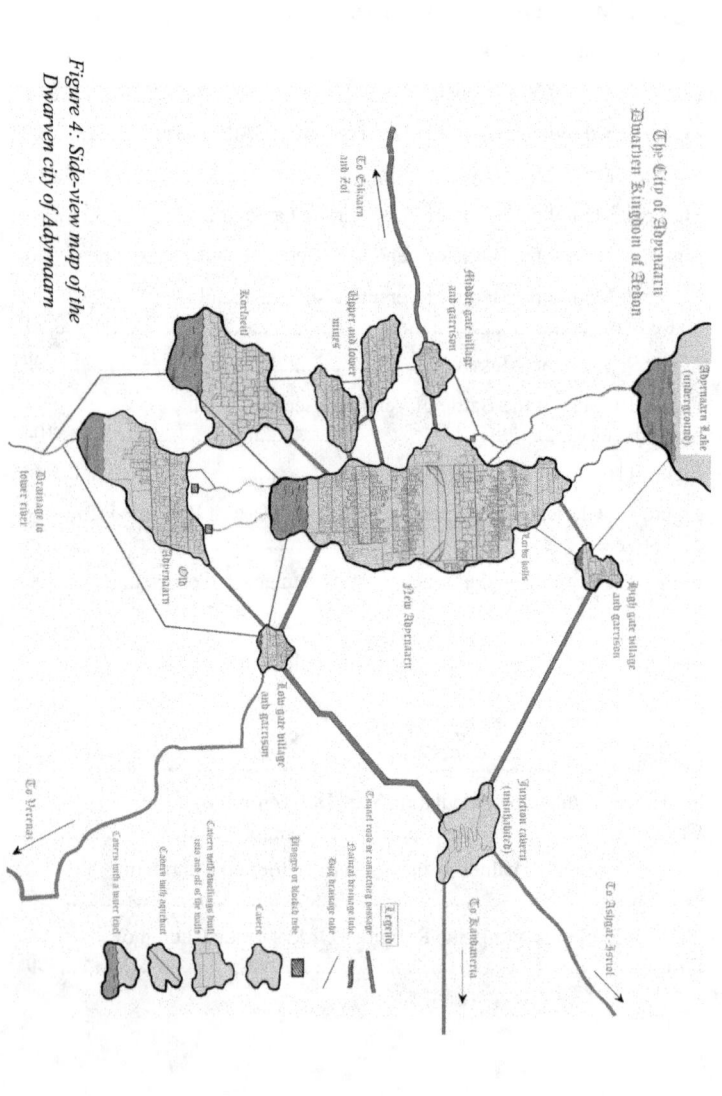

Figure 4: Side-view map of the Dwarven city of Adyrnaarn

Prologue

Junction Cavern, near the Aedon Dwarven City of Adyrnaarn.
Two miles beneath the surface, deep in the Kaskev Mountains.
By the Dwarven Calendar, 122nd day of the 10,484th Year.
By the Human Calendar, Twosday (second day of the week), first week of
Darri (fifth month of the year), 794.

The columns of dwarves marched forth from the mouth of the road tunnel and into the cavern, passing Gudreka, as the strength of Drenia's legions coiled into it.

"Gudreka!"

Gudreka internally shuddered. He knew that voice. He knew exactly from whom it was coming. He knew exactly what that person wanted. And he knew exactly the conversation he was about to have. And yet, he was bound by duty. The rising officer moved back into the broad mouth of the tunnel road, towards the voice that would not wait.

"Yes, Lord Therog, my general," Gudreka answered his commander.

"There you are, Mud-Vein. Have the pioneers mark the encampment," General Therog barked.

"Yes, my general." Gudreka bowed with suppressed resentment. Gudreka already had the pioneers laying down the markings, posting sentries, scouting further ahead, starting the cookfires, and handling a litany of other tasks necessary to move an army.

"And post sentries! Even a mud-vein like you should have thought of that! Why do I have to tell you everything?" Therog stalked past.

"Yes, my general." Gudreka remained bowed until he

1

passed from Therog's immediate presence, before trotting off to the side under the pretense of accomplishing tasks that had already been done. He grumbled to himself darkly. *I have a bad feeling about all o' this.* The ceiling of the large cavern soared overhead, slashed with striations of hard rock. The walls were dry and there were spikes from the ceiling reaching to the floor, where water had dripped over millennia and built up minerals. The tunnel's mouth entered the cavern near the floor, and an additional passage was built up to the entrance of a higher road tunnelling into the cavern. That would be the road to Ashgar-Isriol.

Gudreka closed his eyes. He could hear Therog's voice pounding in his head, demanding that his legions be the ones to smash the gates of Ashgar-Isriol; nevermind that the king desired control of Adyrnaarn as a route to Ezkaarn and Zol. The king wanted to cripple the scheming Aedons for invading Drenia while Drenia was fighting to regain what the Medrians had stolen from them a hundred floods ago.

Therog was single-mindedly intent on impressing the king so that he would be showered in praises, titles, and lavish rewards, which was not a particularly strange goal for any of the generals in King Nerim's grand army. The problem with Therog was his method, which was to achieve things that were not asked of him. Gudreka supposed that it might make sense to Therog in his own head, if Therog assumed that he would also accomplish what was asked of him, namely the conquest of Adyrnaarn, Ezkaarn, and Zol, and to prepare for other legions to march through and conquer a weakened Aedon.

How did I find myself with this idiot? Gudreka asked himself as he moved about the growing camp and supervised the Dwarven captains settling their companies in the places marked for them by the pioneers. But he knew that answer. He knew it well.

No one could say when this all started. *A bit more than two flood seasons ago, mayhaps?* King Nerim had sent a bundle of decrees fluttering off of his desk and across Drenia. *He reminded us all of what we had lost. What was taken. What was owed.*

Gudreka remembered some of those times, himself. While not old for a dwarf, Gudreka was not young, either. Having one hundred twenty-three flood seasons in his time, the dwarf recalled all too well the sprawling mines and furnaces of Mezar Rin and Rael Dol-Buen. He remembered when Drenia lost them to floods, and those thieving Medrians came with false kindness to buy the value of gold with handfuls of copper. Soon after, the Medrians built Ren-Gol and the other new border towns.

Even before the orcs took Ikria, the throne did nothing, the highborn did nothing, and Drenia was left to soak in its shame as even orcs spat upon her. Gudreka had nearly cried in relief when the levies came. *Finally*, he remembered thinking to himself, recollecting the joy he felt as the forges were called upon to stop and hear the king's decree. The quotas were filled entirely by volunteers, and the recruiters had to turn many back. 'Someone had to run the forges and farm the mushrooms and the hogs,' the highborn had said.

Well before the next flood, Drenia had marched into Ren-Gol only to be surprised. It was not only the Medrians that cheated. They had conspired with Aedon and Dranomar. As Drenia reached to take back its rightful possession, the thieves of Aedon and Dranomar pressed on Kerolus and Grednir itself.

'Better to take on all the thieves at once,' the highborn had said, but Gudreka knew what this really was. This was just like a knife fight behind a drink hall: when three come at you, the only way to win is to fight harder, cut deeper, show no mercy, and make no mistakes. The king raised more legions and Gudreka marched out of Medria and into Aedon. It was not until the king's legions had broken the gates of Kandaneria and several of Gudreka's superiors had died to serious injury that he was promoted directly under General Therog.

After his promotion, Gudreka had written to his wife in Goroboln. She was overjoyed, and had written back of how enthusiastically she had been bragging that her husband was a major captain under a general, and of what a fortunate chance it would be for them. *What a chance*, he chuckled bitterly. *What chance?*

3

"Major Captain?"

Gudreka roused himself from his bleak reverie to face one of his senior scouts, a younger dwarf with a beard that strained to reach below his neck. The barely-scruffed soldier wore light armor of boiled hog and orc hides, and boots made of the same. His steel-spined crossbow creaked on its leather sling, hanging over his shoulder.

"Ah, Rangli. Report."

"Thank you, Major Captain. It is as you said. No water here," said Rangli.

"Eh, that's fine, it is; what about the banners on the gate?" asked Gudreka.

Rangli shifted uneasily. "There were a few, but there was one with a downward axe on it."

Gudreka's eyebrows crept up his forehead. "The King of Aedon, is it?" Rangli nodded. Gudreka exhaled through his mustache. *What a chance...*

"Is the banner on both gates?" Gudreka asked. He had to be sure.

"That it is, Major Captain," Rangli responded.

"Right. Go on, then. Fetch me the quartermaster and the master engineer. We'll have to fix the water problem 'afore setting into the siege." Gudreka unconsciously cast his gaze to the far end of the cavern, toward the tunnels' ramps to the upper and lower gates of Adyrnaarn.

"Yes, Major Captain."

Rangli moved off to find the two officials while Gudreka approached the tunnel gates. The scouts had already cleared out the sentries from the Adyrnaarn guard, but there was no real hope of surprise in any case. By now, the Adyrnaarnans would have known about the Drenian legions' approach for several days. Without water, the siege camp would have to catch water at the last stream, two days' march to the rear and move it up... *I wonder if we could be puttin' them in the same problem. Hm.* Gudreka looked over the rock striations canopied on the ceiling.

Gudreka was yet again roused from his contemplation as the quartermaster and the engineer found him. He gave instructions to the quartermaster to begin shuttling the water. For the engineer, Gudreka directed him to devise plans for digging to the Adyrnaarn water source and plans for constructing a crude aqueduct to the stream, to determine which method would be more efficient. Gudreka had formed the basis of a plan to break the gates of Adyrnaarn, but it required time.

Time to get the ugly business on, he thought after dismissing the other two dwarves. He scanned the area and found General Therog's banner marking his location: a red banner hanging downward, with the embroidery in the middle of three gold medallions arranged into a triangle. Gudreka moved towards the banner, neither rushing nor dragging his feet. The cynical dwarf knew the impending conversation would be important. And difficult.

The general's guards and Gudreka nodded to each other as he passed. He found his general lounging on a metal chair that folded upon its hinges for travel. A silver goblet of mushroom brandy dangled between his jeweled fingers as he was doted upon by the interloping prostitutes he had hired as his servants. All of the dwarves had to leave their wives, wenches, and strumpets behind when they volunteered, save Therog, the only soldier of Drenia here with women.

"Ah, there y'are Mud-Vein. Took you a bit, eh?" Therog laughed.

"My General," Gudreka bowed.

"Out with it, Mud-Vein! Where are those scouts?"

"They've returned. They ran off the sentries. Adyrnaarn knows we're here, my general," Gudreka said, dropping to one knee and planting his fist on the ground.

"Good an' well. Maybe if ye'd been artful on it, we'd have those sentries in hand and them none the wiser," Therog scolded.

Until Adyrnaarn changed out the sentries in a day or two, Gudreka noted silently. But there was no point in arguing. Gudreka knew his general knew that. It was about–

"What's the hold up on the siege?" Therog asked, swirling his brandy. "And get up."

"Water, my general. I've tasked the quartermaster with setting up a relay for water from the last stream, and the engineer to give a choice on how to get water closer." Gudreka rose as he answered.

"Hm." Therog found something interesting in the depths of his goblet and eyed it thoughtfully. "What banners did the scouts see? What's the senior one?"

"The King's banner, my general," Gudreka said, as his eyes drifted up the skirts of Therog's serving women.

"The King's!?" Therog lurched forward in his chair, and his goblet clanged to the ground in his surprise. "With the *axe?* What're we waiting for? I want those rams up now and assembled!"

This was precisely the direction Gudreka had feared the conversation would take.

"My general, going at the gates right on… it outs the boys in a bad way. We can get the city in a better way if we tunnel–"

"Tunnel!? That'll take until the next flood!" Therog bolted to his feet and leaned towards Gudreka as he bellowed. "No! Rams up *now*, Mud-Vein! Get those rams up before the water!"

"My general." Another voice approached. It was Therog's war wizard, Aemzon. Aemzon was an older dwarf with a fine lizard-hide coat inlaid with silver in blocky patterns. He was fully bald and his charcoal-grey beard dangled to his belt. The very bottom of the beard had a faint brownish tinge. "Listen to Gudreka, eh?" He walked with a pained but well-worn limp as the guards admitted him. "Think on the tunnel, eh? It'll save a lot o' the boys."

"Save the boys? What're we supposed to be doin' here? The Aedon king's right there! King Naurom's right on the other side o' that gate! You want us to dig a tunnel?" Therog demanded.

"The king won't leave his people, my general," Gudreka said.

"Nor will they be leavin' him! Bust the gate, we fight the city, their king, and the king's chosen. Dig the tunnel an' we fight that an' whatever legions show up, too. Dig a tunnel an' we give time to the Aedons to raise more legions and move 'em," Therog challenged.

Dig a tunnel and save lives while Kurelig gets to Ezkaarn first, eh? That's what this is about, ain't it, ya turd skid? Gudreka glowered as he drew a deep breath. "Very well, my general. We will bring down the High Gate and flush them out."

"*And* the Low Gate, Mud-Vein." Therog poked Gudreka in the chest with a thick finger.

"… We'll be losin' a lot of boys goin' through two kill boxes, my general," Gudreka said levelly.

"An' what're we supposed to be doin', Mud-Vein? You're bein' so kind to the boys, maybe you want to be their woman and serve them brandy and other things, eh?" Therog barked, spit flecking Gudreka's face.

"Eh, my general, maybe I could be makin' a stone creature with a scroll. That'll help the boys get through the kill box and crack the gate. I could maybe make two of 'em?" Aemzon suggested.

Therog's body and head reeled over toward Aemzon. "I say 'no tunnel, it takes too long' and you say 'how's about something else that takes a long time?' What do you two not understand?" Therog demanded incredulously. "How's about you," he snapped, pointing at Aemzon, "go figure out what you can do to help the rams crack the gates?" He stabbed a finger back

7

at Gudreka. "And you–how's about you get those rams up, eh?" Therog looked between the two of them as they both avoided his gaze. "Right, then GET OUT," he bellowed. Aemzon scurried away, still limping. Gudreka left at his deliberately measured pace. He heard Therog's voice recede behind him."Girl! Come here an' sit."

Typical, eh? Gudreka glowered and then sighed. "Rangli?" Gudreka called. The fatigue was pouring into him suddenly. "Rangli?" he called again.

"Uh, yes, major captain?" Rangli answered after a bit of searching in the camp.

"Go and fetch me the quartermaster and the engineer again. New plan. Need the rams up first," Gudreka said.

"Uh, yes, major captain, but what about the water?" Rangli asked, his feet shifting in uncertainty.

"Rangli. Just go and get them, eh?"

***

At the entrance to the kill box cavern outside the High Gate of the Dwarven City of Adyrnaarn.
By the Dwarven Calendar, 130th day of the 10,484th Year.
By the Human Calendar, Restday (tenth day of the week), first week of Darri, 794.

Another loud clang echoed in the tunnel, and another inward dimple appeared on the broad, thick shield mounted to the front of the ram frame. The ram was made from a huge, hollowed bronze tube, filled with lead and capped with steel, suspended from chains inside the frame of steel and mounted on spoked bronze wheels. These dwarves had been pushing this ram up the slope of the tunnel road for three days bombarded by the great siege crossbows guarding the gates, hurling their long bolts of steel, but the worst was yet to come.

"Push, boys!" Gudreka bellowed over his shoulder, and scanned the scene through the narrow slit in his shield. "Almost there, boys! They can't stop us now!"

CLANG.

That one hit the shield right by Gudreka's head. His ears rang after the echo subsided. "Push!" His ears still ringing, he could barely hear the grind of the wheels of the ram frame on the tunnel's stone floor. Through the metal-on-stone grinding, the faint sweep of the oil brush on the bottom of the front of the frame made scuffing sounds with each push. He could not hear the grating and jingle of the chains as the body of the ram bounced in its frame.

They were about to push the ram into the cavern by the High Gate. As with any city, the approach to the gate would be overlooked by numerous vantage points, allowing the defenders to shoot their crossbows at the ram crew from all sides. The crewed siege crossbow would continue to bombard them all the way up to the gate. The shield mounted onto the ram was barely enough for the attacks from the front, and worse yet, the sides were unarmored in order to keep the ram frame light enough to travel the great distance it had come and had yet to go. More armor on the sides now was not a possible solution the way it might have been for the other crews going on a downward slope who were advancing on the lower gate.

"Put the stop on, boys! Fresh crew! Double crew! We need to push fast. *Hear?* Ready with the shieldbearers," Gudreka shouted. That was the answer. Push the ram through as fast as they could and take the losses. Ranks of shieldbearers followed the ram and would chase the ram crew, trying to protect them from flank shots. Gudreka wiped away the sweat from stinging his eyes as the crew of exhausted dwarves let two additional crews take the load of the ram. Gudreka looked over them. He guessed that most were barely over forty floods old, their beards short and untouched by grey hairs.

"Right, boys. This is it! We're gonna push this ram and make it rumble like the deep stones. We're gonna break this here gate! And we're gonna bring honor upon ourselves, eh?" Gudreka called to them. They panted from the exertion of taking over the ram. They were rested, but by no means were they fresh. They had been on the same grueling push over the last three days, and that was after the march here from fighting in Kandaneria. But he could see the light in their eyes. The fervor. They would return Drenia to glory. They had the will to fight. They were young, and the young were always the most eager to fight.

"Ready, boys? Ready." Gudreka watched their faces harden as they steeled themselves. "GO!"

The dwarves gritted and braced their bodies and pushed with their collective might. Gudreka pushed against the frame as well. The ram frame slowly lurched into a faster motion up the slope. The air cleared slightly as the frame pushed past the mouth of the gate cavern. The kill box. A fresh breath was all they got, before the air was thick the acrid smell of oil on the ground, the buzzing, pinging, and clanging of the crossbow bolts surrounding them. The defenders were shooting at them from the sides and the ram crew could do nothing but take them at this vulnerable part of the approach. This was the price of making the ram lighter. Gudreka felt the air sear past him from a crossbow bolt and jerked to the side, stumbling, as another glanced off the edge of his plate pauldron. Some of the ram crew were lucky like Gudreka, others not so lucky.

Yelps of surprise and howls of pain sounded behind him. The hurried shuffle of the feet of replacement dwarves blended in with the steady clop of the remaining crew. The shieldbearers squeezed between the ram frame and the tunnel wall, out into the kill box cavern. Their broad, tall steel shields dragged and skipped on the ground as they rushed to their task. The shieldbearers on the left moved faster than those on the right, and crossbows of the High Gate of Adyrnaarn claimed some of their numbers as they rushed into position. The Adyrnaarnan defenders on the right shot at the Drenian crew, some bolts missing the crew and finding the backs of the shieldbearers on the opposite side of the ram frame.

The wounded and dead lay on the ground as the remaining crew barreled the frame through them, stepping over their fellows feebly reaching for rescue. The crew and shieldbearers that rolled on the ground, crying out in pain, were soon silenced by the defenders, sprouting a bolt or two from each of their bellies as if they were dirt mounds spawning metal mushrooms.

"PUSH, BOYS!" Gudreka's legs burned in the push as the frame creaked forward. More shieldbearers moved forward and the ram's crew was mostly protected. The defenders' bolts sounded against the tall shields like sharp fragments of rocks bursting from heat. The crew pushed and strained as the ram crawled across the cavern floor towards the steel doors to Upper Adyrnaarn. Maybe it was for a few minutes. Maybe it was for a few hours. Gudreka could not tell how long, but it seemed an eternity, where his boys sweated and died while that buffoon Therog sat in safety, running greasy hands over his filthy whores.

TANG.

Gudreka's world flashed white and spun as he slammed to the ground. *Just when the ringing was almost done, eh?* He could not hear anything at first. His vision was blurry as he crawled to his hands and knees. Slowly the blur of voices surfaced. It was not the first time the Gudreka had taken a blow to the head, but it was always a hard hit when a bolt slammed into one's helmet. Gudreka was glad the helmet was still there. The pain in his head warred with his concentration and he knew his neck would be dreadfully sore in a bit. *If I can manage to live through this.*

"RIGHT BOYS! PUSH!" Gudreka felt the vibrations in his throat more than he could actually hear himself over the ring or distinguish any individual sound over the muffled, distorted cacophony of dwarves' shouting voices and metal striking metal. He squinted through the small aperture in the front shield plate of the ram frame. They were almost to the gate, now. He chanced a glance over his shoulders. Hardly any of the original crew remained on the ram frame. The rest were replacements and he could see the unmoving silhouettes of bodies in the trail behind the ram frame.

"PUSH, BOYS! A LITTLE MORE!" Gudreka called. Light caught the corner of his eye. His gaze darted to it. The cavern was lit by flaming braziers, but this was a new light. A light in the stone slits that the defending crossbows shot from. Gudreka closed his eyes as more lights appeared in other slits. *This is when they bring the fire. They must've wanted to beat us before this. Or maybe, this is where they push back the hardest.*

"BURN 'EM DOWN!" Gudreka heard one of the defenders shout from behind the wall. It was a woman's voice. Before the war, Gudreka had heard that the Medrians and the Aedons gave weapons to their women, but he had not believed it until the first battles in Medria. Gudreka was initially troubled by cutting down women with his axe, but they fought, and so they also died.

Tiny flames leapt down to the ground of the cavern or pinged off of the ram frame. As the bolts landed, the ground steamed and smoked for a few breaths before flames leapt up and tore across the cavern floor. It was as if the ground came alive. The flames spread through the cavern. Smoke choked the air. The ram slowed a bit as its crew struggled for breath, but they were *almost there*.

Gudreka was thankful for the brush on the bottom of the front of the ram frame. Its stiff-bristled, wedge-shaped head scraped against the floor, pushing the oil off to the sides. Gudreka and the engineer had insisted upon this improvement right before their march on Kandaneria–because the Medrians did the same thing with oil and fire, and the Drenians had lost a lot of good boys from being burnt to death. The thin slick of oil that remained smoked, but Dwarven feet stamped out the flames as they pushed on.

No good for the shieldbearers, though. Their boots were soaked in the oil and readily lit when the fire came to greet them. Their tall shields tilted and wetly flopped into the flaming oil as they thrashed about, screaming as they burned. One by one, they would slip, falling into the burning oil, rolling and writhing as the fire ate them alive. The sole blessing bestowed upon these unlucky victims was the fire of their own immolation made it too bright for the enemies' crossbows to accurately aim.

The ram frame had made it, finally, to the last few paces before the doors of the High Gate of Adyrnaarn. Gudreka's throat vibrated. "STAND CLEAR!" He was not certain whether his crew could hear him, but they turned their gazes. He snatched a hammer from one of the surviving crew behind him, as another one of the forward crew members drew one from his own belt loop. They hammered at the retaining pegs for the forward shield. They were close enough to the enemy's gate that the defenders' great siege crossbows could not mark them, and the other crossbows from the side slots had shots on them from the flanks, not the front.

The first pair of pegs came out and in a desperate frenzy, they hammered at the remaining two before casting the hammers aside, lost in the inferno surrounding them, and pushed the plate. The plate, once free of its retaining pegs, rested atop two small shelves on each of the front legs of the frame. Once it began to tip, its momentum carried itself, thudding down into the burning oil slick. Burning globules of hot oil sprayed in the air, coating Gudreka and the other crew members. The other hammerman hollered, clawing at his face and stumbling blindly into the fire screen. Gudreka grimaced and tried to ignore him—and all the other torment raging around him—as he kicked the oil brush off the frame before throwing his shoulder against one of its legs.

"LAST BITS, BOYS," he hollered as the frame once again skidded into motion. His men strained and grunted as the brightness of the flames and acrid smoke concealed them against the defenders. Gudreka and the remaining crew heaved and pressed until the ram frame thudded against the door.

"MORE CREW," he shouted back towards the cavern opening. He had enough of a team to move the ram for the moment, but he knew that they would not last much longer. They were exhausted and some would still be taken by the crossbows. Gudreka wanted fresh men at the ready for when the gate cracked.

"ALRIGHT, BOYS, GRAB IT. ONE. TWO. THREE. PULL!" Gudreka and the rest of the crew grabbed the handles or the chain shackles on the ram's massive bronze body and collectively pulled back on his command.

"PUSH!" Gudreka shouted and the group pushed the ram ahead from its back position. Most of the ram's power was in its weight, though, which swung on the chains and slammed into the doors of the gate. It was the first sound that Gudreka was sure he actually heard since taking the bolt in the helmet, though he felt it too. The stone underfoot shook with the vibration, and dust swirled off of the door.

"GRAB IT. ONE. TWO. THREE. PULL!" The crew repeated the drill and on Gudreka's command, again slammed the ram into the doors. Over and over, they pulled the ram back and heaved it forward, offering their paltry support to the mammoth weight of the ram's own inertia. They gasped from the exertion. The metal of the High Gate strained and screeched like a dying beast of the deep. Sweat mixed with the soot to form a greasy, ashen mud caking their faces and sliding down their bodies.

"PUSH!" Gudreka bellowed. A thunderous twang echoed as the warping metal snapped and gave way. They had slain the spirit of the High Gate. Or rather, half of it. One of the doors slammed against the interior wall of the gatehouse and fell off of its hinges, shaking the ground with another resounding clang. Beyond it was the secondary interior gatehouse and a secondary gate. Overhead were murder holes for the defenders to rain all kinds of unpleasantness upon their invaders. Gudreka braced himself for more death to stare at.

"PUSH, BOYS! ONE MORE GATE AND YOU TAKE THEIR WOMEN!" The men cheered behind Gudreka as they pushed the ram frame into the gatehouse. The frame had a roof of steel sheets, but they were thin. Large rocks and crossbow bolts pinged in the frey, making divots or perforating the metal covering. Some penetrated the roof and clanged off of helmets or pierced the mail on the necks and shoulders of his men.

"PUSH!" They repeated the drill, drawing the ram back and casting it forward again. The inner gate whined in agony as Gudreka heard the thick patter of liquid hitting the roof of the ram and pouring off of the sides, dripping through the holes made by the bolts.

"MORE OIL! PUSH BOYS! THEY'RE GONNA TRY AND BURN US AGAIN! PUSH IF YA WANT THOSE TASTY TREATS ON THE OTHER SIDE!" They pushed once more, but light flared around them before they could pull the ram body back again. Hollers and screams of men burning alive sounded behind him as the ram shed the strength of so many men at once. It weakly nudged the gate, slightly torn ajar.

Curses! Gudreka looked back. There were more men rushing into the gatehouse, but he needed their strength to fight what laid ahead on the other side of the gate, not to spend it on the ram. The men whose strength should have been spent on the ram were being devoured by the hungry fire. Gudreka coughed and choked on the smoke before blowing it out through his mustache.

"LET'S GO, BOYS," he shouted. This was the best way, because it was the only way. Hustling past the capped head of the ram and pulling his fighting axe free of its belt loop, he forced himself through the gap between the breaking point of the doors. *Two more hits and the gate would be done*, he lamented.

Spears immediately demanded his lifeblood as they coursed for his neck and face. Sweeping them aside with a reflexive whirl of his axe, he pushed the spear shafts up and kicked one of the onrushing defenders, while fresh men squeezed through the gap behind him. The first two gave their lifeblood to the indignant spears of Adyrnaarn, but more followed them. Gudreka fought for his life for innumerable heartbeats, barely keeping speartips and axe blades off of him, sometimes slapping them aside with a gauntlet. But as more men entered through the gates, they took the fight from him.

Gudreka stepped back and bent over, heaving for breath. The air inside the upper gate garrison cavern was much clearer since there was no open fire trying to claim anyone here. He was vaguely aware of the rush of more dwarves surging through the gap in the gate, others prying the remainder of the intact gate open. The light of the fire from the gatehouse and the kill box cavern washed over him and danced in the shadows of more men flooding into the High Gate. Soon the twang of defending crossbows ceased as the Drenian soldiers silenced those who had been feasting on Gudreka's flanks for so long.

He pushed himself off of his knees and rose to his feet.

15

"FORWARD, MEN!" Gudreka walked with less urgency now–the worst was over. There was yet a great deal to do, but they were inside the High Gate, his main force was flooding into the garrison, and the defenders would not be able to tell that the push on the lower gate was a ruse.

He stopped in his tracks as he saw a pair of his men pulling one of the defenders down and stripping off their armor. He already knew the situation before he came upon them. One soldier was pinning down the defender while the other one was working on his trouser belt. Gudreka kicked over the man working on his belt.

"OI!" the belted man angrily yelled before realizing it was Gudreka. "Oh, Major Captain, eh?"

"FUN LATER. FIGHT NOW," Gudreka shouted firmly.

"Eh, boss, it's just a snack to keep us going," the other protested while the defending soldier, a Dwarven woman, writhed and screamed curses at them in her native Aedon tongue. Gudreka drove the spike on the butt end of his axe shaft through the ribs under her collarbone. The surprised light in her eyes died.

"OI!" The other man leapt back from holding her down. Gudreka wielded the axe menacingly at the belted man and then slew it over to skim the other man's face.

"Fight now. Fun later," he repeated. This time, he did not shout, but was unwavering. The two men gulped. "Aye, major captain," they said.

***

Upper levels of New Adyrnaarn.

Hrene grabbed a young dwarf newly draped in the Adyrnaarn livery. "You! Report to the major captain that the garrison is lost to the Drenians."

He gawked at her wide-eyed, "But–but–" he stuttered.

"Captain," she corrected.

"Captain–cap–c–" he stuttered more.

"Captain Hrene," she supplied, gripping him with her gaze and staring into his eyes with pointed intent. She spoke loudly and slowly. "I need you to tell Major Captain Havrali that Captain Hrene says that the Drenians are inside the city. We have lost the upper garrison completely and they are coming into the city. Do you understand?"

The young dwarf gaped at her for a breath and she was about to shake him again when he nodded and scampered off towards the closest stairway.

Hrene climbed the steps to one of the halls on this level, to see out over the heads of her soldiers as they clamored into their positions near the mouth of the tunnel to the High Gate. Stone walkways hugged the perimeter of the cylindrical cavern that was the largest space of Adyrnaarn. Water fell from a hole in the ceiling and fell the length of the cavern to supply the reservoir at the base of the city. More water trickled in from a smaller stream a few levels beneath them, creating a gentler waterfall over the section of the city that housed the lords' halls. The lights of the city glistened off of the falling water, making it sparkle.

The soldiers formed ranks across the entirety of the walkways framing either side of the tunnel's large opening. On the upper floors and balconies of this level and further parts of the walkways, she had positioned her crossbows so as to strike the invaders from all sides as soon as they tried their way into the city proper. *How could we have given them the upper garrison so easily?* She chastised herself internally.

"Alright, you broad axes and bright spears!" Hrene's voice carried over their heads and echoed off of the ceiling of the cavern. Some heads turned towards her, but most remained fixed on where the enemy would emerge.

"This scum's the worst of all Dwarvenkind. They take

children as slaves, turn proud women to whores, and throw the men to the mines alongside their goblin slaves an' work them to death! YOU'RE the bulwark. YOU'RE what keeps their base kind at bay. YOU'RE the King's shield! No matter how many o' that filth come through that tunnel, you give 'em a chop in the throat or a poke in the eye an' let the ranks behind them see what we've got for 'em. When there's too many o' them dead on the ground, give 'em a toss over the side."

They all had a grimness about them and there were no cheers. They knew that many of their company were about to die.

"They have no golems wit' 'em," Hrene continued. "They puttin' nothing but flesh forward here. Give 'em enough pain an' they'll fold."

A loud, metallic clunk echoed from up the tunnel. *That sounds like...* Hrene's thoughts were interrupted by a blur of motion smashing into the ranks at the tunnel mouth, sending the bodies of six of her dwarves spinning over the side of the walkway, plunging into the depths of the city. Some of them screamed as they fell, though one of them fell soundlessly, a large steel bolt impaling his body as he plummeted down.

They're using our own siege crossbows from the gate, Hrene realized. "CLEAR THE TUNNEL PASSAGE!" She tried to contend with the cacophonous panic, as soldiers were already already scrambling away from the entrance to the city, pushing back against the ranks that had formed behind them. The Drenian soldiers came after that and fought a bloody stalemate for what seemed an eternity. The wounded and dead from both defenders and aggressors piled upon the walkways and pooled over the railings. The upper levels had already been evacuated and everyone that could bear an axe or a spear pressed into arms, but a seemingly unending stream of Drenians kept coming. Adyrnaarn was not a big city, and it seemed the Drenians had brought enough to pay in blood for all of them.

And they've got a wizard, Hrene remembered from one of the briefings from the days before the Drenians broke the upper gate. One of the king's spies had gotten a message through before the Drenians arrived. They had a wizard and it was only a question of when the Drenians would put him forward. *What kind o' person is that?* she wondered. Spying was widely considered a dishonest and dishonorable profession, yet Hrene was thankful for every bit of information that had been provided before the Drenians closed off the upper and lower gates. *An' that's another thing.* The Drenians were still pressing on the lower gate and they could put all of the King's Legion against the High Gate in case they broke the lower gate.

Hrene had come with the king's own legion to reinforce the homeguard of Adyrnaarn and, the king had hoped, throw the Drenians back at the gate, break their momentum and drive them back through Kandaneria. *But there're so many o' them… for all o' the spies the King had, big still beats small. 'Specially when they haven't shown their wizard yet.*

The Adyrnaarnan defense concentrated around the Great Stair, a spiral staircase, smooth ramps, and a central shaft normally utilized as a cargo hoist that connected most of the levels together. There were secondary entrances encircling the periphery of Adyrnaarn, but they were small and could each be held by fewer numbers. Bit by bit, the defenders of Adyrnaarn, homeguard and the King's Legion alike, ceded their ground until the Drenians controlled the upper levels of the main city; enough so that they wheeled down the siege crossbows from the upper gate and began bombarding the defenders, forcing them to give further ground.

They were losing another level, suffering losses at every level where the entrance to the Great Stair could be seen and angled by the siege crossbows on the higher levels, when the stuttering young dwarf from hours before, his scant beard struggling to break through the skin of his face ran up, stumbling to a stop and panting for breath.

"What?" Hrene demanded irritably. The boy-dwarf held up a rolled scroll for Hrene, leaning on a knee with his other hand. Hrene took the scroll and unrolled it. *Finally*, she grumbled. She shoved the scroll back at him. "You tell them not to wait. We'll be getting' out o' the way when they come."

19

The boy-dwarf ran off, squeezing his way through the defenders and down the Great Stair to deliver Hrene's reply. Hrene and her soldiers were too many levels below the top for the stolen siege crossbows to bombard them, and so they could openly fight on the stairs. But because Aedon fought openly there, so did Drenia, and right then, the line was buckling at the left flank. Two, three ranks were folding, dead and dying laying at the feet of the Drenians as the invaders started to press the king's soldiers on two sides.

"C'mon!" Hrene strapped her shield to her arm and snatched her battle axe out of the loop as she ran, grasping her shield in her other hand. She always had a few soldiers reserved out of the line for just this kind of thing. Tried and tested veterans. Their feet pounded on the paving stones, plates clanging against the rustling jingle of the mail, felt more in their bodies than heard over the din of fighting.

Hrene's first overhand strike took a Drenian soldier by surprise. His spear was mid-thrust over the shoulder of another Drenian. Hrene's axe blade forcefully met the vulnerable gap between his pauldron and helmet. The blade did not break the mail, but it jolted him to the ground. She raised her shield in time as a Drenian axe blade skittered off of it. Adyrnaarnan soldiers surged behind her and crashed into the other Drenians as she stepped on the weapon arm of the foe she had lain prone and drove the top spike into his open-faced helmet.

He feebly clutched at the axehead as she pressed it in. He shuddered and twitched as she pulled the spike out. The soldier fell limp, but she had already moved on in the space of two breaths, driving the butt spike of the axe between the plates of the Drenian axeman who had been protecting the spearbearer she just killed. The spike passed between the plates and parted some of the rings of his mail. The spike did not drive deep, but the axebearer still fell, and her soldiers finished him off.

Holding her shield high, her shoulder tensed and she felt a pop in the joint as the axe squarely rang on her shield. Sweeping widely with the hook-end of her axe blade, it passed through the air until she hit the ankle of another Drenian soldier. Pulling hard, she brought him down and used the momentum to swing the hook-end around and bury it in the Drenian's chest. The outrage of being killed by a woman showed on his face as he lost the strength to hold up his head.

"Captain! The golems!"

"Finally," Hrene impatiently called back, in the midst of beating back the Drenians and restoring the right flank. Then to her soldiers in front of her, "Make a hole! Golems! Make a hole!"

The rear ranks looked back to share witness with her. Four massive bodies, sharing Dwarven proportions but three times the mass, and made from stone and clay, climbed the stairs in great, lumbering strides. Two robed dwarves trailed them, shouting at the blocky creatures and waving their arms as they scurried about. These would be the King's Wizard and the Wizard of Adyrnaarn. Hrene had never met Adyrnaarn's wizard and never gotten to know the King's Wizard. There had been no need. *I'll buy them both drinks everyday for the next three floods if they can pull this out of the fire*, Hrene vowed to herself as she shouted for the soldiers to clear a path.

The Drenian's frenzied pace paused as the golems entered their view. The front ranks of Aedon soldiers had not yet parted when the first golem reached over their heads with a huge hand of living stone and grabbed one of the Drenian soldiers. Its enormous hand easily enveloped the armored, thick-bellied soldier, raised the feebly flailing invader over its head, and smashed him to the ground still encased within his closed fist. Blood and bile squirted from the lump of flesh hanging in the golem's hand before it through the heap of gore into the ranks of the Drenians. Aedon's ranks parted and the other three golems joined the first, crushing, smashing, picking up Drenians and using them as weapons against the other Drenians or throwing them off of the walkway to plummet to the bottom of the city cavern. Aedon soldiers followed and mopped up the flanks, eliminating and finishing off the surviving pockets of Drenians that the golems swept past.

As quickly as they had lost them, the King's Legion was

regaining the levels forfeit to their invaders. After retaking a fourth level, the siege crossbows the Drenians had taken from the High Gate could manage the angle, and began bombarding the golems, and the Aedon soldiers with them. One of the constructed giants took several direct hits, with one long steel bolt lodged in its torso, the other two hits taking one of its arms. Despite this, the soldiers of Aedon, the two wizards, and their golems were able to fight past the entrances to the Great Stair on each level and managed to lose only a few soldiers to the siege crossbows on each floor.

The golems mauled and crushed the enemy in their march up the Great Stair. The two wizards drove the golems, and Hrene's soldiers hurried to keep pace, protecting the wizards from the few bypassed Drenians. Hrene looked down at the remains of a Drenian as she kept order behind her soldiers. The bloody ruin of a Drenian oozed down the stairs. One of the golems had stepped on him. The legs and one arm were the only pieces easily recognizable; his other arm, head, and body were mashed together with bits of crushed metal and garments in a wet pulp that someone would have to clean later.

Hrene grimaced. They were nearly where they had been only hours earlier: three levels below the top of the cavern. The golems were making great progress, but it was merely a dent in the Drenians' numbers. What was actually important was luring out the Drenian wizard. Ruin enough of their gains to force him to commit. Once they could flush him into the open, the two Aedon wizards could crush him and then commence grinding up the remaining Drenians.

Flying rock fragments pelted against the walls, sprinkling Hrene and her company with dust and sharp stones. Shielding her eyes, she peered back towards the Great Stair to see the two wizards arguing. Three of the four golems were continuing past this level's entrance to the Great Stair, but the fourth golem had broken into pieces from the assault of the siege crossbows of the higher levels. A pair of tenuously attached legs stumbled amok, seeking footing to continue its march. Hrene could not hear what the wizards were arguing about over the sound of the fighting and shouting of hundreds of dwarves and the rampaging golems, but one of them seemed like he had made up his mind about something.

No, no, nono, "No! NononoNONONO!" Hrene tried to make him hear over the noise once she realized what he was doing. She watched him produce a wand from the folds of his robe. Energy crackled around the tip, forming into a fiery bead. The bead grew into a ball and shot upward, growing in size and brightness. The flaming ball shot past the siege crossbows, impacting explosively on the wall behind them. Mangled wrecks of the siege crossbows, mangled bodies of the Drenians, and bits of shattered masonry quietly fell from the great height to the echoing sound of the boom.

"Now ya've gone and done it!" Hrene shouted at him, but her protestations were drowned out by the answering impact. Dust, shouting, and blood everywhere. Hrene could not see clearly.

"Fight on! Keep 'em on the run and throw 'em out of the gate!" Hrene shouted and took the line herself amid the confusion. *This was the opposite of what was planned. The golems were supposed to make the enemy wizard show himself, so our wizards could crush him.* The smoke and dust cleared only slightly as she fought alongside her soldiers, hacking at silhouettes in the dusty haze that shouted with different accents. Sure enough, she saw the corpse of one of the wizards, half of his face charred away, his two golems standing dumbly with no one to drive them. The other wizard sheltered in the arch of the Great Stair, peering around nervously. Hrene fought on with her soldiers and the other two golems. They were moving towards the broad spiral, when a light flashed behind her and she heard a thunderous crack.

Looking over her shoulder, she saw one of the golems still standing dumbly. The other one was a smoldering pile of stone and baked clay. As she was turning back, a searing light burned a line in the edge of her vision as the Drenian wizard destroyed the other idle golem. The Aedon wizard, close behind Hrene, cursed at the enemy but his voice was drowned out by the din. This was Adyrnaarn's wizard. She knew because she did not recognize him.

Aedon's warriors reached the entrance to the next level from the Great Stair. The golems, oblivious to danger, continued to smash and drive through the Drenian ranks. They were breaking from a withdrawal into a rout, even with only two of them. Invincible titans against puny axes and spears. The Drenians ran, but the golems easily kept pace with them, crushing and maiming or hurling them to fall the screaming height of the cavern. Until they crested the archway of the entrance.

The golems moved ahead of the soldiers and the Aedon wizard. Another bright, searing light, and one of the golems exploded into a rain of rocks, pebbles, and burning clay. Hrene only heard a ringing. The rest of the world was muffled and so it barely registered as a sound when another bolt of energy destroyed the last golem. The soldiers of Aedon paused, as did the Drenians. The tide could go either way.

"Fight on!" Hrene cried. She could not hear herself over the ringing in her ears, but she pressed forward and her soldiers followed her. They pressed the Drenians past the archway and continued to drive their rout up the stairs. The Aedon wizard clung to the edge of the covering archway. Hrene was barely aware of him. She could not spare anything for him. She had to lead her soldiers with her own axe.

Scorching air and concussion knocked her forward onto the stairs. The helmet took much of the impact, but she could feel hot blood trickling down the side of her face. Hoisting herself to her feet, she spared a glance behind her. The Adyrnaarnan wizard and a dozen soldiers lay smoking and unmoving.

Oh, no... She stared at them wide-eyed for a moment. She shook herself and turned back to the only problem she could do anything about, but the tide was already turning. With no golems to crush them, the Drenians were realizing that they still had more soldiers on the field than all of Adyrnaarn and began to press them back downwards.

Hrene had no idea how long she fought, but she knew that the Drenians pushed her soldiers all the way back down. Time always passed surreally in long fights. She distantly puzzled as to why the Drenian wizard did not lay into them, having killed both of the wizards on her side. But, she and her soldiers were allowed to live, at least by him. The other Drenians, however, were eager to pay back the pain dealt to them by the golems. They took no prisoners, except for the women. Of the soldiers that got separated from the main line, they threw the men over the side. The soldier women were stripped bare and carried into one of the evacuated halls. Hrene bit back bitter tears as she fought and commanded her soldiers, their numbers now ever so precious, as she did her best to withdraw them to the lower levels.

They fought down to another level on the Great Stair when Drenians poured in from that level and began rolling up the flanks of Hrene's soldiers. They must have finally gotten down one of the other stairs. Hrene's force split. Most continued fighting a withdrawal down the Great Stair, but without their leader. Hrene and a hundred or so of her soldiers were pressed onto the walkway on this level. The Drenians pressed them from two sides, one coming down the Great Stair and through the archway, the other Drenians pressing her soldiers from one direction along the walkway. So, they continued their fighting withdrawal.

Hrene had hoped to reach another smaller stairway, but they were blocked from the other side and forced onto one of the many bridges that spanned the cavern. The bridge had made a quicker route across the cavern for merchants and officials that normally served its function well on this level. But for Hrene, it was certain death in front of her as the Drenians pressed her backward across the bridge, certain death from the fall on either side, and a glimmer of hope at possibly finding a stairway on the other side of the bridge before the Drenians came the long way around the cavern behind them.

The bridge was narrow and it gave some of her soldiers the chance to rest on their feet after fighting for hours. Hrene kept at the front. Her hearing had improved, but the ringing was still there. They were almost across the bridge and it looked like the Drenians were not going to cut them off at the rear. *Just have to deal with the ones in front then*, she resolutely grumbled. Her soldiers were getting onto the main walkway on the perimeter of the other side of the cavern when the bridge shook with a blurred motion from below. Another blur and the bridge shook again. Hrene staggered, as did her soldiers and the Drenians.

"They're bombardin' the bridge from below! Keep 'em on the bridge!" she hollered. Hrene's soldiers fought backwards to the mouth of the bridge, perpetually shaking from the large bolts of the great siege crossbows from below, still controlled by Aedon crews. The Drenians sneers turned into desperate snarls, ferociously trying to fight their way onto the perimeter avenue and save themselves.

A bolt thumped the bottom of the bridge. A chunk of masonry broke off. That was all it took. The bridge needed its integrity to bear its own weight. A chunk of that size, half of the width of the walkway, and it crumbled. Large sections broke off and plunged into the abyss. The Drenians scurried. Enough of them had scampered back to the side they started on, but not all of them—scores of invaders hurtled to the depths as the collapsing bridge gave way.

The ground gave way under Hrene, as the mouth of the bridge fell in on itself. Two soldiers fell with her. Her own fighters grasped to save them, catching Hrene and one of the soldiers. She met the eyes of the soldier that fell. He looked back at her as he plummeted, face was grim, but without regret. She wanted to reach for him, but he was already too far and her soldiers hoisted her up. She had lost her axe and shield, but was handed a readily available replacement axe from one of their fallen.

She heaved a heavy sigh. "Let's find us another stair."

***

Roughly one hour later,
Two levels below the Middle Gate of Adyrnaarn.

Hrene and two other soldiers burst out of the entrance to the minor stairs, alert and weapons readied. Echoes of the fighting thundered above them.

"Why here, Captain?" one of the soldiers asked anxiously.

"Dreadful close to whining, there!" she scolded, "but here's the rally area that was in the major captain's instructions. Now get the rest of the boys down here." Her shoulders and knees ached, but she stood upright and proud for her soldiers. Their wills wore thin and would wear thinner before the end. *That be where it's headed. The end.* She thought bleakly. Those buffoons, the two doddering wizards, bumbled their last chance to throw the Drenians out of the city.

Hrene's remaining soldiers piled out of the stairway. About a hundred of them. Most of her soldiers would still be fighting in the Great Stair, but they were separated. Hrene's best hope was to reunite with them at the rally area or fight for their relief. *But to what end?* She stood rigidly by the arch to the minor stair. No matter how much internal effort she was exerting to remain vigilant, her soldiers saw her standing straight, and in turn straightened themselves as they passed by her. She waited for them to file out completely.

"Last one," said a dwarf woman from behind a closed helmet with a recent dent decorating its visor.

"Good. Form a column," Hrene commanded. "We'll not be walkin' back a mess. Show 'em we're still gonna fight, eh?"

The soldiers meandered at the base of the stairs wearily, but a bark from one of Hrene's few remaining sergeants put a bit of mettle back into their march.

"Fine, then," Hrene muttered to herself and moved off over the bridge spanning the cavern on this level. It was wider than the bridge off of which they had fought on the higher levels. The column should be able to march across with five soldiers shoulder-to-shoulder. She heard the sound of the column marching behind her, sluggish footsteps. Soldiers on the march would often sing, but in their current circumstances, they were unable to muster the hope to do so.

"Sing *To the King's End*," she called over her shoulder.

There was an exhausted silence behind her, only the

clopping boots on the cobbling of the bridge.

"You heard the captain! Eh? You filthy worms better make 'er proud!" yelled the sergeant.

"What. Does. The King. Say?" The sergeant punctuated the words with each step, timing them so the other soldiers could mark their step off of his.

"The King. Says. The orcs. Came. Today," sounded the soldiers in response. Echoes of the fighting sounded from above. Now and then, falling bodies of warriors plummeted past them, having fallen from the higher levels. Some of the bodies struck the bridge and bounced off, leaving gory splats on the stone masonry.

"And. What. Does. The King. Do?"

"The King. Fights. He kills. With axe. And spear. He fights. With. His own."

"What. Does. The King. Need?"

"The brave. And. The strong. By. His side."

"And where. Were you?"

"We were. There!" The soldiers cheered.

"*Where?*" the sergeant screamed at them. Hrene always liked this song, but found it bitterly ironic now.

"We were. There! Atop. A pile. Of broken. Bodies. Green. Skins. With. Dead eyes. And. More. To come!"

Hrene could hear them cheer on more, their spirit somewhat restored, but stopped listening. More bodies were falling, but they were not the bodies of soldiers and warriors laden in armor. They were children, elders, new mothers and fathers clutching their babes as they careened downwards. Hrene's eyes went wide at the rain of her people.

She marshalled her face to calmness. *That's the way o' it*, she thought bleakly. Mass suicide of civilians was for when the savages broke the gates, when they were overrun by orcs, hobgoblins, goblins, ogres, trolls, and the like. Death was a better fate than the life of enslavement that otherwise awaited them. Guard the secrets of the craft, rather than let the beasts cut them out of you, or worse, force you to perform the miracles of Dwarven craft for your kinsmens' butchers. It was long recorded in the histories that dwarves taken prisoner suffered horrific fates, being tortured to work, but those that had it worst were not tortured themselves. Dwarven families taken prisoner were compelled to work for the savages or bear watching their children be tortured and killed.

Better this way, but it was normally reserved for the filth. *Not... not for other dwarves.* But Hrene had already seen what the Drenians would do. Any other Aedon did not trust a Drenian for their word, and it was common knowledge that they kept slaves, but Hrene had seen with her own eyes the invaders stripping captured women soldiers and carrying them off.

Shaking the recently branded memory from her head, Hrene focused on the work in front of her: get these soldiers to the rally area and get them back into the fight. Her column marched into the marketplace on this level, cleared of the carts and stands. The marketplace was bustling with soldiers and messengers running about frantically. The taverns hummed with activity as the King's Legion had taken over its kitchens to feed soldiers that were not fighting.

"Rest them here," Hrene called to her sergeant and hurried off to find anyone that knew what was happening. Forcing her way through the crowd, she found the headquarters of Major Captain Turiotli and several of his clerks.

"Major Captain!" she called as she forced her way through the crowd.

Turiotli glanced up from a scroll he was reading as another messenger was talking to him in urgent tones. He held up a hand to silence the messenger. Sweat and nerves painted the messenger's face.

"Hrene! You live!" A smile split his face of worn stone and

bent his beard of wires.

"Major captain! I was separated from my main unit in the Great Stair. I–"

Turiotli held up his hand again, this time to pause Hrene. "I know. I had a report on it."

"I have a hundred axes with me. We're ready to rejoin the fight, captain," Hrene said.

"You and yours need to be eatin' before you're goin' anywhere," Turiotli said.

"But, Captain–" she protested.

"No. Look," he pointed. Hrene followed his direction and saw tired soldiers congregating in clumps around the marketplace, sitting on barrels or merchant carts or on the ground. They drank soup from bowls or tore meat with their hands and teeth.

"Need to eat to fight. Who wants to die hungry anyways?" he chuckled. "Go and get them fed and come see me."

Sour-faced, Hrene left the command post, found her sergeant, and pointed him towards the nearest tavern, directing him to feed the troops. She watched as the sergeant goaded the soldiers to their feet and marched them. She was almost back to Turiotli's command post when her sergeant's hand pulled on her shoulder through the crowd. She half-turned and looked in annoyance only to have dried meat and bread thrust at her.

"You need to eat, too, Captain. Can't have ya fallin' over in the middle of it," he scolded her. Hrene took it sourly and turned back toward Turiotli's command post.

"Ah, good. You ate, too," he said. He glanced up anxiously at the higher levels.

"Where can we fight, Captain? Is my main unit still up there?" Hrene asked urgently.

"Chew your food, captain. Finish eating before you rush

off to die again," Turiotli said, wiping the sweat from his brow. His surcoat, emblazoned with the mark of the King's Legion, was smeared with ash, mud, and ink; Hrene's own surcoat was mainly colored with blood now. Hrene scowled as she bit off the end of bread that her sergeant had pressed upon her.

"It will be different for ya. King's orders. You're to take some soldiers and get the wounded and the gnomes out o' here." Turiotli's head leaned forward to look her pointedly in the eye.

Hrene could not believe her ears. "And run from the fight?"

"King's orders," Turiotli said, trying to quiet her a bit.

"And is the King leaving this city!?" Hrene's voice rose with outrage. "Where be the King?"

"The King fights in the Great Stair, Captain," Turiotli said.

"Then I will go an' fight there, too. Beside the King," Hrene said and started to move off, but Turiotli yanked her back by the shoulder.

"You will not." He pointed a low finger at her chin.

"But, you said the rest o' mine are down here. I take 'em back up and give it to the Drennies," Hrene said.

"No, you don' have anything besides those hundred over there," Turiotli said. "Ya've been relieved o' them."

"Relieved!?" The words slapped Hrene. *How? What did I...?*

"King's orders," Turiotli said.

Hrene looked around the floor. "What… what–have I angered the King?"

"No. Th' opposite," Turiotli said solemnly.

"THEN WHY!" Hrene shrieked in anger, blinking back tears. "Why does the King shame me? Spurnin' me at the last?"

31

Turiotli took a breath. "The King trusts you to do the job. He needs the wounded out of here. He needs the gnomes out of here. An' the siege crossbows on the Middle Gate do no good here anymore. Ezkaarn and Zol are next in Drenia's path, so take the crossbows there, tell them how the Drenians came at us, and fight with them."

They argued a bit more, but the king's orders determined the outcome. Numbly, she shuffled her feet through the crowd back to her soldiers.

"Sergeant Marchag," she mumbled, her voice lost in the bleak energy of her surroundings. She lifted her voice and called again as she came nearer. "Sergeant Marchag."

"Captain? Have we orders?" her sergeant bounded to his feet.

"That we do, sergeant. Get them ready. I've bad news to bear," Hrene said.

Sergeant Marchag guffawed. "Bad news, eh? Worse than this?"

Hrene nodded solemnly, "Worse it is. These orders, I mean."

Chapter 1

Upper levels of the Korlaeith district of Adyrnaarn.
By the Dwarven Calendar, 124th day of the 10,484th Year.
By the Human Calendar, Thirstday (fourth day of the week), first week of
Darri, 794.

udreka grimly watched another slew of families jump to their deaths, plunging from the middle levels of Korlaeith into the dark reservoir at the bottom of the cavern. These Aedons were curious to him. In Drenia, suicide to avoid capture was only when defense against the savages, orcs, goblins–that kind–was principally to prevent invaders from torturing craft secrets out of prisoners. Gudreka was surprised when the first families jumped, and was even more astonished that it did not stop. Gudreka had a nagging feeling that Drenia had underestimated the fighting spirit of Aedon. *But today! Today the day is won*, he shrugged to himself.

"Rangli!" Gudreka called, raising his voice to boom over the sounds of lingering fighting.

"Major Captain! On the way!" Rangli's answer faintly sounded. Moments later, Rangli loped towards him, flecked in blood all over to match his commanding officer. "Yes, Captain."

"Tell the minor captains that they're on their own authority to finish up here an' bring me the trophy. After that, you can help yourself to the prisoners," Gudreka instructed.

"Yes, Major Captain." Rangli trotted back from where he came to carry out his orders.

Gudreka had been delaying this, ironically taking refuge in combat rather than face the task that lay ahead. He knew Therog was furious at Aemzon's intervention, but it was also very clear to him that Therog would have denied Aemzon's intervention had he been asked. *Ah, well. It ain't wine. It ain't gonna taste better with age.*

33

***

Therog's command post, Lord's Halls of Adyrnaarn.

"That wasn't your place, either!" Therog bellowed, spilling wine from his cup.

"And what was *your* place, general? Eh? During all the fighting? With your men doing men's work, or laying under a whore all the while the boys of Drenia be bleedin' dry and gettin' smushed by Aedon's golems," Aemzon retorted, his tenor raising to match Therog's in volume. "An' what was the purpose do ya suppose the King had when he sent me with ya?" Aemzon continued, raging. "Do ya think the King's like, 'ah, that boy-o there, Therog, needs someone to paint his whore's nails. Better send him a wizard!' Certainly not to save the blood of Drenia, eh?"

"Oh, inpretin' the King's will is one o' your skills, now, is it?" Therog retorted.

"High Captain Gudreka," the guard announced. A stony-faced Gudreka entered. He was stained in dried blood and bore a cloth bag over his shoulder, its bottom caked in dark mud.

"Oh, just in time, Gudreka! Maybe you've got an eye for the King's will, too, eh?" Therog baited.

"The fight's about done, General. Korlaeith's done," Gudreka said. Aemzon could tell he was spending a lot of effort to keep his voice measured and his face calm. Aemzon knew that Gudreka hated Therog, as deeply as he himself did.

"That's good an' all, but how do ya answer for this?" Therog jabbed a finger towards Aemzon.

"How do ya mean, general?" Gudreka asked evenly.

"Oh, don' play stupid. Aemzon interfered with the fightin'

and took the glory away from the boys!" Therog rounded on Gudreka.

"As he did, the Aedons were goin' to push us all the way back to the High Gate, if he didn't," Gudreka said.

"Ah, so ya *asked* him ta–" Therog hissed.

"The good captain did nothin' o' the sort. I took it upon myself to fight. An' they had two wizards that woulda burned the boys to ashes, too," Aemzon talked over Therog.

"Ah, so good thing, that I only be needin' to throw one o' ya in shackles for disobedience. I get the relief of the other bein' thrown in chains for incompetence at not bein' able to crush the Aedons an' their small garrison. How about–" Therog spat at Aemzon, but cut off as a large object thunked on the floor wetly and rolled at the edge of Aemzon's vision.

They both jumped. A bloody head rolled on the floor and came to a stop between them. Its eyes stared up at Therog.

"King Naurom of Aedon," Gudreka said.

Therog stared at the head for a moment before shaking himself, "if ya think this changes things, you'd be makin' a mistake. You're on thin tolerances, Major Captain!"

"Ya've orders, General?" Gudreka asked in a neutral tone, not having moved from where he stood.

Therog glared balefully at Gudreka before he spoke his next words. "You're to get the boys ready for Ashgar Isriol and be sendin' scouts to Ezkaarn. An' no mistakes at Ashgar Isriol," Therog warned. "We're to make good time and break the gates of Ezkaarn before Kurelig is done with Zol. Understand?"

"I understand your orders, General," Gudreka said.

"An' you!" Therog stabbed a finger back at Aemzon, "since you're so understandin' o' the King's will an' takin' care o' things, you're goin' to... fix the plumbin'... yeah, here in the Lord's Halls first." Therog smirked to himself self-satisfiedly.

"The plumbin', general?" Aemzon said dumbly.

"Yeah, the plumbin'. Work your magicks, master wizard. Begone," he waved them away. Turning and sloshing his wine a bit more he lumbered to the back of the hall. Aemzon knew he was going to the bedchamber to lay with his whores some more and shook his head in disapproval. Never had he seen a general so unwilling to fill his station. He was so intently focused on his loathing, his face contorted into a glower, that he jumped in surprise when Gudreka nudged him.

"We should be goin', Master Aemzon," Gudreka said. Aemzon nodded and they both left, quietly passing the guard. The guard nodded ever so slightly to both of them.

"The plumbin'," Aemzon blustered in outrage when they were at the Great Stair.

Gudreka heaved a sigh and looked over at Aemzon, "whether you agree with the general's priority or not, the plumbin' does need to be addressed to bring this place back into use. I can't say anything for your decision to fight, but I know ya killed two wizards and I know the boys are mighty grateful. They might give ya some o' the women if you went by the taverns at the Middle Gate," Gudreka suggested. Aemzon stopped walking and Gudreka took a few more steps before stopping and turning back.

"You're a good man, Gudreka," Aemzon said earnestly. The two parted company without a further word. Aemzon found his way back to his own hastily furbished dwelling. The soldiers in the headquarters detachment had delivered Aemzon's trunks of books into another chamber of the Lord's Halls.

"Leave me. Take your meals and find your women." He waved off the staff. The young soldiers smiled and thanked him as they left, but Aemzon was only listening for the receding sounds of their footsteps.

Aemzon pulled a chair up to a table next to his trunk of books, "Ryn. It's safe."

A pinprick appeared in the air in front of him and slid,

forming a line before splitting and making a hole in the air. A tiny red face peered through before equally minute red, clawed hands wrapped around the edges of the opening in space and spread it further. A miniature, slender woman, red-skinned with wings and horns, no larger than one of the wizard's fingers, crept through and stood on the table in front of him. Aemzon gave her a tired smile and affectionately stroked her lithe body with his finger.

"I dunno if I can keep servin' the King's will under this idiot, Ryn," Aemzon said glumly.

"I see how hard you work, Master. I see your brilliance and your cunning," she kissed his fingertip.

"I love ya, Ryn," Aemzon said, emotion filling his voice. "I'm glad we made that contract all those years ago."

Chapter 2

A small hamlet south-west of the town of Serna, west of the town of Keppa.
By the Human Calendar, Twosday, first week of Darri, 794.
An overcast, humid midsummer day.

"**W**e have enough problems without your like coming here," snapped the headman.

Julian took a long, deep breath. "I understand this is hard, Headman Oris, but the Lord Serna needs your support–"

"Look here, young man! We've already had conscription patrols from Keppa, from Garber, and Yvel itself! And now, you're coming here for more!? None of those patrols, *and definitely not you*, even bothered to keep those scoundrel bandits away when they came through last week!"

"Bandits?" Julian muttered to himself curiously.

"Master headman, we're not here for conscription," Liri began in a conciliatory tone, "we're looking for–"

"I DON'T CARE! Get off with you! Out!" the headman insisted.

"–volunteers," Liri finished.

"You don't understand? Get out. Get. *Out*. There's no one left to conscript. 'Volunteer.' Whatever you want to call it. Look around." The headman gestured to the small hamlet. Liri and Julian stood on the tiny patch of grass that passed as a village green, though with only six houses around it, the hamlet hardly needed anything larger. The houses were made of clay and straw daubed on frames of wooden planks and sticks, with larger timbers bearing most of the weight. The roofs were thatched except for one, presumably the headman's house, which sported a tile roof. Proof to the headman's point, Julian could only see very young children and oldsters minding the work and keeping the village operating. He could see three farm houses in the distance around the hamlet, but only one of the fields showed signs of activity. *This is going to be a very rough winter*, he thought bleakly.

"You've made your point," Julian said, turning to mount Pine, his chestnut roan mare.

Liri was mounting her own horse when the headman called after them. "This is your own fault for bringing the war here in the first place, Serna!" Julian's head hung, staring at the ground as he absently guided Pine out of the nameless hamlet.

Liri caught up to him a moment later. "You ready to go back?"

"Yeah," he answered blandly. They rode on in silence for a few miles, no sound but the wind occasionally rustling the leaves and the clop of the horse hooves on the hard-packed dirt road. The air was brisk and smelled clean.

"Are you going to take Sir Merik's offer?" Liri said abruptly. Julian was quiet. More than a minute passed in silence. "Julian?" she asked again.

"Nah," he said, wiping sweat from his brow.

They rode further in silence for a while until Liri spoke again. "So you're staying?" Again, Julian was silent. "Julian!"

"Huh? Yeah. Staying."

"So? What is it?"

"What's what?"

"Listen. I don't have time–none of us have time–for your mopey scat. We've a job to do."

"Right, tenleader," Julian murmured dejectedly, "whatever's needed."

The pair plodded along to the northeast, towards Serna and Keppa, for a few hours in silence until the next tiny village came into view. It was quiet. Julian sat up in the saddle, suddenly alert. *Very quiet*. He and Liri came to a halt, surveying the area. The nearest house was four hundred or so paces away, but they would have still been able to see movement or maybe hear something. Nothing. Julian looked to Liri and she motioned for him to circle left, to the north around the settlement. Julian walked Pine on, skirting the houses, quietly picked their way through the fields.

And he saw them. Three, at first. People dead in the fields.

Slashed or bludgeoned. A few with arrows in them. He cautiously continued, seeing them, mostly in groups of two, three, or four, the closer he came to the village. He counted twenty-seven in all. He joined a grim-faced Liri on the far side of the village. She nodded to him and they walked their horses through the center, seeing more bodies. They exchanged a glance before turning their horses out of town. "They didn't burn anything down this time," she commented.

They were most of the way out until Julian noticed Liri staring at something. He followed her gaze. He had to squint for a moment, but saw it too. Movement in one of the buildings. He looked at her and she nodded. He dismounted and drew his hand axe from a loop on his belt and crept towards the house. It was a small cottage with mud and timber walls and a thatched roof, like most modest houses situated in rural Yvel. Julian crept in through the open doorway. A few bolts of fabric lay scattered and unrolled on the floor, some torn or unfinished garments, and an overturned cabinet of thread spools marked this a tailor or seamstress' house. He looked around. He was sure that he had seen something. And then he did. A pair of eyes–two pairs of eyes–three pairs of eyes– fearfully staring at him, hidden in the piles of fabric with a broken chair on top. They did not look like orc eyes.

"It's fine. I'm not here to hurt you," Julian reassured them. He slowly put the axe back in its loop and held his hands open and in front of him. One of the small figures shuffled. Then another. All three of them revealed themselves slowly, with two additional figures coming out of hiding from under the straw-mattress bed.

There were two children, both boys, and three adults; two women and a man. "Who are you?" asked one of them. He spoke in Eklendan, an adult male with a characteristically Eklendan narrow jaw and red hair.

"My name is Julian. I am from Serna. It's not safe for you folk here. Come back with us. We'll take you to Serna where you'll be protected." Julian's Eklendan was stilted, but passable. He brought them out to Liri, who was holding an arrow she had collected. "What's that?" Julian asked.

"I don't recognize it. Maybe someone else does," she said, stuffing it into one of the leather saddlebags. The villagers gathered their scant remaining belongings and joined Liri and Julian to travel back to Serna. The adults, Jana, Sontrin, and Molok, were tailors, but the children had been from other families. Julian was not sure, but they seemed like they were related, or at least very familiar with each other. Jana, her hair kissed by greys, seemed a bit older than the other two, though they were all in their thirties. She rubbed her hands often, though it seemed to stem more from shaken nerves than from pain. Sontrin was on edge the whole journey, looking over her shoulder and around the fields for threats to leap from the grass. Molok would engage in conversation but trail off at odd times, his eyes taking a far-off light to them.

"Greenskins, right?" Liri asked.

"What?" Sontrin jumped in surprise at Liri's question, breaking the silence. "Oh. We didn't see them," she said. "They came at dusk and it was too fast." They were quiet again for a while. "Do they really have green skin?"

"Yeah, lots" said Julian, "but some have blue."

It took three days to walk back to Serna with them, though they would have made it in less time had they been prepared to accommodate a larger party. Possessing more horses, or a cart and mule and supplies for five adults and two children, would expedite their journey, but they did not, so they had to forage, hunt, and lay snares overnight. A pair of rabbits and some wild chives and henbit fed them for the trip. Prey was starting to get scarce with the start of winter.

Julian and Liri had been out recruiting for the Serna Regiment with little luck. Maybe some of their new companions would join. Lodging would be difficult, but they could be put to work, either in the regiment or with their craft to supply the regiment. At least one would have to care for these children that were not even theirs.

At the end of the third day, the increasingly foreign sight of Julian and Liri's home came into view. New buildings had sprouted up where the old had burnt down. They were all four-floor buildings, the fifth one nearing completion with four more to go. The ground floor was for craftsmen and shops, the upper floors housing apartments and barracks. The palisade, completed late in the summer, was now having a layer of stone sent by Prince Arnold laid with the much-appreciated help of engineers. Liri took the new arrivals into the quartermaster's office while Julian waited outside with their horses. Liri came out a moment later and walked with Julian over to the training field.

The training field was at the base of the hill by the Covendran Manor. It had several archery targets set up, sparring dummies, and quintain. The young Serna Militia Company had reformed into the even younger First Company of the Serna Regiment, which was drilling on the practice field. Liri led them, walking towards Lady Judane, who, under the instruction of one of the elves, was practicing alone with her polehammer. Judane was the second child of House Covendran after her brother, Lord Dareum, who was probably out recruiting, since he would normally be put through the paces alongside his sister. Like him, Judane had fought and somehow survived the Battle of Serna Hills, picking up the polehammer she favored from a fallen soldier during one of the skirmishes of the battle. Julian thought the elf training Lady Judane was named Bierien, and was mildly surprised to see her out on the training fields. Normally, she spent her time training blacksmiths to be weaponsmiths and armorers.

Julian peeled off without Liri noticing, dropping Pine's reins. Julian strode aggressively to put a stop to something as soon as he saw it."Just what do you think you're doing?" he demanded. A squad of soldiers stopped drilling.

The tenman, Baryn Kevr'ail, stared in surprise. "What?" Julian roughly reached in, seized the shortest soldier, ripped off the leather-veiled helmet and cast the soldier on the ground.

"What the scat, Julian!" Ziek angrily yelled from the ground.

"You watch your mouth! You're too young for this and you know it! Twelve years and a soldier!?"

"I'll be thirteen in two months," Ziek muttered as he stumbled upright.

"Julian," Baryn stepped in calmly, but assertively. "It's not up to you. The lad made his mark on the papers and it's his choice. You know the greenskins don't care how old they are."

Julian looked past Baryn to Ziek, who was sheepishly averting his eyes. "A mark on the papers, Ziek? Or did you not mention that?" Julian asked.

Baryn slowly turned and looked at Ziek expectantly. "Well?" Ziek said nothing and turned further away.

"All right, boy, if you didn't mark the papers then you're not in the militia or regiment. Doff all that right there and be on," Baryn patiently chided.

"Don't see why everyone *else* gets to fight," Ziek grumbled, as he removed his gambeson and thigh-length leather coat that reached to his calves and stormed off.

Julian watched him go and then stepped to follow, but a hand on his shoulder stopped him. It was Baryn. Tenman Baryn. "Don't do that again, Julian. You have a problem, you bring it to me."

"Right, tenleader," Julian looked at the ground, feeling ashamed at his rudeness. He could not look Baryn in the eye. After all, the man had lost his own wife right before his eyes. Julian had no idea how he could still go on. Julian walked away only a few paces before he noticed that Liri was standing not far off, maybe thirty paces, holding the reins of her horse, with Lady Judane and Bierien. All three of them were looking at him and Liri had her 'you-made-a-mess' face with her hands on her hips. *Great.*

Liri walked towards him, leaving the other two to resume their training. "Save all of the Gersh, yet?" Liri asked sardonically, "or just the town?"

"The boy's too young to soldier," Julian muttered.

"Fine, but next time tell me and I'll talk to the tenleader. I have to go apologize to Baryn now because, apparently, I've got a hot-tempered soldier of my own."

"Sorry, Tenleader," Julian said.

They walked in silence for a bit before Liri spoke again. "Are you going to your family's farm?"

"No," he said flatly. *Why would they want that? Need another reminder of how Ervan's dead?* Julian thought for a moment of his late cousin, set to marry a woman named Terah here in town when the war started. Ervan was full of hot blood and they both went off to fight. Julian was supposed to look after Ervan.

Temper that hot blood. *It should've been me...*

Liri glared at him from the corner of her eye, but remained silent as they walked. Julian was unsure where they were going, so he just kept pace with Liri and their horses. They passed through the busy town green, turned supply dump, bustling with evening activity. They passed the new multi-storied buildings. One featured a soup kitchen with a small counter for townsfolk to sit. It was run by an oldster, too old to fight, but not so old that he could not offer soldiers and workers some meat and vegetables in a warm broth to ward off the cold gusts of wind and the coming season. They passed Mkaela's closed up bakery and another row of houses.

"Where are you going?" Liri asked.

"I was following you," he said, confused.

She made a vexed sound. "Get your business together," she huffed. "C'mon. Let's get some soup." They turned around and walked back. They tied the horses to a post and sat down at the soup counter. The old man nodded to both of them and started cutting thin slivers of meat from a rump on a cutting board next to a large pot of broth.

Julian laid head in his hands, covering his face while he waited. He could feel Liri's irritated glare.

"Smell anything good in there?" piped a familiar voice. Julian looked to his other side.

"Garven!" Julian exclaimed. Garven, one of the huntsmen and trappers who was apprenticing under Korane before the war, and his Elven friend, Arynn, were seated at the counter. "What are you doing here? I thought you both went up to Borly." He had a little bit of scruff coming in, though he was younger than Julian. *About Ervan's age.* Julian did not know what to make of Garven's silver-haired friend, Arynn. She wore her locks tied back in a cord to keep it out of her face. Like most of the other elves, Arynn kept her face calm, almost emotionless. But what Julian found most unnerving about Arynn was her golden eyes. When the sunlight shined at a certain angle, they almost seemed to glow.

"We're done at Borly. We came back," Arynn said. "We hear there's a regiment forming," she grinned.

"Anyone else come back?" Julian asked.

"Korane caught up with us on our way into town. She picked up some supplies. I don't know what. She's here for only a night and leaving tomorrow," Garven said.

"Korane!? Where's she going? Was she with you in Borly?" Julian asked excitedly. He did not know why, but Julian had not felt more lively in months. He struggled to understand what was so interesting about Korane. *Maybe I'm just happy to see Garven?*

"No, I don't know where she was. I didn't think to ask too much. She didn't seem to want to talk much about it. She did have a prisoner, though," Garven said.

"Yeah? What kind? She'd get the meanest ones and grind them up," remarked Julian.

"Actually, she had a little goblin," Arynn continued, " and she hates the poor thing, too."

"Poor thing!?" Julian said incredulously.

Arynn made a skeptical face, which was very expressive for any of the elves. "You did not see how she treated it."

"What do you make of this?" Liri broke in, handing the arrow she took from the village over Julian and Garven to Arynn.

"Why do you ask?" she said.

"I showed it to Bierien and she told me what she thought, but said that I should ask another elf, or someone else well experienced, for another opinion," Liri answered.

"That sounds like Bierien," Arynn agreed. "Let me see." She turned it over, checked the fletching and glue briefly, inspected the length of the shaft, but seemed to focus her attention on the shape of the arrowhead. It was fashioned with its single blade on one side, the other side being flush with the shaft. "Goblin," she said slowly, "Northern Goblin, would be my best say. But, Irduin would be the best to ask, and she stayed at Borly."

"Hm. Thanks," Liri said" "Were there goblins at Borly?"

"Oh, yes, quite a few," Arynn replied, "Never seen so many at once." Arynn paused thoughtfully, "although, that is not unique to goblins. This journey has had a lot of first times."

"Hm. Goblins all the way down here. Wonder where

Korane's going. We sure could use her," Liri mused.

"That's from around here? Where?" asked Garven.

"A village about fifty miles from here. Most of the villagers were dead. We found a few live ones and brought them here. They said that the raiders came at night and they couldn't really see them." Liri explained.

"We heard of things like that when we passed through Yvel," Arynn said, "except that it was mostly merchant and supply caravans being raided on the roads further west."

"Hm." Liri said. "Wonder how they're getting so far in."

Wooden bowls gently thudded on the counter as the old man running the soup shop served them. Julian lost his thoughts for a moment with the company of his friend and the hearty smells of the steam wafting into his nose.

***

Ziek had heard everything he needed to. He slunk back in the shadows in the alley next to the soup counter and quietly backed down the alley until he emerged on the next street. He scuttled behind a cart and crossed the bustling, muddy street.

"Finished getting the eggs out of the coop, Ziek?" A voice that Ziek really did not want to hear. It belonged to Imick Rollodran. Since the early summer, when the orcs first came down from the mountains at the beginning of the war and Ziek's family died, he and a few other children in his situation had been lodging under the care of other families around the town. Space inside the palisade was scarce with the growing numbers of farming families trying to move inside the wall, but they earned their keep with chores and work. And there was plenty of work to be done… it was simply that Ziek was not *meant* for chores and work. Ziek was meant for fighting and glory, and he knew where he was going to get it.

"Uh, yeah. I did," he lied. She looked at him skeptically. "Uh, well," he lamely stammered, "I might've dropped a couple of them," he falsely admitted.

"Ah, I knew it," she said, sure that she had caught him trying to pass off the mistake. "You're sure to be cleaning that up."

"Yes, mistress," he said with well-feigned sullenness. She watched him go as he meandered in the direction of Imick's family home, near all of the Rollodrans. The Rollodrans were one of the big clans in Serna; most people were either related to the Rollodrans by marriage of a cousin, or else had some old grievance with them. Often enough it was both. Conveniently, the chicken coop was on the far side of the house and he was able to walk past it, all eggs safely nestled where they had been laid, and out of the town. Ziek walked through the field of stumps. The forest line had been cleared back by the town after the first raid and they had used the timber for the construction of the palisade. It was a barren field for over two hundred paces. He crossed it in the best way to avoid questioning– as if he was meant to.

"What are you doing out here?" called another voice. *Almost.*

Ziek turned to see Sedra Torin'ail. "Uh, Auntie Imick sent me out here to gather chives," he lied.

"Oh," she said, satisfied. She had a basket of berries in hand, freshly picked. Short, like other Marins, and very lean, unlike some of the other Torin'ails, Sedra had a stern, grandmotherly air about her despite only being in her forties, abetted by streaks of grey coming into her hair. "There's a patch I saw yesterday fifty paces in the trees that way," she pointed. "Don't stay out too late or the Bog Knight'll get you."

"Thanks!" Ziek said excitedly and ran off. The excitement was genuine, though not for the purpose Sedra would think. Ziek skipped into the woodline, passed the patch of chives fifty paces in and hooked to the left, toward the direction he had been heading before his second interruption. He steadily climbed up the hill through the trees. The needle trees pricked at him and the broadleaves, having lost most of their foliage by now, scratched at him, but he brushed them aside, stopping occasionally to flail a spider off of his sleeve or out of his hair.

He reached his destination just under a mile later. Sure enough, smoke billowed from the chimney of Korane's cabin. The solitary house was built mostly from timbers, with red clay filling the gaps. It had two shuttered windows on each side. Ziek heard indistinct voices coming from the inside. He crept closer and could make out two different voices. One was probably Korane's, but he could not recognize the words. They were neither Marin or Eklendan. Nothing like either language. The other voice was timid, hoarse, and slightly muffled. Creeping closer to peer between the cracks of one of the shudders, he adjusted a bit to see around the room. He could see a small figure, maybe his own size, tied to a chair with a bag over its head, but no one else. No Korane.

And then Korane's hand was on his shoulder, spinning him around and thrusting him against the side of the house. She had always been a little scary, but it was worse now. There was something in that unwavering gaze of hers that forced his eyes to the ground. Her hair black like a hidden moon and tumbling like the waters of a river. She had a scar on her cheek that he did not remember. Ziek had a bit of an infatuation for the huntress and would sometimes daydream about her, even if she was older than the age that most women married. But, there was something different now. She had lost her husband and her son months ago when the orcs came. Now, she was leaner, but not gaunt: like unneeded things had been burned away or left behind. It felt like she did not blink. She stared at him, eyes boring into him, neither speaking a word.

At last, she broke the silence. "No. Go back."

"But, I–"

"No," she interrupted, "You do not want any part of this. You will need to trust me."

"I just wanna–" he tried.

"No."

He chanced an upwards glance. If iron could be carved, that would be her face. He looked down again. Reluctantly, he started to move back towards the town. He really did not want to deal with those stupid chickens and their scatty eggs.

***

Korane watched Ziek retreat back into the woods until his slight figure disappeared into the brush. She felt sadness for him with no one left to turn to and wanting to join the fight, but being too young to do anything besides get in the way. *Well*, she thought, *there's plenty someone his age can do to help. Just none of it's fighting.* She waited for him to be gone before heading back inside, wincing from a sudden pain in her leg where that cursed hobgoblin had slashed her months ago.

She took the bag off of her captive's ugly little head and sat down at her small table and returned to slicing the meat from the carcasses of a tree rat and a fox that she had shot with her bow on the way back from her recent adventure.

She spoke in Marin. "Tell me how to say what just happened in your language." Korane hated the little scatbag, but he was useful, at least for the time being. He was a lying coward, who had pretended to be utterly dumb to the Marin tongue. The beastly little savage had finally admitted it after several days of her abusing him for the crimes his kind had committed. She hated him for what he was and what he brought with him. But he was an oddity.

His surprising fluency in Marin came out when he started begging for mercy from her beatings in the language. He concocted an unlikely story that he used to be in a group of goblins that 'traded' with Markians, though in reality more likely raided Markian villages and took prisoners for slaves. But, he never resisted her, and promised to help in every way he could–not that his promises were worth much.

At first, Korane had taken to beating him daily, but she grew tired of it, and the delays made for slower travel. She realized that she was taking her other angers out on the creature, and decided that past the purpose of establishing dominance, it was a waste of effort. He was much like a wild dog that had been tamed.

The whole time since she had picked him up two weeks ago, she prodded him, when she was not beating him, for how to speak his filthy language. In the evenings, she learned their letters. She chuckled to herself bitterly. She never had a use for learning letters and only knew enough numbers and coins to sell meat and pelts. That she was learning Goblin letters before those of her own kind rankled her mightily.

"Do you want that instead of letters?" he asked.

"No. We do them both."

"That will take most of the night."

"That's fine."

"So, we are staying here?" he asked optimistically. The hope was very obvious in his voice. He was clearly tired.

"No. We still move at first light," she said, plopping the meat into the stew pot along with some chives from a nearby patch and some roots and mushrooms. He groaned. This was the first roof over their heads for weeks and he was visibly exhausted from the pace that she set, just from the difference in stride. He was only a little more than half her height.

She slammed her fist down on the table and he jumped in fright. She gestured at him with the hunting knife. "No whining or you get less food." He was silent and waited patiently. She scooped the stew into a bowl for herself and a mug for the little wretch, putting it down in front of him. She untied one of his hands so he could eat. They ate in silence.

Curiosity struck her at odd times and this was one of them. "How did you learn your letters, anyways?"

"I needed them for my function," he said, greedily slurping the stew.

"What function?" she prodded.

"I was a mining engineer where I am from," he said, "then Fndeyet answered the call and formed a fist of engineers."

"Who's Fndeyet?" she asked.

"Fndeyet? Fndeyet the Great is the eldest of the Talz clans of Berkasliryig," he said.

"What's Berkasliriyig?" she asked through a mouthful of the stew. The stew was the best meal they had had in the two weeks. She had not had rat before, but it had a tangy, gamey taste like most animals that find their own food. The fox meat, strangely, tasted a bit like mutton. The roots and mushrooms gave it an earthy taste and the chives added another tang complementing the rat meat.

"It is a city," he said.

"A city? On the other Side of the Mountains?"

"No, on this side," he said, "under it, really."

"Under it? Further north? I've never heard of it."

"It is within the Mountains."

"In the mountains? I didn't know there were humans that lived in the mountains,"

"No, it is a city of goblins, mostly."

"What!?" Kovane was genuinely surprised. *A whole city of these little scats?*

"Mostly goblins. Plenty of others for trade. Sometimes that is where some of the humans come to trade," he explained.

"… Is it far?"

"It is further than Kogylar, but we could probably see it before the end of the moon after this moon." The goblin sounded like he was starting to regret his answers.

"Then we'll go to Kogylar and see how far deep under the mountains we can go," she said. He groaned again.

***

Deep under the mountains, on the road to Ikria.
By the Goblin Calendar, sometime in the Eighth Moon Cycle, 3114.

Oygariyet missed riding his wolf. At this moment in particular, he missed riding his wolf by the ache in his knees. The great one, his throbbing knees, and his Hobgoblin company wended their way along the road to the Place-called-Ikria, though to call this a road was a term of convenience. Really, it was a networked, winding labyrinth of caverns, tunnels, and dug passageways that had supported trade between the Place-called-Ikria, the Stone of Rykooth, and other places of the hobgoblins, goblins, or even orcs.

His company consisted of his honor guard of twenty seasoned Hobgoblin warriors, Zirn, the small orc named Grotis, his Fourth from his own staff, a motley collection of orcs and goblins, both warriors and slaves alike, including the sword dancer given

51

to him by the Donbat-Karang, a few from his harem, and some humans for a special purpose. The slaves and some of the warriors took turns pulling the baggage wagons that held most of their supplies, tools, and spare weapons.

Despite the condition of the road, peppered with collapsed bridges over bottomless chasms, narrow ways, and the disintegration of the path in more open caverns such that it was difficult to determine which outlet was the true route to the Place-called-Ikria, the recurring dilemma of food and drink, it was the humans who proved to be the largest obstacle. Their inability to see in anything short of blistering light of the coward in the sky meant the troop had to keep torches lit, which created problems of fodder, and oil to burn, and choking on the smoke in smaller passageways.

Curse them, but this had better be worth it! Oygariyet grumbled.

"We should rest for the day, Great One," Grotis said to him.

"How much further do you think?" he asked Grotis. Oygariyet noticed his Fourth's ears perk up. He knew that she did not like to travel without a clear sense of the passing of nights. She kept a tally, but it was based on when they slept with no clear sign like the rise and fall of the moon.

"Another two moons, Great One," Grotis said.

Oygariyet sighed. "Very well. Next large cavern will be our place for the rest. Water, if you can find it."

Oygariyet was not sure if it took a few moments or an entire winter to reach the next large cavern, but he knew his feet ached for the entirety of the passage. Some of the slaves fell to the laborious task of foraging the bizarre, whorled trees that grew beneath the surface, all knots and bulbous growths that had to be cut into something resembling logs for burning. Sometime even later, they had a fire going. Slaves roasted some unlucky lizards over the fire while also setting pots of water to boil.

With the work of pitching the camp done, the honor guard posted sentries while those off duty cleaned their weapons and armor, ate, took sport, or slept. The slaves continued to work busily, but some of them rotated for shifts to eat and sleep.

"May I take sport with you, Great One?" his Fourth said. It was against normal convention, since great ones took sport with their own harem, but he knew that his Fourth was in an awkward position. She was not part of his honor guard and, though more skilled than common warriors in any host, she was not skilled enough to match the honor guard–and that mattered to them. Similarly, she was not a great one, herself, and had no harem. Two of Oygariyet's own slaves curled around him in the relative privacy that could be afforded in these circumstances.

He gave her a friendly smile. "You may. My harem is open to you, Fourth." She smiled in return and began to unbuckle her belt.

As his Fourth joined and partook, the Orcish woman sword dancer approached them. Oygariyet looked up from what occupied him. "Speak," he said in Orcish.

"I would like to provide entertainment," she spoke in accented, but clear Goblin of his own dialect from the Liberator Side of the Mountains. "I would like to dance for you and your harem, Great One."

Oygariyet smiled. *Such a treasure. The Donbat-Karang can provide one that truly understands the honor of being a slave to a great one. Even an orc can do this, yet somehow Arkiban's redskin and that human woman, exotic as they may be, cannot seem to understand it.*

"Begin," he said.

She pulled her swords out of their back scabbards and left in the direction of the fires. He would later find out that she went to coat them with fat from the lizards and then dipped the blades into the cookfire to set them alight. She returned with both blades hissing in low flames. She walked in front of them and stood fifty or so hand-widths away. She assumed a pose, half bent at the waist, most of her weight on one leg under her, the other bent out and touching the ground with her toes for stability. The flaming swords were held low by her knees and high overhead. She began to dance and twirl. Oygariyet, his Fourth, and the harem watched the dance for a few moments, awed by the sword dancer's strength and grace before returning leisurely to the sport.

Most nights were like this. Marching for the waking hours, pitching camp, foraging, and the like became routine. Twelve nights later, the road broke. It was another bridge that had collapsed with disuse, shifting in the rock over time, and whatever else happened down here where no one could see or hear it.

When it was intact, the bridge would have been two spans, employing a central supporting column, whose design was based off of stalagmites unified through masonry. Oygariyet recognized the construction as Dwarven. Each span was as long as the height of three or four hobgoblins, but the furthest span had collapsed. His company spent hours that dragged on to seem like days establishing a bridge by implementing an intricate and very gradually built mutually reinforcing rope system looped over the bridge moorings.

Soon after beginning this process, Oygariyet ordered a handful of slaves and some warriors to return to the Stone of Rykooth with orders to send some Talz and workers to assist in repairing the road. Oygariyet was sick of it. It was a huge chore to get to the Place-called-Ikria and it would be an even mightier task to bring their hordes back with him to the surface.

At last, after nights of work, the task was complete. The elaborate system of ropes closed the gaps between the fallen bridge, albeit tenuously. Crossing was still dangerous. One orc and one human slipped and fell into the chasm. The supply wagons could not be carried over the tenuous rope bridge, so most of the supplies and tools were now carried strapped to backs. Despite the danger and the setbacks, Oygariyet was relieved that the gap was behind them, and they continued on.

Three nights later, by his Fourth's count, they had stopped to rest in a large cavern, somewhat larger than the courtyard at the Stone of Rykooth, to take what they guessed would be their midnight meal of dried lizard meat and fungus. . Grotis said he needed time to determine which exit passage was the correct one. They had been marking their way the whole time with ash from torches and arranging piles of rocks to find their way back, but this particular cavern possessed numerous entry and exit passageways.

The ground rumbled and Grotis seemed nervous as he made off. Oygariyet shrugged. Something did feel off, but, aside from rumblings in the ground, there was no clear threat. Oygariyet knew that if the ground here was unstable, there was no outrunning it. Had they known the true path forward, they would not have stopped here, but they did not. They would move on as soon as they knew the proper exit passage. Though there was a stream, it was strangely humid in this cavern, too. Quite humid.

Oygariyet finished his meal, as had most of the company. Grotis approached.

"Great One, I believe I have the way forward. We should leave as soon as we can," he said. He seemed more nervous than before.

"Very well," Oygariyet called to the rest of the company. "Prepare to march."

"Great One! Look at this. A purple rock. I daresay that it might contain gemstones," Oygariyet and many of the company looked over. Some of the slaves had found an outcropping of what appeared to be purple-looking rock with a deeper indigo mottling.

"That is–No! Do not–!" Grotis called just as one of the slaves touched it.

The slave pulled his hand away from the purple rock, threads of slimy secretion trailing from his hand back to the surface. The slave's face curled in perplexed disgust.

The ground rumbled again.

"Oh, no," Grotis moaned as he pulled an arrow from his quiver.

"What is this?" Oygariyet asked.

The purple surface rumbled and began to move. Expanded, as if it were heaving a breath, and rolled, crushing the slave that had touched it beneath it. Then it curled and reared up: a great worm, long as a wolf could run in ten breaths and big enough to swallow one whole. The end of the great worm turned down to look at them. A maw of three intersecting, jaw-like fleshy bits parted to reveal rows upon rows of jagged teeth. It roared and a foul smell of acids in its gut filled the air. Oygariyet choked on the fumes as it plunged into the company. Grotis loosed his arrow, but he was one of the few calm ones. The arrow stuck into the great worm's skin, but it was like throwing sand at a citadel.

The rest of the company scattered like ants. The great worm crushed some warriors and consumed others, swallowing up slaves whole. They hollered and shrieked in fear until the trifold jaw closed around them. The worm lunged towards Oygariyet, but he dodged out of the way. One of the humans, mostly blind in the darkness of this whole terrifying encounter, fell into the worm's jaws. The sword dancer leaped to snatch the human out, but misjudged the worm's momentum as it swallowed both of them whole.

"Curse it!" Oygariyet hacked at the worm's body as it went by, but to no avail. His people continued to scatter about, some running for the supposed safety of the many exit tunnels, not grasping what Oygariyet had instantly realized. The many tunnels were from the worm's tunneling and they were no safer in the tunnel. Oygariyet managed to draw the beast's attention by smashing its tail with his mace. The worm let out a small shriek. Small for its size. The shriek was still very loud and ear-piercing. It turned to look at him and lunged at him, maw open. Again, Oygariyet dodged aside and took the chance to smash the worm again, this time in one of the trifolds of its jaw. *Curse it!* Oygariyet realized that he could not hurt the great beast of the deep rock, but only to annoy it. It reared up and looked for him again. Oygariyet could tell that it found him and was looking right at him when it abruptly arched its body and collapsed. It writhed on the ground shrieking and emitting piercing screams, if Oygariyet could call the high-pitched noises coming from the great worm as 'screams.'

It continued to writhe, but the motion slowed and then stopped. Oygariyet and some of the other warriors approached the limp form cautiously. There was a thudding tap coming from the side of the worm. Oygariyet got closer and located the rough area from where the tap was originating. He slid the flat of his sword along the worm's side to try to find the exact location, when the skin of the beast began to part from the inside. A bit of steel sparkled in the faint firelight as it jutted through the worm's thick hide. The steel rocked, levered, and withdrew only to emerge again. Oygariyet understood. The motionless worm was much easier to work on than a tense one on the move to feed upon them. Oygariyet hacked at the worm's hide at the same place where the steel blade had poked out. He worked it into a hole and then widened it with the assistance of what was within the worm.

The sword dancer of the Donbat-Karang, one human, two goblins, and one orc emerged from the hole with smiles of relief, though the smell of the worm's innards released caused many witnesses to vomit.

"Quick! Into the stream and wash off," said Grotis, "the stomach juices from that thing are still strong enough to kill!" They washed in the stream in the cavern. It took a while to gather up everything that had been scattered about in the commotion. In all, two Orcish warriors, three human slaves, and four goblins had perished. As they prepared to move, Oygariyet went to the maw of the worm and smashed out two of its teeth. He washed them in the stream himself and approached the Sword Dancer.

"You have done yourself and us a great honor and service this night. Take these as trophies to your glory and that you may have them shaped later to your liking," he offered.

She swept back her wet black hair behind her head and accepted the cleaned teeth. "Thank you, Great One. You, too, do me great honor, just by your words."

He looked at her more closely. She was older, or at least seemed so for an orc. Most orcs died before they showed signs of age past adulthood, due to their violent natures, even amongst themselves. The lines of exertion and care were etched into her face from training in her art, and wielding the strength that was needed for it.

"I am given as property, Great One. Serving here with you is different and better than serving with the other orc tribes. I only wish to serve here."

They rested for the night soon after they left the worm's cavern. The following rest, the Sword Dancer again offered to entertain with her art while others took sport. Instead, she was invited to join.

Chapter 3

Somewhere near Krogen.
By the Human Calendar, Laborday (seventh day of the week), first week of
Berenk (sixth month of the year), 794.
By the Elven Calendar, sixty-seventh day of Summer, 18031.
A humid, unseasonably cool late summer evening.

ak checked that his arrow was firmly nocked in the bowstring.
He sat on a convenient stump in the fading sunlight, concealed in
the mud and tall grass, thirty or so paces from the road. He looked
around and saw a few of his crew. Most were doing what they were
supposed to be doing. Most. He would have to talk to Jawn again
about getting sleepy while waiting. But for the time being, they
would wait. The talk with Jawn would have to come later. Jak's
mind was drawn to the oddity of the last six or so months compared
to his previous years in prison.

Jak did not know his parents. He was unwanted and
abandoned, and his earliest memories were on the streets of a
town—though he did not think it was Yvel, it may well have been.
Around that time, he had been taken in by an orphanage, but the
other children had given him a hard time. A hard time until he
broke one of their legs, that is. Jak had no illusions about the fact
that it was his own fault for breaking the other boy's leg, but as a
fair counterpoint, the other boy had earned it by being such a scat
burglar.

His days at the orphanage were done soon after that and he
was out on the streets again. Most of that time, he lived surrounded
by ridicule and hostility, and had learned quickly and definitively
that no one took care of you better than you. Keppa was the first
place that he remembered with a specific identity, though not
necessarily where the orphanage or other memories were housed.
Jak lived that way on the streets of Keppa—by then he was sure
of the locale—on the wrong side of the law more often than not.
Sometimes because of what he had done in the heat of the moment.
Coarse words quickly led to blows and broken furniture. Jak rarely
started the incidents, but became increasingly proficient at finishing

them and leaving the scene before the constabulary arrived, often preferring to do most of his living at night and sleeping during the day. He increasingly found–

Is that it? ... No.

–found himself accused of things with which he had nothing to do, and the cause for it was obvious at the start–the color of his skin. Jak's skin was brilliant green, like leaves in the summer. He did not know what that meant, or why it was that way, for a long time, but discovered early on that no amount of washing, cutting, beating, or burning got the green out. So that was that. He was just green and everyone else was not. He also remembered being told that his overgrown canines were for eating babies and that other people were watching him for the time when he surely fell to his secret cravings for infant flesh.

Jak had been sent to prison, accused of murdering a man of his acquaintance in Keppa. Jak knew the situation. That man's wife wanted to be with another, and had conspired with the other man to kill her husband while keeping his money and avoiding the shame of...whatever the word was. Simply put, Jak mused, he went to prison because some woman wanted to jump on another man and because Jak was green.

Still, it was peculiar to Jak, to send a man to prison for being green. It was not until Jak was out of prison that it became clear. It was strange that people hated him for his skin until Jak saw what was called an 'orc' after he was out. It was a dead orc, and it was a lot greener than he was. Taller, too, and with larger teeth. Jak had looked around at the other men and women he was with and figured that he was halfway between an orc and a regular person, however that worked out, though this realization did not make anything easier. The reasons for them being pulled from prison were also strange to him, but those also became quickly clear.

There were still hard times in his group of about thirty, all former prisoners. All of the people that were in the wagon coming out of prison with Jak were in his group, but they were joined by additional wagons of people. Jak remembered on that strange morning he was pulled out of prison, being able to pick out the sound of at least two other departing wagons.

First, the prisoners had been checked–

Hear something... No.

–checked to make sure they could work. Then, they were taught how to fight. How to fight with swords, spears, and axes. How to shoot bows. How to hide and wait, like he was right then. How to uncover information. Plenty of other things. Then they were sent out with instructions. Jak found it ironic that he was sent to prison because someone else killed only to leave prison after, maybe, three years, to go kill people.

From the east, Tansher waved from her lookout. This would be it. Jak waited. He could hear them. Then he could see them. One. Two. Four. Six. Nine. Nine wagons. *Are there more? No. This is it, then.* Jak pulled his bowstring and loosed. It was an awkward shot, but he hit his mark. One of the two horses on the first wagon, right in the neck. The horse screamed and scrambled in a panic, startling the other horse and their driver. The wounded horse stumbled and fell. The others in his band were loosing their arrows on the drivers of the other wagons. Tansher and a few others shot and killed the drivers of the rear wagon. The fallen horse on the lead wagon flailed wildly as the other horse tried to pull the wagon in the other direction, away from Jak and most of his band. The wagon started to lean, came up on one side of its wheels, and tipped onto its side. Most of the other wagon crews fared no better, either being maimed by arrows, trampled by panicking horses or crushed by overturning wagons. Jak noticed a few of the drivers managing to dismount their vehicles from the other side and running away, but he knew that the five band members he had positioned on the far side would get them.

It was over as soon as it began. A small amount of motion remained in the few survivors trying to crawl away or rolling on the ground in pain. Jak got up, adjusted his belt, and grabbed his spear, clutching it in one hand, his strung bow in the other. Arrows rattled in his quiver as he walked, but the others in his group ran towards their quarry. Wails of the wounded cried out before being cut short. Horses shrieked and fell silent. Jak strode up to one wagon driver, chest heaving with the labor of breathing. He beseechingly held up a hand. "Plea–" but Jak thrust him in the chest with his spear. They made quick work. Eviscerated everyone. It was ghastly work, but it was needed. Apparently. Jak reflected again on the oddity of him being taken out of prison to do far worse things than that for which he was sent to prison–crimes which he did not even commit.

By now, the group was looting needed supplies and a few extra treats and prizes. *Wait.* "What are you doing?" Jak called. It was Jawn. *Again, with Jawn*, he thought irritably.

"What boss? I'm just takin' somethin' for later. Just a little snack," Jawn grinned. He had a whimpering woman, bleeding from the arm. He was forcing her to walk along with him with a strong grip on her other arm. Jak casually nocked an arrow, drew the string, and shot the woman. She yelped once and hit the ground dead. Jawn jumped in startlement. "HEY, WHAT THE SCAT!?"

"You don't take any of these," Jak motioned to the wagon crews, "not for any reason. You wanna have fun, try your luck with someone in the group. Pay up with a whore next time we're in town. Go stick it in a tree, or curl it around to your own scat hole, I don't care. But no prisoners."

"Eh? What's it to you? Ya scatty greenskin!" Jawn challenged. For all of the oddness, Jak had appreciated the last few months. He especially appreciated the efficiency of the knife techniques he had been instructed on as the belt knife glided out of its sheath at his belt, beneath the folds of his tunic and, with a flick of the wrist, raced towards Jawn's mouth. The blade was a hand long, from palm heel to fingertip, and it broke Jawn's front teeth before entering his head at the roof of his mouth. Jawn's head snapped back from the force of the stab, gurgling briefly before falling off of Jak's knife. Jak looked around at the rest of the group that had congregated to watch. Each of them carried a small box or sack of what they had scavenged from the caravan. There were no other challengers.

"What should we do with Jawn, boss?" asked one of the others.

"Leave 'im. Whoever finds this will think he was one of the caravan crew," Jak said. He bent down to pick up Jawn's forward-curving sword. Jak was told that this was an Orcish sword. He cast it into the midst of the wreckage so it did not seem like it was Jawn's sword, but that an attacker had dropped it elsewhere. The last five of Jak's group appeared from the other side of the road. "You get the runners?" he asked.

"Sure did, boss," Bisin replied.

"Good. Take your share and let's go," he said. He motioned to a few others, "go hack off some horse legs. That'll be food for a few days."

The five went for their pick while others butchered the horse meat. Jak thought about the meat roasting over an open fire later in the evening. The fire would be good. The wind brings the cold autumn sooner than normal. Tansher caught Jak's eye and gave him a playful look for what was to come later. *That'll keep the cold away, too.* Life was good, for a change. A big change.

Jak did not particularly like the work, but why should he really care. No one else in the world ever really cared about him or was ever kind to him, except for maybe one or two people in the orphanage. He went to prison for something that he did not do. So why should he care about these people he was supposed to kill? He had to kill people and make sure it looked like orcs and goblins did it. But he was free. These other normal humans did what he said. Most were afraid of him, but a few even respected him. He generally got his pick of the women in the group. Sirid was eager to be his girl, but so was Tansher and he particularly liked Tansher. Tansher was the only one with freckles. And the freckles were everywhere.

***

Crown Sorcerers' Proving Grounds, west of Yvel, on a farm.

In the dark of the morning before sunrise, Tyrnimar, a bookish elf with disheveled hair, stuffed a notebook into his saddlebag. He fixed his right foot in the stirrup and hoisted himself up. Gripping the scabbard with his right hand, he held the saddle with his left as he swung his other leg over and was seated, his other foot fumbling for the stirrup. He sighed, breath frosting in the humid air. The humans would call this moon 'Berenk,' the sixth month of the year, though they used to call it Soppi before Beren the Great had changed it. But to elves, the year was just beginning, since they counted the new year with the beginning of summer. Tyrnimar lost himself in a daydream for a moment of a place far off in a high tower with a warm fire, lamps for light to read by, and two cups of freshly brewed tea–

"Oohoo!" called a grating, musical voice. *How galling and loathsome!* The voice was like a rasp on Tyrnimar's pointed ears as he shuddered in vexation. He twisted in his saddle to see Zaya, already mounted with a leather bag slung over her shoulder, walking her horse up to his. He had risen very early. Very early. Specifically, to avoid exactly this encounter. She smiled coyly at him, which he returned with a tired glare.

"Can you be helped?" Tyrnimar said flatly.

"Well," she began melodically, "I knew you were going into the city and I wanted to come along and see my uncle." She was lying. He knew she was. But he had no basis on which to accuse her, and nothing to gain by casting the accusation. From her own saddle, she tried to draw closer to him and seize his arm, but he urged his mount to sidestep, thanking Eevarel once again for her rigorous and unforgiving tutelage. All that ruthlessness and she still had smiled at him... *Task at hand.* Silently, he turned his horse and urged it towards the road to the city.

"You wouldn't want me to wander about in the dark would you?" she called playfully as she cantered after him to catch up. *Then for the light wait*, he grumbled. "I could get lost," she teased" *Threaten me not with a blessing*, he vented internally.

They spent the morning like that, mostly. Zaya continuously harassing him despite his unconcealed eye rolls and irritated huffs. He knew full well what was going on and could only do so much to stop it without specific orders from Holbrin. She chattered at him endlessly and he returned her overtures with silence. For hours. The sun rose and dispelled some of the frost in the air. They entered Trukan and made their way to the docks before catching a ferry to Marin Quarter of Yvel, then made their way up the main avenue towards the palace. Tyrnimar dismounted and grabbed some items from the saddlebags before handing the reins to one of the stablehands and thanking her. Zaya mirrored his actions and followed him.

He made his way into the palace antechamber. As he looked around, Zaya seized the opportunity to latch onto his arm;

he shook her off irritably, her leather bag flopping aside, and she grinned at him. He stalked down the corridor with sidelong, baleful glances at her. "Is there not somewhere to be that is needed by you?" he asked. So focused on his own irritation was he, that he bumped another figure crossing the hallway. He glanced up. *Eevarel!* Zaya again took the opportunity of his surprise–seemingly her weapon of choice–and pounced on his arm, holding it uncomfortably close. Tyrnimar felt the flushing of embarrassment. *Of all the things! In front of her!* His shoulders slumped in humiliation.

Eevarel looked surprised for the barest instant before smiling at the both of them and placing her hands on her hips. She leaned close on Zaya's side, away from Tyrnimar, and whispered. Tyrnimar was not sure if he was supposed to hear or not, but without ambiguity heard Eevarel threaten, "get your own toys." They smiled at each other in a peculiar way for a moment before Zaya detached herself and cheerfully begged off to see her uncle. Eevarel, hands still on her hips, leaned to one side, and said in Elven, "I am going to kill her."

"Gah," breath escaped Tyrnimar. "As much of a relief as that would be to me, and incredibly helpful also not to be mentioned by me, that approval would be granted by Holbrin would not be thought likely by me," he answered in Elven. "Not to be mentioned, against the Ways."

"Hm? Well, I've been missing my tea. You brought me some?" she asked.

"Oh," he fumbled. "Yes, um…"

"Not *here*," she scolded as he was producing the first tin cup. They proceeded to the apartments that the elves shared, though most were out of Yvel now.

As they walked, Tyrnimar asked, "what was that about toys?"

"Tsk, nevermind that," she airily dismissed as they entered the apartments. He was glad to see Trinien.

"Ah, Tyrnimar! Here with my weekly delivery?" he laughed in a friendly greeting.

"By the Way," Tyrnimar said, producing the notebook he

had packed. Trinien tossed it into the fire and handed Tyrnimar a blank notebook.

Eevarel was clearly confused by the exchange. "What are you doing!?"

Tyrnimar tossed the fresh notebook on the table before producing the gourd bottle and two tin cups, pouring Eevarel's serving first. He nudged it towards her before answering while pouring his own. "Zaya of House Yand'ail was the lady in the hall. Observations of the sorcerers and myself have been made by her. My notes and, perhaps, one of my books has been copied by her. Now, decoy notes are made by me. That she does not know Elven is certain to me, so the ruse can be continued for some time."

"How do you know she does not read Elvish?" Eevarel asked.

Tyrnimar blushed and looked away as Trinien grinned and answered, "because Tyrnimar writes all kinds of nonsense in there. Everything from roast chicken recipes to how to diagnose health problems in lizards from the color of their dung," he chuckled.

"That some of that was fabricated by me must be admitted," Tyrnimar mumbled into his tea. "Still, this is serious. A serious attempt at espionage and that she has copied at least part of one book is to be certain. Which one, I am not sure."

"Well, Holbrin will not be too pleased," Trinien said.

Eevarel was surprised. "He does not know yet?"

"No," Tyrnimar said glumly, "not yet. This letter will be sent by me." Tyrnimar held up a rolled letter, sealed with wax.

"I will take it, then," Eevarel said. "Holbrin sent me off to check on something and needs my report."

"Oh, you will?" Tyrnimar asked.

"Wonderful," Trinien said at the same moment. "Holbrin has me on task here advising the Prince's Merchant and Guild Council. Greedy, short-sighted lot there. I was getting worried about making time to bring all these other goods down to him in Serna."

"What other goods?" Eevarel asked tentatively.

Trinien gestured to four wooden travel chests, "Tyrnimar's traveling library. He had to evacuate them away from the espionage risk and they're not much safer here."

"Wonderful." Eevarel deflated, clearly displeased to be charged with the transport of four large trunks of books. "Did you not only have three saddlebags of books when we arrived?"

"Oh, yes," Tyrnimar said, suddenly giddy. "Those two are notebooks full from the sorcery observations." He waved the fresh notebook. "And this one will be filled in by memory and go with the rest. Also, more books have been bought by me and two more have been written by me regarding the various herbs, roots, and flowers on the western side of the Kaskevs." Tyrnimar chattered on, but Eevarel had stopped listening.

***

In another section of the palace, Zaya pushed open two large, gracefully carved wooden doors into the palace library. She stepped in cautiously. The creak of the doors echoed, as did the dull thud of them closing behind her. She made her way to the fourth table in the main reading area, piled high with books both open and closed. This was her appointed drop spot. She reached into her leather bag and began to lay out the ledgers she had copied from Tyrnimar's room and the portions of one of his books that she had been able to page through. She jumped in surprise when she noticed a man sitting three tables away, peering at her over the edge of a book he was reading.

"Oh! I'm sorry, I didn't notice you there," she began.

"It's quite alright, my fair lady. Please," he said, "be comfortable. I do not get many visitors."

"Erm, I'm sorry. I'm really just returning these for a friend."

"It's quite alright. Please, my name is Nicholas. I'm the chief librarian here. Really," he chortled, "that doesn't say much when I'm the *only* librarian here."

"Um, right, uh, master librarian," she said, "look, sorry, but I have a pressing appointment with my sister. I'm really just dropping these for a friend."

"Oh," Nicholas murmured "Well, of course. Please do come see me some time," he smiled at her. Zaya did not hold his gaze long and excused herself hurriedly.

Nicholas watched her go. It was a shame. He was sure she could be quite charming, even if it was a false charm, but needed more experience at managing surprise. She was too accustomed to controlling the situation and knowing everything about it that she had trouble dealing with the unexpected. Still, her reports were promising, both for her skill at observation and surveillance, but also for what the reports contained themselves. He would make a note in her dossier and talk to one of his handlers, though he did not remember which one. There were three layers between Nicholas and someone in Zaya's position. She had no idea that she actually worked for him or that he was involved in the slightest.

Now, he thought, *let's see what the good Master Tyrnimar has to say*. He picked up the few transcribed pages and scanned them over. *I should've expected they'd be written in his own tongue. Hm. Who could translate... ah... hm... Well, maybe Turin can talk him into it.*

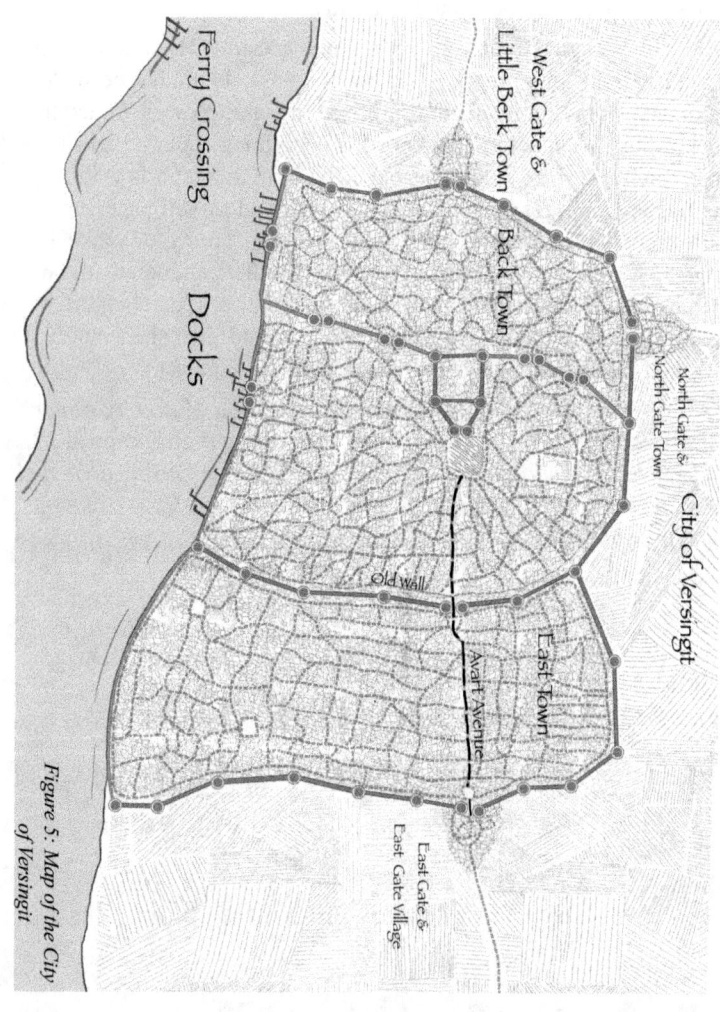

Figure 5: Map of the City of Versingit

Chapter 4

Near the Place-called-Versingit, on the Liberator Side of the Mountains.
By the Goblin Calendar, middle of the Ninth Moon Cycle, 3114.
By the Human Calendar, Playday (ninth day of the week), second week of
Berenk, 794.
A cool and windy late summer night.

"Over there," ordered the subleader. Obeying her
commander, the goblin and her fellows sweated in the cool air and
heaved the timber onto the pile. They had been gathering timber for
almost half of a moon now. She and the others turned back to the
tree line and went to work pulling down one tree after another,
shaving off the limbs and sorting them by intended usages. Some,
the smaller ones, were designated for the cookfires. Others went to
make smaller engines or siege spears. The great timbers were
reserved for the construction of stone hurlers and wall towers.

The subleader's lash seared her side. "Ah!"

"Put your back into it!" the subleader yelled, lashing her
fellows. A young goblin boy fell to the ground, writhing in pain.
Barely old enough to join, and he had been swept up by Bindeyet's
call. Bindeyet had come to her clan and said that salvation was
at hand. The mighty Oygariyet the Great would lead them all
gloriously to the lowlands of easy living, where no one froze during
the winters, the beasts were mild, and easy prey populated the
lands. She had only heard stories of places like that, and had at first
been skeptical, but enough merchants passed through Kogylar with
the same stories of flat ground, many trees, warm rain, and easy
hunting that she could not altogether dismiss it. She had heard these
stories for many Longnights. *Longnight…* they would probably
take this Longnight feast here in Place-called-Versingit. It was only
three moons away. She was just barely old enough to participate in
the feasts and festivities of love, though if she had her own family,
she could have. But that was postponed for… this. When Bindeyet
spoke to Jireyet, the leader of her own tribe, the Venjeer, and their
clan elders, it was like a child's story coming to life. They had all
happily agreed.

Who knew it would be like this? Endless marches and back-breaking labor every day for the incomprehensible plans of some Talz engineer. The nights were starting to get longer again, but with the comfort of darkness, came the chill on the drying wind from the cold rolling off the mountains. Even though they were not the heights of Kogylar, the gusts still whipped and chapped the crew, and they shivered at night and huddled close.

The subleader had informed them that they would have a new home in the easy lands by Longnight. That quieted most of the discontent, at least for the meantime, but it did not give rise to much working spirit when they had to gather timbers for three wall towers, fifteen stone hurlers, the same number of great siege crossbows and the siege spears they threw, plus enough firewood to feed the entirety of the great host assembled before this Place-called-Versingit. Not much working spirit indeed, when the youngest of her fellows lay on the ground, twisting away from the lash.

The boy was very young, but like the rest of them, he had leapt at the chance for a life of his dreams. The subleader turned towards the onlookers with her lash in hand. The foreigner with the red skin of goblins from far to the right along the mountains, where it was even colder, the man with the once-broken nose, the man with purple eyes, and the woman with gold earrings on both sides; herself, too, and the youngest. She bore the subleader's lash alongside the rest of them. They cowered from the sting until the subleader tired, her chest heaving with the effort of lashing the whole crew.

"Ten more timbers today! We have to have enough to start building tomorrow. You understand? We don't build fast enough and those stupid greenskins will eat us out of boredom!" she hollered at them. The goblin understood; she had heard about orcs and their appetite for anything that moved, even one other. The crew felled ten more trees, but the subleader made them cut three more just to be safe. Collapsing in exhaustion just as the sun was rising, they huddled together for warmth next to the pile of timbers for mutual protection against the cutting winds. They slept as the sun rose, invading the sky, and began to retreat over the edge of the land, far from the mountains. Nearly a moon ago, she had flushed with anticipation and excitement about sleeping so close to the red-skinned one from further on the right of the mountains, with his beautiful sunset-red eyes. Now, she was so tired after so many moons of toil, that she was asleep nearly instantaneously as soon as they were given permission.

The subleader kicked them awake when the sun was running away. The first job was building a stone hurler. They took two great timbers the length of about four goblins' height, twice the height of a hobgoblin or human, drilling three evenly spaced holes in them and setting them with smaller timbers to build the frame. The drilling lasted through the sun's retreat and well past the rescue of the moon. She chanced a look over at the other half of the crew, building the second stone hurler. Mindful of the lash, she did not allow her eyes to linger for long. They drilled additional holes and mounted four wheels made from disks cut from the trunks of trees. The goblin appreciated mounting the wheels sooner before it became very heavy, which also allowed them to push the frame over to other piles of timbers. They broke for a brief meal of boiled possum and snake with roots: food that would have made her crinkle her nose up just two moons ago, was now a welcome meal. It was still hot.

Next came the two upright beams on either side of the frame, close to the middle, with a thick crossbeam connecting them at the uppermost point. The subleader stalked about, doling out a sharp kick or rebuke here or there, but the goblin guessed they were on schedule because there were further no lashings. She furtively watched the subleader move about the other crews building their own stone hurlers or great siege crossbows. Two more holes on opposite sides of the frame base let them install the rotating beam for torsion and then affixing the throwing arm. Gods knew where the rope came from, but they had enough. The throwing arm went in as others in her crew were finishing carving the stone basket out of a stump, whittling out the wood with sharpened carving spoons, stopping periodically to whet them on stones. They drilled a hole into the basket and carved down the throwing arm to mount the basket on the arm, then fixing it in place with a retaining peg. With the arm and basket installed, they rested. The night was almost done. The moon was retiring and it was yet quite bright. It would be fullest soon.

The very unlucky ones were building wall towers, tall enough to be wheeled to the walls of the Place-called-Versingit and to mount the top of the walls of the Place. After the first night of working on the stone hurler, a rumor traveled around camp that some goblins had fallen to their deaths while working on one of the towers and that the orcs had laughed and eaten them.

The goblin glanced around to make sure there were not any orcs nearby, but was being kicked awake by the subleader before she realized she had fallen asleep. The sun had invaded a while ago and they needed to finish the stone hurler today. The upright beams were braced on the frame on both sides. The rest of the crew wrapped rope around the torsion bar, installed a hook on the stone basket, and wound rope around a winding beam that had been installed yesterday–but the goblin had been too tired to notice. As they continued coiling the rope around the winding beam, they installed the cranking arms on both sides to charge the stone hurler.

The goblin watched the progress as she had been set to a different construction task. She built a cart of smaller timbers and scraps to carry the stones for the hurler. First the bottom frame, with two short beams ending in handles on its rear, a wheel between the beams in the front, and a pair of pieces on which to set the cart down. Then came the bottom of the cart, resting on the frame, then the sides. Apparently, since she made the cart, that meant she got to go find stones. She grumbled dark thoughts at the subleader as she walked further into the woods.

The only nice part was picking stones with the red-skinned foreigner with sunset eyes. She would have flushed with excitement, had she not been so sore and exhausted from the unending toil. The first few days of the march, she would have been embarrassed by struggling to keep up, though most of the new recruits had struggled to keep pace. Even him. She would have been embarrassed by being whipped by the subleader in front of him, but then, he was always whipped, too. They all were.

She smiled. He would not judge her. He would not because he had suffered the same hardships. The same humiliations. They both had the same dreams. She remembered when he had arrived at Kogylar a few winters ago, covered in mud from travel. Jireyet had graciously welcomed him into the Venjeer. He had raised swine far to the right of the mountains, where the winters were very long, before the humans came to his village and destroyed everything. He told the goblin that when he had to flee his burning village, none would give him a chance to be useful, not even by using his hide and bones. No one gave him a chance until he came to Kogylar.

When Bindeyet came with the call, the redskin cheered as loud as Jireyet–almost to the point of rudeness. She was happy for him. Happy that he could be useful to those that he had to leave behind, even if it was not against the same humans that had come to his village. Or maybe it would be. This Place-called-Versingit was also further toward the right of the mountains. Who knew for certain?

The two goblins gathered stones in silence for the stone hurler, piling them into the cart, then wheeling full carts back and making a pile. Three cartloads later, the subleader told them it was time for the end-of-day meal. The goblin unpacked her stone bowl and got in line with the rest of her crew by the cookpot. Apparently, the rumors of a goblin falling from the wall tower was at least partially true, or else someone had gotten themselves killed in another way, judging by the stew served into her bowl. She was not sure if it was the Bindeyet and his kindness allowing him to be useful by feeding the army, or if it was Maglaban who had been generous this time. She did not know much about Maglaban. He and his odd, purple-skinned Barituul, from the Invader Side of the Mountains, had joined them on the march from Kogylar. They were a strange lot. Exotic-seeming at first with such a sensual color natural to them, yet they acted like it meant nothing.

They ate. Some of the others joked together, but she ate alone until she looked up to see the purple-eyed goblin was offering her something. Bread. "Where did you find this?" she asked.

"In a human dwelling when we were gathering timbers," he said. He looked away sheepishly, "I wanted to give this to you yesterday, but we didn't eat together."

"Oh," she said. She smiled. The purple-eyed man had always been nice to her. When the older spawners of the tribe died, he had saved bits of their skins and bones and made her some clothes and tools with them. She broke it in two, offering half back to him. They sat and ate it together. It was strange. The air pockets

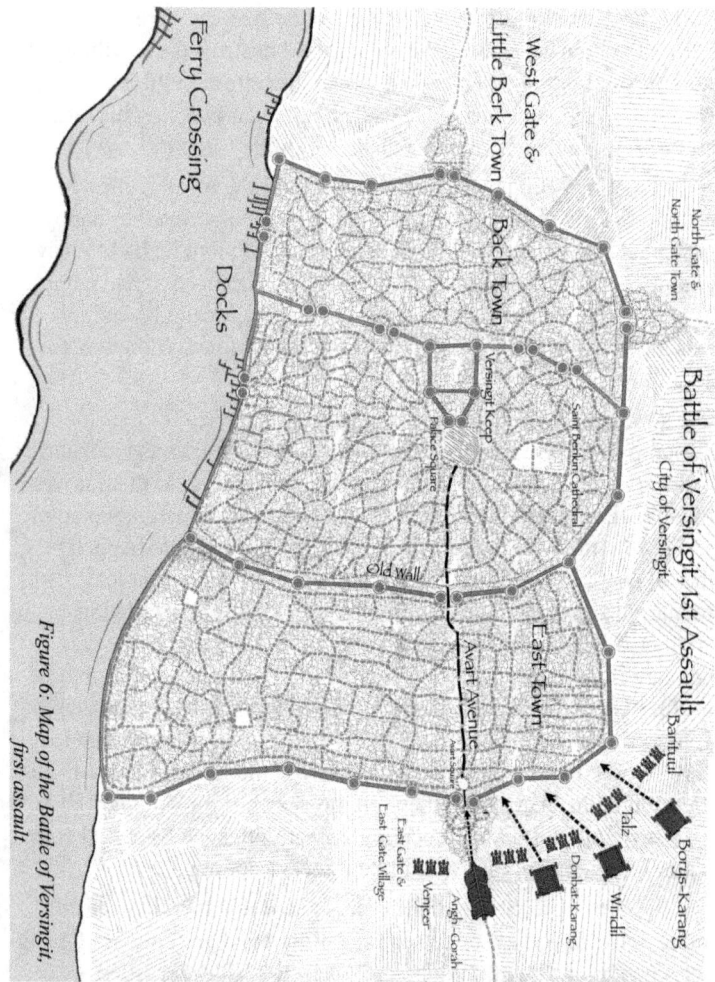

Figure 6: Map of the Battle of Versingit, first assault

from baking were smaller and it tasted of nuts. They were both used to the airier, sweeter bread they made in Kogylar from the flour of ground roots. They finished the bread and slept, since the sun was about to invade.

The subleader woke them when the sun was high and attacking. It was time to prepare. The goblin and the rest of her crew pushed out the stone hurlers through the light screen of trees into the open. This was the first time that she saw the Place-called-

Versingit. It seemed like a silly place. A city–it must be a city–built with no mountain or hill around it? She supposed that was how the humans had to build things, since they did not live in the mountains, at least not these ones. They had to make their own mountains with high walls, but the walls were stone, which came from the mountains. It seemed quite nonsensical to build something far away from the materials needed for its construction. Humans (she assumed they were humans but could not tell from the distance) gathered on the walls and watched the approaching host.

A river flowed by the Place-called-Versingit. That created a different kind of protection and the goblin decided that maybe it was not entirely nonsensical. She had plenty of time to ponder this as she and the rest of the goblins strained, grunted, and sweated against the weight of the stone hurler. They pushed and lagged until reminded of the task by the subleaders whip. The subleader lashed so often, she imagined she enjoyed it, or at least did it when she was angry or frustrated, judging by the way she yelled.

Then she saw an odd thing. A house, made of wood, floating on the river. It seemed like the house was made to float on the river. It was hundreds of paces away, but it seemed to have a body like a blade. Two tall posts had large blankets hanging from them that puffed and ruffled, she guessed with the wind. It was quite strange. Then she saw another. The water-houses floated on the river away from the Place-called-Versingit as if they had a will of their own.

"They are called 'boats," said the subleader. "Maglaban says that they are operated by human crews to move things." This generally made sense to the goblin, *but what made it better to move it on the river instead of carrying it? They had to move the stonethrower. If the human crew operated the 'boat,' would they not still have to push it?*

"Over there!" the subleader yelled. The goblin and her crew pushed the stonethrower over a small rise in the ground, cursing the tiny ridge. The other stone hurlers and siege crossbows moved up, forming a line. Carts of stones and siege spears followed. "Aim for the first tower away from the gate," the subleader ordered.

The crew rotated the stonethrower, lining up the throwing arm with the tower to the left of the gate. She cranked the throwing arm down with another goblin on her side of the crank, and two others on the opposite side. The rope around the torsion beam groaned. Two other goblins loaded rocks into the basket. The man with the once-broken nose pulled the lever, releasing the lock on the crank. The rope around the torsion arm creaked and moaned as it pulled the throwing arm up, slamming into the crossbar. The stones soared through the air and thudded into the wall in a cascade as the other stonethrowers unleashed their first volley at the wall, eliciting a startled cry from the humans who had congregated on the wall.

The sun's beating and passing blurred as the crews reloaded the stone hurlers and slung more projectiles at the wall. She noticed the three wall towers slowly approaching the city's wall, one near the gate and the other two further to the right of the gate. A ram with a shelter approached the gate itself. She had heard some of the Talz talking about the wall towers, but these seemed simpler. They had four ladders on the tower, straight to the top, a platform for attackers to stand, and a wooden board to make a bridge from the tower onto the defenders' wall. Each of the platforms held maybe three or four of the hobgoblins shoulder-to-shoulder. This was the first chance that she had to get a clear look at the wall towers and barely looked at the ram. The goblin had not noticed the ram being built, but she had been too busy inspecting the stone hurler to make her way over to the wall towers as they were being built.

The crew labored over the stone hurler as the sun blazed upon them. The moon rose to banish the cowardly sun as the wall towers reached the walls of the city and the ram reached the gate. Thin streams of green-skinned orcs flowed up to two of the wall towers, and a purple stream of hobgoblins up the third. The purple would be the Barituul, the only tribe from the Liberator Side of the Mountains in the siege. The goblin did not know which orc tribes were climbing the towers and which were pushing the ram. She heaved against the crank, pulling the throwing arm down, as the ram began to thud against the gate. Crew members loaded stones in the basket, but they were running low on stones.

As they released another shot, stones began to hail down upon them from behind the enemy's walls. The humans had their own stone hurlers. She wondered why they had waited all daytime to start using them, but maybe it was because they had to gather stones as well. The subleader screamed at them to keep steady and work the engines. They placed a shot, and another, and another. Their opponents in turn rained stones down upon the hurlers. They launched their last shot of stone when a cluster of rocks flung by the human stone hurlers smashed into one of the other goblin stone hurlers, smashing the beams and spitting the broken bodies of some of the crew away.

"Away!" screamed the subleader. She ran amidst the stones, raining ever closer to the goblin's own stonethrower, kicking and pushing the other crew away, "Move! Away!" The subleader kicked the goblin hard and she fell. The Goblin woman with two gold earrings pulled her up as they ran back towards the tree line. The subleader had hurriedly disappeared toward where Jireyet and the other leaders were. She appeared moments later as they caught their breath. "Build some ladders," he ordered. *Ladders?* She was puzzled. *What for?*

The orcs had rammed through the gate itself, but were fighting hard to gain entry and were dwindling under a blizzard of arrows launched from atop of the gate wall. Even as they struggled at the gate, and orcs and hobgoblins alike toiled with the wall towers, the goblin and her crew gathered more timbers–long, young trees with narrow trunks–and lashed them together with shorter, stout branches. The subleader had hurried off, but returned to check on them periodically. She was hardly yelled at, and the lash never came off of the subleader's belt. *Does she feel sad for beating us?* The subleader told them to make the ladder taller. It almost sounded like a request to the goblin, rather than an order. They lashed more narrow trunks to the top, reinforced them with extra rope, and extended it before the subleader told them to rest.

***

Amidst the blustering wind, Peregan shot another arrow into the thrashing green crowd amassed at the bottom of the wall. Another orc clutched its shoulder and reeled back into the raging swarm below. This was not how Peregan had thought things would end for him.

Three months ago, he drove wagons for his uncle, hauling grain. Then the raids came, and they moved to the city. Prince Eron said they needed more soldiers and Peregan signed enlistment papers while his uncle was off hauling grain by himself. His uncle was out on the roads when the attackers came a few days ago. He hoped his uncle got away. Another arrow down into the mob struggling to push the wooden tower forward. *Three towers.* They had pushed three towers. Peregan could not conceive of how they managed to build those towers. *Towers as tall as the wall. Where did they get that wood? How did they even build them? Are they not just a bunch of inbred savages?*

The tower swayed as the orcs climbed the shielded ladders on the other side. He loosed another arrow at one that climbed to the top of the ladder, but missed. The arrow whistled off into the distance, free of the chaos. Peregan, offset directly in front of the tower, noticed that it had a wooden bridge that was folded up, shielding the orcs from the front. Soldiers with axes, swords, and spears piled in to block the attackers. Loosed another. The first orc was already behind the bridge, but Peregan got another. The arrow lodged into armor made of thick overlapping hides and leather. Some of them even had mail. *Did they steal those?* Peregan loosed another arrow. And another. And another. But it seemed to not matter. The orcs lined up behind the bridge-shield. Twelve. Sixteen. Twenty. He could start to hit them, but some had shields and blocked his shots. Another arrow, got one in the top of the head, peeking out from over the shield. Twenty-four, not twenty-three. Now twenty-four.

The bridge landed on the wall with a resounding thud, and the orcs stormed over it, but ran against a wall of sharp steel, cleaving the lives of the first rank. Peregan was almost dry on arrows as more orcs swarmed up the ladder. He ran along the wall ten paces to a barrel of arrows, grabbed two fistfuls and jammed them into his quiver as he ran halfway back and began loosing arrows onto the crowd of orcs massing at the tower's base. More orcs were streaming from the woodline toward this tower and the next one over. The soldiers held as valiantly as they could, but were falling one by one.

The orcs rushed on with frenzied abandon. Their size and

their number would wear the soldiers down eventually. Maybe forty soldiers held against the tower, with more archers culling the horde below, but there were so many. Already six, no, seven soldiers lay bleeding and motionless on the parapet, their bodies ceaselessly jostled by the hustling of feet in the melee. A new rank of orcs topped the ladders. Peregan loosed an arrow at one, catching the orc through the forearm. The greenskin dropped its weapon, clutched its arm and howled as the arrow protruded halfway out the other side. It glared in furious pain at Peregan before the orc next to it punched it out of the way, and it stumbled and fell backwards off the tower.

The orc that had just struck his compatriot shouted at two other orcs, and in unison, the three of them bounded forward, slamming into the backs of their fellow soldiers. The force of the impact cascaded forward as orc bodies slammed into each other. The orcs in the rear continued to push the middle and front ranks of orcs forward, impaled on the defenders' spears, and drove them all ahead. The colliding bodies bumped some of the defenders off of the wall on the back side, four of them falling to the grounds within. The rear ranks of orcs crawled over the dying bodies of their fellows, laying waste to the human defenders with axes and square-tipped or forward-curving swords. Peregan loosed another arrow, catching another one in the armpit as it raised its sword for a strike.

They fought to a stalemate for an intense instant. Maybe seconds. Maybe minutes. It might have been all day for what Peregan could tell, but he was out of arrows again, his muscles burned from the urgency, and the skin on his fingers was raw and chafed from pulling the bowstring. He ran for more arrows.

"YOU!" Another soldier emerged from a door set into the nearest turret, forty paces up the wall. "HELP ME WITH THIS!" The soldier was rolling a barrel on its side along the wall's inner edge. He was well-armored, with plates of embossed steel covering most of his body. The wind gusted and howled. Peregan ran to him and helped him steady and roll the barrel. The soldier had three buckets, clutched by the rope handles in his other hand. They rolled the barrel towards the melee.

"WHAT ARE WE DOING?" Peregan called over the din.

"FIXING PROBLEMS," the soldier called back. They neared the writhing mass of angry humans and orcs, struggling for dominance of the wall. "PUSH THEM BACK! THIS IS VERSINGIT! YOU TAKING THIS LYING DOWN!?" With much thrashing and struggling, the human defenders pushed the orcs back a pace, maybe a pace and a half. The soldier halted with the barrel, "NOW." Peregan helped him set the barrel upright. "WRONG WAY," he shouted, and they turned it back onto its side and rolled it to the other end . He broke the seal, revealing a viscous, yellow-tinged liquid inside. Flax oil for lamps, discernible by the vaguely fish-like smell. He thrust a bucket at Peregan and threw another to one of the other archers, "YOU! TAKE IT!"

"WHAT ARE WE DOING?" Peregan called again.

"THIS!" the soldier said, dunking the remaining bucket into the barrel, the liquid resisting the bucket slightly. The soldier ran to the edge of the wall and cast the liquid onto the tower. "HURRY UP!"

Peregan and the other archer set to work feverishly casting the yellow liquid down the wall, bucket after bucket as the wall defenders surrounding them perished. "YOU!" the soldier shouted at two other archers, "MAKE TORCHES! NOW!" Peregan, the other archer, and the armored soldier heaved the contents of the barrel at the orcs' siege tower, splashing its wooden siding, the orcs climbing onto the top platform, wherever they could reach. Most of it splashed on the near side of the wooden tower. "LIGHT THEM! NOW! THROW THEM!"

The archers tried to light their hastily constructed torches. Peregan noticed that they had ripped off shreds of their own clothes, soaking them in the oil before knotting them around arrows. The wind made it difficult to light torches with only flint and steel. The archers huddled against the wall and continued to struggle in their task, as Peregan and the other two heaved liquid at their attackers. More defenders died around them. They would break soon.

The torches slowly sprang to life and then suddenly burst into vigorous flame. They hurled the torches at the tower. One landed on the platform, the other bounced off and fell to the ground at the tower's base. "MORE, CURSE YOU, MORE! I DON'T CARE IF YOU HAVE TO STRIP NAKED TO MAKE MORE! CURSE YOU TO THE PIT! HURRY UP!" The others hurriedly assembled more torches as the soldier kicked a few other archers into joining. Peregan and the other archer were nearing the bottom of the bucket. The wind blasted him in the face as they hurled more oil, blowing some backwards onto his gambeson and quiver.

The orcs continued to shuffle up the ladders and forward onto the platform to fight the tired defenders. Peregan grimly noted that both attackers and defenders were having to crawl and climb over piles of the accumulated dead from both sides in order to strike at one another. More volleys of burning torches arced through the air, some landing on the tower, some ending on the ground. But the wait was beginning to show results. The summer had brought little rain to the area surrounding Versingit, and the winds for the past few days had made it even drier. The oil on the dry wood was beginning to heat to burn.

Fresh flames suddenly erupted on the siege tower. First on the platform, eliciting yelps of surprise and fear from the orcs. Flames quickly spread over the platform and down the side of the tower. The wind fanned the blaze and the fire started to climb over the tower. Screams and howls of terror flooded his ears. The defenders redoubled. Arrows from the top of the wall rained on the orcs as the defenders ran them through with sword or spear, cleaved and crushed with their axes, or pressed them into the flames. The attack crumbled at the top of the wall and the smell of orcs burning to death on the tower wafted in the air. Peregan felt it odd that it smelled like any other hunted beast roasting too long over a fire.

The orcs, some still alight, fled the tower and the wall. A drizzle of arrows and cheers of victory chased them, but the commanding soldier that had produced the barrel of oil frantically moved to halt the archers;the winds were blowing the arrows off target at range, wasting arrows waylaid by the wind.

They cheered. They were alive. They had won. Peregan whooped with glee, but felt a hard shove. He looked over and saw the same soldier with a grim expression on his face. "WHAT?" Peregan shouted over the cheering.

"GET MORE OIL." The soldier pointed and Peregan saw more attackers pouring over the tops of the other two wooden towers."NOW," the soldier demanded, kicking him.

Flinching, Peregan lost his temper. "WHO THE SCAT ARE YOU, EH? YOU GONNA GET OIL, TOO!?"

"WHO AM I!?" The soldier seemed surprised at the question, "I'M ERON WRIN'AIL. YOU KNOW? PRINCE OF THESE PARTS AND I HAVE A LOT OF FIGHTING TO DO RIGHT NOW." Peregan stood, agog. "NOW GO! FAIL ME NOT!" Prince Eron shoved him. Peregan fell over in surprise. *The Prince fights on the wall himself? Is this a good sign or a bad sign?*

Chapter 5

Near the Place-called-Versingit, on the Liberator Side of the Mountains.
By the Goblin Calendar, middle of the Ninth Moon Cycle, 3114.
By the Human Calendar, Restday, second week of Berenk, 794.
Mid-afternoon on a late summer day.

*J*ireyet pulled back his hood off of his blue-skinned head as he approached the cluster of tribe leaders. They towered over him, as Jireyet of the Venjeer was one of the only two Goblin tribe leaders amongst the orcs and hobgoblins. The Talz were the other Goblin tribe, but had only sent a warband (this was often a matter of great confusion, as there was also an orc tribe here called the same). Armored, purple-skinned hobgoblins from the other Side of the Mountains admitted him inside the ring of sentries who were loosely securing the perimeter.

The tribe leaders were clustered around drawings of the land, as the wolf surveys. The bald, purple-skinned Maglaban, from the Invader Side of the Mountains, leaned on his glaive, bringing order to the meeting. Some of the Hobgoblin leaders had a small entourage with them–two or three subleaders of one type or another–but the orcs were each the sole representatives of their tribes. Any that the orcs brought with them were their personal property.

"Ah, save the night! The Venjeer are here," said the Ahng-Gorah. A few chuckles dotted the gathering, but Maglaban silenced them with individual, pointed glares.

"Time for stuff and sex or time for skill?" Maglaban asked flatly, his strong accent from his faraway home on the other Side of the Mountains emphasized. Jireyet did not entirely understand, but thought it was some reference to the Orcish religion–he thought they had gods of wealth and prosperity which they referred to as 'stuff,' though was not sure about the others or how many there were. Some of the gathered returned the hobgobin's glare, but others puffed at the rebuke. Allowing time for his gaze to cow the defiant ones, Maglaban switched to Orcish after the pause. "Donbat-Karang, tell us of your plan."

Jireyet's Orcish was not the best, but he tried to follow. The Donbat-Karang stepped forward from the crowd. Two swords hung from his belt on opposite hips. He wore a coat of mail down to his knees over stout leather boots. The sleeves of the coat were covered with overlapping plates of hardened leather down to the wrist. A pair of gloves were stuffed into his belt, and his helmet was carried by one of his properties. Healthy, black, coarse hair grew thickly from his head straight up, but was neatly sheared flat. Designs upon his face, resembling burning swords, were meticulously branded with burn scarring.

"We go to the Versingit-Place again. The Barituul will use what they took on the right wall." He eyed Maglaban, who nodded as the Donbat-Karang pointed to the section of wall that the Barituul had successfully seized. "They will go to the gate and make the defenders give them the gate. The Ahng-Gorah will try to take the gate again." He eyed the Ahng-Gorah.

"You have thing to take?" the Ahng-Gorah broke in. Jireyet could not take the meaning from the words, but gathered from the tone and the steps forward, almost onto the land-drawing, that Ahng-Gorah's question was meant to be threatening. The plan going in required the gate to move most of the attackers inside the city wall, but Ahng-Gorah had failed to seize the gate in the last attack, and the Donbat-Karang was frustrated.

"Yes. I do. You had one thing. Take the gate. You did not take it. You want to take me? You take the gate first. Maybe you can help this time," the Donbat-Karang scornfully dismissed. They locked gazes for a moment before the Ahng-Gorah backed down, diverting his eyes.

"How will the gate be taken with so many defenders there?" Muydiyet asked. Muydiyet led her small tribe of wolf riders, the Wiridil, her host putting only a few fists in the field. They had been effective in closing off the city, capturing a few that were trying to flee on foot, on beast, and on drawn wagon. She did not speak often, but always had prudent and practical points when she did. She was blue-skinned, meaning that she was from the Liberator Side of the Mountains, like Jireyet was. He had known the Wiridil to pass through his home city of Kogylar from time to time.

"Good you ask," the Donbat-Karang said. "There will be

another attack on the left walls. The Talz will take the walls and make the defenders split attention. The Talz will have the help of the Barituul and the Venjeer."

"The Talz," the Ahng-Gorah chuckled. Jireyet caught the difference. The Donbat-Karang meant the Talz, an orc tribe here, not the Goblin tribe, also called the Talz. The Goblin Talz, from Kogylar, was the source of most of the know-how for the construction of the siege machines, specializing in engineering and construction. Because of their knowledge, the Talz were split many ways to help the different attacks, all left and right along the mountains. Jireyet was curious how they came upon such designs and meant to ask their tribe subleader later. Only a subleader was here to represent the Talz.

The Orcish Talz leader stepped onto the land drawing with his horned mace brandished, threatening the Ahng-Gorah. The Ahng-Gorah was drawing his sword from his belt when Maglaban's glaive slowly but firmly lowered between them. "Take the place first," he said quietly. "Then you fight after we have the city."

The two backed down before the Donbat-Karang continued. "With the defenders divided, the gate will fall. When the defenders know we took the gate, they will give up the left wall or be killed. There will be no way for them to keep the left wall from the attack on the ladders and an attack from the gate. But they have to know that they do not have the gate anymore, so the Ahng-Gorah will have to keep some warbands back and ready to attack after the gate falls. Move inside the wall to the left and attack the left wall defenders."

Maglaban shifted his weight and looked at the leader of Borys-Karang, who had been silent throughout this exchange. To say the Borys-Karang was a tribe leader did not capture it. The Borys-Karang was the mightiest orc tribe in both strength and numbers. That the Borys-Karang was here himself spoke to the importance of the matter, as Jireyet had heard that the Borys-Karang fought in many places and had their own kind of subleader, which he believed were called 'garad-dai.' Jireyet watched the silent exchange of mistrust between Maglaban and the Borys-Karang. The Borys-Karang smiled at Maglaban. The Borys-Karang

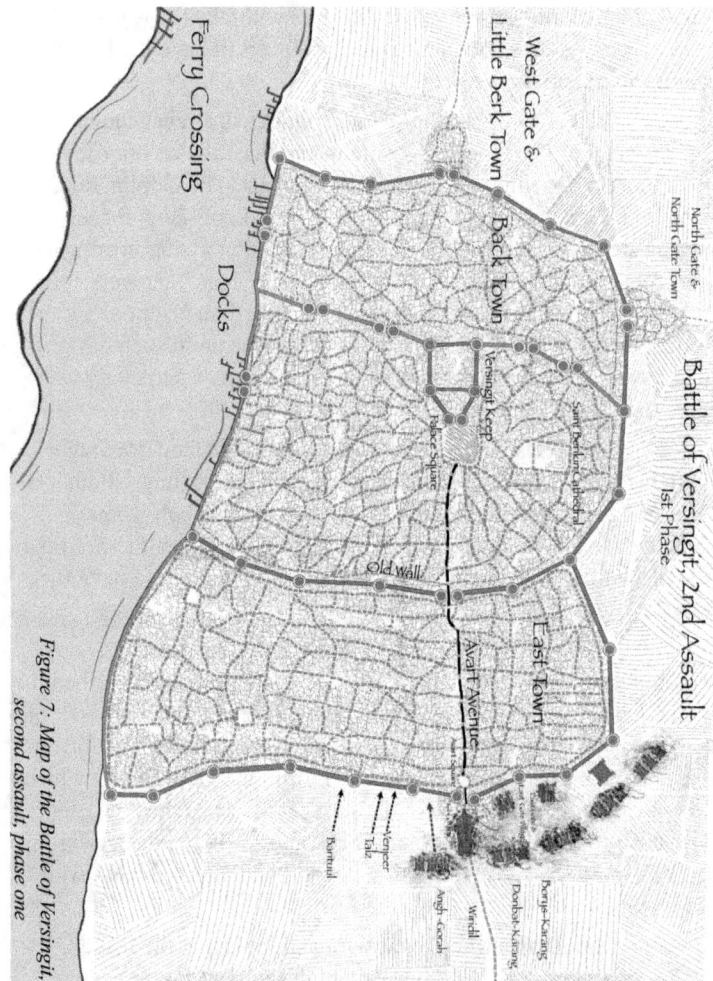

Figure 7: Map of the Battle of Versingit, second assault, phase one

was a near opposite in temperament to the other Orcish leaders there; where the others were youthful, quick to anger and challenge rivals, the Borys-Karang was the only orc Jireyet had ever seen that was balding on the top of his head from age. He was quiet, reserved, and sharp-eyed.

Maglaban shifted his weight and gaze back towards the Donbat-Karang with a meaningful look. The Donbat-Karang turned away uncomfortably for a brief instant before speaking. "The

Borys-Karang will pass through the gate after the Ahng-Gorah takes it. The Borys-Karang will do most of the fighting inside the city. The humans will move to defend the inner wall." He pointed with the stick to the map's depiction of an interior wall within the main structure. Within the interior walls, were more buildings and the innermost fortress. "The Wiridil will move quickly through the gate ahead of the Borys-Karang and take control of the gate to the inner wall before the defenders can control it fully. Keeping the gate will remove the problems we have now from happening again later, and it will trap many defenders between the walls for the Borys-Karang to kill them or take them. That will make the inner fortress easier." The Donbat-Karang sighed. He was not looking forward to the fortress, Jireyet guessed. "We will try using Maglaban's humans at the fortress first." He continued brooding for a moment before shaking himself out of his thoughts. "Are the ladders ready?"

Jireyet stiffened, *since we can be more helpful than those filthy Ahng-Gorah*. "The ladders are ready! More than we can carry."

The Donbat-Karang looked at Jireyet. "Good." They discussed some more details about timing, supplies, and troop rotations through the fight before concluding the meeting and dispersing. Jireyet overheard the Donbat-Karang speaking in hushed Goblin. "Thank you for mediating," to Maglaban. And then to Muydiyet; "I am depending on you."

***

The goblin did not remember falling asleep, but she knew she was dreaming. Dreaming of being home, dreaming of being a great one and having her own clan hall at the bottom of Kogylar, away from the sun, where the crops had better flavor. And her own family like the Hobgoblin great ones. She would be the head of this family with the redskin and his sunset eyes, the purple-eyed man, and the woman with the gold earrings. The goblin would adorn the earrings-woman's whole body with golden rings. The goblin would buy her even more earrings and let her put other rings in. Her family would feed her sweet root bread, mushrooms, and Goblin cheese that she did not have to make herself, and serve her root tea every day.

She woke abruptly as the subleader kicked them awake in the last harsh light of the fleeing sun and yelled. It was time. *Time for what?* Time to get ready. *Get ready for what?*

"Forward, you! You think we have forever!?" Jireyet ran up, berating the subleader. The subleader cowered before Jireyet and pushed the crew to motion.

"Come on! Pick up the ladder," the subleader barked impatiently. She took a place in the middle of the ladder, "Hurry up!" Along with her other crew members, the goblin grabbed a portion of the ladder. The remaining ten or so of the crews of goblins from the two stone hurlers were carrying additional ladders. The subleader motioned and they started to move forward. The goblin soon paid no more mind to the other crews and their ladders.

She saw them as soon as they cleared the treeline. Two of the wall towers had been burnt out. The one next to the gate was crumbled in glowing embers at the base of the wall. The other one was still burning, but collapsing beneath its own weight. The third tower stood, a steady stream of purple-skinned hobgoblins moving between folds in the land to hide from the arrows before getting close enough to rush for the ladders. Hobgoblins continued trickling into the Place-called-Versingit. Orcs crowded the base of the wall near the gate to hide from the arrows, but none were pressing on the gate at the moment.

Clearing the trees, they walked on until they reached the ruined frames of the stone hurlers before starting to run. It started as a trot and it stayed that way for a while. A few other stone hurler crews were carrying ladders. The goblin chanced a look behind her and saw streams of green and blue warriors following behind. *We're putting the ladders on the wall!?*

Her apprehension was cut short when the first projectiles drizzled down upon them, growing into a torrent of arrows and bolts. They ran. Hard. The wood soles of their hide shoes pounded the ground as arrows screamed into the ground. The subleader staggered, clutching her leg. Her arm was still linked in the ladder as she tumbled to the ground. The man with the broken nose tripped over the subleader and the whole lot of them collapsed into a pile with the ladder falling on top of them in the snowy mud. The goblin stumbled away and fell to the ground, facefirst. They wailed in panic as arrows whistled towards them.

The ground thudded near the goblin's head as arrows planted themselves in the ground around her and sprayed dirt in her eyes. The subleader was not yelling anymore. "GET UP!" the goblin screamed. She groped for the ladder. She could not see it. More screaming and yelling around her. She grabbed onto something. A ladder rung! Clutching it blindly, she tried to pick it up blindly. "GRAB IT!" she yelled. "MOVE!" She felt the ladder lighten as the other goblins got out from beneath it and picked it up. "GO!" She barked. She lurched as the other goblins moved again. She could smell hot blood and fear as she ran with no clear sight, trusting her fellows, arrows barely passing her by.

They jerked to a stop. "WHY DID WE STOP!?" she demanded.

"WE ARE AD DA WALL," called back someone with a strange voice. It sounded like the man with the broken nose.

"PUT IT UP, THEN!" She hollered. The crew dropped the ladder. She could hear the twang of the human bowstrings preceding the pelt of arrows hitting the ground around her. The goblin scrubbed the dirt and mud out of her eyes as she heard a gurgled scream. She blinked against the muddy water still on her face and hastily wiped it with her tunic. The redskin was lying on his side, clutching an arrow through his neck. He rolled, gasping and spluttering. The goblin reached out for him, but a hand yanked her back. It was the broken-nosed goblin. Arrows spattered on the ground, two killing the redskin. *No!*

The broken-nosed man heaved. His face was covered in blood where his nose had been torn off by an arrow. "WHAD SHOULD WE DO?" His words made bubbles in crimson snot, which he fruitlessly attempted to wipe away on his sleeve as they huddled at the base of the wall.

"I SAID PUT THE LADDER UP! THEY ARE WAITING FOR US!" She shouted through the noise. The broken-nosed man, if he could still be called that, glanced apprehensively up the wall.

"NOW!" She kicked him. He jumped with a start. She pushed the Goblin woman with the earrings and pointed at the purple-eyed man, "WE ARE NOT GETTING WHAT IS OURS AT THE BOTTOM OF THE WALL!" She pushed him and the woman with earrings again and they all risked the dash to the ladder.

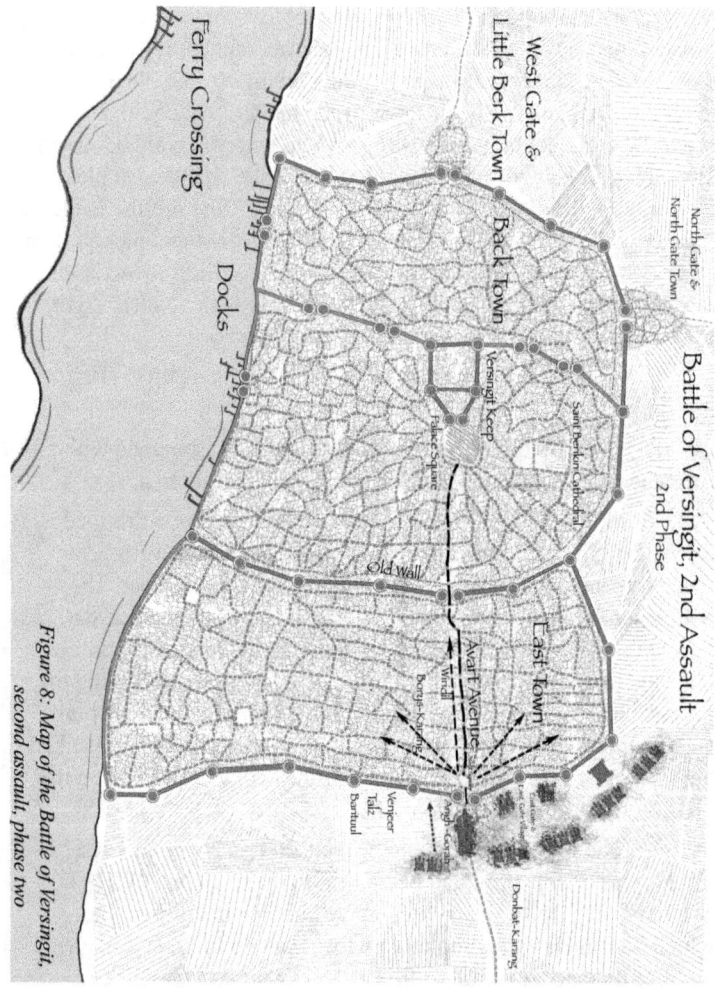

Figure 8: Map of the Battle of Versingit, second assault, phase two

She heard the humans' cries of alarm as the four of them planted the ladder in the dirt and began to hoist it upright. Three of them. The Goblin woman with the gold earrings limply dropped to the ground with three arrows protruding from her back. *It's heavy*, she internally groaned as the three of them strained. *Is this it?*

A cry came from the top of the wall. A different kind of sound. She chanced a look. It was a cry of pain. Arrows clattered against the wall. Sparsely, but steadily. She laughed with hysterical relief. The soldiers behind them were covering them. "KEEP PUSHING! IT IS ALMOST THERE!" A pair of soldiers rushed up, purple-skinned hobgoblins, the harsh light of the coward sun gleaming off of their mail and helmets, reaching head, shoulders, and body over the goblins, grasping the ladder and pushing.

"COME ON, LITTLE ONES! MAKE A NAME FOR YOURSELVES TODAY!" He shouted over the din of arrows, trampling of feet, and moaning of the wounded. She strained and the ladder's top arced to clunk against the wall. Immediately, they felt a jolt as some kind of fork on a pole started to push the ladder away from the wall's edge. "GET ON THE LADDER! HANG ON IT FROM THE BACK!" the hobgoblins yelled.

Another hobgoblin bounded up from cover amidst the hail of arrows from the wall and heaved a javelin. It flew true between the battlements, slaying the defender pushing the ladder away. It fell back to the wall and the three goblins hung onto the back. Arrows clattered against the wall and the humans at the top shot less arrows, but one did find its way into the back of the purple-eyed man. He stiffened, but hung onto the ladder for a moment. It was too much. Blood poured from his mouth and his grip weakened. He fell to the ground. *No!*

The Hobgoblin arrows raked the walls, silencing the defenders as hobgoblins and orcs clambered up the ladder. The goblin prayed the rope would hold. She had not considered that so many soldiers would be on the ladder at once. From the side of her vision, she saw orcs carrying another ladder, plant it in the ground, and raise it to the wall before scaling it. Her arms and back ached from hanging onto the ladder to keep it steady as tens and tens of soldiers pounded up the rungs.

It seemed like an eternity, but the sun had just barely fled and twilight was fading when Jireyet ran towards them. He looked around, seeing the goblin and the broken-nosed Goblin man, now the no-nose Goblin man, holding the ladder steady while more soldiers ascended. The pace of Hobgoblin soldiers was slowing. The goblin supposed that they had fought their way onto the wall and had a good hold of that section of it. "Drop off," Jireyet said wearily. The fighting had drifted away and they weren't getting shot with arrows anymore, so no one had to shout to be heard.

The goblin and her no-nosed companion both dropped off and heaved in sore relief. The goblin got up, rubbing her hands. Jireyet spoke. "Find a weapon, maybe a shield, and as many of us as you can and meet over there," he said, pointing at the gate. The orcs had gone in through the gate after they had laid the ladder, but the goblin had not noticed when. She had looked over and seen them, only for them to be gone when she next glanced. *How long ago was that?* she thought blearily. "We are forming into fists to attack," he continued.

"Attack?" she said numbly.

"There is much fighting in the city, still." Jireyet looked around, as if expecting to see someone else before looking back to the goblin. "You are the new subleader. Where is the rest of your crew?"

"Dis is id," said the no-nose goblin. He had balled up a piece of cloth and stuffed it into the hole where his nose had been and wrapped another piece around his face.

Jireyet sighed. "Another one," he muttered to himself. "Then you will be in another crew. I have lost a few subleaders today."

***

Peregan watched the goblins emerge from the tree line; he was not sure how many. Maybe a hundred. They were carrying ladders and running for the wall. *Not good.* They were already close enough that he could aim at groups instead of firing at a faceless mass with high arcing shots. He had drawn his bow seconds ago and loosed an arrow, catching a trailing goblin in one of the teams. He let go of the ladder, staggered, and fell. "GET ONE IN THE MIDDLE OR THE FRONT, DUMMY! THEN THEY'LL FALL," called one of the other soldiers.

Peregan drew another arrow from his quiver, nocked it, drew the string, and released it. The arrow flew true in the midst of another ladder team, catching a goblin in the leg. She seemed to be in the midst of yelling at the other goblins when she clutched her leg, staggered, and fell, bringing the rest of the team down. Peregan and the other defenders shot arrow after arrow, but the goblins made steady progress over the field. They were close enough that he could aim at individual goblins as they neared the wall.

Planting the ladders down, the invaders raised them to the wall, a few ladders thunking on the wall only a few paces to Peregan's left. The other soldier grabbed a pitchfork, probably taken from stables in the city, and started to push the ladder away. Peregan shot another arrow, as orcs and hobgoblins climbed up. The orcs brought more ladders. Enemy arrows began to clatter on the wall and find the flesh of some of the defenders. Hobgoblins were hiding in shrubs or folds of the land and covering the ladders teams.

A strangled cry and a wooden clunk told Peregan that the nearby ladder was planted firmly back on the wall. The defender who had been pushing the ladder away had taken a javelin to the chest and was exhaling his last breath. Peregan aimed at one of the ladder teams, but missed. He was nocking another arrow when he noticed the hobgoblins helping some of the Goblin ladder crews hold the ladders steady or covering them with bow shots and javelins. Other ladders had orcs and hobgoblins already scaling the walls.

"WHERE'S THE REST OF THE COMPANY?" Peregan called.

"AT THE GATE," someone hollered in reply. "THEY'RE MAKING ANOTHER BIG PUSH FOR THE GATE." A hobgoblin bounded up from cover as Peregan shot another arrow into the mass of enemies clambering up the ladder. Another soldier took up the pitchfork and desperately tried again to push the ladder off the wall, already heavy with the weight of the enemies climbing it. The hobgoblin heaved a javelin, striking the second soldier with the pitchfork, the tip piercing his mail and protruding from his back. The ladder fell back to the wall and rattled as enemies clamored up the top rungs.

"GET BACK!" another soldier called. Peregan loosed another arrow, striking one of the goblins holding the ladder steady. It hung for an instant before falling to the ground. Someone pulled Peregan hard and he stumbled. "I SAID GO! NOW!" The first orcs peeked their heads over the edge of the wall. Soldiers lunged to attack them, sending the first few falling while clutching head wounds or already dead, but cover from attacking archers forced the soldiers back, and more orcs kept coming.

Peregan loosed three more arrows into the crowd of orcs as they fought their way onto the wall. Soon joined by purple-faced hobgoblins, they pressed the defending soldiers along the wall's walkway. Swords flashed in the twilight. Spears thrust. Axes swung. Another arrow from Peregan's bow sought the face of an orc, but his target was struck down an instant after the arrow had left the string, and accidentally found the back of the defender who had slain the orc. Peregan let another arrow fly, finding a hobgoblin's knee. The arrow bounced off of its mail trousers, but the impact twisted its knee and leg. It fell and was trampled by friend and foe alike. The hobgoblin crawled out from the melee to the edge of the parapet, but was kicked off, falling twenty paces to the street below.

Peregan did not see or care about the hobgoblin. Grimacing through having killed one of his own, Peregan drew and shot his last arrow. It did its job, parting links in the mail of another hobgoblin and finding the space between the ribs of its chest. It fell back against the ranks of its own as Peregan raced in search of a barrel of spare arrows or the quiver of a fallen comrade.

***

Muydiyet tossed the quiver of javelins to one of her soldiers, an old and grizzled balding hobgoblin.

"You are certain that you do not want them, Great One?" he asked, tying them to his own saddle.

"I am. I will not have the time to relish in it." She smiled wearily as she mounted her impatient wolf. "Second. Make ready." Muydiyet was looking down at her scabbard and adjusting the straps as she spoke to her Second. A strapping, blue-skinned man nodded and obediently trotted towards his own mount before cantering off. Behind them, the Second spread the word among Muydiyet's host, the hobgoblins of the Wiridil. They checked their saddles and weapons or sat astride their beasts, anxiously waiting for the moment.

Muydiyet sighed, quieting her own anxiety, forcing it deep below the surface. She looked towards the commotion by the gate.

"It is nearly time," said the old soldier. The lines on his face deepened as he squinted to see the distance.

"Leriyet willing, it nearly is, if the Ahng-Gorah can manage to do anything and the Talz somehow do not fail at being helped by the Barituul *and* the Venjeer," Muydiyet muttered bitterly.

The soldier chuckled. "Patience, Great One. It will be time soon. Leriyet's rules tell us that we cannot rush victory. It will come to us willingly with the right patience."

Muydiyet glared at him. *This old man*, she grumbled internally. She had known him her whole life. He supported her rise to Great One of the Wiridil and rode in her guard, though he should have been the great one or one of the numbered to be named a great one. He had passed on every offer, 'preferring the life of a simple soldier.'

"You told that the plan by the Donbat-Karang was something that could be done." The old soldier glanced at her before returning his gaze to the gate. "Great One. It is time. The gate falls." His voice rose slightly.

Muydiyet again looked toward the gate. Two orcs waved banners of white cloth strapped to tall staves so as to be more easily seen. Muydiyet did not need the banners, though. Looking past the orcs, she could see the gates hanging open, their mighty timbers and wrought iron splintered and warped by the ram and light emerging from behind the interior door of the wall.

"The Donbat-Karang are the sole redemption of their entire kind, a log too heavy to bear by so few," Muydiyet muttered under her breath as she twisted in her saddle and drew her long, curved sword. "Onward!" Snapping the reins, her wolf stirred to motion. The beast, irritable under its plated barding, needed little urging to move. It picked up pace from a trot to a lope to a sprint. The sound of hundreds of paws pounding the dirt behind roared thunderously in her wake. She called back to her troops. "Remember! Kill only those in the way! The goal is more important and there is plenty of fighting to be had!"

Over the fields, past the ruined stone hurlers, the Wiridil ran astride their great wolves. The walls of the Place-called-Versingit grew tall as she drew near, her host filing behind her as they neared the gate. The shadow of the walls passed over them. The gates had been forced open from the inside after the human defenders had been forced to surrender it. Inside the gatehouse,

Figure 9: The Avart Massacre

she spared a glance for the arrow slits and murder holes that would have been difficult to fight past. Moving through the gatehouse and the interior door of the wall, signs of recent fighting were still apparent in the bloodied bodies, some still alive, decorating the streets.

A broad, mostly straight road stretched before her, buildings of wood and clay standing on either side, three and four stories tall. Muydiyet had heard from some of the Goblin siege engineers that the humans did not build underground; at least not dwellings. Cries of terror echoed off the buildings as throngs of unarmed humans fled before her.

Curses! Filth! Muydiyet grumbled. The humans accepted that so many of their own kind would not fight, yet those non-fighters were so fascinated with the fighting that they turned up to watch their own soldiers be ground to paste. *And be in the way!* The long, curved blade, designed for mounted combat, arced like wind. Muydiyet grunted as her sword briefly met resistance and a head spun away from a man running in front of her beast. Another human futilely ran for his life, barely dodging the spikes of her wolf's barding. To her left, the old soldier drew a javelin from his quiver.

The javelin wetly lodged itself into the man's back. He staggered and rolled onto the ground as the first of hundreds of wolves trampled him. Muydiyet glanced over her shoulder. *They are enjoying themselves too much*, she noted, as other riders threw their javelins or took mounted bowshots at the humans who were running away from the main avenue. There were others that were veering off the road to chase down fleeing, terrified, unarmed, not-in-the-way humans.

"Third! Marshal them! There will be time for fun later. We have many tasks ahead of us," she called to her Third, who was riding ten paces behind her. He nodded, urged his mount to the flank of the column and slowed to police the riders' bloodlust. Muydiyet grimaced. *They better listen or there will be discipline instead of sport!*

Her wolf plowed through a group of human adults pulling

or carrying children. The wolf snarled and gored them with the spikes on the headpiece of its barding while Muydiyet hacked at them until they broke away or were trampled by the wolf.

"GO!" she yelled, kicking the wolf back to a run, wailing lamentations of the humans in her wake. *Get out of the way, then, weaklings!* she grumbled internally, calling on the Wiridil to keep their pace up.

Muydiyet rode on, the thunder of her host behind her and the screams of pathetic weaklings in front of her. A human woman ran ahead of her, desperately dragging a child at her side. Muydiyet hewed an arm off of a woman and trampled them both. The wolf panted in its exertion, but they rode on. The crowds of humans were getting thicker on the road, but they were learning to cling to the sides of the street. *Good. Be good hogs and line up for the slaughter. Useless filth.*

Muydiyet spared a glance upwards. The higher towers of the citadel of this place were barely visible above the inner wall. *Now, what kind of prize is in there? I will need a great deal of sport when this is done and over with.*

***

"RUN! THERE'S TOO MANY!" cried a defender. Peregan chanced a look over his shoulder. The defenders had broken. They were running, being slain or pushed off of the parapet, screaming as they fell. Peregan ran. The beating of boots on the stone parapets told him that some of the defenders were escaping with him. Jeers from the attacking orcs and hobgoblins followed them. A detached part of Peregan wondered what they were saying, but his curiosity was cut short when javelins were thrown after them, catching a trailing defender as she ran. Collapsing on the walkway, blood poured from her mouth as she reached for her fellow soldiers and cried breathlessly. Her pleading blue eyes would haunt Peregan for years to come as he and the others left her behind. *There's no saving her. No saving any of them. Maybe we can get to the inner wall and hold them there… and then what?*

Their gait slowed after a hundred paces or so. The attackers were not pursuing, but they still jogged. They could hear a rising wail in the city. *The gate must have fallen. They would be passing into the city now.* Peregan found two more quivers and stuffed them as full of arrows as they would allow.

"Look," one of the other defenders said, gesturing. Peregan followed her pointed finger. Amid the gradually building flow of fleeing citizens and soldiers, they saw blue-faced hobgoblins carrying swords or javelins astride giant wolves, easily loping along the streets, slashing down the occasional fleeing person. *Why are some blue-skinned and some purple-skinned? Does that mean there are purple-skinned goblins?* Peregan thought numbly. A distant, dissociated part of him was still curious about these things.

Curious until he realized something. "They're making for the inner gate!" he cried. That was suddenly motivating. They began to run again, reaching another turret. They entered, finding other defending soldiers. "We have to get to the inner wall!" he shouted.

"What do you mean?" one of them demanded, "we have to hold this portion of the wall!"

"The gate has fallen and they are trying to block the inner gate. We'll be trapped," Peregan insisted. They shifted uncomfortably. "Fine. Stay then." He moved through them to the stairs. More feet shuffled behind him; at least some of those defenders had joined them. They exited the turret onto the streets. Buildings lined the way to the left, right, and straight ahead. Peregan skidded to a halt, but the others ran past him.

"What are you doing!?" one of them called back.

"What about all these people? Someone's got to tell them," he pleaded.

They did not stop. Peregan knew they were right. There was no time to tell everyone. *I can't just leave them to be butchered.*

He pushed in a door to the first house. "Get out! The gate fell. Get to the inner wall. Tell others." The occupants scrambled to movement, grabbing a few belongings and making for the door. Peregan darted to the next door, alerting them, and the next, and the next. He checked over his shoulder and realized that everyone he had roused from their houses were running for the inner wall with their families and scant possessions. He was the only one actively telling people of the danger. More people were joining the flight because they heard the noise and panic outside. Giving up, Peregan ran, too. He noticed a few people split off from the main crowd and ran down alleyways. Peregan was not from Versingit, but he figured that these folks knew shortcuts and decided to follow them.

The tang of garbage and chamber pots assaulted his senses as he ran down the alley. He broke into the throng of the next street over, bowling into a family and tumbling to the ground with them. Cursing him, they got up and kept pushing into the crowd. One of their children kicked him and screamed at him for not keeping the orcs out. Grimacing, Peregan forced his way through the crowd to the other side of the street. He had lost track of the people he had been following, and ran haphazardly through the alleys, crossing the rivers of people. He would periodically catch glimpses of the inner wall, continue running in that direction, and be rewarded with the next glimpse being closer to the wall.

He broke into the main road, Avart Avenue. It was the most direct route connecting the outer wall gate to the inner wall gate– and also the most crowded. Peregan was out of options. He could see the gate over people's heads, and rushed through the crowd as best he could. He shouted, shoved, and nudged forward until the crowd compressed and stopped moving. He shoved a few, to no avail, and some actually elbowed their way back through the crowd, past him, and ran away. *Why are they going back towards the orcs?* Peregan wondered as he pushed and shouted his way to the front of the throng.

The front of the crowd gave a wide berth to the gate. The gate was blocked by the wolf-riding hobgoblins. They had seized control. Bodies lay in the street. Most of them were ordinary people, but a few of them were soldiers that had tried to rush past the wolf-riders, some of whom had been with him on the wall or met at the turret. A handful were fending off three riders who were circling them with curved swords and glaives while another thirty mounted hobgoblins stood ready or prowled. The wolves growled at the humans in the crowd, but their riders held them back.

No other chance! Peregan drew back the bowstring and

loosed an arrow at one of the three circling riders. Catching the rider in the back, it swayed in its saddle and fell to the side. The wolf lurched in startlement as Peregan's next arrow flew towards the second rider. He missed his target, but caught the wolf in its left hind leg. It yelped and staggered, dragging its leg, pitching its rider off. The rider landed hard, and the soldiers took the briefest opportunity to turn the tables. One glaive slashed down, sinking deep into the stomach of the rider before being abandoned by the soldier to make a run for it. The third rider was overwhelmed by desperately flashing swords and another glaive that carved the face and forelegs of the wolf before killing it and the rider.

"NOW!" Peregan shouted, "RUN! IT'S THE ONLY CHANCE!" He loosed another arrow towards the other wolf-riders before running himself. Some of the riders loped after the soldiers that had pressed through, some moved to block the way for Peregan and the civilians. Another hasty shot bounced off of the helmet of the nearest rider. The rider yelled in alarm and flailed to fix its helmet, jerking the wolf's reins. Peregan was able to run by the wolf. It growled and nipped at him, but the rider's thrashing of its reins kept it off balance and unable to lunge at him. Other riders moved and began to hack down townsfolk trying to get through, throwing a few javelins to keep the rest off. Peregan only saw so much. A javelin skipped off of a paving stone near him, giving him another reason to duck into an alley and evade pursuit. A few streets over, he ran into a company of soldiers assembling and joined them.

"They seized the gates!" he called as he ran up.

"Fine, then!" said their company leader, a short, broad man with a trimmed beard hanging out from under his open-faced helmet. "Hear that? Let's go!" The company marched along Avart Avenue until they came within full view of the gate. A few more bodies, mostly townspeople who had failed getting to safety, lay on the ground, gashed by blades or pierced by javelins.

The soldiers leveled their glaives and spears while advancing. Peregan and several other archers shot arrows over their heads to keep the wolf-riders from charging but it was like trying to hold back the wind with his hands. The wolves parted around the soldiers, hurling javelins and pouncing on a gap in the spears. Wading in, they slashed with their curved swords. The line broke, and the soldiers ran, Peregan among them. The choice was either to make for the keep for certain relative safety and to hold out as long as possible, or to run for the docks and try to escape to complete safety. Wolves ran behind him, not even panting with exertion, bearing their riders, swinging and striking the soldiers of the broken company. One of them leapt onto a fleeing defender, smashing him to the ground. The rider shifted in its saddle and hurled a javelin while the soldier screamed as the wolf gnawed on his arm.

Peregan was forced down the avenue some ways before the riders gave up their pursuit and returned to the inner wall gate. Peregan and ten soldiers of the company reached the keep. The officer of the gate ordered the portcullis open for them. They staggered inside, heaving from the prolonged exertion of running for their lives.

"A little longer, soldiers." Peregan looked up to see Prince Eron. "We hold here, getting as many in as we can. The keep has an entrance to the cistern and people are leaving through that. We have to hold the keep long enough for people to get out. If more come, we let them in."

"Your Grace," murmured one of the soldiers, distraught. "What about the rest of the city!?"

The prince grimaced. "Too many of them. Too many orcs. Too many goblins. We'll do what we can." He turned to leave but looked back and patted Peregan on the shoulder in recognition. "Glad you made it."

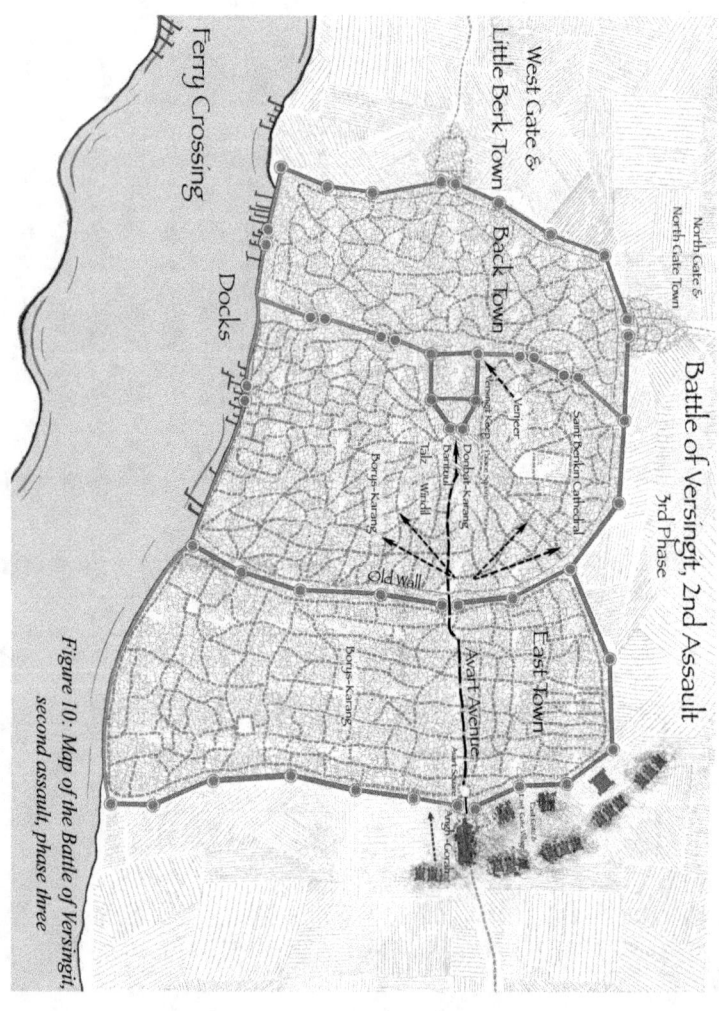

Figure 10: Map of the Battle of Versingit,
second assault, phase three

Chapter 6

Atop the inner wall in the Place-called-Versingit, on the Liberator Side of
the Mountains.
By the Goblin Calendar, middle of the Ninth Moon Cycle, 3114.
By the Human Calendar, Restday, second week of Berenk, 794.
A clear night with a nearly full moon.

"We control the wooden platforms on the water, Great
One," Muydiyet said.

Maglaban gave her a friendly smile. "You do not have to
address me as such. You are a great one, yourself. Perhaps we can
take sport after this?"

She looked at him skeptically. "The Great Oygariyet sent
you here."

Maglaban scowled for a moment. "Yes, but only to see his
will done when others have their own motives and devices, some of
which come to the fore soon, but not before we control this place.
Aside from this matter, I am a tribe leader, just like you. Back to the
way of your words, though."

"The wooden platforms are secure. We captured many
humans attempting to flee on… 'boats." The word was awkward
to her. Like most of the hobgoblins and goblins on this side of
the home mountains, she had never seen or heard of boats before
this encounter. Some of the streams were wide or deep enough in
the mountains to make rafts useful, but it was uncommon in most
places, so boats struck most of the mountain peoples as a strange
contraption. "We were able to sink some of the 'boats' but others
were able to get away."

They stood atop a portion of the inner wall of the Place-
called-Versingit. The blessedly gentle light of the moon washed
them. The cowardly sun had long ago retreated, which made
finishing the fighting in the outer city and securing the inner city,
which was mostly complete, much easier. For all of his doubts,
the Borys-Karang had done their job, though he was not yet out of
tricks and games. Maglaban could see it in his bemused eyes every

time they met. Maglaban appreciated the Great Oygariyet once again for taming the green savage, at least enough to be used, but never to be trusted. Maglaban rued the thought of having to directly keep the Borys-Karang, let alone any of the other tribes, on the task and fulfilling the right goals.

"Here." he motioned her to pause. "We should be with the Donbat-Karang for this."

She looked at him skeptically again. "But, he is…"

"Yes, but the Great One gave this fight to him. I was there when the Great One accepted a tribute gift from the Donbat-Karang for this honor. It is his fight to manage."

"Yes, Great One," she said. He gave her a sidelong glance and she corrected, "uh, Maglaban." They briskly walked along the wall until arriving at the turret that the Donbat-Karang had made into their temporary headquarters. At its top window, they found the Donbat-Karang with Jireyet and the subleader from the Talz goblins. "The wooden platforms floating on the water are secure," Muydiyet informed the Donbat-Karang.

The Donbat-Karang looked away from the window towards Muydiyet, his thick arms crossed and two curved swords hanging at his belt. "Good," he said. His spoken Goblin only had the slightest of accents. He was, by far, the most bearable of the orcs. Clever enough to know his place and succeed, but honorable enough to accept his place and set his ambitions accordingly. He turned back to the window. It overlooked the lower city, with the keep on the right and the harbor barely in sight past it. "This will be difficult."

The assembly looked on at the keep. Its walls were higher. Narrow windows dotted every turret, like a thousand eyes from where arrows would pour. The main gate was thick, and the approach was an open square with no cover from the thousand eyes of death. The Donbat-Karang pointed. "The weakness is the inner wall connecting to the castle. There is no door, but the castle wall is shorter from the top of the inner wall, than from the ground."

"How do you wish to do this?" Maglaban asked.

"We will use distraction and stealth to create opportunities," he began. "We will use a human to distract them, if you would allow me to use one of them, Great Maglaban."

"You may," Maglaban said. Maglaban had brought some humans with him for a special purpose like this. Oygariyet and Indariyet had been careful in selecting them. He took another moment to appreciate Oygariyet's kindness to the conquered by allowing them to be of further use.

"The Venjeer, by way of stealth, will use the weakness there" –he pointed to the same place where the inner wall joined the keep– "and enter the castle during the distraction and weaken the defenses there," he pointed to a walkway connecting the point of entry to the gatehouse at the front of the keep. "In the best way in my mind, they would be able to open the gate and the lowering cage door. From there we will storm the castle."

"Who is 'we'? Who storms the castle?" Maglaban asked.

He sighed. "The Barituul, the Venjeer, the Wiridil, and the Donbat-Karang."

Maglaban gazed at him for a moment. "What of the orcs?"

"The orcs are spent," the Donbat-Karang said, "and they are exhausted. We cannot count on them. If their great ones want a chance at the spoil, they can fight, but their warriors are done with this night." *He is right*, Maglaban considered. *They have fought all through the outer and inner city. They are spent.*

"I am sure that some orcs would be honored to join the fight in storming the stone of this place." They turned to see the Borys-Karang climbing the stairs into the top room of the turret. "Honored," he repeated. *Honored my feet*, Maglaban internally grumbled.

"If the Venjeer fail?" Maglaban asked. Jireyet bristled. "Hold, Great Jireyet; I do not doubt you, but neither do I doubt the defenders." Jireyet settled back to listen.

"It matters in what they do not accomplish. If they can weaken the defenses near the gate, but the gate is closed, then we will attempt to break it. That will be costly, but it could be done. If they cannot do either, then we will have to find another way or wait for them to eat each other enough."

"Humans do not eat each other," Maglaban pointed out.

The Donbat-Karang and Muydiyet both whirled their heads to look at Maglaban in surprise. "They do not!?" the Donbat-Karang asked in astonishment.

"Not even to honor them?" Muydiyet queried, incredulously.

"No. Humans have a very different view of what is and is not honorable. In some cases, they may even value remaining alive more than honor." The latter concept did not register with the Donbat-Karang–he was, after all, still an orc. Even if he was of the Donbat-Karang, and they were the most like hobgoblins in their ways, orcs in general valued being alive and had little sense of honor. The Donbat-Karang was the rare exception in their mimicry of Hobgoblin ways.

Muydiyet, however, was appalled. "More than honor...? Is that why those humans agreed to be with you?"

I never thought of that. Maglaban was suddenly awash with disdain for the humans that Oygariyet gave him. "Perhaps," he said, "it will be hard to know. If they wish to be honorable, they will say so. But, if they wish only to live, they will also say it is for honor."

***

Elbin shakily walked into the stone-paved square, flanked by two purple-skinned hobgoblins. He was internally grateful once again to his parents for their gift to him, bestowing upon him an ear for languages. Elbin had been an assistant to one of the ore merchants and would travel to negotiate contracts. By necessity, he had learned to read and write in both Marin and his own native Eklendan, and was starting to pick up Daearan when the orcs, the goblins, and little horned lizard men came. He thanked his parents again and again that he was able to so quickly pick upon the Goblin and Orcish languages. He had started to learn the characters of Goblin before leaving Kogylar to come here.

Elbin bore with him a banner with a white rag, meant to announce a parlay, and he held it high. Thankful for his gifts as he was, he did not want to be stuck with an arrow from these stubborn

Versingiters. Hesitantly, he walked into the square. His guards were annoyed with his reluctance and nudged him impatiently.

"Slowly!" he cautioned them in Goblin, "or they will think we are attacking and the plan will fail." They slowed to his pace, but were clearly irritated. They reached the front of the castle, far enough back into the square that they could see the top of the wall and the defenders could see them.

"What do you want?" one of the defenders called from the top in Marin.

"We wish to speak to your leader," Elbin answered.

"Get stuffed. What for?"

"To negotiate your surrender."

There was a pause. "Ya, get stuffed!"

"What are they saying?" one of Elbin's guards demanded in Goblin.

"They do not want to surrender," Elbin said.

"Then we waste time!" the guard hissed.

"But *we* waste *their* time. I will keep them talking," Elbin whispered. He called back to the defender in Marin. "Don't you want to live? You can all leave this place with your families."

Another pause. "Who the scat are you? After all this, who do you think you are!?"

***

The goblin crept along quietly. There were very few of them left. All of her crew had been lost except for the man with no nose. Many in their original fist had died securing the outer wall.

Altogether, there were two fists left of the great Venjeer from Kogylar. The man with no nose had been promoted to subleader in the other fist. The goblin and what remained of her fist had painted themselves entirely in a thick, black, greasy substance found at the floating wooden platforms–their clothes, armor, helmets, hair, and everything exposed save for their faces, soles of their shoes and palms of their hands–and crept towards the keep in

109

the moonlight, carrying the ladder with the end wrapped in cloth.

Thankfully, the moon was on the other side of the castle and they were hidden in shadow. From what the Great Maglaban had said, humans could not see at night the way that goblins, or even orcs, could. Above, on the castle wall, they saw a few defenders watching the wall, as if they could see anything. They were close enough now. The goblin signaled to stop by slightly shaking the ladder, then held her hand low and waved. The signal was passed back. It would be passed back to the line until it reached Jireyet. That would be the cue for Jireyet to signal the other fist.

Moments passed, painfully slowly, dripping like tree sap. The goblin felt like the sun would invade again before they could make their move. But she said nothing and barely breathed. Her patience and discipline were rewarded with the quiet whistle of a volley of arrows sailing through the air. Many clattered on the wall, but enough found their marks, bringing forth gurgled cries. The goblin tensed; this was among the greatest risks and she hoped that the ploy with the converted human in front proved to be enough of a distraction.

They planted the ladder as quietly as they could and raised it to rest on the wall as gently as they could. Even though they had wrapped the end of the ladder to muffle the sound, she cringed at the dampened thud of the ladder on the wall and waited, listening for a response. A moment passed with no remark. She patted the goblin in front of her. That was the signal to pass up. Climb the ladder. Silently, the goblin's fist climbed the rungs, consolidating on the wall, signaling the other fist to follow, and moving along the wall. *Now they will pay. Now they will pay for taking the redskin from me. For the woman with gold-earrings. For the purple-eyed man. They were going to be my family, and I will make them pay.*

***

Peregan scowled at the filthy rat man. He had only seen its kind once or twice, and only since he came to Versingit. Apparently, there was a whole nest of the vermin living in the sewers and catacombs. If anyone wanted to use those spaces, they had to negotiate with these things. Prince Eron was haggling with them to take more people through the maze down the secret passage to escape the city.

"Fine! Fine. Just take it and go," Prince Eron said. The rat man said nothing, but looked pleased. It seemed so odd to Peregan that a rat man that lived in the sewers and tunnels beneath the city, dressed in rags, reeking of garbage and chamber pots, held power over the prince in his own throne room, sparkling in his shining plate and mail. *Desperate times, though.* The great door to the throne room was barred. Maybe twenty or so soldiers and some from the Prince's Guard remained with the few civilians that had made it here. The rat man would take them all through the labyrinth of tunnels under the city.

THUD! *And not a moment too soon.* THUD! The orcs were ramming the door. THUD!

"Hurry then!" the prince insisted. He opened a concealed door behind the throne. Peregan could not see the seams or hinges at all. It ground open. THUD! The prince was arguing with his sister and his wife to escape.

THUD! "GO!" THUD! The door was cracking. They hustled. The prince pressed a bag of things, impossible to decipher its contents, into his wife's hands and gave her a shove. The rat man led them through. The prince's family, what civilians had gathered, and then the soldiers followed. THUD! The door cracked open. The barring beam split and the left panel fell off of the hinges, clattering to the floor. "CLOSE IT!" the prince yelled at the other soldiers, as Peregan performed his duty.

***

The door gave way with a resounding crack, the right panel loudly banging the stone floor. The Borys-Karang knew what was next. He shoved the few of his remaining orcs into the anticipated wall of arrowheads. The orcs, and several of Maglaban's and Muydiyet's hobgoblins, took them head on. Grinning, the Borys-Karang leapt over their bodies, with the Donbat-Karang, who had oiled and set his swords aflame, the Talz and the Ahng-Gorah at his side or following in his wake, along with Maglaban, Muydiyet, their fighters, and even the tiny Venjeer.

The Donbat-Karang whipped at the defenders with his flaming swords, slashing and scorching them. The Borys-Karang swung his axe with gleeful abandon, laying waste to the defenders. But a detached part of him remembered how surprised he was at the success of the Venjeer, who had opened the gate for them while the human fulfilled his purpose of providing a distraction. *It will be interesting to see how Maglaban treats the Venjeer after this, with hardly much left of the tribe.*

The defenders broke–most were already dead or critically wounded. Only a handful fought on. Muydiyet locked blades with the one in the best armor except for wearing no helmet. The goblins of the Venjeer creeped through the melee and struck with spears taller than themselves or two-handed axes that would have been one-handed for a taller person. A Goblin woman overtook a human archer that was crawling away after emptying the last of his three quivers. Pulled his head up by the hair. She had the look of deciding whether to take ownership of it or kill it. Muydiyet trapped the armored human's blade against the wall and punched him in the unhelmeted, yellow-haired head hard across the jaw and kicked him in the knee, forcing him to the ground.

"There is a door back here," called one of the orcs.

"Through it! Catch them all!" yelled Maglaban.

Muydiyet reached down and gripped the human man by the chin, pulling his head up, forcing his blue eyes to look at her. "This one will be my prize. He will be very pretty painted in purple and dressed up for sport." The Borys-Karang looked about, noting Jireyet's lifeless body on the floor in the communal lake of blood.

As the others rushed through the open door behind the throne, the Ahng-Gorah stepped to the center. "Challenge to the Talz," he boomed. *Just as planned.* The Borys-Karang contained his amusement. His anticipation. The Talz emerged from the carnage. Everyone else cleared the center of the room. But for all of the Ahng-Gorah's bluster, it was over quickly. They circled briefly before the Talz rushed in for an attack. The Ahng-Gorah, startled by the Talz's aggressiveness, attempted to create space for a counter swing with his forward-curving sword, but he tripped over a dead human and stumbled. The Talz skipped in and kicked the sword out of the Ahng-Gorah's hand and deftly crushed his head with his horned mace.

Clever use of the surroundings. "Good," the Borys-Karang announced in Orcish as the Ahng-Gorah's last breath escaped from his ruined face. "Very good. You have done well, Talz."

"I took what I did," the Talz answered.

"And you take what you can. What will you do with the Ahng-Gorah?"

"I shall take them as my own. There are no more Ahng-Gorah," the Talz announced.

"Good, and I shall take this place–" The Borys-Karang was cut off.

"No, you shall not!" Maglaban broke in.

The Borys-Karang barely suppressed a scowl. *Cursed meddler!* "Surely? Is it not my right for having done most of the fighting?"

"You well know that the Great Oygariyet gave this honor to the Donbat-Karang. You even went to the Great Oygariyet with a gift *from* the Donbat-Karang." The Borys-Karang said nothing, but regarded him calmly. "How you choose to let the others organize. Who owns whom. It does not matter to the Great Oygariyet. If–" he said, and pointed at the Talz, "you are going to destroy a tribe, fine. That is your concern. But you had better be ready to appoint a Garad'dai, unless you think you can be in two places at once!" Maglaban turned back to the Borys-Karang. "You have cooked this meal and you are going to eat it! The Donbat-Karang have the right to claim this place, as granted by the Great Oygariyet–a right that cannot be transferred!"

Hmph, the Borys-Karang grumbled. *Not quite to plan.*

***

Eron's wife, Fyon, and his sister, Brindi, raced through the tunnels with the small crowd of civilians and soldiers, led by the rat man, barely able to see by the light of carried torches. The temperature underground was much warmer than the frigid autumn air, especially at night. They could hear the shouts of their pursuers behind them. *Eron has fallen*, Fyon thought bleakly. She pushed down the pit of despair growing in her guts. *But he will be avenged!* Fyon stumbled on the cobbling of the passage, staggering into the wall and cutting her arm on a jagged stone. She felt a trickle of blood drip and cool down her arm as she lurched to a run again, vaguely aware that it would scar, if she lived through this.

"They're gaining!" called a panicked man in the back.

"We cannot lose them here," called the rat man in front. "They are too close and there are too many of you. You have to fight."

"Will you help?" Fyon asked.

"No. That was not in the agreement. I will come back for you if you live," he said, as he sprinted ahead and darted around the corner into the darkness of the unlit tunnels.

Fyon hissed in frustration and pulled two items out of the bundle that Eron had shoved at her, passing one to Brindi. They were her most precious possessions, though she never thought she would have to use them. Not like this. She and Brindi stopped and wheeled about, pushing through the running civilians. "Keep going! You! Soldier! Fight! We have to protect them!"

Brindi fussed with one of the gifts, her forearm muscles taut with effort, as she tossed her head to flick her braids out of her face. The first pursuer reached the corner and rounded it. She could barely see it, save for its sweat glistening on its green skin in the torchlight. Brindi squeezed the lever-trigger on one of the possessions, sending a steel bolt searing through the humid air, driving into the orc's face.

No sooner had the first orc fallen, than a blue-skinned goblin with a flat, bloody bandage where its nose should have been appeared, brandishing a spear taken from one of her own soldiers. It darted through the soldiers' legs and thrust its weapon directly at Fyon's torso. Hobgoblins and orcs crashed into the other defenders. She brushed the spear thrust aside with her own gift, an arming sword Eron had given her during their courting period. She slashed the goblin up his side and kicked it away before ducking into a side tunnel. Her suspicion was correct–it was connected to another passage in the back.

She emerged from behind her pursuers. There were not that many. *Why chase us with so few? They could have poured through in numbers.* She took them from behind, slashing at them or running them through. Seconds later, the defenders stood heaving with exertion. There were some not standing, and some no longer alive, but the casualties were a minority of their group.

"Take their weapons, we will need to arm the rest of the people. We may have to fight again. Bring the wounded with us." Fyon, Brindi, and the defenders were shuffling off to gather the civilians who had fled and hid, and to find the rat man who was their key to escape. She heard labored breathing. It was the goblin with the spear. He glared at her bitterly while he struggled for breath. Fyon looked at him for a long moment before bending down and taking his spear. She left him. He may live or die, but she did not want to become the butcher that they all were.

Catching up with the others, she made her way to the front of the pack, where the rat man was waiting. *Convenient. He knows exactly when to show up or hide*, she thought bitterly. "What now?" she demanded.

It made a face that might have been a smile, though if it was, she was unsure of what kind. *Is this friendly? Or is this smug because he has the power?* "My friends are preparing boats for you."

"They will see us," Brindi objected.

"There will be a large cloth covered in tar for each boat. It is most important that you hide under them. They cannot see through the tar. They see the warmth of your body. Hide under the tar and they cannot see it in the darkness."

"How do you know?" Fyon asked.

"We have the same eyes, my friends and I, as the invaders," the rat man explained.

They moved on in silence. "Where will we go?" Brindi probed.

Fyon sighed. "I think our best option is to row out to the lake and up the River Guth to Yvel to plead for aid and asylum."

"To Prince Gerald?" Brindi asked.

"No, Gerald died fighting the orcs a few months ago. His son, Arnold has the Crown, I think, unless it's one of the other children, but Arnold is the oldest. Or was it Oswald? I only met him once, when we were both children. He might help."

***

The Stone of Versingit
Two Days Later

Maglaban entered the rooms of one of the castle's turrets. There were no walls in these rooms–one floor of the turret was one large, round room. This is where what remained of the Venjeer had settled. Many of them were nursing their wounded, fixing armor, bringing in more pillows, blankets, and other soft things taken from elsewhere in the castle for bedding, beating their slaves or sporting about. Maglaban waded through.

As much as the goblins tried, they could only emulate the hobgoblins. There were some things about goblins that were wholly of their own nature and ways. They too could choose life over honor. Many chose stability over change, and Maglaban had been surprised that so many tribes from Kogylar had joined, and was even further surprised at how passionately they had fought. Surprised at their commitment. But no matter. They had done their job, and earned their rewards.

The two surviving subleaders of the Venjeer dwelled on the top floor of the turret. One was in a very bad way. He had lost his nose in the early part of the siege, then earned himself a very honorable wound pursuing the fleeing defenders in the tunnels under the castle. Some of the other goblins were tending his wounds or piling loot from the castle around the room, setting their treasures aside to build their new home.

The Goblin woman that stood before him was also changed, though in her manner more than her physical appearance. Maglaban had briefly met her a few days ago when he had helped her and some of her crew push the first of the ladders onto the outer

116

wall. Before she was young, fearful, plaintive. Naïve. The skin on her face was still young, of course, but her eyes were old, now. She had seen much in the last few days. Done much. Lost many of her friends. Taken on new responsibilities. She held something in her hand. Behind her was a human man strapped to a table and stripped to the skin, rasping haggardly in his slumber. His face was stained purple from berries she had crushed on him. Droplets of the human drink, wine, were soaking into the wood of the table around him. *And there they are, again. Emulating us.*

"Yes, Great One?" she said. He caught a glimpse of what she was grasping in her hand. Six small golden rings. *Earrings?*

He looked at her grimly. "The Venjeer have fought bravely and gathered great honor upon themselves."

She regarded him numbly. "Jireyet is dead, Great One, as are the clan elders that were with us. The only other clan elders are back at Kogylar and too old to fight. This is all that is left of the host of the Venjeer."

"Yes, I know," Maglaban said. "You are the leader of the Venjeer now. Your accomplishments override their age." She stiffened. That surprised her a bit. "What will you take as a name?"

"I... can choose my own?" she said. Flecks of surprise showed through her numb delivery. She closed her grip on the handful of earrings. She was exhausted. Not physically, but she had been through much and was a young soldier. The young soldiers always needed more time before they could fight again. Before their eyes and hearts hardened.

"Yes. The Great Oygariyet granted me the decision of things like this. I give you that right."

She thought for a moment. "Then I ask something of you, Great Maglaban."

"Just Maglaban. You are a Great One, yourself. You have earned it. Even the Donbat-Karang can be known as a Great One for his work here, but only *that* Donbat-Karang. But, yes, ask."

"Hear me, then," she began, pointing to the goblin without a nose. "He, too, shall be named. We shall lead the Venjeer together."

"Oh? You ask much," Maglaban said. "Why ask this?

117

What is the purpose? Will it not lead to confusion?"

"We are of the same heart," she answered. "We will form a new clan in the Venjeer as brother and sister."

"Yes, Gread Wud," the no-nosed goblin murmured from where he lay, "we agree on mosd everydig."

"Granted," Maglaban smiled, "but there are so few of you remaining."

"Give us slaves," the no-nose murmured from his bed.

"Yes," the Goblin woman agreed. "We will take slaves for our own purposes."

"Very well." Maglaban thought for a moment. "What will be your names?"

"Erseyet," she declared.

"Ig'Pon," he croaked.

"Is'Pohn? '*No nose?*'" Maglaban's words were full of skepticism.

"Id will be whad they call me adyways," he shrugged from his pile of furs and blankets, another goblin washing the long, stitched wound on his side. "Ad I losd id here, hodorably."

Maglaban chided him. "Honorably, truly, but you need a proper name. Need I pick one for you?"

The no-nose goblin pondered for a moment. "Kogleyet, then," he said.

"Kogleyet?" Maglaban asked.

"I am a son of Kogylar," Kogleyet replied.

"That you are. And Ereseyet, after the legend?" Maglaban asked, directing his attention back to the first goblin.

"Yes, Great One," Erseyet answered.

"Perhaps you will make another legend," Maglaban smiled. "There is a need for the Venjeer here, in this place," he continued thoughtfully.

"What need, Great One?" Erseyet asked.

"This place is far from Kogylar. Far from the forges and fletchers and weavers and tanners. The Donbat-Karang have earned their say over this place, but Oygariyet needs this place to be a place like Kogylar."

"But–" Erseyet stammered in surprise, the most emotion Maglaban had seen in her this day, "–but what about honor and fighting?"

"There will be new chances for honor," Maglaban offered, attempting to allay their fears, "including fighting. There will be times where the Venjeer will be called to battle. But, it is important that the Venjeer do here in this place what Bindeyet does in Kogylar. Will you move the Venjeer here?"

"Yes, Great One," they said in unison, though Kogleyet's version sounded more like 'Gread Wud.'

"So be it," Maglaban concluded. "It is done. Erseyet and Kogleyet lead the Venjeer, though… I will come to Erseyet first." Kogleyet made no objection, and Erseyet looked at him impassively.

"And we take the slaves we need," she insisted.

"Yes, take three hundred for the Venjeer. By my blood, I will speak with the Donbat-Karang. The Venjeer will sort out all of the new slaves to find the crafters. The Venjeer will take them on and give them the honor of being useful."

"Very well, Gread Wud, bud we do nod know the humad laduage."

"I will give you one of my humans for that, though you will have to learn their ways enough to manage them." He paused looking at them, "can this be done?"

"Yes," Erseyet answered.

"Good. You should celebrate," Maglaban suggested.

Erseyet relaxed a bit. "Good. Yes. Then we *should* celebrate." She walked to the table and picked up a bottle. She uncorked it and held it over her head, pouring a few gulps into her mouth, letting some of the wine down her chin. She dabbed her fingertips in the juice and traced runes on her face for vigor and endurance, then offered the wine to Maglaban. "I must beg your pardon, but we must discuss if we are in the same clan or we each have our own clans and then start picking members for the breed family. We cannot properly celebrate without a breed family, you understand, Gr–uh–Maglaban."

"By the way of things, please do. I will be on to other things," Maglaban smiled. *I wonder if Muydiyet would be willing for some sport. Maybe with her new prize...*

Chapter 7

The Stone of Rykooth
By the Goblin Calendar, early in the Tenth Moon Cycle, 3114.
By the Human Calendar, Restday, first week of Banreni (seventh month of the year), 794.
Late at night, howling winds from the mountains bringing early autumn snow.

Indariyet watched from the balcony overlooking the courtyard. She pulled on her collar against the cold wind whipping at the ramparts. It was well past the Longnight Festival, and had been a strange one for her. It was the same music, the same feasting, the same sport, yet there had been a palpable atmosphere of anxiety clashing with hope. *Moreso with Oygariyet being gone for the Place-called-Ikria for nearly four moons, now.*

Shaking herself from those thoughts, she looked on below and surveilled the humans. Indariyet was genuinely curious to see how they would perform. These were humans taken as bounty from the Place-called-Ardara that had pledged to fight in Oygariyet's cause, securing themselves a place of honor. They understood. They understood that the mightiest honor would be in fighting and laboring for a great one. THE Great One. Lucky that they had come upon such an opportunity. All other honors were lesser. If they became wounded or frail, they could help in contributing ways, but the honor was lesser and it was usually granted at the kindness of a great one or someone in a prominent position that was able to provide those opportunities.

Oygariyet truly had a beautiful gift of finding ways for everyone to be of use, even when they had already given everything they could in life. Even if they refused, through lack of vision or understanding, honorable ways in life, he granted them such a kindness to use their skin and stomachs for leather and parchment,their bones in tools, their hair as cord, rope, thread, and fabrics. Their jaws and teeth for tool handles. Indariyet had not seen the limits of Oygariyet's kindness and remembered the mercy that he had paid Arkiban, herself, and the Okaramine.

The humans drilled, mostly with spears or swords. Soon, they would earn enough trust to wear armor and the partake in the honor of battle. These were the humans that had volunteered to form clans within Oygariyet's own Zirn. Others had joined other Hobgoblin or Goblin tribes. Indariyet did not quite understand what appealed to them in the Goblin tribes, except perhaps for the Talz, but it did not matter, so long as they were honorable.

Then there were the others. Oygariyet had set other humans aside and insisted that Indariyet take them in, which she did. They had another purpose. They were to go back to the human lands. They would learn the plans of their human opponents. For some of them, they would do more than just learn.

"Great One," greeted one of her staff, the Second, climbing the stairs to the balcony. "A messenger arrived from Kogylar."

"In the map room, then," she said. Indariyet entered the map room a few minutes later. A fire blazed in the central pit. She walked to the map table where the rest of her staff had already gathered. "And Oygariyet's staff?" Wordlessly, her Third scampered off to find Oygariyet's senior retainers, his purple cheeks flushing with embarrassment. *By my blood! How could they think that the others would not need to be here?* The Second strode through the main door with the messenger in tow, a blue-skinned female. She was no stranger to travel and hardship. She walked with a slight limp. Indariyet recognized her, but she did not acknowledge her. She could not. It would be rude to both of them and Indariyet did not envy her. No future, no opportunities. No redemption. No honor.

"The messenger, Great One," her Second announced. Indariyet motioned the messenger forward.

The messenger bowed her head respectfully, "I bear two messages, Great One. The Donbat-Karang made victory at the Place-called-Versingit."

"Very good!" Indariyet clapped. Her staff fussed over the map, updating the markers. "Do you have more information?" The messenger produced a roll of parchment, presenting it with her head still bowed. Taking it, Indariyet unfurled it and scrutinized the figures. She grimaced at the losses. She did not mind the orcs, but the losses of the Barituul and the Wiridil were concerning. There was a note from Maglaban written that the Venjeer had new leaders and would move their home to the Place-called-Versingit. The Ahng-Gorah were no more, consumed by the Talz. *He must mean the Talz orcs.* She suppressed a smirk at the thought of the tribe of Goblin sappers and engineers consuming the Ahng-Gorah. She read on. Plans for the winter. Plans for the melt. Concerns about the Borys-Karang. All noted. She handed the parchment to her staff, so they could update the maps. "What still?"

"Defeat at the Place-called-Borly," the messenger said.

Defeat. Again. All around the Place-called-Yvel. "You have information," Indariyet said flatly. It was not a question. The messenger produced another rolled parchment. Indariyet took it, perusing the figures. *Incredible losses. There the humans fight with honor and glory. But in the Place-called-Versingit, they fall. In the Place-called-Ardara, they fall. Why here? What is it for the Place-called-Yvel?* "You may go," she stated, waving the messenger away. She finished reading on the parchment, but kept her gaze on the parchments as the messenger left. She could not look up or give her any kind of recognition. Even to ask her what she knew.

Indariyet turned to her staff. "We are losing too many of the named. We must take additional measures," she said.

"What type of measures?" her First asked.

Indariyet leaned on the map, looking at the marks of lost battles in the Place-called-Yvel. *Too many being named before they are ready to lead.* "We need an academy. There has to be a... a reward for attending. Hm. Slaves. Yes, graduates would be allowed to own slaves before being named... And honor gifts for learning well. I would even give my human slave, the man from the Place-called-Serna, to the best."

***

The messenger walked away from the gathering. Indariyet's Second paid her a couple of silver coins with leaping wolves stamped upon them, three brass coins with spears on them, and a couple of bronze mountains, but mostly copper coins with pine trees or hogs stamped upon them. The Second left her at the door without a word. They knew who she was. They all did. She was supposed to be dead. She should have died moons ago on the side of a hill near the Place-called-Serna, at Dariyet's side. But she did not. She had missed the battle, having been wounded while scouting, her wolf mount slain beneath her.

She still remembered the face of the human scout that had wounded her and killed her wolf; hair and eyes smoldering black as ash, filled with a burning hatred. The messenger made her way through the halls and down the stairs,wondering what she would say to the human with so much hate in her eyes. She strode through the main door of the keep to the courtyard where her wolf waited. This was a new wolf. She had leased the creature from one of Jolaban's merchants in Kogylar to use in fulfilling her contract work, such as couriering messages.

She idly rolled one of the silver coins over her knuckles. It was a new coin, one side stamped with a leaping wolf, and the other with the face of Oygariyet the Great, glinting in the light of the fire from the mounted sconces. The coin was thicker than most used throughout the tribes of the mountains, and was worth its greater weight. The heft served as a promise. A promise from Oygariyet that times would be better under his leadership. That there would be renewed prosperity. No more scratching out an existence. She sighed as she put the coin in with its fellows and stuffed the pouch into her saddlebag. *A promise that I have no part in keeping, and no way to gain from.*

She rested her hand on the saddle and watched the humans as they drilled in lines with weapons. *How bizarre*, she thought wryly, *humans serving with honor while a hobgoblin feeds on scraps at the bottom of the pile.* She fitted a foot in the stirrup and swung the other leg over. Tried to. Searing pain shot from her knee in the stirruped leg and brought her back down. Wincing, she tried again, swinging the leg over, and successfully mounted. She had tried mounting from the other side a few times, but her scabbard had kept getting caught, and she preferred the occasional pain over the annoyance of tangled weaponry. She pulled her fur-lined hood forward as the wind gusted. The Longnight festival had been a lonely one.

She had been passing through Kogylar during the festival. She could not sport or even take meal with her own kind. It was improper, given her dishonor. The goblins would not take her in. Most goblins did not sport–at least, not the way that hobgoblins did; while they sported mightily, it was generally confined to inside their own clan, of which the messenger had none. Disdaining the orcs and what they thought of sport, she had spent Longnight alone with a bowl of soup and a bottle of ridin. It would be a long, cold ride back to Kogylar, with no one waiting for her on the other end, and only the fond memories of being the Cavalry Leader to keep her company.

***

Three days later, Indariyet received some welcome good news. Oygariyet's First returned with twenty-five ogres. She greeted them in the courtyard. Most of the ogres lazed about, even in the cold, while the castle staff and soldiers, especially the humans, gawked at them. The newcomers were quite tall, between two and three times the height of a healthy hobgoblin, mostly garbed in a rough patchwork of animal hides, cured to varying degrees. They had very large noses and round ears, with tufts of hair poking out of them, and their skin was various colors. Their skin reminded Indariyet of the underside of a mushroom. For all of their size, their eyes seemed comparatively small. One ogre stood, a female, with a paunch that matched her bosom in size and sag.

"Welcome back, First of Oygariyet," she greeted cheerfully. "The Great One pledged a name to you for completing this feat. Do you wish to choose?"

"Uh, no, not yet, Great One," he said. He seemed nervous. "Please, this is Urazor." He gestured towards the standing female ogre. She had a regal sense about her, in her own way. "Urazor is the Priestess of her tribe," the First explained. The ground shook with each step as Urazor strode towards Indariyet.

"You must be this 'Indariyet,' I am told of." Urazor spoke in accented Goblin, her voice rumbling in the air. It was a peculiar accent, but Indariyet had never met an ogre before and had little to compare to. *Really, I was surprised it could speak. I heard they are quite dumb.* It struck Indariyet that Urazor spoke the dialect

125

of Indariyet's home, on the other side of the mountain, where the cowardly sun first beats each day. The First seemed surprised as well and it seemed to increase his nervousness. *She must know both dialects and changed to the other one when she saw my purple skin.*

"I am Indariyet. I am glad that you have decided to join our honorable fight. There are a great many rewards for hard work and the Great Oygariyet is very generous."

"And just where is this great Oygariyet of yours?" Urazor asked.

"He has traveled to a Place-called-Ikria to gather more soldiers," Indariyet answered.

"Hm," Urazor mused noncommittally.

"You know this Place-called-Ikria?" Indariyet asked.

"Hm. It has been a very long time, and I am sure it has changed," she said dismissively. "I am sure that what I knew is of no use."

She speaks very well. I thought most of her kind to be at the grunting and groaning level. "Well," Indariyet began hesitantly. Indariyet was not sure of the ogres' customs. This was a bowl of mixed morsels for her–there was both good and bad in there, and she was unable to sort it out. She did not want to give up any of her staff to the mission of recruiting the ogres, and indeed, had never wanted anything to do with their kind. Indariyet found them unpredictable. Difficult to read, with costly consequences.

She was surprised that *anyone* was able to achieve something approaching cooperation with a group of ogres. *That means that this First has a special, unchangeable, indispensable place,* she grumbled. She had no illusions. The First was clearly the only one that the ogress was willing to tolerate, but that reduced the First to merely a go-between. The ogre priestess had the authority and would abide by Oygariyet's wishes at her whim.

Still, she came, which means she thinks she has something to gain. So I must involve her in planning. At least some. Indariyet was becoming frustrated considering the practical logistics of hosting Urazor, as a fresh gust of cold wind whipped over the walls. The ogress and her kin would not fit through most of the doorways in the castle. *That would* probably *be insulting.* Bringing maps out to her in this wind would be fruitless.

"Go, then, little man. Come to me later and tell me what your man-god wants of you and we will see what I will let my children do," Urazor said.

Indariyet concealed a deep sigh of relief. *She would actually let the First be her communicator. This seems so expertly done, so why is this First so nervous?* She ushered him inside with urgings toward the map room, but her curiosity got the better of her. "Tell me. What is it that she wants? How did you convince her to join? And why are you so nervous? You are Oygariyet's *First*."

He was silent for a few steps in the hallway, his eyes pointed towards the floor stones before looking at her sidelong. It was a very direct, exhausted expression. "Do not ask. Not even a thousand drownings in the coldest stream of the Mountain will ever wash it away, and it is a task that I will never finish."

Indariyet's curiosity ended in a quick death as they walked in silence. As they neared the map room she said, "I will never doubt your courage or devotion. You may choose a name."

"If only I had known," he said bleakly. They stopped at the door and he thoughtfully continued, "I am undeserving of a name. It is by knowing their customs and speech that I came upon this. Not the honorable ways. And even still, I knew too little and I cannot say what I learned. I have been sworn in a way that I cannot change, even if I wanted to."

"Oygariyet said that you would have a name if you returned. You were grateful for the opportunity. Oygariyet said that you would be named. And he will need to make room on the staff to train someone new. You are committed to this task."

"Committed, I am," he murmured. "Fine, then. 'Ogrekin.' That will be my name."

"Ogrekin?" she said quizzically.

"That is what I am now."

***

127

Several Hours Later

Sometime after the sun fled from the moon and the safety of darkness, Ogrekin walked to where the ogres had encamped away from the Stone of Rykooth. There was no safety for him. The ogres idled about and snored or lazed, wrapped in blankets made from animal pelts stitched or tied together. They ignored him as he walked past. He saw his wolf and went to pet it. Ogrekin yearned to be free; to feel the wind rushing in his face as his steed loped down the mountain. But there would be no freedom, not for him, not here, not with this wolf. The wolf was not tied. There was no need anymore. Urazor had destroyed its mind. It was more of a tool than an animal, like a water mill was more a tool than the trees it had been made from. The wolf laid there and slept, yet it seemed more like a stone than a resting beast. He petted it. *I am sorry, my friend, I did not know enough.*

He walked on towards the rocky side of the mountain and found the spot that Urazor would be. He turned a corner and saw her. She was still in her ogre form, but as soon as she saw him, she began to shift. Briefly, she held the silhouette of a great, winged, and long beast, even bigger than an ogre, before shrinking quickly, like water falling from a bucket, resolving into an outline roughly his size. The hide clothing of the ogre form fell limp and she emerged as a hobgoblin with odd coloring. Blue skin, like others of most tribes on this side of the mountain, but with purple hair. No hobgoblin had naturally purple hair, not even the ones from the other side. Purple coloring was added to hair with berries or other dyes, usually in women, to signify that they desired sport of some type. He looked away.

"Oh," she scolded softly, "do you not like it?" She spoke in his own dialect of Goblin still. He said nothing. She stepped delicately towards him, wrapping her arms around his shoulders and hung on him. She smiled poison at him. "Be not a chore, or I will skin you alive and leave you out for the vultures."

Chapter 8

Palace of Yvel City, Yvel Principality.
By the Human Calendar, Morningday (first day of the week), second week
of Banreni, 794.
By the Elven Calendar, eleventh day of Autumn, 18031.
A rainy, autumn morning.

The Blue-Eyed Man leaned back in the chair in the sitting room of his apartment, sipping coffee and regarding his new guest as his brother and sister nursed their own coffees, seated around a round wooden table decorated with ornate carvings. Praxia's delicate and otherworldly frame loomed in the doorway. She coughed and hugged a blanket about herself, looking on the assemblage before her equally sickly twin, Pantaria, ushered her away.

Those two need something to do. They've spoken to the Prince several times about wanting to be useful in some way as everyone around them struggles so hard. They study and help Stanis and the other such things when they're not too sick, but maybe... A servant stoked the crackling fire, pouring its warmth into the room to combat the cold seeping in from the seams of the closed windows.

The Blue-Eyed Man spoke. "You really should try this. One of the towns to the south brews their coffee in goat's milk."

"Yes, I know," the guest responded, rather curtly.

"Oh, you do? You've already been to Serna?" he asked.

"What? No. I mean the brewing in goat milk is how it's done in Markia," she said, her tone still laced with an edge.

"It is?"

"The water method is Eklendan. Yvel has always been more Eklendan, at least to us."

Bewildered, he continued. "Yes, surely. It's just–"

"Is this *really* important?" she cut in.

"I suppose it is not in comparison," he admitted. "Please,

have a pastry."

"I'd rather not," she said flatly, glaring at him. "Can I rely on–"

"Of course," he interrupted, taking his turn to cut her off. "The Prince supports intervention and the safety of our neighbors to the north." She sighed quietly. The Blue-Eyed Man sensed that it was a sigh of simultaneous relief and exasperation "Are you sure you are willing to go to these lengths?"

"If I must, yes. And so will she," she said resolutely.

"Let us hope it does not come to that. It might make things more complicated later." *In some ways. Easier in others.*

"She's already quite set about it," his guest said.

"Oh, yes, she is," added the Blue-Eyed Man's sister.

"What? Just by seeing the Prince and some passing pleasantries?" the Blue-Eyed Man asked incredulously.

"Yes, but she took the sight in at the practice yard," the guest said.

"The practice yard?" the Blue-Eyed Man raised his eyebrows. *What could she have seen in the practice yard to sway her heart so?*

***

That Afternoon

Jovaela wearily dismounted in the courtyard of the palace in Yvel, brushing her thick black braid behind her. It had been a long while, marked by a rain-soaked road worn by every return. Months ago, she had left to report to the Guardian Council on Holbrin's behalf, requesting supplies, proper armor, and further guidance. She had returned with all that was sought, and then some. Over a hundred elves dismounted horses or climbed down from drawn wagons behind her. Brushing off the dust on her breeches that had been gathered from the road, she looked up to see Trinien hurrying down the steps, boots splashing on the wet stone, to jovially greet them.

"It is so good to have you back, my dark-eyed friend," he

smiled at her, clasping her shoulders.

She let out a vexed sigh. "I wish it was good to be back, but at least I can say it is nice to see you, Trinien."

He chuckled. "I see you are energetic enough to keep being yourself."

"Where is Holbrin?" Jovaela was not one for forced pleasantries and brushed past Trinien's warm welcome.

"Ah, so good that you arrive just now. There will be a council session soon, and Prince Arnold has asked Holbrin to attend," Trinien said as he hurried after her. "I am sure that Holbrin would like you there, once he knows that you have returned."

"Good."

"And it will really help you understand events and activities that are currently happening."

"Good."

"And I am certain that you will be the most presentable at the council."

Jovaela abruptly halted on the steps and slowly turned to glare at Trinien over her shoulder with one eye. She could have burned a hole into him with that gaze.

"At least a minimum," he continued, "let us get you off and dusted over, and changed, so that you do not track mud in. The staff can heat a bath for you." He chuckled.

"The bare minimum," she said flatly.

An hour later, Jovaela emerged from the apartments in the palace allotted for Holbrin's affiliates, the dust and mud of the road washed off of her, and stuffed into clothes that Trinien had arranged for with the palace staff. She was towed through a labyrinthine set of passages she had never seen before, that Trinien insisted was the fastest way to the council chambers.

Jovaela tolerated being towed; she did not have the advantage that the others of her original company had of being at all familiar with the palace. Her guide continued to lead her through the maze of passages and stairways, weaving past walkways that overlooked a central courtyard now transformed into a well-equipped training ground before arriving at a waiting room outside what was, presumably, the council room. Holbrin was there in front of a pair of carved double doors with that infuriatingly placid smile of his.

She spoke in Elvish. "Do you have any notion of what I had to accomplish for the Guardian Council to *not* be dragging you back in chains right now!?"

The only reaction he gave was a slight arching of one eyebrow. "I have a vague idea and I greatly appreciate your accomplishments. We have done much, and much remains."

She glared at him. She had a bag full of glares for everyone.

Holbrin continued after a pause, fully taking in Jovaela's scowl. "What were the difficulties on the road? Knowing the rigor you take in your duties I imagine there would have been some in the amount of time that you have been gone."

She shifted a bit. *At least he understands that there have been problems.* "I made the journey twice before. We had to fight our way through Vostind, the north pass, and Markia, and gave a wide berth to occupied lands," she said. "Versingit has fallen."

"I heard a few weeks ago. That is one of the things that Prince Arnold wishes to discuss today." Holbrin looked pensive. "How are matters further north?"

"Not well," Jovaela explained. "All along the mountains, they come down like thawing ice. This is happening on both sides of the Kaskevs, too. We did not have problems in Vostind, but we have reports that orcs, gnolls, and goblinkind are pressuring Vostind and occupying parts of Gilliam. We have rendered assistance to the Markians, as well."

"What about the Vostindin and the Gills?"

"The Gills, yes, but it is already in a very bad way. The Vostindin are too proud to ask or offer help."

"I see," said Holbrin.

Unbothered as ever, she grumbled to herself. The carved doors, one decorated with the Yvel crest and the other with the Torg'ail crest, creaked as the Prince's Guard opened them. "My Lord. My Lady," one of them said. "Please enter. The Prince will arrive soon."

"Holbrin?" Jovaela caught his attention.

Holbrin turned, catching a hint of anxiety in her tone. "Yes?"

"This is Abrasian Darkmoon," Jovaela started, gesturing to another elf looming behind her–not over her; the looming over was reserved for Holbrin in particular. Of course Holbrin had noticed, but there was a tacitly-observed protocol to handling situations such as these. If a traveler entered into a situation in which there was already another traveler managing the situation, courtesies had to be observed.

"Ah, good. We meet again, Abrasian. It has been some forty summers, yes?" Holbrin smiled, unphased. Jovaela hid her surprise, but was unaware that they already knew each other. Abrasian had been bemoaning the situation with the human's rediscovery of blood magic on full display at the Battle of Serna Hills and Holbrin's handling of it, twisting the words in her reports to reflect his own interpretations. Holbrin could be infuriating, but still, it was odd for her to encounter an elf that meant ill towards another of their own kind, especially one such as Holbrin.

"Nearly, yes," said Abrasian. "We shall talk soon?"

"Yes, as one lead traveler to the other." Holbrin's voice was smooth and pleasant.

"I am here as a lead sword. Not a traveler. I will introduce my Second, Arcaezhia Moonwhisper, at the nearest leisure," Abrasian said. Informing Holbrin about his role here was something Jovaela had been a bit nervous about. The Guardian Council had sent Abrasian here with a different set of mandates, some of which were in conflict with the ones they had given Holbrin. Jovaela was anxious about how the two of them would reconcile the Council's conflicting directives.

"Oh? Well, I am certain we can smooth out any ripples in the water. Our main purpose this afternoon begins soon." Holbrin was pleasant, remaining unphased. He turned back to the main event unfolding in the palace's council chamber. It was a dismissal. Abrasian glowered into the back of Holbrin's head, but Holbrin feigned ignorance. Jovaela considered the exchange that she had just witnessed. *Perhaps Holbrin knows Abrasian better than I credit him for...*

Holbrin's interpretation of 'soon' meant time enough for the comfortably fat merchants and guildsmen to waddle in and find their seats at two long tables placed on either side of the round room. They were followed by the few nobles who happened to be in Yvel, the prince's siblings–Oswald, Velthuria and Aered–his staff, and the usual retinue of the Crown Guard. Marshal Mot Gundr'ail arrived, as did the Chief Librarian, Lord Nicholas Machidran, Bishop Belifar, Chamberlain Dorrels, Sir Merik, Mistress Mkaela from Serna, and several others. The prince arrived last, flanked by an armed Crown Guard. The prince wore an arming sword with familiarity as he individually greeted nobles and guildsmen.

"Alright," he called for order, "only a few items to discuss, but important ones." The chatter in the room subsided. A pair of servants followed the prince as he sat at his table, situated at the end of the long tables for the council members. The servants brought out coffee and a pastry, served with a fork, and already cut to pieces. Chairs that had clearly been borrowed from other rooms had been brought in to accommodate the large attendance. Holbrin and Jovaela settled into the mismatched seats near the edge of the room.

Behind the prince, the elderly chamberlain whispered to an older servant as he idly snacked on the pastry. Stewards moved through the chamber with plates of berries and warmed, spiced Marin dark wine, though some of the prince's retinue also took coffee when offered.

"Versingit, its city, has fallen. Their people are in a grievous need." The prince looked around, "and Yvel will fill it."

"Absolutely not!" one of the council members exclaimed, slapping a meaty palm down on the table.

"That is Erbasil Halifar; he owns several farms between here and Borly for grain, cattle, and the like," Holbrin whispered to Jovaela. Erbasil was a large man, larger than his bones would have liked. His features were different from most in the room. He lacked both the narrow Eklendan jaw as well as the pinched Marin nose, but had very yellow hair, blonder than any other in the room.

The prince turned to regard the council member. "Master

Erbasil. Good day, and why not?"

"They can defend themselves. We have our own problems!" Erbasil insisted.

"Those that died in their city might disagree, as might those now bearing the yoke of slavery at the hands of those greens and those blues," the prince said.

"They have their own soldiers, we have ours. We do not have enough to both rescue them and defend ourselves. The Versingiters would never fight under a Yvelian banner–and you know it–and we have no legal method to intervene. It would be an invasion!" he ranted, "and what's more! What *about* our own problems, my brave Prince? When was the last time that a caravan of goods got through without being raided?" His last point received scattered cheers from the other council members, even some of the lords.

The prince turned to one of the nobles that had encouraged Erbasil's challenge. "Do you agree with Master Erbasil, Lord Bers?"

Bers stood from his seat against the wall and puffed out his chest to rival his impressive belly paunch. "I do, Your Grace. The enemy raids our supply lines and the army is bogged down chasing the ugly vermin all over the place."

"Yes, without you, I would add," the prince chided offhandedly.

"Here now!" Bers began.

"Really, Bers, if you want to help, then help instead of bleating about it like these coinmongers," the prince dismissed. The other council members snorted and hollered in outrage.

"Here now, yourselves!" The prince brought them to rein quickly. "You say we have problems at home, Your Prince hears." He turned to Bers and smiled, "I am certain that House Der'ail would bask in the honor of being part of the solution."

"Your Grace?" Bers was slightly flustered.

"Take some of your own soldiers down to the garrison at Serna. Speak with Lady Judane and Lord Dareum down there. I will send a letter with you. They are to send detachments to patrol the roads. If they do not have enough soldiers, they will need to levy more, but you are going to help them, Bers."

"Um, well, uh, Your Grace, I have some delicate matters that require my direct attention here..." Bers muttered sheepishly.

"Yes, yes, Bers, send one of your trusted, then." The prince rolled his eyes in disdain. "Does anyone else of the court have an objection?" The other nobles were silent, but the merchants and guildsmen were visibly disgruntled.

"What is it now?" the prince asked their sour faces.

"It is not enough," Erbasil, who seemed to be the de facto opposition leader.

"It will have to be. Patrols from the Serna Regiment, with some very *generous* assistance from the Der'ail, will cover all of the main roads to our borders," said Prince Arnold.

"Well, then who will be going into flaming Versingit with the army stretched that thin?" Erbasil questioned.

"The First Yvel Regiment with Koval Covendran, along with several other regiments that I know so many of you have been working *so hard* to raise in time," the prince said while eyeing Marshal Gundr'ail.

"Your Grace," the Marshal began, "who will take their place on the line?"

"More of these glorious new regiments that the houses have been raising. Especially the Toliodrans. We have good Sir Harl–Now Baron Harl–at Borly doing the same thing. Oh, and of course to make the liberation an assured victory, Your Prince's own Crown Guard will join the fight," the prince said.

Holbrin sighed.

"What is it?" Jovaela asked quietly.

"The Prince is creating an excuse for more of his gallivanting misadventures. Just wait for it," Holbrin said to Jovaela, under his breath.

"Who will guard you, then, Your Grace?" asked Chamberlain Dorrels in his trembling, wispy voice.

"What? Oh, why the Crown Guard, of course! The Prince will wet his blade at the head of the army," he grinned.

"See?" Holbrin whispered as the Marshal made a vexed sound. Jovaela could understand. No general would want his sovereign strolling through the army he meticulously administered and maneuvered.

"Anything else?" The prince left the floor open.

"You still haven't said anything about those people to the north. They will not fight under a Yvel banner!" Erbasil demanded.

"Indeed, Master Erbasil, Your Prince has it on *very* good authority that they will."

"Oh? And just how is that?" Erbasil prodded. The air in the room had been tense since the beginning of this exchange. Lord Bers Der'ail had melted into the crowd to avoid attracting any additional tasks at the cost of his own health or coin.

The prince wryly glanced at the floor for a moment before looking directly at a pair of women who had remained unannounced and quiet up to this point. They were seated next to Oswald and Velthuria, in the seats on the other side of the room from Jovaela. "They need proof. Could you please?" The two women were both blonde, but not like Erbasil; not anywhere close. The shade of blond, their narrow noses, and their brilliantly deep blue eyes marked them as Marin in a purer way than most others in the room.

One of them stood, "I am Fyon Wrin'ail, Princess of Versingit, and I have asked Prince Arnold for help liberating my people. They will fight under a Yvel banner."

"There. You see?" the prince said.

"There is still no legal method! And there is no lasting interest! What is there for Yvel if we help Versingit? More raids on the farmers near Borly?"

"Listen here, people are dying by the hundreds, while scores more are made to fan the flames of industry for the enemy," the prince said firmly.

"*You* listen here, Your *Grace*, people *are* dying by the hundreds. Right here in Yvel!".

"Well, for one, we will have favorable relations and can put a stop to those raids. For a second, we are getting something out of all of this afterwards. Lands will be conquered in the mountains.

New opportunities and new resources. New trade. What we conquer that would otherwise be a Versingit share would be ours, if that helps to convince the coinmongering among you. But, if you need a legal path for this," he looked to Fyon and the woman next to her. He left a long pause as he looked at them. They looked at each other and then both nodded to him, "then, I will adopt Princess Fyon's sister, Brindi, as my own sister. This makes Fyon Wrin'ail, Princess of Versingit, my sister-in-law by her marriage to Eron, and establishes a claim for House Torg'ail. With this new closeness, the likes have not been seen since the Imperial Secession War, we will be able to secure favorable trade arrangements after the war."

The council members gaped at him. The prince eyed each of them before glaring at Erbasil. "Happy?"

Jovaela noticed the woman on the far side of the council room, Brindi, now sister to Prince Arnold, gazing intently at him.

***

After leaving the council chamber, Holbrin led Jovaela and Abrasian through the corridors to the apartments the elves had shared up to that point. "Things seem to be relatively well in hand here," she said in Elvish.

"They are not," he replied. His ever-serene expression did not shift, but Jovaela had known Holbrin long enough to know that his concern on a topic was reflected more in how direct and unceremonious his words were.

"Then, I must know," she pressed, "I am really only here to deliver these reinforcements and supplies and to take back an updated report on these matters. Particularly–"

"I know what in particular you speak of, and we shall wait a moment until we are in a safer location," he broke in.

She bristled at his interruption, but she also knew that he would not be rude without cause. Holbrin was a very odd person who had grown more polite with age, rather than less. He had explained it to her once–having gone through periods of varying rudeness, he had found that people were ruder to him in direct relation to how rude he was to others. Since he would live on, regardless of how short- or long-lived those around him would be, they would be more tolerable to be around. Jovaela had not found this to be true in her own experiences, but Holbrin generally seemed satisfied with that notion he had constructed.

They walked down tight, spiraling stairs and crossed through some servant corridors. "Is this the way we are meant to travel?" Jovaela asked.

"No. It is the quickest. The other way is grander, but longer," Holbrin explained over his shoulder. His gait appeared natural, but he was in a hurry. Upon their arrival, Holbrin closed the door behind them. Tyrnimar waited for them, sipping his tea and conversing with Trinien.

"Where are the others?" Jovaela asked.

"Spread to the corners of this Principality," Holbrin said, "helping the humans fight better and fighting alongside them." Holbrin waited while Tyrnimar poured all three of them a cup of herbal tea. Jovaela took the cup Tyrnimar offered. He looked friendly, but tired. They all looked tired. Just as tired as she was.

"Who is this?" Tyrnimar asked, referring to Abrasian.

"Abrasian Darkmoon. Lead sword of the new contingent," Trinien said.

"Ah." Tyrnimar nursed his tea some more.

Jovaela decided to resume the conversation from the hall. "I said that things seemed well in hand because this area is the only one on both sides of the mountains that is not being overrun, and I cannot even imagine how the Dwarven Realms are faring." She looked around. "And while that is good for the people here, the Guardian Council is very alarmed at humans wielding magic again."

"Word of the dwarves is had by you?" Tyrnimar said eagerly. Jovaela and Abrasian glowered at him and Tyrnimar deflated. "With each new day, sorcery can be used better by the humans," Tyrnimar said quietly.

"The Council would like a report," Jovaela said.

Holbrin looked at her. "The Guardian Council or the Seer Council?"

"The Guardian Council. Although, I suppose the Seer Council will want it, too," Jovaela continued, "but what difference does it make?"

Holbrin smiled wryly. This was the smile he made before he would take it upon himself to educate the youth. Jovaela hated that look. "Out with it, then," she snapped irritably.

"The Guardian Council will want to know what is going on and all of the things that it affects, so that they may act." He paused to clarify the difference. "The Seer Council will want to know the factors that allowed it to happen in the first place so that we are not surprised in this way again. Because of this difference, the report would be very different, depending on for whom it is written."

"Fine, then, since the Guardian Council is the one dealing with this mess, then they would be the ones needing the report the most," Jovaela offered.

Holbrin looked at Tyrnimar. "Both should be written," Tyrnimar suggested.

"I agree, but the one for the Guardian Council first," Holbrin decided, "Trinien."

"I will have it done in two days, Holbrin," Trinien agreed.

Holbrin looked back to Jovaela. "The one for the Seer Council will take longer to write, but we have already started. Tyrnimar has been studying their sorcerers as they train."

"They train!?" Jovaela was not amused.

"How could you have let this happen?" Abrasian asked quietly.

"Their prince directed it. I have never seen anyone with such a vigorous personal training regimen. He believes training fixes nearly every problem, directly or indirectly–and while I tend to agree with that–I have never met anyone that takes it to such an extreme. Most humans, I imagine, when they learn they have a new weapon, such as sorcery, they will use it as soon and as often as possible, before it is ready, and lose it. Prince Arnold has shown exceptional patience by placing them out of fighting to train enough that they can employ their powers effectively and safely."

"*How*, Holbrin, *how* could you have let things come to

this?" Abrasian pressed.

But I know Tyrnimar better. Jovaela was skeptical of Tyrnimar's academic motives, and fixed a disapproving look upon him. "You have not been helping them discover their powers, have you?"

"Am I to just kill off the humans with awakened powers?" Holbrin asked.

"If that will–" Abrasian began.

"Lead to many more humans dying because they did not have protection against overwhelming odds and suffered complete surprise at the mercy of an alliance between the orcs and hobgoblins?" Holbrin took Abrasian's sentence away from where he had wanted to go.

Tyrnimar looked everywhere besides Jovaela's direction. "Uh, well, no, I–"

Jovaela made a vexed sound but Holbrin raised a disarming hand. "It is much worse than that," he said.

"What do you mean?" she accused.

"The Prince is spying on Tyrnimar's studies, and Tyrnimar had to defend himself from one of the sorcerer's outbursts."

"So, she saw him deflect," Jovaela looked from Holbrin to Tyrnimar and back. Tyrnimar nodded sheepishly.

"Ow!" Tyrnimar was on the ground, his teacup overturned. Jovaela had struck him before she realized it.

"YOU FOOL!" Jovaela shouted as she stood over him.

"It is done, Jovaela," Holbrin said. He looked so very tired. "And it cannot be undone. The sorceress saw Tyrnimar defend himself, but we think we have concealed it from the spy. We have also moved all of Tyrnimar's notes and traveling library."

Jovaela sat back down, with her face in her hands. "Anything else I should know of?"

"Well," Trinien said as Tyrnimar was warily rising, "some happy news is that Eevarel and Tyrnimar have initiated the marriage ritual."

Again, before Jovaela realized it, her foot was streaking

forwards Tyrnimar's face in outrage. He was ready though, catching it and brushing it aside. "Very rude of a greeting is to be punched and kicked by you," Tyrnimar snapped.

"What are you thinking? Are you an idiot?" Jovaela said sternly. Abrasian's eyes blazed at Holbrin in contempt, outraged that he had allowed matters of young hearts to distract from the demands of society.

"And after the tea was served," Tyrnimar said sullenly. "That tea was made for you by me."

"Well?" Jovaela demanded.

"And my tea was spilled by you!" Tyrnimar continued.

"Do not ignore me!" Jovaela was angry.

Holbrin stepped between them, "Tyrnimar, go wait in the other room." He turned to Jovaela. "This is also done. Striking him solves nothing and, I would add, is unbecoming of a proper gentle elf. I have sent Eevarel down to Serna with Arynn, since they cannot seem to govern themselves when they are together." He glowered at Tyrnimar. *So he is frustrated*, Jovaela observed, *at least he is trying to not run a troupe of fools.* "That did not bring levity, Trinien," Holbrin scolded. "What Jovaela really needed to know is that Lierialuth passed to the next life at Borly."

"Lierialuth…" *But she was so young!*

"Lazura and Erensed are with Irduin at Borly," Holbrin said.

"I met with Irduin, but she would not say much. You let her ride a wolf?" Jovaela asked.

"A wolf? Oh, that must have been what she meant. She was vague in her letter. I do not mind. I trust Irduin's decisions, especially in matters like that, and she likely blames herself for letting Lierialuth die." Jovaela was quiet and Holbrin continued, "Bierien is here helping train new weapon and armor smiths." He held up a hand to silence Jovaela's protest, "She is only teaching them to the level that they need, without revealing anything. Sieraean and Parendien are further west, helping the Prince's nobles form more regiments."

Jovaela sat back in her chair and let out a long breath.

"Well," she said after a moment, "we should decide where these reinforcements go and get them moving in those directions while Trinien writes this report."

"Let us take thirty of them to Serna. Trinien will be done with the report when you return, and Tyrnimar will have at least the first portion of his report ready. I have not had a chance to check on them since the beginning of the season, and you have not seen them in almost two seasons."

"You run a traveling circus here, Holbrin," Abrasian said. "I must insist that one of my people bring reports back to the council from now on, even if some of them are written by your group. And *I will* be writing my own assessment. Perhaps the gravity of this requires that I send my own Second, Arcaezhia Moonwhisper."

Holbrin sat down in Tyrnimar's seat and repoured himself a cup of tea from Tyrnimar's kettle, wearing his placid smile. "Perhaps that is for the better. Send whomever you wish. I could well benefit from Jovaela's presence, certainly… well, then… now that you have expressed your disapproval of the situation, I would be most entertained to hear the solutions that you would have enacted were our positions reversed."

***

Earlier, at the recess of the council.

The Council Members and other attendees gradually filed out of the room. They mingled and chatted with one other, and the Blue-Eyed Man wove among them with kind words, pleasantries, promises of support, well wishes, and an understanding ear. Most were gone and now was the time. "Master Minderl, a moment?"

Minderl Radidran was one of the other council members, a guilder. He owned several workshops for pottery, tanning, garments, and the like. His olive skin had wrinkles about the hands, eyes, and neck, speaking to long years in the shops, as did the plain cut of his breeches and tunic. But the lightness of his skin and a paunchy roundness through the middle suggested that it had been some time since he had done that work himself. His eyes were such a light shade of brown they almost seemed golden under his red hair. The Blue-Eyed Man knew he owned additional enterprises outside of the city, but it did not matter. He was hurting enough to be in need of security. That was why he supported Erbasil. The Blue-Eyed Man was about to change that.

"Yes, y–" he began.

"No need for that. It is only us two," the Blue-Eyed Man said. "I understand your reluctance to support the Prince's eagerness to liberate the walls of Versingit."

Minderl hesitated, taking a step back.

"But. But. Hear this first before you object further or withdraw," the Blue-Eyed Man continued. "Once Versingit is freed, there will be a vacuum in it. All of their guilders are dead, gone, or enslaved. It would be a gem for the plucking."

"… And you are saying–" Minderl started.

"Yes. Yes, especially for those who support the Prince and the army's needs, there are a great many opportunities."

Minderl looked away, scrubbing a hand through his hair, "Erbasil will be difficult."

"Don't worry about Erbasil."

"But–" Minderl objected.

"No. Really. Don't oppose him. Not here. The meaning is that the Prince and the army will have needs, and the Prince needs to know that he has someone to rely upon. *You* can be that someone, and that will position you and, perhaps, a few others of your choosing, to be in some very advantageous positions later on," he said. "Though, in truth, there will be some very difficult times along the way."

Minderl's smile was grimly cynical. "What needs to happen?"

"Oh, nothing for now. Nothing. One of the Marshal's staff will contact you," the Blue-Eyed Man closed confidently.

"Security is a problem, though," Minderl pointedly objected.

"Yes, yes. The Prince will have the Serna Regiment on it,"

the Blue-Eyed Man reassured. They exchanged a few more words and then both departed pleasantly. The Blue-Eyed Man made his way through the halls to the library. Opening the doors, he was greeted with the sight of freshly laid out coffee and pastries and his friend immersed in a very old book.

"How did it go?" Nicholas asked without looking up.

"It went well. Minderl is skeptical, but agreeable," the Blue-Eyed Man answered with a smile.

"Good," Nicholas said absently.

"Another good performance by Bers. Send him a bonus," the Blue-Eyed Man suggested.

Nicholas reached over, dipped a pen in the inkwell on his desk, and scratched a note on a ledger without looking away from the book. He turned a page as soon as he dropped the pen. "On bonuses and money, we're running out."

"We just need to close the gap more with the teams raiding caravans. We are able to build a good portion of the army without having to pay for many of the materials," the Blue-Eyed Man explained.

"Yes, and let's hope that none of the Council pays close attention to how their workshops are being fed materials," Nicholas said, eyes still glued to the book and turning another page and squinting at a diagram.

The Blue-Eyed Man leaned back in his seat, sipping a coffee. He picked up a pastry. He savored the sensation of the flakes breaking under his teeth and the buttery-sweet moistness of the dough. Chewing for a few moments in silence, he watched Nicholas squint and turn more pages.

"We have some teams here in the city?" The Blue-Eyed Man asked.

"Yes. Two. They are here just in case. I have them mostly training and holed up in one of the warehouses the ministry owns."

"Good," the Blue-Eyed Man said.

"Why?" Nicholas looked up for the first time. "You want them to do Erbasil in?"

Sipping his coffee again, he paused. "What? No, no. We

need to be able to create problems and be the ones with solutions to them. For that, we need there to be opposition."

"We could recruit him and direct the opposition," Nicholas suggested.

"Hm. If necessary, but that would not work as well. People–the Council–will believe the situation better with genuine opposition. If we try to direct it, it will be more clumsy," the Blue-Eyed Man pointed out.

"Like the difference between a conversation amongst people and that of an acting troupe?" Nicholas reworded.

"Right," the Blue-Eyed Man agreed. The conversation died there as Nicholas went back to his book. Curiosity got the better of the Blue-Eyed Man. "What is that?"

"Valnos' explanation of how to create solid, dense projectiles out of dust in the air," Nicholas said.

"*Really.*" The Blue-Eyed Man was rapt with interest.

"Yes, it actually seems fairly simple. Relatively speaking, that is."

"Do you think you could do it?" the Blue-Eyed Man eagerly prodded.

"I can give it a try." Nicholas paged over and over until he found the correct diagram. Looking back to it for reference, he inscribed mathematical symbols onto a small patch of parchment and mumbled an incantation. The air in front of him grew darker, forming into the shape of a long spearhead. Nicholas reached out and grabbed it.

"So, what? You make it and throw it yourself?" the Blue-Eyed Man asked.

"No. I stopped the incantation. There is a second part to propel it. Valnos describes being able to create and propel multiple spears at once, but it seems like it would be difficult to manage."

"What do you mean, difficult?"

"Uh, it's hard to describe. Really, you'd have to do it yourself, and–" Nicholas started.

"Splendid idea!" the Blue-Eyed Man interrupted. Nicholas looked annoyed. "Oh, come now. You can spare a few of these.

What's good to start with?"

Nicholas sighed, vexed. "I have been working on this for a month and I can barely do that. You don't even read Old Paetic."

"Ah, meaning to pick that up, anyways. Send someone over to help that along. They won't see any of these," the Blue-Eyed Man picked up one of the books, "and we'll use some historic text."

"Fine, fine. Just not those," Nicholas pointed to a small pile.

"Why not?" the Blue-Eyed Man asked.

"Well, for one, they're Zaya's notes from the proving grounds," Nicholas said.

"The Tamark girl?" the Blue-Eyed Man asked.

"You always remember the women," Nicholas rolled his eyes. "She's half Tamark, yes. The notes are hardly anything to begin this endeavor. Valnos makes quite a few notes about safety in these incantations. Really, Zaya's notes are more useful in determining what the elves know and are hiding."

"Right, right. What about this and those?" The Blue-Eyed Man pointed to the stack next to Nicholas.

"Kolus brought them from the ruins where you found that carving," Nicholas said.

"Ah, yes. He has quite the following now. Where did you put him?"

"I have him in one of the ministry's country estates in the west. By Krogen."

"Ah. And that's his only task?"

"Yes," Nicholas said. "Though," he added thoughtfully, "he has been different since this last trip."

"You mean the Goblin harem?" the Blue-Eyed Man joked.

"Try to contain your jealousy. And, no, besides that."

"Really, more curious," the Blue-Eyed Man said.

"Liar," Nicholas muttered.

"Hm. Well, keep an eye on him. Maybe the Prince will pay him a visit," the Blue-Eyed Man said.

"Not with many, I hope," Nicholas cautioned. "He really needs solitude. With what's going on with the war and all, what would it look like for a company or a regiment, even a ten-man, to walk up and find a man working with a bunch of goblins? It would be a bloodbath, though I'm not sure which way. Kolus has had more success than I in these studies, and with fewer distractions."

"Fine, fine. Maybe only a very small visit. As soon as he's ready, he should train others to use this magic," the Blue-Eyed Man said.

"Ugh. More with the training. All the time with the training," Nicholas muttered. "Alright," he relented, "but I must insist that Kolus has to agree. He has a hand up on us right now and we are relying purely on his loyalty."

"Fine, but get a hand and a half up on him," the Blue-Eyed Man said.

Nicholas put the book down and walked over and got himself a cup of coffee, "I'll be up late with this. I don't know how you drink it all the time."

"Better than wine," the Blue-Eyed Man said.

"How can it be better than wine!?" Nicholas exclaimed.

"Wine dulls the reflexes and balances. Can't train with wine," the Blue-Eyed Man said.

"Again, with training," Nicholas said. "Well, anyways, quite lucky that the Princess of Versingit and her sister came along to freely offer a claim to their throne."

The Blue-Eyed Man smiled, "Yes. Quite lucky indeed."

"Be careful," Nicholas chided.

***

Turin suppressed wrinkling his nose at the smell of garbage and street refuse left to rot for months, for a third time. The odor emanated from the guest's skin and fur, and was probably strong enough to kill the prince's sickly twin sisters by itself. The situation was almost comical to Turin, to have such an undesirable person visiting the guest quarters at the palace in Yvel. It was also undesirable to recruit a new contact in their place of dwelling as it could threaten revealing Turin's identity and task, but with this particular contact, it was actually less risky to meet this way than his normal method of consulting in a public place.

"Something bothering you, Garrick?" the rat man asked. His Marin was strangely accented, probably from living underground and having a differently formed mouth from other humanoids, but Turin could make it out well enough.

"No, Master Smeld, thanks for asking," Turin said, putting on a good face. "You were saying? The number of people like yourself living under Versingit?"

"Yeah. A few thousand," Smeld answered.

"That is quite a bit," Turin noted. "How do you survive?"

Smeld looked at him flatly. "From the scraps and leftovers."

"But, surely, you have your own industries. Your own enterprises," Turin prodded.

"Surely, we do," Smeld's bitterness shifted to pride. "And a fair bit we can do. We grow mosses and mushrooms, raise rats, moles, and hogs, and we farm many different crawlies."

"That's quite a bit," Turin repeated appraisingly. Turin was trying to sound impressed. Indeed, he was, at what basically amounted to a city under a city with its own agriculture, but it still was made of rat-faced, scat-smelling people, eating scat-stained food, wearing scat-stained clothes.

"Surely, it is!" Smeld said smugly. "We can turn any trash of the surface into something better."

Turin paused in feigned thought. "So, with all that you have, what would you and your people want out of this arrangement?"

"We want to live on the surface." His flat statement made it seem simple.

Turin was not quite expecting that. "I think we can come to an arrangement of some type on that, but what about the grand city you have that you were telling me of? Will you abandon it?"

"No. Some of us will stay, some of us will move," Smeld

explained.

"Won't it–" Turin began.

"You can let us worry about that, Garrick," Smeld cut in.

Turin smiled internally. *Fine that you feel you have control.* "Very well… though I worry that the humans on the surface may have a hard time with this."

Smeld sat upright, black eyes smoldering with years of resentment. "That would be something that I–*we*–expect you to do something about! They don't like living next to ratfolk, they can have the orcs and goblins back. Surely, they just love that right now!"

Turin nodded appraisingly. "You make a fair point, Master Smeld, and we can come to an arrangement on that," Turin soothed in a conciliatory tone, "and we can help with that, but it will take a lot of doing. I can make the argument for that with the ones I work for, but I really need it to sound attractive to them, you know? They don't always see a good deal when it's right in front of them. So, what I really need is a bit more in this deal to make it tastier."

"What did you have in mind?"

***

Tyrnimar handed the reins to the stablehand. "Thanking you for work done by you," he said. The stablehand looked at him in blank noncomprehension. Tyrnimar realized he had spoken in a different language. He repeated himself but in Marin. *In trueness, which language was spoken by me cannot be remembered by me*, he pondered as he absently walked towards the farmhouse.

"Tyrnimar!" Kora called. Tyrnimar looked over to see the two sisters in the field of the proving grounds. "Look what I can do," she beamed with a smile and turned away. Fiery glow coalesced around her, focusing into a sphere and then shooting out in a sputtering beam of melting, flaming air. The beam shot out more than a hundred paces, spalling around it the whole way, and roaring loudly.

Tyrnimar's eyes sparkled, fascinated. "Wow," Tyrnimar said breathlessly, and far from his mind were any thoughts of caution, or recollections of the awful history of humans wielding magic.

Chapter 9

erik, the broad-shouldered Church Knight, and Mkaela, the one-time baker and apprentice apothecary from Serna, turned the corner towards the guest rooms reserved for clergy visiting the palace. Mkaela felt out of place just being in such a lavish room, nevermind having one to call her own, even if only temporarily. Merik's room was next door to hers. These were their rooms as long as they were in the capital, and by default their own private quarters as no other clergy had visited Yvel since the beginning of this. *I never wanted any of this.* Mkaela slumped down in a cushioned chair. *I just wanted to bake bread and pie, marry some happy fool, have some children, and get old and fat. That's all. Too much, I guess.*

"Lady Mkaela?" it was Merik's voice.

"What?" she called back.

"Could you please come here?" He had an odd tone. Curiously, she went into the room next door. Merik stood with his back towards her, but Mkaela looked past him to two other people in the room, one sitting and one standing. Mkaela recognized the one standing; he was one of the Kostrian knights who had sided with Merik and herself after Merik's trial by arms months ago. The other one was a muscular blond woman in her thirties sitting in the chair. They were both fresh off of the road in muddy riding breeches and sweaty tunics. The air was tense.

"Lady Mkaela, you remember Sir Reverend Arami from a few months ago," Merik's voice was tense with anxiety.

"Yes. I remember him," she replied, uncertain.

"And this is Dame Reverend Risit Aselifar of my same order," he continued, "my wife."

"Your…" Mkaela began.

"Yes," Risit confirmed, "and I would have a word with

you. Arami. Merik. Wait in the hall." Arami seemed to know not to question. Merik's appearance was haggard. They were gone. Mkaela looked from the closed door back to Risit.

"Is it true?" Risit asked. Mkaela was uncertain what she meant, and looked at her quizzically. "The healing," Risit pressed.

"Yes."

"Show me," Risit ordered briskly.

"Uh, there are no wounds," Mkaela said.

Risit drew a dagger from somewhere Mkaela could not see. One moment her hands were empty; the next, the blade was in her grasp. She nicked herself across the palm and thrust her hand at Mkaela. Mkaela took it and started concentrating. "How long does this take?" she demanded.

"Longer if you fuss!" Mkaela snapped. She immediately felt sheepish for the outburst, but Risit held her hand still.

A moment later, the purple light glowed faintly and closed the wound. Risit rubbed it in wonderment. "So… you're not just trying to steal my husband."

"What!? No!" Mkaela exclaimed incredulously, "I mean, I'm not trying to steal him at all!" Risit looked at her for a long minute.

"Fine. Merik wrote a lot of things about you in his letter. Better live up to them," she said. "Merik!" she hollered, "you can come back in." The door opened. Merik and Arami reentered.

"Satisfied?" Merik asked, his voice calm but plaintive.

"Satisfied," Risit agreed.

"Good. Arami tells me things are not going well.""Oh, no. They are not," Risit replied emphatically.

Mkaela looked between them. "What do you mean?"

"The Primarch at Clovis is moving against us," Arami said. "There are some of the brethren that are siding with you, Lady Mkaela."

She blinked. "*Siding* with me? What do you mean?"

"It means that what you are–and what you can do– threatens the Church's power. Some side with the Church, some side with you."

"Because I can *help* people?" Mkaela's voice rose. "Isn't that what they're *supposed* to want?"

"It is because you can do things that they cannot, yet the scripture and the histories say that they used to be able to. For them to acknowledge your abilities, they would also be acknowledging that they cannot fulfill Orneth's Will. The only two ways out of this. You could join the clergy–but even then, you would be a problem. You can do things that they cannot, and that alone would set you apart." She paused. "The easier option? They declare you a witch. An unholy being to be cleansed with fire and steel, and that anyone that you help, tainted by association."

Mkaela shook herself in disbelief. "So, what is so bad…?" *That they all want to kill me…*

"The Primarch has the Tamarks and the Berks on her side, along with the Princess of Kotara… as well as the Prince of Clovis, if that counts as anything," Arami said.

"That sounds like a lot of people," Mkaela muttered bleakly.

"It is. We were going to inform the Prince," Merik's voice indicated that it would be another unpleasant conversation.

"I don't want to put the Prince through any of that. None of this should be his problem," Mkaela tried to bargain with the situation. " He's done so much for these people. They need him. He can't fight on both sides."

"He should know all the same," Merik resigned. "Besides, he's using other witches–*actual* witches, that is–and word is spreading. The Church will come for him eventually anyways. And he's a prince. It's his choice which fight he gets into–or not."

***

The Grand Audience Room of the Cathedral-Palace of the Western Reformed Church of Orneth, Clovis.
The afternoon of the same day.

"No, Dum'ail, I *never* wanted this! But the Church cannot ignore it at this point, now, can it?" The Primarch's face, its skin loose from long years of incense and tobacco smoke that she took while administering her duties, shook from the motion of her outburst. Her voice was tired from suppressing her rage and she had run out of patience. The Primarch, Seer of Orneth's Wisdom, Hand of

Orneth's Will, garbed in the purple and gold collar of the office over the white dress embroidered in red of the clergy, leaned forward in Saint Gristan's chair. While the seat was not the original chair made by Saint Gristan, this one, with its graceful, ornate carvings and inlaid gold, was more befitting of the office of the Primarch, and impressed upon those that viewed it the propriety of the office of Primarch, the highest title of the Church.

The Primarch buried her face in one hand. The purple and gold braided garland on her head slipped forward to rest on her hand. In the other hand, she limply held Elder Dum'ail's report of charges leveled against a handful of peasants and some country nobles. The accusations were something the Church could handle easily, even if the weight of the charges were heavy, and even fantastical–magic, of all things. But the addition of the Prince of Yvel to the charges of heresy, most of his staff and retainers–not to forget the Bishop of Yvel–some of his soldiers, made this very, very difficult for the Church to prosecute. *But now this fool forces our hand with the rebellion of five knights between two orders, and more will certainly follow. Dum'ail should have left it at the trial by combat, but this has a life of its own now. The fool has a following among the Order of Acrist, especially. No, it cannot be ignored at this point,* she thought bitterly.

"Holy Seer, would you have me turn a blind eye to this heresy?" asked Dum'ail, a thickly bearded Berk man not quite the same age as the Primarch. His tone skirted the edge of insolence.

"Your eyes are already blind if they cannot see what you have brought upon the brethren," she said coldly, looking up and adjusting her garland. "A divided Reformed Church will be weaker against the Easterners."

"But, Holy Seer–" Dum'ail broke off when the High Elder held up her hand.

"I do not want to hear it, Dum'ail," she said, beckoning another forward. Dum'ail sheepishly pressed his hands to his heart and sank back to his corner and sulked, flanked by two stoic Acristian knights.

Lord Bandal Oklaifar, emissary of the Kingdom of Berkmar, stepped forward. "Yes, Holy Seer?"

The Primarch let out a long, vexed sigh before speaking. "In these times of heresy, wherein brethren knights turn upon one another out of confusion of truth and lay lords, even a prince, take up arms against the Church, the Church must call upon faithful nations more urgently."

"Yes, Holy Seer, faithful Berks will answer–*have already* answered–the call, as you have asked of us," Bandal replied dutifully.

"Yes, Lord Bandal, but I fear that three regiments and a baron will not be enough." *And I can squeeze a bit more out of them.* "The Tamarks do not seem to have any crisis of faith, and have pledged twelve regiments."

"Twelve?" Bandal appeared earnestly surprised. "It would be difficult for the King to match such a pledge with the problems in Markia right in front of us, Holy Seer."

"The Church is not blind to your grievances with your neighbor, but that does not change the situation at hand nor the ready piety of the Tamarks," she chided Lord Bandal.

Bandal pleaded with her. "The King will have to raise new regiments, Holy Seer, and there is a great cost in that."

"Surely, there is. The Church can provide assistance with that, and help the good and righteous King in other ways," the High Elder suggested, offering a compromise.

Bandal looked directly at her. He was being appropriately humble, but the air about him made it clear that he needed something to offer to his king in order to facilitate her demands. Reading his expression, Primarch continued. "The Church is prepared to bless exclusive rights for ore traded by the heretics on the river routes."

He pursed his lips. "That will help, Holy Seer; Berkmar is a poor country. But I am skeptical that it will not offset the cost enough. Our coffers are shallow, Holy Seer."

He's really pushing for this. Well, no surprise. And no difference with what is happening in Markia. "The Church may bless Berkmar regaining some of the territory it lost to Markia, but only if we are successful in crushing this uprising of heretics."

"Truly, Holy Seer?" Bandal's face lit up.

"*If* the good and righteous King of the Berks can provide twelve good regiments, then the Church is prepared to bless such an endeavor. Twelve, mind you," she said pointedly.

"Yes, Holy Seer, of course," Bandal eagerly replied, before she had Lord Bandal and Dum'ail shuffled out of the nave. They would be put up for lodging at the palace near the Clovis cathedral, though billeting was starting to become scarce with the gathering of so many Church Knights and their retinues, minus those that were not splitting to join the heretics and those she had hunting them.

One of her aides approached from the side. "Your forgiveness, Holy Seer, but the Queen of the Tamarks has only promised eight regiments."

"Yes, I know, but he doesn't know that," she said, "and now, we can tell the Queen of the Tamarks that the Berks have promised twelve regiments."

"Ah. You are most wise, Holy Seer."

She waved him off. "Just come up with something to promise them–and I don't want to hear it again about an archbishopric! And remember, we already promised the Yvel fishing rights to that precocious little girl from Kotara."

***

The town of Roven, northwest of Heath.
The afternoon of the same day.

"They have Ja'Kend!" Kozain whispered. Her knees ached as she crouched in the alley behind the inn where she and her small household had been lodging, a miserable downpour raining upon her. Kozain's knees had just started to ache within the last year. She was still relatively young, in her thirties, though old for an unmarried dame reverend knight. But being unmarried kept her more active on expeditions, which led to the aching knees to match the lines in her face as she squinted through the rain.

She had intended to meet Ja'Kend when she arrived, after which they were to move on from this town, Roven, through Heath and onto Yvel. But, Ja'Kend was pursued. Kozain watched as Ja'Kend, flanked by a few servants and house soldiers, were surrounded by knights wearing Acristian designs in red livery.

"My Lady, we have to *go!* We can't save them," one of the servants said to her between shivers.

"We can't just leave them!" she hissed back. "You. You. And you." She pointed at one soldier to another, then to her huntsman, Goss. "Go around. Kill some of their horses, cause a diversion and draw them off. We'll surprise them, grab the four of them, and get out. You ride out as soon as you draw some off. We'll meet at the docks of Heath. If you don't see us by Restday of next week, get to Yvel without us."

The soldiers and the huntsman grimaced but saluted, clenched fists to heart, and led their horses northwest through alleyways around other buildings. Kozain turned to see her servant, Sarl, head in his hands. "What's the matter? Problem with the plan?" she whispered impatiently.

"No, Your Ladyship, no problem excepting that you sent the only two soldiers you had on the distraction. That leaves myself, one other servant, and Your Ladyship to ride your warhorse and two baggage horses to rescue four people." Sarl was a timid man in his mid forties that would have been content to fold bed sheets and serve brunch for the rest of his life.

"Good that you have a quick mind, Sarl, otherwise I would have to explain it again," she snapped. Sarl was sullen and silent as they waited. Yelling came from the encirclement. There was an argument. Kozain could make out Ja'Kend's voice, but could not understand what she was saying or with whom she was arguing. The circle started to close.

"No time!" Kozain sprang up from her crouched position, and bound towards her impatiently stamping warhorse, Persis. She fit her foot into the stirrup, and despite the weight of her armor and her protesting knee, mounted in one fluid motion.

"But–" Sarl stammered.

"Now! Go! Mount up!" Kozain demanded and kicked Persis into motion. Persis indignantly grunted and lurched into motion, turned the corner and quickly gaining speed. Kozain thundered toward the encircling Acrists, as they turned to the sound of clattering hooves and shouted in alarm. She crashed through their line, swinging her horse mace. Helmets crumpled and shoulders snapped. Glaives and swords arced towards her as the two baggage horses lumbered closer to the fray amid the shouting and ringing of steel. The baggage horses reared in fear, pitching Sarl onto the ground.

"Come on!" Kozain shouted to Ja'Kend and her retainers. Kozain fought around them as Ja'Kend and her soldiers tried to break the encirclement. Ja'Kend, wearing mail but no helmet, got to Sarl's baggage horse, seized its reins, brought it down, and mounted it. One of Ja'Kend's soldiers took the tip of a glaive as it plunged into him through his mail. He cried out as he sank to the ground. One of Ja'Kend's servants climbed onto the other baggage horse and they lumbered off, trying to gain speed. Ja'Kend helped another servant onto her new, humble horse as they also galloped away at as brisk a pace as the workhorse could manage.

Kozain hauled a disoriented and stumbling Sarl onto Persis and he laid across the saddle in front of her. Ja'Kend's lone remaining soldier and her other servants fled. Kozain stayed ahead of them, doubling back now and then to trample a pursuer or dent another helmet, sometimes with a small spat of blood spraying down from beneath the steel rim or mail. They soon lost their pursuers in the streets, and departed Roven with a handful of servants, one of Ja'Kend's soldiers, and the two Knights of the Order of Saint Kostray, with just three horses between them. They traveled with urgency, not sparing breath until they were at a safe distance. Kozain went back to coax the stragglers on more than one occasion.

"Thanks, Sister," Ja'Kend said an hour later.

"It needed to happen," Kozain shrugged.

"We lost all of our baggage back there. No supplies," Ja'Kend said grimly.

"We had to leave ours to get you out of there," Kozain echoed the concern.

"Sorry," Ja'Kend looked away sheepishly.

"Better this way than talking to clean clothes," Kozain replied. They rode in silence for a bit, thankful to be out of imminent danger.

"A cloud." Ja'Kend pointed. A cloud of dust approached them from the direction of Roven.

"Hide," Kozain commanded. The party moved off of the road, concealing themselves in the trees and bushes. She gave Persis to Ja'Kend's soldier, instructing him to take Persis further back, and to keep away from his teeth. Persis would make more noise and needed to be further away for them to conceal themselves successfully.

Kozain and Ja'Kend hid with the servants in the brush. Moments passed before they heard the approach of hooves clopping on the hard-packed road. Kozain winced as she crouched lower, but as their pursuers approached, their horses slowed and stopped. She heard someone dismount. Kozain dared to peek around the tree trunk, and felt a wave of relief.

"Goss," she called to her huntsman, emerging from hiding.

Goss smiled. "You changed the plan, My Lady."

"I had to," she smiled back. Looking beyond Goss, she saw one of her soldiers and four horses, three of them loaded with baggage. "Where's...?"

Goss shook his head grimly. "At least we got away with some of their horses."

"Good," she admitted, "we have some supplies for the road to Heath."

"And some Acrist red to wipe our scat with," Goss joked. "It might be better to skip Heath, My Lady. He was still breathing when we got away. They might be able to get it out of him that we were going this way."

"Fine, then. We'll go west to Boaz, over the Tald, and up the Guth to Yvel."

"What about the others?" Ja'Kend asked.

"They'll have to make their way to Yvel separately. Smaller groups will be easier to move, anyways."

She persisted. "Right, but how will they know to do that?"

"Same way with you," Kozain said. "You knew to leave if we didn't meet you in a few days' space."

"How many did we end up getting?"

"Besides us, four more from our order, and two from Graffin."

Ja'Kend pursed her lips wryly. "Only a few thousand to go."

Miles away, Dame Reverend Olavy walked among the bloodied square in Roven. The other knights' soldiers had caught up and were bearing away the wounded and the dead. *What a disaster*, she thought. *They fight with such abandon, once they give over to heresy. Maybe they think that witch can save them from death.* Olavy removed her right gauntlet and looked at the two stumpy fingers that had been severed beyond the second knuckle a few months before. She tried to make a fist. *The axe hasn't felt the same since.* She wiped away some blood from where Kozain had dented her helmet in. *Thank Acrist that the heretic's blow glanced off the helmet instead of landing properly.* Around her, her brethren remained unmoving. *But Acrist and Orneth will win in the end*, she pledged to herself.

***

A well-furnished apartment, Palace, Yvel City.
That Evening

"That seems like a lot." The Blue-Eyed Man raised his eyebrows appraisingly.

Merik looked at him incredulously. "That understates the situation by a bit, sir."

"So, the Tamarks, the Berks, and Kotara, all under Clovis' banner?" the Blue-Eyed Man confirmed.

"Under the *Church's* banner, sir," Merik corrected.

"Yes, yes, same thing," the Blue-Eyed Man said, waving his hand. "I'm sure the Prince will think of something."

Merik leaned forward to emphasize the gravity of the report. "You don't seem very alarmed, sir."

"These problems are not here right now," the Blue-Eyed

Man looked at Merik sharply. "We have battalions and regiments in the field fighting orcs and goblins right now." He squared his shoulders towards Merik. A few others sitting at the table shifted uncomfortably at the Blue-Eyed Man's tone.

Merik looked to the floor. "Of course, sir, you have a great many problems at hand."

The Blue-Eyed Man forced his face to soften. "The Prince will not make light of this problem, and it is understood that the Church has several thousand well-equipped knights and their own soldiers." He sighed. "But, while not as well-equipped or trained, the armies of orcs and their fellow kinds rain down upon us from the mountains now–and, mind you, it does not just happen here. Versingit has fallen, Ardara has fallen. Soorin is encircled from the north, and is pressed against the Chessa." The Blue-Eyed Man pointed at the air in emphasis. "Once they fall, they'll come at us from the south, and Keppa will feel it. As Yvel continues to hold, they will move on Heath and Vidara, and we'll be a pocket of resistance against the shores of the Tald."

"Of course, you are correct, sir," Merik said lamely, trying to find a way out of the conversation.

"And it extends beyond," the Blue-Eyed Man continued. "Things go no better in Markia and Eklenda. The only reason the Church can do this is that they're further west; otherwise, they would have been helping like they should have been all along."

"Of course, sir."

The Blue-Eyed Man grimaced. "Thank you for providing this information, Sir Reverend Merik. The Prince will find a way."

The Blue-Eyed Man begged their leave, taking his still-steaming mug of coffee with him, and wound through the corridors until finding himself in front of the office he sought. The guards bashfully admitted him and he waved off their announcement to greet the aged Melz Belifar, Bishop of Yvel. The bishop rose from his seat behind his desk, a well-made, wooden piece of woodwork, its front legs carved in reliefs of fruit and wheat on one, and the silhouettes of buildings and cities on the other, symbolizing the domains of Ornethian saints. Despite its impeccable craftsmanship, it was still entirely wooden and lacked any other ornamentation. It was a far more mundane piece of furniture than those he had seen used by other clergy.

"What can I do for you, y–"

"Please, Melz, sit. Thank you. Please." The Blue-Eyed Man dismissed the offered formality.

"Yes, indeed, then," Melz retook his seat. "Well, what is the occasion?"

"A question comes to mind?" the Blue-Eyed Man said.

"Yes?"

"What if the Prince declared you to be the rightful Primarch of the reformed Church–on the basis that the Primarch in Clovis had lost the way as was written in scripture, and that the clergy in Clovis were merely a grouping of self-serving bureaucrats?"

The bishop, in his red-cuffed white clergy robe and a royal purple-edged white collar, paused, his eyes fixed on a spot on the floor. He stayed frozen for a long moment as the Blue-Eyed Man fought to contain his own anticipation to hear the old man's response. The Blue-Eyed Man sipped his coffee that he had been nursing since his meeting with Merik, Risit, and Arami.

"I fear that I am not the man to be the object of such an undertaking, sir," Melz said at last, settling into his high-backed wooden chair.

"No?"

"No, sir. While I do not always agree with what the messages out of the Cathedral dictate, it is a far cry to say that they decidedly do not care for the plight of people, and, more directly, if I were to say that I am better suited than they are for the charge, then I prove that I am indeed worse because of my own pride."

"Your *pride!?*" the Blue-Eyed Man said in surprise.

"Yes, sir," Melz said.

"Well, it would have been good if you could have used that position to pull some of the knights of the orders onto our side, or at least convince them not to fight for the opponent."

Melz frowned at an upper corner of the room where early winter moonlight streamed in through the window. *Strong winds coming tonight, by the look of those clouds*, the Blue-Eyed Man noted to himself. "You make a good point, sir, and I will do what I can to make your intent come to pass," Melz said, "but I cannot usurp the office of Primarch. I am grateful simply to be elevated to this not-humble office, yet look what it has gotten me? One of my own parishioners bringing the weight of the Church down upon us, from what Merik tells me."

"Merik's already been to see you?" the Blue-Eyed Man asked.

"Oh, yes, he's a good young man. Him and his wife, Risit. Fiery one, that Risit." The Bishop beamed. "In any case, I will do what I can to see to your will."

"The Prince's will," the Blue-Eyed Man corrected.

"Yes, yes, the Prince. Why so formal suddenly?" Melz was curious. "And why are you drinking wine from that kind of cup? It's very undignified."

"This? Oh, it's coffee," he shrugged.

"Coffee?" Melz was incredulous, "oh, right, that's all you ever drink. Why is that?"

"It's the Prince's most favored drink, Your Grace," the Blue-Eyed Man raised the cup in mock toast with a smirk, "and most of the Prince's close retainers have taken to drinking coffee over wine, at least in one form or another." The elderly bishop frowned and shrugged, mumbling something the Blue-Eyed Man could not hear. "So, what will you do?" the Blue-Eyed Man prodded.

"About what?" the Bishop asked.

"… about what we just talked about. You said that you would do something to meet the Prince's will," he said patiently.

"Oh. That. I will talk to as many of the militant brethren I can find and convince them this is Orneth's Will." Melz settled back into his chair. "I haven't seen what these witches of yours can do myself, but I do know that I had made what I thought was the last visit to Mot Gundr'ail. I have talked to both of the *Prince's* surgeons about what has transpired." Melz nodded, "and, again, while I have not witnessed their feats firsthand…"

Melz shifted in his seat. "I have met and talked with this young lady Mkaela. I am just not convinced that they are here to do evil, when so many lives have been saved. So much of Orneth's Will and the writings of her disciples lean on simple, observable truths, or truths understood within the context of timely circumstances." Melz leaned back in his chair and folded his hands over the belly that bulged against the voluminous robes in this posture, "those truths may be twisted by some for a momentary purpose, but I really cannot see how Orneth would allow these people to be created, live among us, never hurt anyone before this way, and save so many now.

Melz's hands rested on the edge of his desk, "I just cannot make sense of how that could be evil. I think I can explain that to a few groups of rich children with metal sticks."

The Blue-Eyed Man smirked at the explanation. "Very well, good sir. The Prince shall trust your discretion in this matter and he will offer any support required for traveling." Again, the Blue-Eyed Man begged his leave and made for his third destination, the library. He found Nicholas there, still poring over more arcane texts.

"What do you tell people that come in here and ask about your research?" he asked Nicholas.

"That would require people to come into a library during a much-more-exciting war, good sir," Nicholas said, not looking up from his book.

"Fair point," the Blue-Eyed Man chuckled, "but lend me your ear for a moment. I have news." The Blue-Eyed Man recounted what Merik had told him, as well as his conversation with the Bishop.

"Really!?" Nicholas exclaimed.

"Yes, really," the Blue-Eyed Man said. "But I have to admit, my friend, this was a bit of a test."

"Oh? How so?" Nicholas asked.

"Well," he said, "you are really the spymaster, you know. This *is* the Ministry of Information–and all that such."

"What a garish title." Nicholas smiled wryly. "You're right. I should be the one telling you this."

"My point is that those studies are distracting you from your main tasks," the Blue-Eyed Man said.

Nicholas was defensive. "Well, yes," he retorted, "but these can really help with matters."

"Yes, they can," the Blue-Eyed Man agreed, "but your main duty to the Prince as the Minister of Information comes first."

"Yes, but this *is* information," Nicholas protested.

"It is, friend, but *the Prince* needs you to balance. If you want to be booger deep in this, fine. The Prince probably fancies doing a bit, as well, to make a good show on the field with the knack of it," the Blue-Eyed Man said, "*but*, it is a growing, unusable capability now versus the need that the Prince has for current information in a sea of enemies."

"I see," Nicholas conceded. "Very well."

"Now, what you say is right, though. This will be useful," he said.

"Yes," Nicholas agreed.

"Unless you disagree, pull Zaya off the Proving Grounds and have her study. Maybe send her to Kolus," the Blue-Eyed Man suggested.

"No, not to Kolus," Nicholas said. "You're right, though. We're not getting anything better out of the Proving Grounds. The elves have tightened up their practices and we cannot get any good notes off of it anymore. Just more wind howling and stuff burning. We shall rely on official reports from the Proving Grounds of their training progress. Kolus has gotten very bristly, though–he still takes orders, but he doesn't get along with anyone except his pet goblins now. I've another spot for Zaya. If you don't mind, I'd like to put a few more people on this. Learning it. There are plenty of other applications besides warfare."

"You mean medicine? Healing?" The Blue-Eyed Man's curiosity was piqued.

"The little that I've read on that is actually very complicated and quite beyond me at present," Nicholas clarified. "I mean roads, building, guild work."

"Indeed. Yes, then. Put as many on it as you want, *but* we cannot have a loss of people in the field," the Blue-Eyed Man insisted.

Nicholas' shoulders slumped. "Recruiting will be difficult, but you're right. I have a few ideas." Nicholas' eyes briefly twinkled.

"What's that?" the Blue-Eyed Man asked pointedly.

"What? Nothing," Nicholas put on the innocence of an assassin.

"Fine, then, keep your secrets," the Blue-Eyed Man relented before changing the subject. "How are the teams doing?"

"Fine. Still have two in the city if you need them. The others are working the caravan routes and keeping supply costs low and council members anxious. Oh, to go back, there is something."

"On recruiting?" the Blue-Eyed Man asked.

"The Kad Rang," Nicholas was nearly bouncing in his glee.

"The who–or what?" The Blue-Eyed Man was puzzled.

"They're a gang of thieves from Verdunsk, the best run this side of the Kaskevs," Nicholas explained excitedly.

"Better than your Eklendan counterparts?"

"No, no, no, best run *gang of thieves*, I said," Nicholas emphasized.

"Ah, yes. Right, right," the Blue-Eyed Man nodded. "So what of them?"

"You hear how bad things are in Markia: they'll come south, and I want to recruit them. At least contract them," Nicholas proposed.

"You think they will?" The Blue-Eyed Man was skeptical. "If some of them want to leave the gang and they look promising, go ahead, but we can't have another entity inside the Ministry."

"Understood, sir," Nicholas agreed, looking pleased with himself.

"Can we talk about the teams now? There's a great task," the Blue-Eyed Man asked, broaching a new topic.

"What task?" It was Nicholas' turn to be skeptical.

"The King of the Berks and the Princess of Kotara need to die, and it needs to look like they were assassinated by our friendly neighbors from the mountains," the Blue-Eyed Man said. "There also need to be failed assassination attempts on the Queen of the

Tamarks and the Primarch, herself."

Nicholas thought about it. "So you want them to continue mobilizing, and then fight the hordes instead of us?"

"Yes." The Blue-Eyed Man pointed his finger in agreement. "They're not doing anything helpful otherwise, and it helps move the plan along. We need those two to survive and make the decisions that they probably would. While the teams are at it, get the Prince of Heath first."

"You're planning on moving on Heath, too?" Nicholas asked.

"As soon as there's enough regiments available, we will move to protect the peoples of Heath. After those, to Versingit to gain access to a broader levy base," the Blue-Eyed Man said.

"Well, this certainly sets things up nicely for after the war, too," Nicholas surmised, "assuming we survive."

"Yes, assuming. We'll need to make provisions that we have the right forces and weapons in place to ensure that happens"

***

Crown Sorcerers' Proving Grounds
Late Afternoon
Cold and damp after the rain.

"Is readiness had by you?"

"Yeah," Ayza called back. Tyrnimar loosed an arrow. It whistled towards the target beside Ayza before stopping mid-air. "Again," she called. Tyrnimar shot another arrow and it stopped short of the target, hovering next to the first. Tyrnimar fired four more arrows before Ayza collapsed, heaving in exertion.

He walked over. "So well a task was done by you," he congratulated. "Your readiness for more should be told to me by you." He smiled at her and walked over to Kora, his bow slung. "Is readiness had by you?" he asked her. She nodded; Kora's face had a determined set. "Please," he said, gesturing to the open air in front of her.

She reached her hands forward and flames began to drip

from her open palms. They sputtered a bit before she was able to project them into focused fans at shoulder height, spreading twenty-five paces in front of her in a broad arc. She maintained the fan of fire for almost a minute before tapering it off. "Good," Tyrnimar commented, "and the other thing?" Kora nodded and held her hands open and facing each other, fingers arched as if she were holding an invisible globe. He saw the muscles in her arms tense and her brow furrow in concentration. Slowly, a small marble of flame appeared in the space between her palms. It grew slightly and then shrank before disappearing altogether. He gasped for breath, similarly heaving from the exertion. "Fine it is," Tyrnimar said. "Wait! Your dress! It is being burned by fire!"

Kora looked up suddenly, raising her hands. The cuffs of her sleeves were burning and the flames started creeping up the sleeves. Kora shrieked and started running, flailing her arms.

"No! Stop!" cried Tyrnimar. *This was anticipated.* He grabbed a bucket of water and chased her as she waved her flaming arms about until upending the bucket on her.

Kora stood there mortified and sopping wet like a cat during a bath as the autumn wind gusted. "Argh! Cold!" she cried. She shivered and glared balefully at Tyrnimar as Ayza laughed.

Chapter 10

Along a road outside of Krogen, Yvel Principality.
By the Goblin Calendar, late in the Tenth Moon Cycle, 3114.
By the Human Calendar, Thirstday, third week of Banreni, 794.
A rainy, early autumn afternoon.

*J*ak waited on the rock, the hood of his waxed cloak pulled over to partially shield himself from the rain. Droplets pattered on his hood and in the puddles around him. He had spent much of his time waiting since his bizarre release from prison. Waiting for caravans to come through. Waiting to transport stolen supplies. Waiting for replacement fighters.

That was an odd one, too. Jak had never been a bandit. Not until now, at least. But he had always been under the impression that bandit gangs did their own recruiting. Here, he was specifically forbidden from doing so. Orders. Every month or so, he got one or two new pairs of hands, always able-bodied and capable of handling themselves well. Discipline had improved, too, since he had killed Jawn, the man in his crew that had turned on him.

Discipline was a new concept for him. Jak had been in plenty of fights, even a few knife fights, but was not much of a killing man until after prison. But it was the training after prison that made the importance of discipline clear. The memory was still fresh of the argument with his superior regarding his altercation with Jawn. That was another odd thing about this bandit crew. Jak had never considered it before, but had assumed that bandits decided for themselves what to do, that is, their leader decided. As far as Jak knew, he was the leader of this bandit crew, yet every few weeks, he would meet outside of Krogen with a hooded man who went by the name Darent. The two of them would discuss the raids since their last meeting, raids they anticipated in the near future, problems with the crew, equipment, and pay and privileges.

It was Darent who gave Jak the orders for the next week or two, but Jak sensed that Darent was not the person in charge, either. He did not seem the type. That was something Jak had a very good feel for–he could sense when someone really owned the room. The situation. Darent seemed more the type that did not want to be noticed in the room at all, which meant that Darent worked for someone else. That someone else might have multiple Darents running around, managing other people like Jak. But this was only a guess.

Finally. Jak saw the signal from Tansher. *The things I am going to do to her later…* Jak mused. He shook himself and focused; *work first.* And waited. More waiting. Tansher had probably seen the caravan some ways off, and now they had to wait for it to enter the ambush.

Jak hated waiting. He was surprised at how much he hated waiting. He figured that he would have realized how much he hated waiting while he was in prison, but it was different. In prison, there was nothing to wait *for.* You were just there. Period. Now, he was always waiting for something, someone, sometime, and it was never fast enough. He glanced in Tansher's direction again. Her hair was in thick, red braids to stay out of her way on the raid. *Some things are worth waiting for, though…*

The caravan came into view. Jak could see it was well-escorted. Lots of guards with some on every wagon and a few separately mounted on horses. *Wonder where they found all of those with the war going on. Then again, wonder why we didn't get sent to the war from prison instead of doing this.* Some of the crew were looking towards Jak, waiting for the signal. Jak squinted at them. *That's where they found them.* The caravan guards were laughing and joking with one another. Trained guards would also do that, but they would simultaneously be looking around with a keen eye to spot people like Jak, and avoid places like exactly where they were. These were not trained guards, just caravan drivers in gambesons or mail with some weapons. That meant that Jak and his crew were getting some new gambesons and mail.

Jak raised his arm high and brought it down lazily. This was all routine for them by now. Jak had lost count of how many of these they had done. He supposed that whomever Darent worked for was trying to strangle the war effort, since all of the supplies seemed as if they would be very useful in keeping an army going. Metal ingots, grain, lumber, bolts of cloth, salted meat, crushed herbs, occasional livestock, and all manner of things that would be incredibly useful for any town or village, but especially for a country supplying an army in the field.

Ah, well. Jak gave up for the moment on trying to figure it out as the archers on the flanks of the ambush filled the wagon mules and lead drivers full of arrows. The archers in the middle brought down the mounted guards before his crew stormed the remaining survivors with axes, swords, and spears, all of which had been taken from orcs months ago. This was meant to look like orcs raided farther west. Jak supposed that the army and Prince Arnold would look to the east for the raiding parties instead of their own countryside and towns.

"All done, boss. Just cleaning up the last," Bisin called.

"Good," Jak got up to walk down.

***

Kudre winced as the arrow shifted in her thigh. It was caught in the twigs of the bush behind which she was hiding. She watched as the bandits came down from the rocky outcropping that the road curled around. They were killing everyone. Everyone. Kudre squeezed her eyes shut, stifling sobs that would give her away. She heard a cry and a scuffle. She dared to peek and saw some of the other caravan drivers trying to flee, only to sprout two or three arrows from their backs and fall into the mud.

Kudre had been in a bandit raid once before, years ago, and they all were yelling and laughing. The bandits were neither cheering nor jeering; they were mostly quiet, other than conversations or calls between one another. Her eyes flitted around and stopped on one bandit. The last one coming down from the rocks. His skin was greenish under the hood of his raincloak. *Like an orc?* She thought orcs were supposed to be really big... he was big for a man, but still reasonably man-sized. And he was wearing clothes, too, like a man.

The green-skinned marauder pointed and she froze. He did not point at her. But where he had gestured, arrows followed and pinned a crawling driver to the ground. She kept her eyes on him and could not look away as he carefully picked his steps down the rocks. Another small scuffle erupted as the bandits hacked at a few more of her fellow caravanners with their axes and swords.

They were talking now. She strained to hear them. "Alright, leave an axe there. Yeah. A spear there. Good."

"That all of them?"

"Yeah."

"You sure? I thought I saw one over there. And I can smell 'em!" said a man's voice. Kudre's heart skipped a beat.

"Yeah, I'm sure, Bisin," a woman's voice said irritably.

"Don't eye me, Sirid. I swear I smell something. You sure?" said the man's voice.

"Yeah," the woman's voice became more subordinate. "I'm sure. Checked 'em all."

Kudre squeezed her eyes shut again.

"Alright," said a second man's voice. "Haul it over to the other wagons and get ready to move."

***

Outside of Krogen
Sortingday (sixth day of the week), two days later.
Evening

Jak pulled his hood close like before, this time against the chill wind of the oncoming season. He could see the silhouettes of some of the taller buildings in Krogen on the horizon. Though he had never actually been into Krogen, going there was not an option these days; not with the color of his skin and the war. Not that he really wanted anything in there in particular other than satisfying idle curiosity. This was the place he was supposed to meet Darent, by the road, west of Krogen, near the tree that had the lightning-split branch. *More waiting.*

A single, mounted figure approached from Krogen. He could tell it was Darent without looking closely; the way he sat in the saddle, the gait of the horse. It was past twilight, but Jak had

172

his Orcish father's keen eyesight and could see very clearly at night, though without color. He could see the warmth rolling off of Darent and the horse. Jak could see heat very clearly, except around fire. Winter was difficult, too, but right now, it was clear. Moments ticked by and he briefly thought about how he could see the heat in Tansher's cheeks. How he planned to later on that night.

"Ah, there you are," Darent said as he pulled the reins of his mount and dismounted. Like Jak, he kept his hood pulled low. Jak got that sense that he always did when talking to Darent–that Darent would one day send him on an impossible task as a way of disposing of Jak and his band.

They talked about the last three raids and bickered about the drop off location of the supplies from the last raid, finally agreeing that Jak would pick up three more fighters at this same location tomorrow.

"But why tomorrow? Why can't it wait until we meet next week?" Jak asked.

"Because we won't meet next week. Or the week after. Or for some time," Darent said calmly.

"What's this about?" Jak asked.

"New assignment. Far away," Darent said.

"Where?"

Darent named the place.

Jak had never heard of it. "Where? Where's that?

Darent produced a rolled paper from his shoulder bag and unrolled it across the dusty road before flinting a fat candle and setting it on the road next to the paper. Jak recognized a map, but did not recognize anything about it. He could not read, but could still decipher that this was not like any of the other maps that he had seen before.

"Where are we?" Jak asked. Darent pointed to a place on the map.

Darent pointed.

"Well, fine, but that doesn't tell me anything. Give me something that I can tell the distance by. Uh, where's Yvel?" Jak said. Darent pointed out Yvel, then pointed to the place he named on the map. "Whoa…" Jak said. "That's a long way." Jak thought for a moment, scrutinizing the map. "It'll be winter before we even get there."

"Perhaps. You might make it before the change of the season, if you hurry," Darent suggested, thumbing an itch on his nose.

"What about the raids?" Jak's brow furrowed at the change.

Darent shook his head. "Don't worry about the raids for now. Don't worry about anything but this task."

"What's the task?"

"You read?"

"No. But, I've got a couple that can. Only Marin, though, I think. I don't think any of them read Ekie."

"That's fine," Darent blinked as he nodded, handing him an envelope sealed in wax. No stamp embossed in the wax, just sealed with a plain dollop. "You should learn your letters, though. It'll only help you."

"Yeah, maybe. For now, I've got someone to do that for me," Jak said.

"As long as you trust them and they manage to stay alive," Darent shrugged.

"What happens after this task?"

"When the first snow falls here, I'm going to put another letter in that hole of the tree," Darent directed, pointing to a hollow in the tree with the lightning-struck branch. "It will have instructions. Make sure that you take the letter with you."

"Yeah. Alright. See you in winter," Jak muttered, studying the sealed envelope as he turned it over in his hands.

"After, probably," Darent corrected.

Jak shrugged. "Fine, after. Bye."

"Good hunting," Darent said as he mounted his horse. "You're going to need it."

Chapter 11

Near the walls of the Place-called-Ikria, deep underground.
By the Goblin Calendar, late in the Tenth Moon Cycle, 3114.
By the Human Calendar, sometime during the third week of Banreni, 794.

ygariyet emerged from the passageway into a larger cavern. For the past day or so, or at least what he sensed to be a day, the underground road showed more and more signs of finishing and past maintenance. The walls were better cut. There was care to provide wide berths against deep holes and gorges. At times, there were even railings cut from the solid stone to guard against travelers and wagons falling into such hazards. But the wear of time and neglect was also becoming apparent. These roads were made by dwarves, but there were none here to care for it anymore.

The passage of time in the depths under the surface was unnerving to him. He thought it was a night. Maybe it was only half. Or two. Without the moon to mark the passing of the nights, Oygariyet could only gauge the nights and days by when he and his party rested for the 'days.'

Stretching before his party was a stone bridge spanning a canyon. He could hear the flow of a river deep at its basin and the sound of water dripping from the ceiling of the cavern, like unending rainfall. The cavern smelled like the deepest, richest mushroom and moss farms of Kogylar. Oygariyet inhaled deeply, savoring the earthy smell.

The underground road had been completely dark and devoid of light by sun, moon, or flame. Two great fires blazed in giant braziers on the far side of the bridge, illuminating a great gate built into the wall of the cavern. It was the first light that Oygariyet had seen in weeks, as they had been conserving their burning oil and there was very little wood or root to burn down there. For weeks, he and the others had been relying solely on their heat sight, which was tiring in its own way. On the surface, objects varied in their heat much more and it was fairly easy to navigate the terrain. Here, the differences in heat were excruciatingly subtle and difficult to differentiate. While their own bodies' heat was easy to see, Oygariyet and his companions had found themselves squinting to see the ground in front of them.

At the far end of the bridge, on the other side of the canyon, was the Place-called-Ikria, one of the great Dwarven cities. Oygariyet possessed a general knowledge of the region, but he had about reached the extent of it. There were different large tribes of dwarves, one of whom formerly ruled the Place-called-Ikria, but had lost it to orcs some time ago; the same orcs who were the purpose of Oygariyet's journey. The bridge was part of the defense, a narrow avenue to besiege the city, no doubt covered by bows, crossbows, or some other manner of projectile.

Oygariyet smiled. He knew they would not be attacked in their approach, despite their mission. There was too much to gain from a dialogue with Oygariyet, with his great legions, his coalition, and grand dreams. And too much to lose by crossing him. Even if they managed to kill him–which would be easiest on this bridge– they would invoke the rage and spite of the thousands of hobgoblins who were loyal to Oygariyet.

He tread across the bridge confidently, his party trailing behind him, slightly more hesitant. He had brought an honor guard of twenty Hobgoblin warriors. Alongside them came few of his slaves–including the sword dancer that the Donbat-Karang had given him, who had delightfully proven quite frisky in sport. A few of his goblins, some orcs, and several humans were with him as well, though the humans had struggled on the journey without heatsight. Grotis, the short orc mercenary, had come too, as had his quick-minded Fourth. Grotis' attendance was necessary as he was the only one that knew the way to the Place-called-Ikria, but the Fourth, despite being the most junior of his staff, was the most learned and insightful,and had proven essential in readying preparations.

Oygariyet could feel the sentries' eyes on him as he stepped off of the bridge and approached the broad steps of the gate. The gate was fifteen paces high, and just as broad. Supposedly built this way by the dwarves. Oygariyet puzzled at why such short people would need a gate so large. Fires burned in large braziers on either side of the entry. Sentries stood beneath the arch, draped in long coats of mail that hung to their knees. Their feet were shod in rough hide shoes, and their bald heads were unhelmeted.

One of the sentries stepped in front of Oygariyet, barring his way. "What do you come to take, outsider?"

"Hear me," Oygariyet demanded. It was a different dialect of Orcish, not the same as either side of the mountains on the surface, but still one of the three that Oygariyet knew. "I come to take the favor of the rulers of the Place-called-Ikria."

Oygariyet looked back at the Fourth, and Grotis and spoke in Goblin. "It was one of their early laws here? The one about not denying a challenger? The Third Law?"

"The Fifth Law, Great One. The Fifth Law of Karap," the Fourth provided.

"What about the one for taking stations?" Oygariyet asked.

"Uh…" The Fourth searched her memory. "That is more of a custom. The same custom of the surface orcs, really, but these ones should be able to understand more nuance."

Right. Oygariyet turned back to the Orcish guard. His hand darted out, jamming a thumb knuckle into one of the orc's eyes. Pivoting on one foot, Oygariyet took a small step forward with his left foot, closing the distance to raise his right leg and slam the sole of his well-worn boot into the stomach of the other guard as the first one staggered away, clutching his eye. The second guard was knocked to the ground, gasping for breath. Oygariyet seized the ear of the first guard, pulling his head down by it. Oygariyet reached over the guard's hip and yanked the guard's own axe from a belt loop. He hacked through the guard's neck, holding both the head and the weapon which had severed it aloft by the time the other guard was on his feet.

"This one was unfit to keep this city safe from an outsider. I have used his own tool and taken his life. His life is mine and what he had is mine. I use his ability to grant access to this city to let myself in," Oygariyet declared. The other guard held his stomach in recent memory of pain as he regarded Oygariyet's entourage passing through the gate, following him.

Oygariyet calmly marveled at the sight inside the gates. It vaguely reminded him of the Stone of Rykooth, though not to this scale. It was well lit–amazingly so, compared to the darkness of the underground wilderness and road–with braziers, torches, pit fires, and sconces dotting the whole place. Avenues spread away from the entrance, further into the city. Buildings of stone stretched from the floor to the cavern ceiling. Some rose only two or three floors, while others climbed ten or more. The higher floors held walkways along their periphery, forming elevated avenues. Archways spanned the streets below, containing their own buildings or open walkways. In places where the cavern ceiling arched higher, streets had two or three archways over each other, each separated by several floors.

The humans accompanying him rubbed their sore eyes, having been unable to see for weeks, while Oygariyet's eyes drank in the sight. Oygariyet could not clearly identify any seams in the stonework. The whole city all seemed to be one piece of stone, as if it were carved of the solid rock.

The streets bustled with activity. It was a bizarre sight for Oygariyet and most of the others. Grotis, however, had been to Ikria before, and was familiar with the sights. Orcs moved through the streets like Oygariyet's staff at Rykooth or the goblins of Koglyar, hawking wares, moving livestock, and hauling carts and crates. Hammers rang on steel and iron. These were the sights, sounds, and smells of urban prosperity.

The streets were dense with orcs, mainly men, going about their daily business. They strolled or hurried along, sometimes accompanied by collared women, and every so often with collared men. Here and there, Oygariyet and his party earned skeptical, disapproving, or curious looks that they walked with uncollared women. Even his sword dancer walked freely. He knew that she would be loyal to him. After all, she was originally of the Donbat-Karang.

Oygariyet had never seen so many orcs together, ever. Thousands and thousands. *And these are the numbers that I need.* Every now and again they would pass a group of mailed Orcish soldiers. Oygariyet marked the uniformity of their appearances; while their trappings were not exactly the same, they had roughly consistent equipment, down to the hide shoes.

"The citadel is that way, Great One," Grotis pointed past Oygariyet's shoulder.

"You mean around that corner?"

"I mean in a few thousand paces, Great One," Grotis clarified.

Oygariyet briefly glanced at Grotis with an appraising eye as they parted the crowds in front of them. "How is it you know so much of this place?"

"Bargains and contracts, Great One," Grotis said. "A few have taken me here."

"So, you know people here?" Oygariyet asked.

"Oh, no, Great One, they all died. That was the contract." Grotis smiled sheepishly. "Though there is a Goblin quarter."

"Really!?" the Fourth exclaimed. She seemed fascinated. Oygariyet paid them no mind as they chattered behind him. Oygariyet guessed the moon would have passed a bit over the sky, maybe two hand-widths, before they stood in an open plaza. The cavern ceiling was at its highest point and the citadel, a square building, stretched all of the way from the floor to the ceiling, hundreds of paces in one piece of stone. Oygariyet noted that there were several different types of stone across the surface, though he still could not detect any seams between the blocks of stone or brick. Other avenues from other parts of the city opened into this plaza, as did elevated arch bridges that spanned the plaza, providing their own walkway to the higher levels.

Without pause, he strode to the base of the citadel.

***

Within the walls of the Citadel of the Place-called-Ikria.

"And what would Ikria be getting out of this arrangement, outsider?"

Oygariyet turned to the questioning orc, perched high in his seat in the audience gallery. It was a circular chamber. It felt like some kind of arena or place of spectacle battle–a loathsome concept–but his Fourth had told him that this would have been the petition or debate hall when the dwarves ruled this city. The room was circular, with a low area in the center, and gallery seating all around. Aisles cut towards an entrance and an exit on both sides of the room for petitioners. The gallery would have been populated by well-to-do and highborn dwarves, representing powerful crafting guilds and clans. Now it was occupied by the Orcish equivalent– and, as far as Oygariyet's experience went, they were a peculiar lot.

The room was lit by evenly spaced braziers and wall sconces, both on the audience floor and in the gallery. It was the most well-lit portion of the city he had seen so far. The smoke escaped through a large, four-pace hole in the ceiling that Oygariyet suspected served as part of the chimney for the entire citadel and, perhaps, the city.

"Certain areas of the surface that soldiers of the Place-called-Ikria are most helpful in conquering and pacifying, as well as the ability to take stuff from the surface and bring it here," Oygariyet said.

"What kind of stuff?" the questioning orc said. Like the other seven tribe leaders here, he wore what seemed to be finery for them. For this particular one, it was a long, baggy tunic with silver beadwork stitched onto it in lines and rows, and a pair of ornately tooled leather boots. At least, Oygariyet thought they were tribe leaders; they spoke like those that were used to holding authority, but they had the statures of... Oygariyet could not describe it. They all had paunches of inactivity. Jowls. Many of them were balding with age, like the Borys-Karang. They had shrewd eyes. And they were vulgar. Four of them had harem slaves with them in the gallery and were lazily cavorting about while taking audience. *And this is the thing with this filth! Even goblins do not do this! You enter into a Goblin clan home and you see it, but it is in the clan's home. Not in an audience hall. Not in the courtyard. Not in the market. Not anywhere but in the clan's home. In hobgoblin fighting units, they have their sport, and yes, it is in the open, but it is wherever the unit is camped for the day. Not in a place for rulership and decisions. This filth just puts it on display... on display... as if...*

"Surface kind of stuff," Oygariyet said, marveling that he should have to further elaborate. This was where the Fourth and Grotis had been very helpful offering insights into the ways of orcs. Of the four-deity pantheon of most orcs, their god of prosperity and fortune–of 'stuff' as they would say–seemed like it would be prominent to them, and material goals would be more important to them for religious reasons, as well as the more obvious ones.

"Like *what?*" the tunicked orc demanded.

"Like *this!*" Oygariyet snapped, stalking to his entourage, who were clustered near the petitioner entrance. He seized one of the humans, a female, since that would be more valuable to this lot. She yelped as he seized her and dragged her into the center of the pit. Her skin, glistening like copper beneath a sheet of sweat, showed her to be one of the many that the Borys-Karang had brought from the Place-called-Ardara. "You trade in slaves, but you only trade in the ones that you can get. You get other varieties on the surface. More exotic varieties. More varieties of weapons, of foods. Stuffs! Why do I have to tell you about these stuffs? Can you not think of it yourselves?"

"What kinds of places on the surface?" asked another orc. This one had discarded his clothes and was being serviced by two of his harem slaves. Oygariyet failed to suppress a shudder of disgust. *The rudeness! Not just to everyone around him, but to his own harem. He talks like they do nothing. Like their work means nothing.* Oygariyet had never even imagined the possibility that someone could be so disrespectful to their own harem. The disrobed orc noticed Oygariyet's disgust and taunted him. "Do my possessions make you angry, outsider?"

"It is you. The sight of you and your rudeness makes me want to cover up your filth with the contents of my stomach."

"*What!?*" the naked orc's paunch jiggled as he rose, his slaves recoiling from him in fear. *Another sign! The harem cowers in fear. They should not be afraid. Pain only comes in the training of a harem slave. He should not be bringing untrained slaves anywhere, and they fear him for he wields pain in a wrong way.*

"I said the sight of you! I come here and make you this offer. The same offer I made to the Borys-Karang, and I come here myself in my own person as a gesture of respect. Instead of returning with any kind of interest, I get countless questions with obvious answers. It tells me that you have no interest in this offer yet you lack the breeder spheres to say it!" Oygariyet cast accusatory glances about his audience, ensuring that each of the tribe leaders met his fiery gaze and were equally insulted. This was the second plan. They clearly were not interested. He had been spelling out his case for some passage of the moon and they had feigned misunderstanding despite his clear words. He was tired of being toyed with, and was following the Fourth's and Grotis' advice. "I look upon you and I do not see equals. I do not see equals to the Borys-Karang. I see filth that is not worthy of the slaves they claim to own!"

"For that, you will die," another tribe leader cried, shaking with rage. "I will take your slaves, I will take everything you bring as slaves as the lizards eat your rotting flesh!"

"You cannot take from me without a challenge! By your own law! And I challenge you! You are unfit to rule! Unfit to lead! You could not lead a piss to a pile of turds!"

"What law!?"

"The Fifth Law of Karap! Your own law," Oygariyet yelled at them.

Some were stunned in anger or surprise or both. Others started to smirk. One by one, they craned their heads, as if listening to a voice Oygariyet could not hear. One by one, each of them, even the ones surprised or furious, calmed as their filthy lips curled into smiles.

"I accept your challenge," one said. Then another. And another until they all had. Oygariyet understood that they knew he had implicitly laid his entire holdings on this gamble, but so had they. But each of them would be unable to offer a sufficient challenge, even all of them at once. Not in that state of softness. "You shall await the arrival of our champions," another tribe leader said.

"What champions?" Oygariyet demanded.

"By the Eighteenth Law, people of our status, too concerned with the good running of the city to train for such menial matters, may appoint a champion to answer challenges such as this."

"*Menial?*" Oygariyet was surprised to hear the word. It was actually a borrowed word from Goblin tongue. He was genuinely surprised at them expressing the idea that this filth was above anything as much as to hear them use the turn of phrase.

"Yes. All eight champions you shall face," the tunicked orc said. On the inside, Oygariyet smiled. Perhaps he would get a chance to take out his annoyances of the journey after all. He had thought this would perhaps be a boring one, but it was turning around.

As they waited, Oygariyet took food and drink that one of his own Orcish slaves carried. The hosts offered none, not that Oygariyet would not have accepted any given. He watched the orcs as they snickered amongst themselves, leering at Oygariyet while they ate and drank and rudely displayed their slaves. Oygariyet and his companions drank the meager rations that remained to them. They had hunted some prey and foraged mushrooms on the journey to supplement the dried, salted meat that remained. They had finished the bread and biscuits in the first week, as well as the ridin.

His mind wandered. Oygariyet missed the ridin, most. That and his favorite whom he did not want to risk on this journey and, should something happen to him, that she would be safe from this filth. *Ah, the favorite. To have her and the swordbearer here together. To drink deeply of a cup of ridin while she–*

The door to the other side of the petitioner pit finally opened, and the eight supposed champions of each of the tribe leaders filed through. Five of the eight wore mismatching shirts or suits of mail, reinforced with plates at joints and other critical areas. Some wore helmets that were broad at the top of the head and slightly tapered towards the bottom and the front, making a gentle corner in the center of the front, reminding Oygariyet of a toad's face. The five in heavier armor and one very lightly armored, wearing two broadswords at his waist, walked to Oygariyet's left.

The remaining two reminded Oygariyet of the Baki-Norn. They wore very little, but had grown beards and shaved the sides of their heads. Strange designs were tattooed onto the sides of their heads and down their necks. One wielded an oversized axe; the other grasped a long-bladed sword. Much more than a longsword, it was simply a very big sword with a lengthy, heavy blade, as tall as Oygariyet himself, with an equally considerable handle. Maglaban had told him once that the Vostindin or the Daearans would use swords like this. Oygariyet wondered if this was made under that influence, if not taken from a field of battle, or if they had thought of the idea themselves.

Smiling, Oygariyet took up his spiked mace, offered by his Goblin slave, and strode into the center of the pit, drawing the sword bestowed upon him by Leriyet the Great, infused with soul of one of Oygariyet's own warriors, the Soulblade.

"Ah! The challenge has not yet begun," one of the orcs in the gallery chided.

"But your champions are here. Do you doubt them?" Oygariyet said.

"Oh, no. Just a moment," the orc replied.

Oygariyet looked back to the orcs in the petitioner pit. One of the two bearded and tattooed orcs was stuffing the remains of what looked like a large mushroom in his mouth. The other one was fiddling with a leaf pipe and lighting it at one of the braziers.

"Time to relax or time to fight?" Oygariyet called.

"Patience, outsider, the time will be soon," the tunicked orc said from the gallery with a grin.

"And so, when will it begin?" Oygariyet said impatiently.

"Soon. I will call it when it begins."

Oygariyet waited in annoyed silence. The six armored orcs alternated between watching Oygariyet for signs of weakness and eagerly glancing at the other two orcs. The one with the pipe puffed on it while glaring back at Oygariyet. The one that had eaten the mushroom did the same, but Oygariyet noticed after a while that his eyes glazed and he was just staring in Oygariyet's direction. Oygariyet looked at him for a long bit and noticed that he had started drooling and staring off blankly. His body slowly began to lean against the wall of the petitioner pit, right under the gallery.

"Argh!" one of the gallery orcs cried in frustration, "he grabbed the wrong mushroom!" Reacting to the sounds of the gallery's irritation, the smoking orc dropped his pipe and began coughing in increasingly violent wracks until he began to foam at the mouth. The coughs turned into yells and howls. He growled and looked up at Oygariyet, his eyes widely dilated, tearing and bloodshot. He leaped towards Oygariyet with broad, sweeping arcs and swipes from the long axe.

Finally! To be alive!! Oygariyet dodged a few of the axe swipes and flicked some of the strikes into the ground with his Soulblade, banging loudly and sparking on the stone floor. The other six orcs looked on. *So that was it. They wanted to see if he would fall to this before they engaged.*

Oygariyet brought his sword to a middle guard, blade in front of him, tip toward the raging orc's head, crossguard protecting his middle. The spiked mace draped over his left shoulder. He grinned as the orc moved laterally and lunged with a powerful axe stroke. Oygariyet stepped well inside the axe blade's reach, jamming the strong of the blade and the crossguard into the axe haft, stealing all of its momentum while heaving the mace down with an easy, overhand blow to the orc's head.

The spikes visibly and bloodily dented his orc's bare head as he dropped. Oygariyet chuckled as he gave the orc one more mace blow to cave in his skull. With a spatter of blood and grey matter on his face, Oygariyet grinned at the six armored orcs as he calmly approached the seventh orc in his drooling stupor, and thrust his blade through his face. The orc dropped, blood spilling quickly, weaving through the unswept dust and dirt like water.

The remaining six sprang into action, moving quickly to surround Oygariyet and attack from all sides. The first orc easily blocked Oygariyet's diversionary sword stroke with his own longsword, but Oygariyet's spiked mace smashed his elbow, sending him staggering away, howling in pain. Oygariyet's blade reached under his mail skirt, cutting large veins before Oygariyet kicked him off to the side to bleed another river. One of the toad-faced helmets was almost upon him with an overhand axe chop. Oygariyet deftly sidestepped and a flick of his blade tore through one of his leather gloves and severed one of his attacker's hands. The quick one, wearing the light armor, came at him, his broad, short blades flashing in the firelight.

Oygariyet gave ground. The other named champions seemed to favor either raw strength and speed, or the protection supposedly offered by their armor. The strength left them clumsy and the armor made them careless and sloppy. This one's fighting style seemed different from the others; there was a quickness and agility about him. *That is it.* His light gear, a simply quilted heavy jacket, gave him speed and flexibility, but also left him vulnerable and forced him into caution. *Simple solution.*

Oygariyet swung his mace in a wide stroke. The agile orc leaped to the side, out of reach of the mace, but straight into the arc of Oygariyet's sword stroke from the other side. The blade tore across his right knee. He fell, clutching his wound. Oygariyet kicked him onto his side, then kicked him in the chin. The orc's head snapped back. Oygariyet stepped on the back of his neck. He struggled weakly against Oygariyet's foot, looking upon him fearfully through the corner of his eye, as Oygariyet drove the swordtip through his skull.

Three remained. Three and a half, counting the one nursing a stump where one of his hands used to be. The orcs in the gallery stared in stunned silence. Of the three remaining orcs, one had a spear, one a broadsword and small shield, and the last a large, round shield with a short, thrusting sword. The three of them, advancing on Oygariyet, formed a triangle, with the spearman in the rear and the two shields up front. *A triangle has three sides and three corners... only one of them can land on me.* Oygariyet smiled to himself. He advanced on them quickly, meeting them. The spear thrust came between them. Oygariyet feinted a step to the left before leaping to the right, dodging the spear thrust and using its haft to block the left orc's maneuver. Oygariyet battered the small shield as he thrust under it at the belt line. Mail links broke under the strain and blood and urine poured from the abdomen of the orc as he crumpled over.

"NO!" cried one of the orcs in the gallery, as the dying orc's breath bubbled in a pool of his own bloody urine. Oygariyet swiped away a spear thrust and stepped on it, ripping the attacking orc's head from its shoulders with the Soulblade. All who remained was the orc with the large shield and the thrusting sword, wearing a toad-face helm. Oygariyet kept the orc's sword busy blocking swings and feints while he abused the orc's shield with his spiked mace, backing him towards the wall. The orc's back brushed against the wall of the petitioner pit, surprising him. In his moment of startlement, Oygariyet mightily smashed the shield, bending it and breaking the orc's forearm and hand. He hollered in pain, but his cries were cut short as the Soulblade came in from under his shield. Oygariyet drove the tip of the sword upwards, into his victim's throat, bursting through the top of the helmet.

Ripping his blade free in a spray of blood, Oygariyet panted, grinning widely. This was the most fun he had known in moons. He eagerly strode towards the one-handed orc, still clutching his stump. "I submit," he cried. "I am yours."

"CURSE YOU!" screamed one of the gallery orcs.

NO. CURSE YOU ALL. A voice boomed in Oygariyet's head. His gaze darted wildly seeking its origin. The gallery orcs and harem slaves shouted in terror, falling over themselves to climb the stairs to the exit. The one-handed orc cowered on the ground. *This is it*, Oygariyet thought as he thumbed a small axe loose from his belt.

A bulbous object floated down through the large hole in the ceiling. A mass of many lidless eyes glared in every direction; two sinewy arms extended from the creature, one on each side. "DO NOT LOOK!" shouted Oygariyet's Fourth. Oygariyet felt a pressure he had never felt before. On his gut. On his mind. On his chest. He squeezed his eyes shut. He heard the others, all of the others, friend and enemy alike, wail in despair, some retching up their last meals.

TO THINK THAT YOU WOULD–

The voice cut off as Oygariyet heaved the small axe toward where he last saw the disgusting eye creature, aiming as best he could with his eyes screwed shut.

SSSSKKKKKKKKEEEEEEEEEEIIIIIIIIIIAAAAAAEEEHHH.

Oygariyet became aware that he was prone, dry heaving into a pool of his own sick. He unsteadily rose and blearily regarded his surroundings, weakly scrubbing the vomit from his face with a sleeve. Most of the orcs had died from whatever that was. He cast a quick glance towards his entourage, noting that they had not managed much better. Some of his honor guard and slaves were stirring or getting up, but others lay motionless, blood seeping from their mouths, ears, noses, and popped eye sockets.

The Fourth and Grotis had fared the best; Grotis claimed to have seen the eye beast before and his Fourth had read of them extensively before this journey and they must have been better prepared. The sword dancer lay on the ground breathing raggedly. Oygariyet looked in the direction of the eye beast's carcass. It lay on the ground, twitching. He could see that it had a mouth on one side, spiked teeth blossoming in rows. Oygariyet staggered over to it and hacked at it with sword and spiked mace until he had popped all of the eyes and ensured that it no longer moved. The one-handed orc shuddered on the floor by the wall of the petitioner's pit. Oygariyet walked over and seized his stumped wrist, thrusting it into the flame of a brazier. He cried weakly as the fire sealed his bleeding stump.

Oygariyet kicked the one-handed orc to make sure he stayed awake and then yelled towards the direction of the vent from which the eye beast had emerged. "HEAR ME!" he cried in Orcish. It was the surface dialect that he knew, but it seemed to suffice, despite differences in the accent. "I, OYGARIYET THE GREAT, HAVE KILLED ALL YOUR LORDS AND LEADERS. YOUR TRIBES ARE MINE! THE PLACE-CALLED-IKRIA IS MINE!"

***

Oygariyet was tired, but they had cleaned off. He had appointed the one-handed orc as one of his staff, but lower than a fourth. He was an orc, after all, but seemed to be the only one still alive that knew enough of the general situation and with whom to speak to get things done. The orc had procured new clothes for Oygariyet's survivors, since what they wore was soaked in blood and vomit. Oygariyet had lost almost half of his entourage, including the human woman he had shown in the center of the pit, and more, including the sword dancer, were seriously wounded.

Oygariyet and his able-bodied followers sat in a lounge of sorts, a square room higher in the citadel with windows overlooking the city. Most of the furnishings consisted of stuffed, hide pillows, but there were a few chairs and a small table. His Fourth sat at the table with him as the one-handed orc stood attentively.

"I suppose I should not be surprised," Oygariyet muttered as he put his head in his hands. *Of course they would have their own problems and conflicts.* "When do you think they will be returning?"

"We do not know, Great One." The one-handed orc shifted his footing as he made this last addition to Oygariyet's brief he had just completed. Dwarves. *Of course, the dwarves want their city back. These dwarves of this Place-called-Drenia.* Oygariyet sighed deeply.

"Very well. It is what it is. I want several things," Oygariyet resolved. He rose from his chair and began to pace.

"Yes, Great One." The one-handed orc's nervous fidgeting gnawed at Oygariyet's sense of certainty.

"First, change the instructions to all who guard the entrances to the city. Do not admit anyone that does not already live here, except for those that I send," he stated firmly. "Make exceptions for merchants and normal trade, but anyone that comes in saying things like 'I want to win the favor of this city' should be kept out."

"Yes, Great One."

"I want the harems and other slaves of all of those sacks of piss." Oygariyet leaned forward to emphasize the importance of his declaration.

"Yes, Great One."

"What will you do with them, Great One?" his Fourth asked.

Oygariyet steepled his fingers and peered at his Fourth. "Give them a choice."

"A choice?" She was puzzled by the ambiguity of his statement.

Oygariyet pursed his lips. "It sickens me that they were treated that way. You saw how it was. So. I will give them a choice. They may be free. They may join my holdings, where I will show them the proper way of respect for the honor of being a great one's slave. They may form a warband, maybe one big enough that we might call it a fist. Or they may form some kind of guild to produce supplies." Oygariyet thought for a moment, "I suppose they will not all choose the same thing, so it will be a combination of all of those. If any of them want something else, grant it within reason."

His Fourth hesitated. "Great One, you speak as if I will be overseeing this."

"Ah, that you will, at least for the ones that do not join my holdings," he dictated, unceremoniously springing this surprise on his Fourth. "Oh," he said, turning to the one-handed orc as well. "That reminds me… there will be rules enacted for the decent treatment of slaves here. No sport in public like that. It is indecent. Of course, harem slaves have a specific use–but it is a private use." He gestured to the Fourth. "Write some other rules that you think are within reason." She nodded as he continued. "I must name you for this task."

Hesitantly, she looked up at Oygariyet from her seat. "Great One. I… I feel as though I am unready."

He pointed a finger and rested it on her forehead. "You are more than ready for this task. I share your concerns about managing a battle, but you can handle this, surely. I want you to consolidate our hold on this Place-called-Ikria." Withdrawing his hand, he smiled approvingly at her. "I will send another to replace you and you will return to the surface, or you may reply that you have further endeavors here. In the meantime, do whatever you wish to ensure we do not lose this city. In that time, make an estimate of how many orcs can leave the city to fight on the surface without endangering security here."

"Yes, Great One."

"This one," he said, gesturing to the one-handed orc, "will be a tool to you."

His Fourth smiled, pleased with the turn of events. "Is he mine?"

"You want him? He is damaged. You can have whoever and however many you want. Oh, right. Your name. You wish to pick it?"

"No, Great One. I wish you to choose." She rose from her chair, nearly bouncing on her feet.

"Hm. Well. I name you Dyiriyet," he said.

"Thank you, Great One." Dyiriyet rose and strode towards him slowly with a new smile. "To celebrate, will you take sport with me, Great One?"

He rose to meet her. "It would be my honor." The one-handed orc glanced around anxiously as Oygariyet and Dyiriyet began to partake of each other before awkwardly leaving the chamber.

***

The Low Gate of the Dwarven City of Zol, Kingdom of Aedon.
By the Dwarven Calendar, 214th day of the 10484th Year.
By the Human Calendar, sometime during the first week of Ongkanir
(eighth month of the year), 794.

"Ye should turn back," warned the guard in the gatehouse.

Sergeant Marchag called up to him, "Sure, when we've unloaded the siege crossbows to ya."

The guard waved them off, "Naw. It's lost here. The Drennies are ramming the gates on the other side. The siege crossbows are no use. Try Ezkaarn."

"Ezkaarn didn't want them. Maybe we can fight for you?" Hrene offered.

"They didn't want them? Oh, why's that d'ya suppose?" the guard jeered.

"Listen, Friend, we're here on the King's orders to deliver these an' help in any way," said Hrene, shifting her weight. *He ain't gonna let us in.*

The guard called down to them, "The King's orders, eh? From the King himself?"

"No. By way o' Major Captain Turiotli of the King's Legion," Hrene said. She knew where this was going: the same way it had gone at the gates of Ezkaarn.

"Ah, so, an' where's the King?" the guard called.

Marchah scowled and shouted angrily, "Listen here, man, just open the gate! We'll not stand here an' listen to this insult."

"Ay, man, I'm the minor captain o' this gate, an' I say no. Where's the King, eh? Ya come 'ere an' tell me ya left the King in Adyrnaarn with the Drennies. Where's the King, eh? Where's your major captain? We don' be needed anyone that runs from the fight an' leaves the King an' his people," the gate captain said.

Marchag raised his arm, pointing at the gate captain, but Hrene laid a hand on his shoulder. "Let him be."

"But–" Marchag puffed in rage.

"It don' matter," she said quietly.

"Captain!" Marchag backed away from her in outrage, "what do ya mean 'it don' matter'?"

Hrene looked back towards their dwindling caravan. They had started with a hundred soldiers, a few scores of wounded dwarves, and the hand cases for the gnomes to travel in. Only the gnomes remained in their entirety. Some of the wounded had died on the journey to Ezkaarn, where the guards at the gates had used much stronger words than this gate captain had. More than half of the soldiers and wounded had run off to try to rejoin the fight or committed suicide at the shame of having abandoned their king.

"They don' want our help, Sergeant. Neither did Ezkaarn. Take a guess at any o' the other places. We don' have the numbers to make a difference. What do we have? A couple score of soldiers an' the gnomes," Hrene said.

"Ay! From the wounded we had a mathematician that stayed with us an' an apprentice wizard," Marchag protested crossly at his captain.

"The boy? Does he know any spells at all? Listen sergeant, we got a choice to make. We can't go back an' we can't go forward," she said to him. The gate captain, seeing that he was being ignored, abandoned his perch and disappeared from view.

Marchag sighed, his anger deflating. "I'll pull everyone together, captain. We probably all need to hear this from you an' we got to go somewhere, don' we?"

"That we do, sergeant," Hrene nodded grimly.

Chapter 12

Stone of Rykooth, Kaskev Mountains.
By the Goblin Calendar, late in the Eleventh Moon Cycle, 3114.
By the Human Calendar, during the third week of Ongkanir, 794.
A snowy, windy autumn evening.

he guards opened the doors to the throne room of Rykooth for the Borys-Karang, trailed by a few nameless underlings. He gestured for several to remain in the hallway with the gift as he entered. *This had better be worth it. I had to pay Muydiyet handsomely to wrest her prize away from her.* A fire roared in the central pit; the same pit, apparently, where their precious Luriyet, Loriyet, Leriyet, whatever his name was, appeared to them and gave Oygariyet his greater purpose in life. *What a farce!* The Borys-Karang chuckled to himself, unaware that the term 'farce' was a term borrowed from Goblin that had been assimilated into Orcish.

None of the stuff gods had ever appeared to any of the orcs. You just knew what you were supposed to do. Know about stuff, kill stuff, have stuff, sex stuff. Simple. No books of contradictory rules or useless ideas like 'honor.' Then again, maybe it is useful to them, as they live longer. The Borys-Karang passed the tables of maps flanking the central firepit and approached the throne. Indariyet, wearing a coat of mail with plate pauldrons and sporting several weapons at her belt, was seated there in Oygariyet's stead. He recognized several of her subordinates with whom she was conferring standing near the throne, some holding ledgers and quills, others with more rolled up maps. In the corner, Indariyet's honor guard of wolf riders stood ready, their canine steeds laying on the floor obediently.

"The throne suits you," the Borys-Karang began with a smile, speaking in the accented Goblin dialect of this Side of the Mountains.

Indariyet testily returned his smile. "If you think that you can find your way to putting your face between my legs, I say to you I would rather lose a battle than see my reflection in your balding scalp," she replied with sweet acerbity. "And at your age, I doubt anything else you have works or is much to behold."

The Borys-Karang chuckled lightly. "Perhaps, though perhaps you would mind less sitting on this thing later." He beckoned forth his underlings waiting at the door. They hauled in the gift he brought: an exhausted human man, lean and muscular, with yellow hair, his arms gripped by orcs on either side of him. He had been brought from the Place-called-Versingit and had grown a beard during the forced march. The Borys-Karang smirked, remembering when the man's will broke during the march. His blue eyes had initially been defiant and resentful; now they fell to the ground in resigned submission.

They pushed him forward and thrust him to his hands and knees before the throne. He weakly looked up at Indariyet. Indariyet arched an eyebrow at the human and crossed one leg over another before looking back at the Borys-Karang.

"What is this?" she asked.

"A gift," the Borys-Karang answered innocently.

"Who is he? What is his worth?"

"He was the ruler of the Place-called-Versingit. He has a warrior's body. He will please you well."

She glanced down her nose at the yellow-haired human collapsed on the floor before returning the gaze of her new prize. "I accept this trophy," she said, "but you clearly came here to give *this* trophy to *me*. You know the Great One's tastes fall with females, so you want something from me. What is it?"

The Borys-Karang smiled falsely. "You have an adept eye, Great One."

"The purpose, All-Consuming Flame, what is your purpose?" she prodded irritably.

"Once the Place-called-Soorin is in hand, I wish to take the Place-called-Versinth," the Borys-Karang suggested.

"Absolutely not," she stated matter-of-factly. "The Great One's plan is to seize the Place-called-Yvel, either directly or indirectly."

"Great One," the Borys-Karang plaintively responded,

spreading his hands in a non-threatening gesture (which, generally, was a very odd thing for an orc to do). The Borys-Karang had been exposed to enough of the other mountain's denizens—even a few humans and dwarves—to adopt some mannerisms from other peoples. "The humans near the Place-called-Yvel have magick. We will waste warriors trying to take those places."

"You actually believe that!?"

"The Great Oygariyet does. It decided the battle near the smaller-Place-called-Serna," he said. "Your own Dariyet delivered that defeat. Do you think so little of him or hold the Great One's belief that Dariyet would lose to the humans without some cheating magick or trickery?"

"It was those worthless Pev'Baki-Norn breaking like bird bones that created that defeat!" she snapped. "I will see the Great One's will be done and it will please him and *you* will be part of that." She rose, scowling at him and strode towards one of the map tables. "Look here." She beckoned him brusquely.

"What is this?" he asked.

"The humans that have joined us from the Place-called-Ardara have been helpful in many ways," she said, gesturing to one of the maps that were spread upon the table. The mountains and settlements like Rykooth and Kogylar were easily recognizable, as were some of the human settlements, like Ardara, Yvel, Versingit, and others. They were labeled in Goblin next to what the Borys-Karang imagined were the human writings of their names. Beyond the human cities, further along the way that the cowardly sun flees, was a large area with a border encircling it.

"What is this?" he pointed to the large area.

"A lake," she said. "The Tald Lake."

"That big?" The Borys-Karang was earnestly surprised. He had seen some lakes in the mountains, but he knew them to be much smaller than what the map depicted. "It must be a mistake. Lakes cannot be that big."

"I was also not sure and believed it to be a trick, but several different humans swore to me under great pain that the lake was actually that big. They said that there were no mountains in the way for the lake to grow."

The Borys-Karang stared at the blue splotch on the map labeled as the Tald Lake. *Perhaps I will see it myself to be sure if it is true or a trick*, he mused.

"Are you listening?" Indariyet demanded irritably.

"Hm? No," he said candidly, "I was thinking about this lake of impossible size. As you were saying, Great One." He offered no apology. He was tired of the pretense and wished only to finish the business at hand. She had not liked his proposition, despite the great expense of the gift he had to pry from Muydiyet, and they disagreed on why certain things had happened. He could not force her into agreement, so he had to accept limitations. For now.

"The Place-called-Yvel has proven difficult. So, we will wash around it like water."

"How do you mean?" he asked.

"Seize the Place-called-Soorin and advance to the Tald Lake. Advance to the Tald Lake from the Place-called-Versingit and we will starve the Place-called-Yvel and its smaller places."

"But they can use boats to avoid being starved," the Borys-Karang pointed out.

"I have heard of these boats. You saw them at the Place-called-Versingit," she said. "I read of them in Maglaban's message."

Maglaban. The Borys-Karang grimaced. *That one thwarted me from a prize of my own*. "Yes, they can use boats."

Indariyet gestured towards the illustrated river which flowed from the mountains, through the Place-called-Yvel, into the Tald Lake. "They must use the river for their boats, and we can use siege crossbows and stone hurlers to destroy them," she dismissed.

He grimaced, pursing his lips, "I still think the Place-called-Versinth would be a better place to go next."

"If work for the Place-called-Yvel fails again–a failure you will not be able to dodge–then the next place to go is this Place-called-Vidara," she explained, stabbing her finger on the map, "to strangle the Place-called-Yvel and its smaller places. The smaller-Place-called-Serna, the smaller-Place-called-Borly, the smaller-Place-called-Keppa, and some others."

He looked up from the map and stared at her. "Do not say

that the Borys-Karang did not warn you," he said quietly.

"Are you finished here?" she asked, "I thank you for the trophy and the good work you offered at the Place-called-Versingit." You have other attacks to prepare for, do you not? Surely, the Borys-Karang will have a not small function in the glory of taking the Place-called-Soorin?"

He glanced back at the map grimly. "After I send some of my tribes for supplies and more warriors at the Place-called-Kogylar, I will need to pull more warbands from Ghetrak. Give me time to contract free fighters from Iliarzin and Golardeg or Berkasliriyig."

"There are no free fighters in Golardeg," she said scornfully.

The Borys-Karang rolled his eyes. "I mean among goblins and orc slaves."

***

Near Kogylar, on the western slopes of the Kaskev Mountains
By the Human Calendar, Sortingday, third week of Ongkanir, 794.
A sleeting, autumn afternoon.

Korane had spent most of her life away from the town and only went in to trade the bounty of her hunting and foraging. She savored the crisp air of the mountains. It made her feel more alive. More awake. The remoteness of the mountains brought other things. Other chances.

The bear pelt curing over the fire was one of those opportunities. As far as Korane knew them, the carcass was on the small side for a brown-furred bear. It must have been younger and foraging one last time before its winter sleep. Might have been a female. Korane was carving the meat away from the bones and cleaning out other pieces of the bear that she would be able to sell. The bones. The fat. She could make a good bag from the stomach and a bowl from the skull. *That will help.* She and the goblin had constructed a crude sled made of stout branches, and piled it high with sacks and baskets woven from sticks and fiber that were filled with the fruits of their labor.

Her goblin, avoiding the smell from the fire, covered its face and kept its distance from it as best it could manage without freezing. Korane was surprised that it was raining in Ongkanir, midway through autumn, this high in the mountains. It would be snowing, normally, from the few times that she had been to the mountains. Winds must have brought up warm weather from the south. Warm weather by comparison, at least. It had been snowing for the past three weeks that they had been in the mountains. The rain was a relief from stinging sleet, but it would certainly turn to ice later.

A gentle stream nearby supplied them with water so pure and cold that her teeth hurt from drinking it. The rain was an annoyance, but the fire was warm enough. Korane was well accustomed to the smell of burning flesh from tanning and curing hides, as well as the cleaning and butchering of animal carcasses, and all sorts of mundane tasks that came with living off the land. Her Goblin companion, however, was apparently unused to these sorts of tasks. He bleated complaints about being from the city of Berkasliriyig and not being used to laboring like this. She forced him to help, though he had retched up his last meal several times over the past two days. She chuckled. He would get used to it, if he wanted to be useful. *And he had better be useful.*

They now spoke entirely in Goblin. He had told her that he taught her the dialect of the language of these parts, but also peppered in some of the words of his native dialect, from further to the right along the mountains. He talked about it being colder there for more of the year and she came to understand that he meant further north. That realization made communication considerably more fluid. Goblins, and most of the other cast-out races of the mountains, viewed the mountains as the center of the world and all other lands with an eye to the mountains. On this side of the mountains, right was north and left was south. Far away was west.

Before making their departure, she donned her disguise. Covering her hands with gloves and wrapping a scarf around her face, the centerpiece of her disguise was the skin of the bear's head over her hair. It covered her rounded ears, to ease passing as a hobgoblin. The last piece of her costume rested in a small tin cup on the sled.

She made him pull the sled, but he did not complain–much. It gave him the chance to get the traveling pack off of his back. She occasionally aided him in climbing the steeper lengths. After another day of travel, they emerged from the pine forest on the mountain slope and stepped onto a hard-packed trail.

"What is this?" she asked.

"A road," he replied uncertainly.

She thwapped him on the back of his head. "I know it is a road. What's it doing here?"

He looked at her perplexedly. "Lying on the ground?"

Korane sighed in exasperation. "I mean, *why* is there a road here?"

"It is the road to Kogylar," he replied, flinching.

"Where does it go in the other direction?"

"Many places. Who knows? Villages. Hunting grounds and trails. Farms."

"What farms?" she demanded.

"I don't know. Farms," he said, recoiling.

"You mean to tell me that goblins have been stealing and killing from farms for years and years?"

"What? No. I do not think so."

"So, you are saying that humans are trading with goblins!?"

"Well, that does happen further to the right along the Mountains, but I think not around here. But I am not talking about human farms."

She shook her head at him. "What other farms are there around here?"

"Farms run by goblins?" he suggested tentatively.

"What?"

"Farms run by goblins?" he repeated.

"What do you mean?" she asked. She was bewildered.

"Goblins have farms," he said.

She looked at him for a long time. "What kind of farms?"

He hesitated. "Any kind you can imagine. Swine farms. Mushroom farms. Root farms. Taming grounds for wolves."

"You expect me to believe that goblins just happily live in the mountains and grow mushrooms and do not hurt anyone?" she challenged.

"It is not easy living for them," he said defensively. "There are raids from rival tribes, especially orcs in the area."

"So, if no one raided them, these Goblin farmers of yours would just live out their lives peaceably?"

"I think so, yes," he agreed.

She kicked him in the ribs, knocking him to the ground. "Then why did the goblins come out of the mountains? Did those raids get worse and they had to leave?" Her attack surprised him and knocked the wind from his lungs. When he caught his breath, he heaved for a bit before speaking again.

"No. I mean, yes. I mean…" he panted, "the raids stopped."

"Then, if they stopped, then why did the goblins attack humans?"

"It," he heaved, "it is what Oygariyet the Great wanted."

"Who is that?" she demanded.

"Oygariyet the Great is the mightiest hobgoblin of our time," he said. "The Great One tamed the orcs and compelled them to work for the hobgoblins. Gave them order to their ignorance. Gave them use to something greater than themselves. He united the Goblin peoples." He paused and looked aside. "Well, *most* of the Goblin peoples," he continued. "And then forged an alliance with the other races whose lands had been stolen from them. The Gnolls, the Kobolds."

"So, you all did this because of this hobgoblin, this Oygariyet person?" she said.

"Yes," he confirmed.

"Why? What does he want?"

"He seeks to reclaim the lands stolen long ago."

"*Who* stole them?" She spread her arms incredulously.

"You did," the goblin said. She detected a tinge of resentment in his voice.

His usefulness is about to change. "What do you mean? *Who* did?"

"Humans did. And elves."

"What humans? When? What do you mean?" She was getting heated. *Is this a joke?*

"Oh, this would be hundreds and hundreds of winters ago. Maybe thousands," he shrugged.

She raised her eyebrows as she confirmed his words. "Thousands?"

"Yes, probably, by the stories."

If they didn't try before in all this time, doesn't that mean they gave up any claim? "So, why now? What made this Oygariyet person want to do this now?"

"I do not know. Some say that he was visited by Leriyet the Great." The goblin squinted and rubbed his chin.

"Who is Leriyet?"

"Leriyet the Great is the greatest hobgoblin that ever lived. At least, for hobgoblins. He wrote the rules that they live by."

"So, why is Leriyet not leading this instead of Oygariyet?" she asked.

"Leriyet? He is dead. Long ago. A figure of legend. Like a god to them. I do not know if I believe that Leriyet the Great actually visited Oygariyet, but that is what I heard."

"Did you tell any of this to the human that gave you to me?"

"The things that he asked, mostly the 'who' and 'where' questions. He did not ask any 'why' questions. He did not ask about farms, so I did not tell him."

"Why not?"

"I was scared from being taken into slavery by humans. It was not the kind of thing that I thought to talk about when no one asked me." He looked at the ground by her feet, occasionally glancing up at her as he answered her question.

She pondered upon what he had shared for a few moments. *I suppose we have our own religion thrust in our faces, what with Mkaela stealing people away from death. Maybe their Leriyet person actually did appear to them.* She abruptly changed the subject. "How far to Kogylar?"

"We can reach it before the sun invades," he judged, assessing the scant moonlight shining through the rain clouds. She gave him the 'I am not traveling at night' look, and he reconsidered his answer. "… Or by the time the sun retreats after this moon's rescue." It seemed so odd to her that they viewed the sun and daytime as a threat and the night as safety, but these things made talking to him make more sense. The pair traveled along the beaten path to Kogylar through the continued rainfall, just barely above freezing, and rested at night. Relief arrived that evening, when it turned to snow, but returned to rain by the next midday.

She could tell by the smell in the air when they were approaching Kogylar. She stopped to add the last piece of her disguise, producing the tin cup from the sled and opening its lid. It was packed with vermilion-colored clay soil from the hills at the base of the mountains. Her unwilling companion had informed her that she would resemble some tribes of hobgoblins of the northern end of the mountains, who had red skin. The persistent rain provided the needed moisture. Wetting the clay, she painted her face.

Korane leaned towards the goblin and whispered a warning. "Let us get something straight. You can probably alert someone and convince them that I am a human and a spy, but make no mistake. I can definitely kill you before they get to me and I might even get away. So, keep that in mind before you try something foolish." The goblin stiffened, but said nothing. "Good," she said. "We will be here for a few days."

The trail gradually broadened over the space of several miles as other trails joined it, all flowing in one direction. It terminated into an arch etched into the side of a mountain. It was not an entirely natural arch–perhaps once a cave, but someone had expanded it, carving out more space and lining the sides with stone. Other travelers had drifted onto the trail with them, lumbering miserably in the misting rain. Their presence sent a shiver down Korane's spine. Goblins. A few orcs or a hobgoblin. The enemy. And she was walking behind them. In front of them. Among them.

Korane and her Goblin companion strained and heaved to pull their sled through the muddy entrance of the archway as other travelers passed them on both sides. The tunnel was about fifty paces long and ten paces wide with cobbled floors and daylight visible on the other end of it. The sound of trickling rainwater draining into the cave echoed around them. Bizarrely, the walls of the cave passage were lined with alcoves carved into stone where shopkeepers, mostly goblins, peddled their wares.

She did not know what to expect, but was still surprised. Kogylar. It was a hollow, roughly cylindrical place. The center of the chamber had been hollowed out, probably whittled down by water flow, judging by the cacophonous sound of trickling water surrounding them. The structure appeared to be that of an immense, cylindrical cavern, hundreds of paces across and hundreds more deep, open to the sky above. Hewn into the walls were cubby holes and rooms with wooden-shuttered windows, stacked on top of each other, floor after floor, for hundreds of paces up and down. The city was linked by combinations of cut-stone walkways and streets lining the peripheries of each level, wooden scaffolding, stairs and ramps made of wood or stone, and bridges of stone, timber, or rope. Additional buildings lined the streets–mostly wooden, though on the broader throughways, some were built from stone.

Warm air gusted forth from the depths of the pit, bringing with it the earthy smell of mushrooms and mold which cut through normal stench of a city and tempered the biting cold of the rain, sleet, and wind that threatened from above. The city seemed to be mostly asleep still, judging by the relative inactivity compared to its scale, but there was still traffic on the walkways and bridges. No. The city was just waking up. The sun would be setting shortly, judging by the light quality perceptible through the clouds. One by one, Korane watched wooden shutters swing open and peddler carts be wheeled out into the streets. *At least I can sell this stuff now.*

Korane was uncertain how much time passed in locating several different merchants, butchers, fur traders, leatherworkers, bowyers, kitchens–and a barber, of all things, who was delighted to purchase their bear fat. She was glad for the bronze-covered scones and braziers lit throughout the city, but it was a strange feeling, looking over the railing of one of the streets into the deep, deep pit and seeing hundreds of torches glittering like gold in the night.

She flicked the last coin she took into the purse at her belt. They had most, and a few more, of the metals for coins here that she remembered from Serna and her one visit to Yvel. Coins of tin were used here, just like in Serna, along with yellow copper and copper, but instead of the faces of dead princes and princesses, the coins bore imagery taken from nature. The tin coins were stamped with a depiction of a mushroom, the yellow copper had a swine upon it, and the copper a pine tree. She also came by a few bronze coins with the image of mountains stamped on them.

She had never dealt with anything more valuable than silver before the war. *Before the war*, she chuckled to herself bitterly. *It seems like so long ago, but it's only been three seasons. Almost a year.* She had seen silver a few times here, but had yet to see any gold, and she wondered if they even used it for coins here. She flicked the purse to hear the satisfying jingle of the coins before continuing on. Feeling a tug at her sleeve, she looked down to see her Goblin slave–she had given up on the debate, he insisted he was her slave no matter how many times she told him he was a prisoner–tugging at her sleeve.

"What?"

"Great One, can we eat?" He pointed eagerly at what looked disturbingly and uncannily similar to the soup counter in Serna, having dropped the towing cord to point and pull on her sleeve. It was a small, horizontal building made of wood, just large enough to put walls around the kitchen, and just enough roof to cover the kitchen and the stools on the other side of the counter, and was run by a handful of scurrying, blue-skinned goblins.

"Fine," she sighed. She was hungry, too. He hauled the sled over to the side of the building, next to a large wolf that growled at him hungrily. They had sold most of their wares, so it was much lighter and he pulled it with neither help nor complaint. They sat on the stools.

Only three other customers were present: two orcs sat at the end of the counter, seemingly not together, one of whom was considerably smaller than any orc she'd seen before, and a Hobgoblin woman. The woman displayed a jagged scar on her jaw and stared dejectedly into her steaming bowl of soup. The rain spattered on the muddy stone walkway behind her, the roof just barely covering her.

One of the blue-skinned goblins approached them. "What do you have?"

"Two bowls of something to keep the cold off."

"Good. Eight tinheads."

Korane assumed that meant the tin coins with the mushroom heads. She fished them out of the purse and laid them on the counter. The goblin had already started their bowls before she looked up from the purse, but was keen to scoop them payment as soon as Korane laid it down. Korane looked down to flip down the closure on her purse and looked back in time to see two double-handed bowls being placed down in front of her and her goblin. The cook also slid along a tin cup of steaming drink for each of them. The drink was sweet and earthy, but tangy. Some kind of honeyed beer of roots that was surprisingly... tolerable.

Korane could smell the pork and mushrooms in the steam from the bowl, along with another strange scent–a sharp, spicy sweetness. She furtively lowered the scarf around her face to eat, leaning forward so that the bear skin obscured her face in shadow. She could taste beaten egg of some kind in the broth, as well. The soup rattled the cold from her bones and the hot drink expelled it. Her goblin devoured it greedily, but she took her time measuring the taste of it. The soup tasted how it smelled, if more intensely, but she could not place the strange flavor even by the time she reached the bottom of the bowl.

Korane pulled up her scarf, turned, and rose from her stool. She nudged the goblin with her fist. He hopped down and scurried to the sled, skirting around the reclining wolf and rushing to make pace with her, hauling the sled and sputtering apologies for making her wait as she discreetly spread more of the red clay over her face under the scarf. They walked around the periphery. Korane's mission was going surprisingly well–to gather information on industry and troop numbers. She had found Kogylar and gained entry, and her disguise had surprisingly held up. Her slave had obeyed her and protected her secret. She had seriously considered killing him before they got to the city to answer that risk, but was pleased that she had decided he could still be of more use. She winced as her old leg wound twinged, as it sometimes did. They wandered only a few moments before Korane froze.

Humans. Marching by in a formation like soldiers. Being led by a hobgoblin. Laughing and speaking in Goblin. Carrying weapons. Wearing armor and something of a livery. Humans working–no, fighting–for the enemy. *Who* are *they?* Korane urged the slave to the side of the path as soon as she could. She was having trouble breathing under the scarf. The mud on her skin felt grainy and filthy and the cured bear head skin felt wet and slimy. She pulled the scarf open a little and leaned against the wall to breathe.

Chapter 13

A soup counter on the upper levels of the Place-called-Kogylar.
By the Goblin Calendar, late in the Eleventh Moon Cycle, 3114.
By the Human Calendar, Sortingday, third week of Ongkanir, 794.
A mid-autumn evening with freezing rain.

The messenger stared bleakly into her soup. No work. No
messages that needed taking, at least none that were not going to be
taken by patrols or someone else. It was not like she was the only
messenger, either. For all of their faults–their laziness, their poorly
veiled cowardice–they did not have the stain on their honor that she
had. So, if it came to a question, all others would receive tasks
before her. No messages to take, no work. No one would hire her as
a scout. She had been disowned, stripped of her weapons and armor.
The only thing to give her a warm welcome was the wolf for which
she had to beg from the houndmaster and the soup in front of her.

Her knee ached. It ached sometimes in the rain or the fog,
where the scout with eyes that glittered with hate had put an arrow
through her leg. The two orcs to her right ate in silence. She slurped
a few spoonfuls and continued to stare ahead blankly. Another
pair sat down a few seats to her left at the soup counter. One of
them was a goblin; the other seemed to be a Hobgoblin woman,
by the height, build, and demeanor. The goblin was fully an adult
in its physicality, but seemed gleeful like a child. The messenger
examined them out of the corner of her eye. There was something
familiar about the hobgoblin's eyes. She risked looking longer and
watched the hobgoblin pull down her scarf to eat. *Red skin! She's
from the right! Or maybe the invader side.* The messenger had heard
that people further to the right along the mountains had different
customs, and not only could enter and leave tribes, but could atone
for past mistakes with hard work. *Maybe… maybe this is a chance.
Leriyet smile on me. I will have to ask to see her, Great One.*

Before the messenger realized it, the hobgoblin and her
companion finished and rose from their seats. The goblin dodged
a nip from the messenger's wolf and retrieved a ramshackle sled
which he clearly constructed himself. 'Great One,' she heard him

call amidst an apology. *That is it. She is the great one of her tribe. That is her slave. Maybe her harem slave? This is my chance!* The messenger hastily finished her soup, and retrieved her wolf just in time to see the hobgoblin disappear into the crowd. She tugged at the wolf's reins and it reluctantly followed as the messenger through the congested streets. Dreading that she may have just spent her only chance at a better life on finishing her soup, she began to get angry with herself and huffed vexedly until she spied the hobgoblin with her slave and their sled pausing against the wall of the periphery. The great one leaned against the stone bricks and the goblin slave waited obediently.

It is now or not at all! The messenger braced herself and pushed through the crowd, ignoring the surly protests at her wolf hindering the flow of traffic. She reached the edge and urged her steed to the side and out of the way. The hobgoblin looked at the messenger and dropped her scarf back in place.

"What do you want?" the hobgoblin from the right asked.

"I… I, uh…" The messenger had no idea what to say. "I heard you are from the right of the Mountains."

The hobgoblin stopped leaning on the wall and stood up straight, on guard. "Who did you hear that from?"

"Uh, sorry, I mean, you have the look. The red skin. And your accent. I saw you at the soup counter."

The hobgoblin visibly relaxed, though the goblin was still eyeing the messenger's wolf warily. "Oh," she said. "Well, I am not from here. What of it?"

The messenger continued, nervously. "So, uh, I hear about the tribes from the right of the Mountains. I hear that people can enter new tribes." She shuffled her feet anxiously and suppressed as her knee twinged and nearly buckled. "Tribes there… you can, sort of, change your life, make up for your past, try new things. Like, you know, if you were given to a smithing occupation and you wanted to try building, then you could change and join a building occupation."

The hobgoblin eyes burned a hole into the messenger as she looked upon her messenger silently. The messenger looked down, feeling foolish. "You have something you wish to change?"

the hobgoblin asked.

The messenger looked up sharply. "Yes, I… uh…" She had still not properly found her words. "I want to change my future."

"Change your future? Is it because of your past?" the hobgoblin asked.

The messenger silently cursed herself. She thought that the hobgoblins from the right had customs that allowed redemption, but she did not want to risk her future on hearsay. "Well, I–"

"Here, now," called another voice, thick with an Orcish accent. They all looked over to see the apparent shopkeeper. A bald orc, wearing a leather kilt and an undyed wool shirt was standing in the doorway to a shop carved into the peripheral wall. "I am open. Come in and see." The messenger's heart sank. She was losing her chance.

"What do you have?" the hobgoblin from the right end of the mountains asked.

"I have the finest selection of slaves in Kogylar," he declared proudly, "all types. Men. Women. Adults. Children. Goblins, orcs, kobolds. We even have some humans!"

The hobgoblin from the right said nothing. She seemed to just be staring at him in the same way, judging by the Orcish slaver's reaction. He looked at them hopefully, eager for the first business of the day, but as the silence dragged on, he seemed to think that he had offended somehow and deferred. "I apologize, Great One. I did not mean to offend," he said in accented Goblin.

"You do not know my customs. I will look past the offense. Let us look at what you have," she said abruptly, and beckoned her Goblin slave to leave the sled. The messenger bade her wolf to lay down by the sled and awkwardly followed them inside. Sconces were lit for customers to clearly see the wares, but they looked to be a relatively recent addition, judging by the fresh masonry around them. If the slaver was telling the truth and he had humans, exotic wares in the Place-called-Kogylar and other cities of the mountains, that would be why. The messenger had heard that humans could not see heat and needed actual light to see anything, which she believed to be true from her few brief skirmishes with them.

The store was deeper than one would assume looking from

the outside in. The front of the store had a narrow space designated for payment, with a broader space in the rear for cages. Two large aisles were lined with cages on both sides. The hobgoblin and the Orcish slaver were already back amidst the cages. The messenger caught up to them. The cages held one or two slaves, each. They were mostly well organized, keeping the types together. Males and females separated. Orcs with orcs. Goblins with goblins. They actually did have some humans. About thirty of them, with pink skin and mostly not-black hair.

"I am surprised you run this place by yourself," the hobgoblin from the right side of the mountains was saying.

"I do have help, Great One, but they do not arrive until the moon is high. Business is usually slow first thing in the day."

"How much?" she asked.

"For what kind, Great One? They are not all the same. The goblins are a black mountain. Orcs are two," he said.

"Black mountain? Be patient, we do not have the same coins where I am from."

"Oh, right. Sorry, Great One. The bronze coins with the mountain stamped on them. Sometimes people also call them black stones around here."

"Thank you. What about the humans?"

"The humans? Well, you seem to have an eye for the exotic, Great One." The Orcish slaver tilted his head back, smug in his knowledge that he had a healthy selection of humans available for sale.

The hobgoblin from the right side of the mountains paused before responding. "There is great demand for humans where I am from." She gazed in that same way into the cages of humans. Each of them shivering, cowering, eating some kind of porridge with their hands from a tin plate, or sleeping.

"Well?" she demanded impatiently.

"Eight black mountains, Great One," he responded, flashing a toothy, welcoming grin, "more or less, depending on which one."

"And what is back there?" She pointed to a door that the

messenger had not noticed at the back of the cage area.

"Back there? Oh, that's mostly supplies and where we dump some waste. There is a rain stream, like most of the shops and dwellings in the Place-called-Kogylar, so we do not have to go out for water. Truly some wonders your goblinkin can make in building this place, eh? At any rate, we have some others back there, but nothing you would be interested in, Great One."

"Oh?" There was an edge to her voice.

The slaver looked down again. "Well, so I would think, Great One. Unruly ones are back there. Brutes. Orcs and a bugbear. If I keep them out in the main cage area, they get very loud and the other ones soil the cages something bad. It really kills me when they do that. The ones in the back area are really only good for fighting pits."

"Fighting pits?" The great one turned her head to look sidelong at the orc.

"Uh, a place where slaves are made to fight each other or beasts as the joy of the show, Great One." She looked at him for a moment and he dropped his eyes. "Yes, I figured that would not be to your taste, Great One. It is beneath one such as you."

"I believe we would just call it something different. I was unfamiliar with the term." She motioned to the door in the back. "Please show me."

The slaver looked apprehensive but headed towards the door with the great one from the right with her goblin. The messenger followed a few paces behind. The messenger passed through the door, waving back the smell when she was suddenly slammed against the wall. The Orcish slaver frantically scrambled against her and struck her across the cheek with an open hand. Before she realized it, the messenger had produced her skinning knife, seized his right arm with her left and drew a semi-circular arc across his throat, over his upper arm, and across his stomach. He staggered back and away from the messenger, clutching his throat with one hand and holding his entrails in the other, spluttering blood from his mouth and throat. He collapsed and squirmed for a few moments before lying still.

The goblin got up from the floor, with labored breathing,

clutching his stomach as if he had been kicked hard. The brutes in the cages howled with glee. The messenger barely noticed the orcs and a bugbear in their separate cages and stared at the dead slaver in disbelief before looking up at the hobgoblin from the right side of the mountains, who was drilling a hole through the messenger with her stare.

"Great One! I–I–I did not mean to–" The messenger was cut off as the great one raised her hand for silence. The messenger fell silent amidst the racket from the brutes.

"It is done. We will dispose of the body. Get an axe from the front. I saw one there." The messenger went to the front area and found the axe that the great one had mentioned. The great one took it and hacked the corpse to pieces, throwing the bits to the brutes. Their howling abated as they gratefully consumed their former captor raw.

"Get this clean," she told the goblin, gesturing towards the blood and gore staining the floor. The goblin briefly disappeared, then returned with a rag and bucket. He filled the bucket in the rain stream trickling down at the end of the back room and scrubbed with a vigor that made up for his limited strength until the floor showed no signs of violence, before pouring it all down the runoff of the stream. By the time he had finished, there was nothing left of the slaver. Not even his clothes.

The great one exited the back room into the storefront, Goblin slave in tow. The messenger followed, full of palpable fear. "Great One, what will happen now?"

The hobgoblin from the right turned to look at her from the corner of her eye. "What do you want to happen?" She did not wait for the messenger's answer before she turned towards a cage of humans. The messenger heard the jingle of keys.

The messenger half-raised her hand in disbelief. "What are you doing?"

"I am taking these humans," the great one replied without looking up. One by one, she opened each cage of humans. They stirred and looked fearfully at their liberator.

"Taking them?"

"Yes. Like I said, there is need for them elsewhere," the

great one nodded to her side without looking at the messenger. "Besides. Orcs come to kill and take. They can enjoy their own practices and see how they like them."

"You are not going to tell anyone about what happened here?" the messenger pressed anxiously.

The great one paused to unlock the last human cage. "Why would I?"

The messenger shrugged plaintively. "Well, I killed him."

The great one shifted her weight to lean on one leg and finished turning the key in the lock. "I suppose you did. You keep your knife very sharp, too."

"My knife? Great One, am I not in a lot of trouble?" The messenger's heart was filling with fear as she further realized what she had just done.

The great one did not look up as she ushered the fearful humans out of their cages as if she were moving goats from one pen to another. "I do not think you are." She looked at the messenger again. "Why are you following me?"

The messenger let out a great breath of exasperation. "I was hoping to join your tribe, Great One. I have a past that I cannot escape here and I seek a new chance."

The great one continued to fix her steely gaze upon her. "What else can you do?"

"I used to be a cavalry leader in a warband of wolf riders, made up of the great Wiridil." The messenger hung her head in shame. "I served under Dariyet the Great before he died in the hills further away from here. I missed the battle. That is my past that I cannot escape."

"Fine, but what else can you do?" the great one said, unfazed.

The messenger glanced up. "What else?"

"Right, what did you do as a cavalry leader and what else can you do?"

"Um…" It was surreal. She was making this description to a great one she did not know, who did not know her, immediately after she had killed a slaver, and the great one was claiming his slaves as bounty. *Wait. It would be my own bounty, if anything, but… I would have to admit to killing the slaver to assert my claim.*

"Um, Great One, how are you claiming those slaves if you did not kill their owner?" the messenger asked tentatively.

"Oh, that is how it works here? I need to kill you?" The great one turned to her and the goblin ducked behind the corner of a cage.

"NO! No! No, Great One, you can have them. I give you my claim. I just want to join your tribe."

The great one sighed from behind her scarf. "You still have not told me what you can do."

"I can lead and train soldiers, mounted or dismounted. I can fight with many different weapons. I can shoot a bow from the wolf at a run. I can track, scout, hunt, skin and tan hides. I know a bit of arrow making and fletching."

"Hm. Fine. I am taking these humans out of here." She turned to the Goblin slave. "We are leaving."

"But you said we would be here for a few days!" he protested.

"We are leaving, if you know what is good for you," she said quietly. He gulped and looked down. The hobgoblin then started speaking to the humans in another language. A strange language that the messenger thought sounded familiar. It reminded her of what she had overheard when she was surveilling the human army in the hills. She did not know the language, but the humans clearly did. At least most of them. The ones that did not looked around in puzzlement until some other one excitedly whispered to them. The great one was making calming motions with her hands open, palms facing down and repeatedly moving them up and down, so as to keep them quiet.

"What about these other ones, Great One? These other slaves?" the messenger asked.

"What of them? You want to take some?" the great one said.

The messenger looked around. The other slaves looked at

her. Some hopeful, some disinterested or bleak and hollow-eyed. "I think I do, Great One, but I am worried about being able to feed them."

"I am sure we can think of something," the great one said.

***

Much later, the moon was setting and they were hours away from the Place-called-Kogylar. It had been a bizarre departure. At least the freezing rain had stopped. So many slaves walking in line up through the gates of the Place-called-Kogylar. They gained many strange looks, but no one said anything about the wealthy hobgoblin from the right side of the mountains that had bought out the slaver's inventory. There were other slavers at the Place-called-Kogylar, but this one was not the least of them and the only one to claim having humans for sale.

They left the road quickly to move through the forest and rough terrain, degenerating from an orderly line into a moving crowd. The great one had spoken to one of the human slaves and left him to walk at the front and keep direction while the great one covered their tracks herself. They were going downhill, away from the mountains, not to the right. The messenger was surprised that the hobgoblin had been able to gain dominance over the slaves so quickly–at least the human ones. She had heard some of them could be quite stubborn, though she supposed that any person in a situation such as that might be. Just like some took to honor of slavery easily.

The messenger said nothing until they stopped to make camp. Some of the humans were digging a firepit with the scant few tools they took from the slaver's office while the other slaves sat amongst the trees. The messenger recognized the technique to conceal the smoke of the fire. The great one had set the goblin to take a few other slaves and gather firewood. The rest of the slaves rested from the walk or constructed rudimentary shelters from pine boughs.

All of the thoughts that had been simmering beneath her shock and fatigue boiled up to the surface. "Great One, where are we going?" the messenger blurted out. "Come to think of it, I do not even know your name! What is the name of this tribe?"

"Watch your tone with me," the great one said. The messenger was silent, but expectant. The great one turned from her and picked up a leather waterskin. "You move like the knife in your hand. I recognized you from before. The scar on your jaw was my gift, just as you gave me a matching one," she said.

From before what? I got this scar from... The great one took off the scarf, but was facing away. She poured some water onto her hands and scrubbed her face before tossing the water bag down and turning back to the messenger. Eyes blazing with cold hate bore down on the messenger. She removed the bear head skin and tresses of hair, black as a raven fell to her shoulders. A small scar on her cheek marked her.

The messenger stared at her in recognition, "You!"

Chapter 14

The town of Serna, Yvel Principality.
By the Human Calendar, Breathday (fifth day of the week), first week of
Nansima (ninth month of the year), 794.
A sunny and brisk late autumn afternoon.

𝕯areum's tall, broad frame slumped wearily in his saddle as they rounded the last bend.

Baryn had a light hop in his step. His jolly belly had become lean from all of the marching from the start of the war. "It'll be good to be home, eh, My Lord?" Baryn had been with Dareum and the militia since their first patrol after the raid where Baryn watched his wife die in front of him.

"That's right, tenman, even if it's only for a day," Dareum agreed. "Looks like they finished the palisade, too."

Serna lay slightly downhill from them as they approached from the west. The town was nestled in a small valley where the mountain streams fed it with fresh water year round. They could see several trailing wisps of the smoke of industry rising from walls constructed of stout logs and evenly spaced wooden towers. There were several gates, too; one each facing the north and south roads, one facing the hills, and one facing the farmlands to the west. His mother, Lady Mariss, had already put the new labor to work.

The prince's sappers were supervising the prisoners from the Battle of Borly in the early construction of a stone wall. That was another feat that Dareum's mother had pulled off, convincing the prince's staff and officers to supply additional assistance to aid in fortifying the town. Dareum imagined that other places might also be in need of some of the help that Serna was receiving–that they were receiving more than a fair share–though he could not be certain. Jovaela had arrived a week ago during Dareum's last stop in Serna with Holbrin and a large contingent of new elves. Some were remaining in Serna, but others were heading further south to Keppa. Jovaela had told him Borly already had a strong stone wall, but from his last visit to Keppa five years ago, he knew Keppa did not have one.

Dareum was joined by twenty militia and elves, in addition to some others they had picked up along the way. Along with Baryn, who was now a tenleader, he had taken the three best trackers still available to him: Arynn and Eevarel; both elves, one laconic, one lively–and Garven, the young huntsman from Serna. Eevarel was an accomplished tracker but far better with her bow and sword. As much as he wanted to rely on Garven first, being a Serna man, Arynn was the best tracker available now that Korane was off elsewhere helping the Prince's Army. Korane had been vague about what her assignment was, but she was clear that she would be gone for a long while.

Dareum turned to take stock of his company. Oddly, one of the female orcs that Mkaela had saved from execution had left her side and joined the militia, naming herself Karsi. It was difficult to say whether she spoke broken Marin mixed with some Eklendan words, or the other way around, but she could communicate in basic terms. Taram, another tenleader in the militia who never seemed to age beyond his fifties with scraggly, greyed hair, said that her knowledge of the Orcish language would help, too.

As a slave, Karsi had never been trained to fight, but she possessed natural strength and a long reach, and they desperately needed people. She stayed in Mkaela's old bakery. Some welcomed her while others openly shunned her, and it was not uncommon for someone to paint nasty threats, and drawings on the bakery, but it was just as common for several folk to be cleaning it off with the Orcish woman.

The rest of the company were militia from the town proper or its outlying farms, and there were many new faces. When Prince Arnold ordered Dareum's father, Koval, to stand up another two regiments from Serna, the task of recruitment had fallen to Dareum and Judane. The militia had split–some wished to remain with the militia; an equal contingent wanted to join the regiment. That meant that both parties had needed to draw from villages well outside of Serna.

The urgent need for recruits was something which Dareum's increasingly bleak task addressed. Dareum and the patrol had been tracking enemy raiding parties, presumably the same orcs or goblins, maybe additional raiding parties of them, that had been attacking caravans and villages. Most often, they would find the aftermath. Razed villages and ransacked caravans, littered with bodies. Every now and again, they found someone that happened to have been out in the fields, hunting in the woods, foraging for herbs, or traveling when the raids came. Dareum and his patrol would take them in and offer them a place to nurse their anger. A place to do something about it. This helped Tenleader Liri's recruiting party, as well.

Dareum and his patrol passed a few new buildings under construction outside of the palisade before walking through the western gate that faced the farmlands. They were greeted by scattered waves and cheers.

"Alright," Dareum said, "muster again at first light." Addressing his company, he continued. "Inspection, breakfast, then we leave. Off with you." The militia patrol dispersed. Some of the militiamen shambled off equally as wearily as they had traveled on the march, while others were suddenly bursting with energy and ran off to see whomever was waiting for them.

Dareum walked his brown gelding, Creasan, towards Covendran Manor. Passing the Moradran, he noted hastily constructed tables and saw that the common room that had been temporarily used as the militia headquarters had become permanent. Wooden awnings had been erected over the tables to shelter patrons from the rain and sleet of the unseasonably late autumn. The first snow would come soon. In the center of the tables, the inn had built a large firepit to keep the general area warmer. It had become a meeting place for the community in the evening. People would tell stories or play music. Old feuds had washed away over the half year since the beginning of the war. People laughed together who would have come to blows in months prior.

Dareum overheard bits of conversation as he passed by. "Baryn? Have you seen Julian?" a woman's voice asked.

"Ah, Terah, I thought he went out on a different patrol..." Baryn's voice answered.

These were a good, strong people, Dareum told himself, not for the first time. Wearing a contented but tired smile, he finished this part of the journey in thoughtful silence.

After brushing down Creasan and handing him off to a groom, he washed the dust of the road and field off of his body and changed into fresh breeches, a clean cotton shirt, and a wool housecoat before joining his mother and sister for dinner.

"I don't know how you did it, Madam, getting every last favor from the Prince's Army. I almost feel bad for the other towns," Judane was saying to their mother.

Mariss smirked. "I have my ways, Darups. Everyone ends up going the way I want in the end," she said, mumbling under her breath. "Even your father."

Dareum took a bite out of the crusty bread. The bread was not the same since Mkaela's bakery stopped providing them. Still, it was far and away better than the same dried rations of salted meat and dried grain biscuits. *Those biscuits*, he grumbled, remembering the multitude of times he had almost broken a tooth on them. Every time he thought he was used to them, he only had to wait for the next meal to remember how sore his jaw got from chewing on them. So Dareum was thankful for the bread, even if it was not as tasty as Mkaela's. Whoever made the bread now, was making bread for everyone, and did not have the luxury of time to put in the niceties that she had.

Niceties. Dareum was lost, thinking about the variety of breads available in the capital. At the prince's victory banquet in Yvel. So lost was he in his thoughts that he did not realize that he had finished his bread, the pheasant, and the turnips until he absently looked down and was surprised to see an empty plate. He looked up and his mother and sisters were both staring at him with annoyed expressions.

"What?"

His mother shook her head wryly, "nothing at all, Darups."

"Any luck on the raiding parties?" Judane asked.

"No. Sadly." Dareum's eyes went wide as his thoughts went back to the scenes he had witnessed over the past week. Carnage. Broken bodies left in the sun for days or weeks. By the road or in the fields. Villages or hamlets, caravans or lone travelers. Usually stripped of usable goods.

Dareum looked up from his thoughts to see the two of

them staring at him again. "Hm?"

Judane raised her eyebrows in concern. "We lost you again. What is it?"

"Oh, it's probably nothing," Dareum shook his head, blinking away the memories, but they both gave him the look. The look that meant 'you had better tell me because I will be annoyed at you if you don't.' "Right, then. Fine, Judy." He was mildly annoyed with himself. "It's just. There seems to be something off."

"Like what?"

"Like... I never find any orc or goblin bodies. I find an axe or a sword or a spear that clearly belonged to an orc. We would find Goblin arrows. Arynn said that you can tell by the notches in the sides for barbs. Never find any bodies of the enemy."

"Maybe they take them with them?" Madam Mariss suggested.

"Maybe that's it, Madam," he mused, "but it just seems... sometimes we find Goblin arrows and an Orcish axe in the same place, but..." He trailed off.

"But what?" Judane prodded.

"It's just that, when we fought them in the hills east of here, yes, there were orcs and hobgoblins working together. But, it wasn't closely together. It seemed like there were groups of orcs and groups of hobgoblins. The groups were working with each other, but the groups were separate. Does that make sense? Here it seems like the raids, some are made by a group of orcs *and* goblins." Dareum paused, considering what he had just said. *And... Now that I think about it, goblins are supposed to be very short. Orcs are very tall... How would they march together? Would the goblins ride in a wagon or get carried? The orcs would probably get sour about that...*

"What do you mean 'the raids are done by one group or another?' What does that mean?" Judane asked.

"Oh. Sorry. I've been talking a lot with Eevarel and Arynn on this and the others," he said.

Judane smirked, "Oh?"

"Eh, come on, nothing like that!" Dareum protested.

"It's… things are too bad for anything like that. Besides. I'm pretty sure their attentions are somewhere else."

"Oh, fine." Judane swatted in his direction and rolled her eyes, "so go on."

"Right. Where was I?"

"You were talking about the raids being done by one group or another," Madam Mariss said.

"Right. The raids are in too many different places for it to be one or two groups. There are a lot of them, but it looks like all of them are orcs or goblins or both… almost… hm," Dareum started, trailing off again.

"Almost what?" Judane asked.

"Oh, nothing. It would be crazy. Don't mind me." Dareum waved off the matter. "How's the regiment forming up, *Regiment Leader*?" he asked Judane.

"Forming two battalions. Both have two companies coming along. Hope to add a third company to each before starting a third battalion. Not to mention the fourth battalion… or the detachments…" Judane suddenly sounded tired when the topic changed. "The recruiting you're doing on the side is really helping. Thanks, Darups."

"Hm. Not much else left for people in a situation like that." Dareum smiled weakly.

Judane sat up straighter. "Well, they're good soldiers. It's awful for them, but it's some kind of awful for most of us. You remember."

"I do," he replied. The conversation naturally died down for a bit after the discussion had turned towards heavier matters. One of the house staff brought steaming tea made from flower petals. It was one of Tyrnimar's concoctions that he had been willing to share the recipe of. Dareum had been skeptical at first, but it calmed the nerves and was good on a cold night like this.

Madam Mariss tried to change the subject. "So, what's next, Darups?"

"Hm? Sorry, Madam, we'll be off in the morning after breakfast."

"Where to?"

Dareum sipped his tea and exhaled ruefully at the reminder of what lay ahead. "More of the outlying farmlands to the east, for those that haven't already evacuated to the west." He was not looking forward to the prospect of another five or ten days of finding the corpses of the people that they were charged to protect. "Then, we'll turn west. There are a few villages that we haven't visited yet, and we haven't gotten out to Bervale yet."

Madam Mariss nursed her own cup of tea. "Have you been up towards Krogen?"

"No," he said, looking at her sharply, "why?"

She shrugged and shook her head slightly. "Just curious. Holbrin said that some of his elves had gone that way to provide support to the area, but I never hear about how things are going there. It's been a while since I've been up that way, so I was just curious."

"Huh," he started to relax back in the chair.

"What is it? What was all that about?" his mother asked, eyeing him carefully, her face bathing in steam from her cup.

"It's just that the raids west of Bervale stopped. At least, that's what I'm told when I check in with the garrisons and ask the merchants. The merchants that are still alive, that is. All around Krogen, they just stopped."

Mariss sipped her tea before speaking, "A place to go, then?"

"Yes, ma'am." Dareum became lost in thought once more and the other two gave up on tempting him into participation.

Mariss turned back towards the only person investing any effort in conversation. "So, what else do you need for the regiment, Judy?"

Judane pursed her lips. "I'm having trouble forming a horse detachment. I might only be able to form the one, and not a very big one, at that. I had meant to have a cavalry detachment and a mounted scout detachment. Really, I wanted the battalions to have their own scouts. Might have to settle."

"Maybe that's a better way. There are a few generals and

rulers that concentrated their cavalry."

"Just as many separated them for use across the line, mother," Judane argued.

Mariss chided her daughter. "Don't get short with me."

Judane grimaced and looked away. "Sorry, mother. It's just that they're light horses and I wanted the battalions to be able to scout ahead more. If they knew what they were getting into, then they might be able to enter the battle with an advantage."

"Reading your father's copy of Beren the Great, I see?" Her mother smiled.

"His techniques worked well." Judane focused on measuring her tone as she argued. "But he did both. He dispersed his light horse and concentrated his heavy."

"That he did. The Panr'ails are helping, right?" Madam Mariss asked.

Judane flashed a sour expression, "Not as much as I like."

"What do you mean?" Madam Mariss asked concernedly. She seemed surprised.

"They've had problems since the Hills. When Ervan died," Judane explained. Mariss nodded in understanding. "They aren't talking to Julian and they aren't willing to do much besides sell us horses," Judane finished.

"Well, we'll see about that. I'll see them in the morning."

"Thank you, Mother. If you can get them to do more, that would really help," Judane made a small, grateful smile. "If you can get that Gunst fellow in Yvel to answer letters about needing battalion leaders, that would be great, too."

"I think I can make a trip," Madam Mariss agreed with a smile. "I'm sure the Panr'ails would be willing to escort the Lady Serna."

Judane chuckled and looked down into her tea before looking up again. Mariss smiled at Judane.

"What is it, Madam?"

"I'm proud of you."

***

Elsewhere in Serna

Turin had been watching this fellow for a few hours. He was not who Turin was here for, but he showed much promise. Turin sat at one of the tables in the common room of the Moradran Inn in the formerly sleepy town of Serna. Turin had previously passed through here a few times, but the war had changed it in just a short six months. One of the inns burned down. Turin could not remember its name, but he remembered liking their parsnip soup better than this one. It had reminded him most of the parsnip soup he grew up eating. *'Course they're not around anymore, either*, he thought bitterly.

Shaking himself, he returned his attention to his quarry. Fair-skinned and blond, the narrow nose sealed him as a Marin. He sat alone in a room full of activity. Where others were glad to be alive, seeking the company of friends or a lover, this one kept the company of an ale and a book while shunning half of his meal. Turin's gaze lingered on him for a moment and then turned to the task that was the primary reason for his journey to Serna.

Turin watched an ageless man get up from a crowded table amid laughs and cheers. The man moved towards the door, pursued by well-wishes and challenges to come back and drink more. Laughing, he waved them off and continued through the exit. Turin followed discreetly, but he knew what would happen, given the ageless man's preceding reputation.

Turin rounded the corner and found himself face to face with the ageless man. Looking like any other with wild, scraggly hair and a lined face like someone in their late forties or fifties that had a difficult life, he irritably sneered at Turin, hands on his hips.

"What? You've been here for hours. What?"

Turin knew it would come to this and had decided to force the issue, leading to this conversation. He braced himself internally. "My superiors are asking you to come in. From what I understand, they have already asked you."

"And did they tell you my answer?" The ageless man was hostile.

Turin had read the limited dossier prior to departing

225

Yvel. He knew that this ageless man had firmly refused before, and also that he loathed this life. *Perhaps it is best to pretend to be conciliatory and then be blunt.* "You know how this would normally proceed. I would make small threats about how we could make life unpleasant for you. I would rather not insult one of your experience. We are desperate." Turin kept his tone even. He could appear plaintive, but not overly so, or the act would become too obvious.

"*Desperate?* For what?" the ageless man demanded.

"Translations."

"Translations? From what?" the ageless man asked.

"Old Paetic, mostly," Turin elaborated. "We have only a few who possess the knowledge, and many of those are on other assignments. And we have lost much of our other people. So we have a very, very limited staff from whom to choose, and sacrifice other needs when we do so. That is why I've been sent for you."

"I see," the ageless man said. He closed his eyes and smiled wryly. "And you have a bounty ready to pull me in on if I don't go?"

"I do, but as I said earlier, I wish to first ask out of respect." *Almost there...*

"Fine. I'll make the arrangements and leave in the morning. You have some document I can give to my company to release me from enlistment?"

"I do, but need to know the name to put in," Turin asked pointedly.

"Taram Karidran." The ageless man sighed and shrugged. Turin went to one of the outdoor tables in front of the Moradran and hastily penned the name onto the document, sprinkled sand on it and blew it away to dry the ink. Airing it for a few minutes, he rolled it up and used the heat from the firepit in the middle of the tables to melt a bit of a candle. After dripping some blue wax onto the folded letter, he pressed Lord Gunst's signet into it and handed it to the ageless man. The ageless man took it and left without further word.

Now, to the extra task. Turin headed back inside to the blond man reading and drinking alone.

226

Turin approached the lonely man. "Mind if I join you?"

The lonely man shrugged and apathetically waved a hand towards the seat opposite him, but continued reading. Turin, after having watched him for some time, felt that a direct approach would serve well. *Lot of being direct for one night*, Turin internally commented.

"You want work?"

"I've got work." The lonely man did not look up from his book.

"Work that takes you away from here?" Turin continued.

The lonely man set his book down. *That got his attention.* "What kind?"

"Lots of travel. Learning some new things," Turin said. "It's for the adjutant of the Prince's Army."

The lonely man looked at him sidelong, "Who's that?"

"Lord Gunst Ver'ail," Turin nodded, trying to keep the lonely man's eye contact.

"Who? Doesn't matter. Nevermind," the lonely man turned back to his pages.

I'm losing him. Time for a gamble. "It's dangerous work."

The lonely man looked up again. "Dangerous?"

"Like I said, lots of travel. Alone. Not settling down anywhere. You hear how the roads are now, these days? Very dangerous."

The lonely man put the book down, hesitantly committing to the conversation. "Alright, fine. I think I can leave the militia. Where do I go?"

"Krogen. I want you to meet someone there."

The lonely man closed his book. "Fine. I'll leave tonight."

"Oh, wait. If you leave tonight... I need a few days to make some arrangements. Can you wait?" *I didn't expect him to be this eager to get out of here...*

"Not here," the lonely man slumped. "You offered me a chance away from this place. I'll take it."

"Can you wait in Yvel?" Turin suggested.

"What for? Yvel's out of the way. Way out of the way. I can be there in Krogen in less than a tenday. Much better to take the road to—" the lonely man started.

Yes. He's a good find. Hopefully he can do what's needed. "Alright, alright, wait in Krogen. I'll have my man come find you. Here." Turin tossed him a small purse of coin. "That will cover the stay in between and then some, plus meals. He'll be there inside the month."

The purse jingled as the lonely man caught it. "Thanks. So, who's hiring me?"

"I told you, the Lord Gunst—" Turin began.

"No, I mean you."

"Oh. Jern," Turin said, careful not to use any of his other aliases. "What name should I give my man to find you by?"

"Julian."

***

Crown Sorcerers' Proving Grounds

"Alright, try it again," said Ayza. She made a pushing motion in front of her and held her arms there. She squinted in concentration and the air between her and Tyrnimar and Ayza shimmered for an instant.

Tyrnimar loosed an arrow from his bow. It sailed through the air towards Ayza and abruptly rebounded with a thud off of Ayza's shield of air. He sent more, each stopped by the air shield. Tyrnimar lowered his bow and Kora outstretched her hands. Flames leapt forth from her palms, cascading over the surface of Ayza's shield. After a few seconds, small arcs of lightning reached from Ayza's palms to the places on the shield where Kora's flames had impacted it.

Tyrnimar squinted through the flames and saw Ayza's aura changing. *Access to more of the powers had by her is being gained.* Glancing to the side, he noticed changes in Kora's aura, as well. *As more control over their powers is gained by them, new layers of*

228

power are revealed to them.

Kora's flames stopped. Despite the cold, she wore a winter dress modified with the short sleeves of a summer garment to keep it from catching fire like the others. She had advanced enough that had she been wearing long sleeves, there would only be minor singing at the cuffs now.

"Would it be tried by you?" he asked Kora. She nodded and turned away from Ayza to face the field. Holding her hands close together, she focused. He could see the energies swirl around her hands before other eyes would see the tiny ball of flame appear between her hands. He watched her summon more energy from her surroundings, pulling more and more heat from the cold ground, as the ball churned and grew. She began to shake.

"It should be thrown!" Tyrnimar called.

"I'll try," Kora said in a strained voice. She lifted her hands and sent the ball of flame into an arc. She did not throw it, literally, but rather directed the swirling energies to push it away from herself, trying to aim it. It flew and began to fall. *Too close!!*

"Look–" he cried, but it was too late. The ball struck the ground about thirty paces away, the shock knocking them all on their backs. Tyrnimar and Kora lay on the ground groaning and aching.

"Are you alright?" Tyrnimar could faintly hear Ayza through the ringing in his ears. It had been a while since he had heard the impact of one of those spells, and he had never been that close.

"What about you," he weakly murmured.

"I'm fine. The shield held," she said.

Did it!? The shield of hers held!? Tyrnimar was surprised that Ayza's shield was already so resilient. He was not surprised at the strength of Kora's fireball, though she would need to work on range for it to be useful and safe. Ayza... she would soon realize her power over lightning. *It is wondered by me if the patterns will be followed by them.*

Tyrnimar was glad that Zaya, the freckled half-Tamark, half-Eklendan woman that Tyrnimar was certain was sent as a spy to observe him, had departed from the proving grounds. She had said something about needing to ask her uncle about publishing her notes as a history of Yvel's discovery of magic, but he suspected that whomever she worked for had reassigned her. Tyrnimar bleakly wondered what could have been more important than the chance of stealing magical secrets from him. He also wondered, if he was correct about her, what other kinds of spycraft her organization was up to.

Chapter 15

City of Kotara, Kotara Principality.
By the Human Calendar, Thirstday, third week of Nansima, 794.
A windy, late autumn morning; snow on the ground.

Liveried guards crossed halberds across Bisin's path, blocking his way. They spoke in a plain and tired tone with him, as if he was far from the first person to try walking right in.

"I have a petition," Bisin said. At least, that is what he *thought* he said. One of the guards made an annoyed face at him and waved him off. Bisin's Tamark was poor. Very poor. He had started learning it from Tansher a month ago and Tansher was not a good teacher. But, she was the only one in the crew that knew any Tamark, *and she's Jak's girl, so no one can say anything*, he grumbled. Still, Bisin got what he needed.

The guards were posted at all entrances to the palace and quite attentive. Bisin made his way through the crowds in the palace square and back into the marketplace. The cobblestones in the square were wet from snow that had been trampled to cold water, but the stone ended once he entered the market. He and everyone else in the city slopped through, the ground alternating between muddy slush and slushy mud. Most of the vegetables for sale were roots, and almost all of the meat available was salted. What to expect? Snow topped the roofs. Icy winds sliced between the buildings. It was winter. No fruit for sale.

A gust of wind picked up a spray of snow from a nearby roof, scattering it over the market-goers. Bisin pulled his felted wool hood closer down over his shaved head and smiled in spite of the cold. It was not winter yet, not actually, but winter came early to mountain cities like Kotara, nestled in the Samziks. Bisin liked the winter best for one simple reason, particularly in cities. The smell. Bisin hated the smell of cities. The smell of people. They way they reeked between baths that were never frequent enough. The smell of the scat and the piss and the trash and the rotten meat. Bisin hated that he could smell when his neighbors were trying to make a child.

He hated it all. Hated hearing them, too, but it was mostly the smell.

Bisin quit the city once he was old enough to leave his family. Hated the lot of them, too. He went to work for one of his cousins on a farm south of Yvel, but things there did not work out and *she* just could not let it go. None of them would just let it go. So Bisin found himself in prison after that. Prison was where Bisin was back around all of those things he hated. Filth. Scat. Piss. People practicing their child-making by themselves. Could hear it all the time.

Once Bisin got out, as strange as that was, he came across quite a bizarre truth. Bisin was almost *happy* working for Jak. Not that he liked Jak or the work. *Well… I don't* mind *the work.* These were all people walking around free and making smells while Bisin had been in prison for such a minor thing, so Bisin did not mind serving back a bit of justice to everyone else. But, anyways, it was the smell. Working for Jak meant that, for the most part, Bisin was out of the city. Out of towns and villages. He liked the smell of the trees in the autumn, the mushrooms of the forest. Even the dust of the road was better than all of the smells that came from or because of people.

Winter made people bearable: the cold dampened their odors. Because of the cold, Bisin hated the city just a little less. Enough that Bisin could keep his temper at people and their filthy stench. He got through the market and into the north square. This city was built on the highest point in a valley. Mountains rose to the northeast and the northwest, but the avenues that stretched north went downhill; in certain places, on certain hills in the city, one could look downhill to the north, see over the walls, and see Lake Volosk sparkling in the sunlight. Bisin loved the smell of lakeshores. Lakeshores away from cities, that is.

At the west end of the north square, Bisin spotted a semicircle abutting a building that no one walked through or near. He parted through the throng to see the reason and found a man completely wrapped in tattered rags over and over so that no skin was showing, sitting on a wooden box with rope straps. The only exposed skin was just a shadowed gap for his eyes to see through from under a deep, moth-eaten hood. The man wore a wooden sign with red letters painted upon it. Bisin could not read the word in Tamark, but Tansher told everyone it said 'leper,' and the approximation was apparently close enough because no one went any closer. On the ground next to him was a small woven basket with a few coins in it. The man made eye contact with Bisin and held the basket toward him. Bisin fumbled with a coin purse and tossed a few pennies towards the hat. One went in, but the other two missed and dinged on the wooden box before plunging into the mud. The wrapped man dug through the muck for the pennies and Bisin departed. He crossed to the south side of the square and entered an alley.

He waited until he was approached by a youth, at least relative to Bisin. Bisin was in his thirties, having spent ten years in prison for that bitch; this youth was between fifteen and seventeen. She smiled at him and said something in Tamark. Bisin was not going to guess and did not care. His more pressing concern was the long knife she had pointed at him. Bisin was not incredibly worried, though; mildly concerned at most. She grew impatient and her smile turned into a snarl as she shook the knife at him threateningly.

He looked past her at the other approaching figure. Noticing his divided attention, she turned to be face to face with the man with leper sign. The second bevel of a tapered blade blossomed through her coat as the man with the leper sign thrust his short-bladed falchion through her. She gurgled in surprise, slid off the blade and fell to the ground. Laying on the ground, her breathing became rapid and shallow as her fearful eyes darted between the man with the leper sign and Bisin.

"Thanks." Bisin leaned over and picked through the girl's pockets until he found her daily bounty, a handful of mixed coins. He then plucked her knife and stabbed her through the throat, wiped the blade on her coat, and rose.

Jak's voice was slightly muffled through the wrappings of his leper disguise, "It's fine. Just not every day, alright? It would be strange if all the muggers here died in the space of a week."

"Fine, fine," Bisin grumbled, looking at the girl who had tried to rob him as she breathed her last. Bisin exhaled sharply through his nose as he stepped away. *Don't want her to get any of that stink on me.*

"Well?" Jak's voice was expectant.

Bison looked at him, perplexed. "Well, what?"

Jak looked at Bisin flatly and lightly backhanded him in the chest. "You know what."

Bisin stumbled backwards and scrubbed his chest where Jak had hit him. "Don't touch me!" he snapped. "Right, right. Everything's guarded. Every entrance. Church Knights and their soldiers. The Palace Guard itself knows what they're about. They're bored, but they're not lazy and they're paying attention."

Jak sighed. "It'll be on Tansher, then. At least for getting in."

***

Tansher picked up a second chamberpot matching the one she held in the other hand and climbed the stairs before tossing the contents out of the window. "Watch the piss!" she called out in Tamark. Walking back down the stairs, she reentered the two bedrooms from which she had taken them. A team of like-dressed chambermaids, wearing dresses of light blue with long-sleeved, white underdresses and grey aprons, were turning down the beddings and changing out laundry. They wore knitted shawls of various colors and thick, quilted bonnets to protect their faces against the cold drafts that crept through the Palace of Kotara.

She left the chambers, proceeding down the hall to a grander set of double doors with guards posted on each side.

"Hey, new girl," one of the guards called.

"Yeah?" She looked at them, one woman and one man, both armed with axes stuffed in belt loops and short, thrusting swords in scabbards. Each wore mail and the green livery of the Kotaran Palace Guard.

"You're not allowed in here."

"I'm just getting the pots," Tansher explained.

"Then go get Vanre," the first guard instructed, a woman. "Vanre's the Princess' maid. Not you."

Tansher made a sour, pouty face of someone who had been foiled from currying favor as she turned to go. *We'll see about this*. The rest of the day passed quickly enough. There was no shortage of work available to keep a castle running. More rooms to be cleaned. Laundry to be washed. Firewood to cut. Fires to feed. Tasks in the kitchen to help with–quietly, and preferably unseen. Lesser nobles to dress. The advances of those nobles, to either fend off or endure. Candles to fetch and light. Preparing for evening meals. And always, a dozen other chores conspiring to eat the day.

With the day's work finished, she fetched three dinners of bread, cheese, and roasted chicken from the kitchen and made her way towards the servants' quarters. The meals were cozily folded in napkins and bundled into baskets, their aromas steaming forth against the cold of the evening. Pausing outside the door, she produced a small vial from the hidden depths of her dress and dabbed a few drops of clear liquid onto each serving of bread before returning the vial to its hiding place and entering the servants' quarters.

"Dinner's here," she announced.

"Oh, that's nice of you!" said Vanre. "Sorry, you're so new here. What's your name again?"

"Miki," Tansher smiled.

"Miki," Vanre repeated. "That's such a cute name." Vanre was the picture of a Tamark peasant woman in her thirties. Red hair, red cheeks, and red freckles contrasted with her smiling blue eyes. She seemed like a nice woman. A nice woman that had never been spurned by a lover, cast out by a family, mourned a lost child, or had to steal or beg or kill. Tansher schooled herself to a calmness. A nice lady.

Tansher smiled back, "I'll be back soon."

"Where are you going?" one of the other maids asked.

"They had more and I wanted to get these to you while they were hot. They're pulling a turkey off of the spit soon and I like turkey better," Tansher said.

"Well, hurry back," the other maid replied with a friendly wave.

Tansher departed and left the palace keep. She headed towards one of the turrets on the castle wall. Finding the door, she opened it and entered. She climbed the turret and emerged onto the parapet. "Juray?" she called.

"Over here, Miki," came a man's voice, a guard.

She approached him and smiled. "How's your day going?"

"Ugh, just getting started. You know my hours. The *really* boring ones," Juray said. "Say, when do you think we could get away for a bit? You're working tomorrow?" He reached for her.

"Oh, not so fast, good master guard," she smirked, dodging his grasp. She looked over the wall. "What's that?"

Dismayed and rebuffed, Juray looked. "Oh, him? That's just some leper that's camped out there. Pay no mind. No one else does."

"A leper?" she curled her upper lip in disgust. She reached into her pocket and pulled out another roll. It was cool because she had fetched it earlier, after cleaning out the chamberpots. She tossed it over the wall and it thudded next to the leper. She saw his hand hesitantly reach out for the lump of bread.

"Nice of you," Juray said.

"Oh, you know," she sighed, "anyone wants a hand from someone when the rest of the world turns their back."

***

Jak shambled through the alleyways, playing the part of the vagrant leper. Deep in the cowl, underneath the wrappings covering his face, he contentedly chewed the last of the roll thrown from the palace walls. He had to admit, the bread was just nicer. Fresher, softer, and still moistened from butter despite being in Tansher's pocket for hours.

Jak peered both ways down an alley before entering the bottom floor of a five-storied building. Structures like these were common in cities, apparently. Jak had been to Yvel a few times, though only briefly, and was vaguely amused that most of his urban experiences had taken place in the past three months, passing through Vidara, Boaz, and even Kotara.

Jak immediately descended the stairs into the cellar. The landlord appreciated the extra coin he received for letting them use the cellar for their own purposes. He had not met Jak, with or without leper rags, and otherwise thought that he was offering a gracious service to people running from the war in the east, looking to make a new start. So far away was that war that the landlord had never bothered to investigate anything they were up to, nor ask what was in the bundles they had carried in from their baggage horses.

The rest of the crew looked up as Jak clunked down the stairs. Tension dissipated and weapons slid back into their sheaths as they saw who it was.

Jak finished chewing the roll. "Tomorrow night's the night."

***

"Yeah, you can go, on account of half the maids being down with the sick," said one of the guards. "Mind you not to get close to me or touch too many things in there! Can't have you spreading it around. Wonder that you didn't get sick."

"Can't get sick on a farm," Tansher replied lightly. "No time for it." She hustled about the ornately decorated chambers and found the chamberpot and some towels in need of laundering before spotting her opportunity. She hurriedly mashed the rotten eggs she had smuggled in with her hands and added them to the pot, then threw the chamberpot down hard, shattering it into a dozen pieces and spreading its liquid cargo over the polished wood floor.

"Aw, now you've done it!" called the first guard. "This is why only the good maids come in here! Honestly."

"Sorry! The handle broke," Tansher cried helplessly, stifling a gag.

"Don't care! Just get a mop and clean it up before her grace gets back! If you think you're working here tomorrow, you better lick it clean!" the first guard threatened. Tansher scurried around the corner to fetch the mop and two heavy wooden buckets she had already positioned there.

"Ah! That smell!" the second guard complained. "Didn't know her ladyship had it in her," he whispered to the first guard.

237

She elbowed him. They were happy to wait in the hall to avoid the smell.

Tansher opened the door of the north-facing balcony. It was a sheer drop fifty paces to the low wall, and another twelve paces from the low wall to the ground. She made a noisy job of slopping the foul muck onto the balcony and over the edge. "Watch the piss!" she called. She paused before reaching into the second water-filled bucket and pulled out a thick rope. Looping the end several times around the stone railing and rungs of the balcony, she tied it in a quick knot and gave it a hard tug. Peeking over her shoulder, she nudged the first bucket with her foot to make a water sloshing sound and then tossed the rope over. Looking down over the railing, a corner in the cut of the stone would conceal the rope to the casual observer, if the smell didn't drive them away first. *Perfect*.

She finished mopping up the mess and carried the buckets from the room.

"You done?" one of the guards asked as she was exiting the chambers.

"Getting some powder to soak up the rest of the smell. Almost done."

***

Breathday, the night of the following day.

Nansima was not the coldest month; it was the last month of autumn and the winter would surely bring more chilling weather, but Kotara was nestled in the Samziks and wind brought the cold down from the mountains. The biting gust cut right through Bisin's coat. He pulled himself up the rope to the top of the low wall. A freckled face was waiting for him. Tansher.

Wordlessly, she reached out and grasped his hand, hoisting him up. He gained his footing and moved aside for the next team member scaling the rope to dismount. They stood on the low wall around the palace. One of the guards lay on the parapet, his lifeblood already drained out of a trench dug through his throat.

Bisin did not have to look at Tansher's hands to know they were bloody; he had felt the stickiness on them when she helped him up. He scrubbed his hands against his trousers until someone slapped him to get out of the way. Bisin moved further over as the rest of the raid team reached the top of the wall.

Bisin looked towards the skies. The dark of the cloudy night made it difficult to see. Might snow later tonight. But that wind whipped at them just at this height. Bisin was not looking forward to that climb. Tansher leaned over the edge of the wall by the keep and pulled back a long rope. Bisin could dimly see the rope oscillating from the pull and the swirling draughts.

Each of the raid team had small sections of rope and were tying them into knotted stirrups around the climbing rope. Tansher took a long, narrow bundle from one of the others and departed back towards the keep as they began their climb. Again, Bisin was up first, after putting on some gloves. The second leg of their climb was easier than the one up the wall–at first. He reached up and pulled his legs towards his body, knees bunching into his coat. Then he simply stood up in the rope-knot stirrups and reached again. Soon, his legs burned and ached.

Looking down, he moaned to himself. *I wish I didn't...* Bisin had *never* been in this situation nor *anything* like it, so he was discovering right then that he was terrified of heights. Tickling fear and nervousness gripped him at the bottom of the chest and in his nethers. His breath became panicked heaves.

"Hey!" a voice called out from below him. Of course, others were on the rope, too, and they all dangled adrift as the wind tossed them about. There was one team member whose job it was to attempt to hold the top tight and steady–a futile effort–but Bisin could not see him.

"*Hey!*" the voice called again, more urgently. Bisin's fingers were starting to lose their feeling. "You better move up that rope or I'm going to stuff so much of this city's gutters up your nose that you'll die from it!"

That was it. The only way to beat a fear was with a greater fear. Bisin was afraid of the city's smells and what they were waiting to do to him, and he was afraid of Jak. He scurried up the rope as quickly as his aching legs and numbing fingers would carry him. It was not that Jak was cruel; he was not–it was that Jak never threw around idle threats.

Bisin shivered as he reached the top of the rope and hauled himself onto the balcony, quaking from the cold. Trembling, he helped Jak and the next teammate onto the balcony before stuffing his hands into his armpits to warm them and shield them from the cruel wind as Jak and the other teammate helped the rest of the raid party onto the balcony. Eleven men and women stood shoulder to shoulder on the narrow stone ledge, pressed close to the railing.

One of them slid a thin wafer of steel between the doors to coax the latch open as the wind rattled the panes of the balcony doors. The teammate held the doors closed by the handles and looked up at Jak. Jak held his hand up with his five fingers extended. He dropped down one finger at a time. Everyone tensed as the second to last finger dropped. When the last finger closed into Jak's fist, the doors burst open.

A startled guard yelped as Bisin's numb hands plunged a knife into his stomach before slashing across his throat. Bisin did not look in the direction of the screaming girl, who sounded to be maybe twelve or fourteen years old. He only went to work on the dying guard in front of him, sawing off his head with the long knife. Have to make it look like goblins did it, Jak had said. No one knew quite what that looked like, so Jak said to make it look bloodier and worse than anything they had seen, and they had seen quite a bit by their own hands over the last half year. But this was to be especially bad.

The doors burst open as two mailed guards stormed in, blades bared. The girl's screaming abruptly stopped with a crunching sound of a skull caving in. One of the guard's blades flashed in the candle light as it whipped toward Jak. Jak always fought best at night. Bisin could see Jak's silhouette dance confidently,batting aside the blade with his own before punching the guard in the face. The guard cried out in pain. The other guard came to her aid, but his mailed head snapped aside as an axe bounced off of his armor from behind him.

Tansher panted and dropped the Orcish axe that they had smuggled in. She picked it back up and tossed it to the other teammates then whisked away before more guards arrived. Tansher was the security for this portion of the raid and as much as Bisin resented her special status as Jak's girl, she came through on this; after she had helped them up the lower wall, she entered the palace with her access as a maid, climbed the stairs while Bisin, Jak, and the others were scaling the walls, and came upon the guards from behind through the doors to the princess's chambers.

One teammate hacked at the dead guards, mangling them further, while others dismembered the girl on the bed. They scattered her limbs around the chamber and used her blood to paint strange writing on the walls, which had been part of their instructions.

One of the teammates vomited. Bisin did not blame him. Or was it her. It did not matter. This was grim work that none of them enjoyed, though there was a small part of Bisin that was pleased to triumph over these people that had never known hardship and conspired against him with the smells of the city.

"Hey! Let's go," one of the teammates hissed in a whisper. One by one, they lowered themselves over the balcony, gripping the rope between their feet and with their gloved hands, and descended. The ride down the rope had Bisin puckered tight and his hands were soon burning with friction from the rope. Were it not for the pool of blood and the dead guard's smell in the way, he would have kissed the stone when his feet met the ground.

***

The Kotara-Boaz Road, east of Kotara.
By the Human Calendar, Fryday (eighth day of the week), third week of Nansima, 794.
Gentle snow, three days later.

Jak's group wearily plodded along the road on horseback, driving three wagons, while a fine snow hissed softly as it met the ground. This was truly Bisin's favorite place. Shivering and flapping his hat to shake off the accumulated snow and frost, he smiled. No smells. It was finally winter, and they had finally left the city. He sneezed and sniffled.

"Hey, Bisin," called one of the others, riding up to him as he drove the lead wagon.

"Yeah?"

"What say? Can we help ourselves to a little extra on the road and have a good time at the next town?"

"No," said Bisin flatly.

"Aw, come on!" the other protested.

"No," Bisin repeated, intentionally not concealing his irritation. "Jak's orders. No drawing attention to ourselves. No raids showing our trail."

"But they'll think it's orcs!"

"And no big parties with the stuff we would've just taken. That'd give it away that it's not orcs, dummy!" Bisin scolded. "We make back for Krogen. Maybe there we can take in a small good time. *Small*, hear? Just like your stuff."

The rider grumbled, making a sour face as he fell back and muttering under his breath.

"What was that?" Bisin called.

From behind the wagon he heard the rider shout, "the best part of you soaked into the sheets!" which prompted a few chortles from the rest of the crew. Bisin scowled as he tried to banish the unbidden memory of the smell of breeding from his mind.

Hours later, the fire crackled in the dark. Jak's crew of raiders laughed and drank around the fire, roasting whatever their bows found at dusk. Inside one of the wagons, Tansher was working at undoing Jak's belt. She looked up at him with a mischievous grin, but it faded. Jak stared off into the distance.

This always *gets his attention. What's he on about?* "What is it?" she asked.

"Hm? Oh, nothing."

"Oh, come on. It's not Sirid is it? Saw you looking at her again," she accused. Sirid was one of the women in the group that coveted Tansher's position as Jak's girl. She knew it. Tansher would catch her making eyes at him. Waiting for him to come to her.

"Huh? No. I already told you," he said. He sat down

wearily, leaning his arms on his knees, shirtless, but otherwise dressed. He looked at her, tired. *I've never seen him like that.* She put her shirt back on and gently pushed him towards the hard back of the bench before sitting sideways on his lap. She wrapped her arms around his neck and rested her head on his shoulder.

"I didn't like this job," he said after a while.

Don't go soft on me, greenskin. You're no good to me soft. "She had it coming. They all did."

"How old do you think she was? Thirteen?"

"Old enough to send people like us to prison for years just because we're trying to live our lives," she said scornfully.

He was silent for a while. "Maybe." He absently stroked her hair and cradled her past the dying down of the laughter outside.

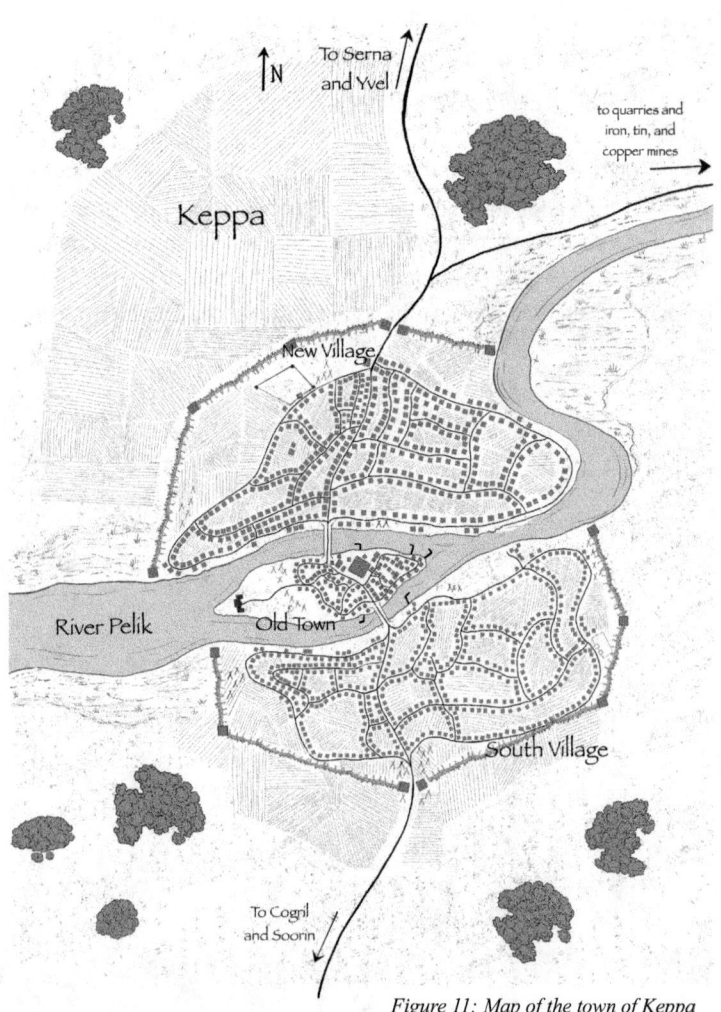

Figure 11: Map of the town of Keppa

Chapter 16

The northern approach to the town of Keppa.
By the Human Calendar, Fryday, first week of Arinochis (tenth month of the year), 794.
A cold and clear evening after previous snowfall.

Koval drew in the reins and raised his hand to signal a halt. Behind him, the three battalions of the Yvel Regiment shuffled to a stop. They were tired, marching from early in the morning, just like the past fifteen days, until late in the day when the sun was almost set. But they needed to push. They needed to get here. Hopefully, they were in time. Koval had needed to push them harder with each day, but he knew that he could only push them so far. Someone would only obey you out of fear for so long before they ran from you. It was a delicate balance, and desertion was not another problem that he wanted to add to the already long list.

It was just the beginning of Arinochis, but it would be over before he knew it. The first snows had come and laid a peaceful blanket over the lands to send them to sleep for the season, but the peaceful setting was marred by what lay in front of them. A few hundred paces off was the north gate into the Keppa palisade. Plumes of smoke, too thick to be from chimneys and industry, rose from the other side of the town. In the distance, Koval could hear the din of battle.

He was surprised at having to relieve Keppa. He had never before admitted it, but he had been jealous of Baroness Kirstan. Kirstan Toliodran. He had his eye on her as a youth before his Mariss came into his life and scooped him up by surprise. He made a small smile, *No regrets though.* It was after he met Mariss that he realized that he only wanted Kirstan to join the titles of Serna and Keppa. And Keppa was a prize.

Was, from the looks of things. Built on either side of the shores of the Pelik, the oldest part of town and the manor sat on an island in the middle of the river. Since then, the town had spread to the north and south banks. The Pelik was too shallow to support river ships, but rafts and small barges would arrive daily from the mines in the surrounding hills. The Baroness of Keppa and several other wealthy families owned the mines and a number of quarries. Those particular quarries were feeding stone to Serna for the construction of the wall being built there, but all of the industry would send the ore down the Pelik to Keppa for smelting and stone cutting. Smelting made a lot of smoke. And yet, the plumes of smoke rising over the palisade and lazily fingering the clouds indicated a bleak situation, probably on the south bank.

"Well?" The prince rode to his shoulder. "What are we waiting for?" The prince's entourage loitered in the background. The young princeling, Aered, though about the same age as Ziek Miykodran of Serna, was maturing quickly. He was preparing for his second battle as the prince's squire, under the mentorship of one of the prince's other, more seasoned squires–Erion, Koval thought to be his name. Oswald and Velthuria, the prince's eldest siblings, were occupied marshalling the Crown Guard and nosing into the regiment's business. Then there were the Crown Guard hangers-on...

"Sorry, Your Grace," Koval said, "just taking it in."

"Well, take it in while *getting* in!" the prince snapped.

"Yes, sir," Koval replied. Turning in his saddle, he motioned for the regiment to continue: Battalion One would lead, with himself and his scouts at the front. The prince and the Crown Guard would follow, positioned between Battalion One and Battalion Two. Battalion Three brought up the rear.

He worried about Battalion One. The prince had foisted one of his Crown Guard onto him, an unwieldy lout named Jof Toliodran. Jof had been in the Arladran Battalion at the Battle of Serna Hills, before it was reformed as part of the Yvel Regiment. He had barely survived Serna Hills, like most of them who had made it out alive, but his company had been mostly destroyed. He spent some time in the Crown Guard 'being mentored,' and then was tossed back into a regular fighting unit. He was high-handed and over-eager, especially when the prince was around, and spent more time wearing his position rather than being it. Koval kept Battalion One close to keep an eye on him.

Koval saw only one guard at the north gate as he

approached it.

"My Lord! Thank Orneth!" the guard cried. Armed with a spear, he wore a thick gambeson, a steel cap, and a collar of mail.

"We march for your relief. Where is your baroness?" Koval asked, forgoing any introduction.

"I think in Old Town," the guard said, pointing downhill towards the river. "That's where the fighting is right now."

The gate was not designed for the purpose of armies passing through, but for the purposes of Keppa defending itself and for moderate traffic. Not armies, either besieging or relieving. The timber doors creaked on their hinges straining to open all of the way, but in the end ranks of ten had to split into ranks of five. Koval rode alongside the regiment, informing the other battalion leaders and the prince of the structural limitations. He arrived breathless at the gate again. Battalion One was mostly through, the last company pouring through the gate. With a few sharp commands, he nudged his horse between the ranks and followed them.

Koval grimaced upon arriving within the gates. They had made the palisade too large, and it was too much to defend. It encompassed the immediately outlying farm fields and pastures, many of those fields dotted with tents. Probably for the miners and farmers seeking refuge in the town.

"My Lord?" a woman called from her mount.

Koval looked. It was Idris Beredran, one of the Yvel nobles that had signed on to lead a company in the regiment. *Wait. Why is she talking to me? Where's Jof?* "Where's your battalion leader?"

"He's gone ahead with the other two companies, My Lord. What should–"

"THAT PISS-DRINKING FOOL!!" Koval bellowed. "FILTHY SCAT FOR BRAINS! CURSE THAT IDIOT!" *I can't leave that vainglorious horse-brain alone for even a few minutes.* Koval kicked his horse to a trot down the main street, ignoring Idris' questions.

Throngs of civilians flowed the other way, fleeing from Old Town and the shores of the New Village, the northern part of Keppa. They parted to make way for him, as they probably had for the two companies that he could now barely see as he had turned a gentle corner. The two companies were crossing a bridge into Old Town. There were two bridges in Keppa: one to connect Old Town with New Village, and the other to connect Old Town with South Village. The smoke was clearly rising from Old Town.

What. Is. That? Koval caught a glimpse of a shape moving amidst the workshops in Old Town. It was taller than some of the buildings. Koval kicked ahead, clearing the buildings on the north bank and riding up the tail of the second company. He spotted Jof. "Scathead! What are you doing running off by yourself?"

"What do you mean, My Lord? We're not alone. We have these brave soldiers with us," Jof called back.

"There are nine companies in this regiment and you want to separate two of them off, unsupported!? Turn them around this instant and get back to the rest of the regiment!"

"But, My Lord, the fighting is here in Old Town and we have to rescue my dear aunt!" Jof protested. He had maneuvered his horse around his second company to face Koval, his first company crossed into Old Town.

His aunt, Koval put his face in his palm, Koval forgot that this buffoon was Kirstan's nephew. The sound of fighting rang out anew as the two companies made contact with the enemy. *Well, it's done, then. This idiot committed them*, he thought bitterly. *After this, I will have to give him back to the Prince and the Crown Guard for some more 'mentoring.' Maybe I should 'mentor' him myself a bit, here and now.*

Jof looked over his shoulder towards Old Town.

Koval gestured in the direction of the fighting. "Don't you have troops to command in battle, Battalion Leader?"

"Indeed, I do," Jof apprehensively stammered, wheeling around his horse to join his soldiers.

Koval turned and started riding back towards the rest of the regiment. He chanced a look back to the south and his eyes widened. The moving shape he couldn't make out before was like a man with reddish grey skin, except that it was maybe ten paces tall, a massive paunch hanging from its waist. It leapt between two-storied buildings into the midst of the companies. Shouts of surprise and fear echoed off of the buildings lining the street as the giant picked up soldiers and hurled them against the buildings and streets, crushed them to a mess in its grip, and trampled entire ranks of soldiers at a time as they feebly hacked and poked at it with their weapons. *What* is *that?*

Koval hastily made his way back to the regiment, which had crossed inside the palisade in good order.

"Well?" The prince rode up, bristling with irritation.

"Idris! Form your company behind Battalion Two. You are now the reserve for the regiment," Koval commanded.

"Yes, sir." He heard Idris, but did not see her.

"What happened to the rest of Battalion One?" the prince demanded.

"Jof, that golden turd you scatted on me, spent them. They're dying in Old Town right now, fighting some giant man!"

"Giant man?" Holbrin asked. "How giant?"

"Uh." Koval squinted, not wanting to answer questions right now. "Maybe ten paces."

"Ten paces? With red-grey skin?"

"Yeah, why?"

"An ogre. Hm."

"An ogre?" The prince turned to regard him.

"Probably. I am surprised they were able to recruit them," Holbrin mused.

"Doesn't matter now," the prince broke in, "they're here. I never knew ogres actually existed outside of stories. What can they do? Weaknesses?"

"They are just big and strong. Their skin is thick–very–but there are the normal weak spots: throat, groin, armpits, and base of the skull. Best to use archers, crossbows, and longer spears on them."

"Fine. Good. Koval, deploy your regiment," Prince Arnold ordered curtly.

"Yes, Your Grace," Koval replied, resigned. He ordered the remaining battalions down the main street and deployed them on the north bank of the Pelik, holding New Village. The two companies that had been led by Jof lay in ruins in the streets of Old Town. The enemy was reveling in hauling away the wounded. Mostly orcs, Koval observed. They had archers skirmishing from the banks of Old Town with his own across the river. He did not see the ogre, though.

A tight pack of orcs emerged from the side streets and moved with surprising speed into a formation, presenting broad shields against the arrows that immediately began coursing their way. They were making for the bridge. The bridge was built of stone and spanned the twenty paces from one bank to the other. The orcs were making their way onto the south end.

"Don't let them have that bridge!" Koval heard the prince shouting. "Push them off! Push them back!"

Koval rode to the front company, holding the mouth of the bridge. "Soldiers! Give 'em the bad end!" he shouted.

The soldiers cheered as blades and points clashed on shields and steel clanged amidst the shouts from both sides. The orcs towered over the defenders from the regiment, but the mouth of the bridge let the company point more spears and weapons at their attackers and the mound of green bodies grew faster than the mound of pink ones. Koval concentrated, shooting baleful stares into the attackers, giving them pause, taking the edge from their boldness and putting hesitation into their attack. It was working. The company was pushing the orcs back across the bridge, step by step.So caught up in the elation was he, that he did not notice until someone punched him in the left arm. He turned. It was Holbrin.

"What?" Koval shouted over the cacophony of the fighting.

"We are being flanked from the north. They landed warriors on the banks with barges from the mines."

"Curse it!" Koval shouted, "Get the reserve over there to reinforce them. Tell the Prince that I *humbly* request Sir Aleksan and the Crown Guard to stand ready as the reserve."

"Yes, Koval," Holbrin cried, and sped off on his white horse to bear his instructions. Despite his early aloofness, and the lingering sense that he was hiding things, Holbrin had always been reliable and a good friend. The two of them had not talked much, but he was always at hand when Koval needed help, and they would not have survived this long without it. *Dareum would probably be dead without him and the other elves, too.*

"NO!" Koval heard another shout, from the south. *The ogre!* It had leapt from its hiding place between some fishing huts on the bank. It must have waded through the river after finishing off two companies from Battalion One. *We're being trapped!* The ogre barreled through one of the companies, kicking bodies aside and pulping anything in reach. Hearing more shouts to the north, Koval turned again to see distant silhouettes of orcs running on the parapets of the palisade. They had seized control of the first palisade tower and were working their way northward. *They'll seize the gate!*

"Your Grace!" he shouted, "We have to withdraw! This is a–"

A great roar behind him startled his horse and a giant hand seized Koval. His horse whinnied in fear and he was vaguely aware of the ogre picking him up and kicking his horse into a line of soldiers. He struggled feebly against the great hand, no air in his lungs, as it lifted him to the grinning face of its master. He felt and heard the bones in his legs and hips breaking. He tried to scream, but there was no air for it. His vision quickly shrank to a dot and he never felt the ground when the ogre let him drop.

***

The Blue-Eyed Man entered the tent. It had been a very long day. Two days, really. They had barely made it out of Keppa's north gate after the regiment's archers and the Crown Guard had forced it open. They had lost Keppa. Catastrophically.

There was almost nothing left of the Keppa Regiment. They encountered its remnants as they swam from Old Town into New Village, but many of them died in the fighting withdrawal. Half of the Yvel Regiment died in Keppa, not to mention a few from the Crown Guard. *It's a good thing that the royal family didn't have any more deaths. What would the Prince do? If Aered... It's a good thing that Brindi did not come. Oh, how we fought about it. She can be nasty when she does not get her way... but if she were here for this disaster…*

The prince was furious at this debacle and there were two men that were chiefly to blame. And they would both pay in the way that the Blue-Eyed Man deemed fit. He would have to apologize to Master Holbrin, too. Some of his countryfolk had died that day. They pushed as many of the townsfolk and refugees out of the gate that they could, to get moving out of New Village.

It was their first chance to rest in two days. The tent had been set up for his friend. Mkaela had been in and out to check on him after stabilizing him as best she could. Even she was doubtful about his recovery. The Blue-Eyed Man looked down on his friend, Koval Covendran, laboriously breathing on the cot. He slept.

The Blue-Eyed Man reached into the folds of his cape to pull his shoulder bag forward. He flipped open the top flap and unpacked several books. Pulling one to the top, he opened it, flipping through the pages until he found the one he had earmarked. Opening another book to an index chapter, he traced the lines of Old Paetic on the page of the first one, whispering the incantation.

Colors began to swirl in his vision around Koval. *This must be the aura it talks about. A deep purple with streaks of black. Which one is that… not that one. Not that one… hm. Maybe this. 'Control of the emotion of fear, ability to incite it in others, both fear of the user and fear of a second or third party.' That could definitely be it. Now, let's see.* He paged over a few clumps of pages in the first book, finding the right one and traced the words, uttering a different incantation. *Just as suspected. His barrier is breached.* The Blue-Eyed Man scrawled notes in a third book, closed all three, and was tucking them back into his shoulder bag when he happened to look up. Koval was looking at him.

"What are you doing?" Koval whispered weakly.

"Testing your aura, Friend. You have a witch power over fear," the Blue-Eyed Man answered.

"You knew?" Koval turned his head away slightly, as if afraid of rebuke.

"*You* knew?" the Blue-Eyed Man said, surprised. "Always had suspicion around you. How you managed to push the men further, and how hard they fought for you, despite their grumbles of resentment toward being many and colorful."

"Can't just let them plod along, sir. The Prince demands action."

"There were even stories about you when the orcs first came and you scared people onto their horses, then scared the horses into charging the orcs. Even before that, your servants were terrified of you. And Dareum and Judane… "

"No need to salt the ground before I die, sir," Koval murmured.

"Right, friend. Sorry." The Blue-Eyed Man continued. "Much study about this," he said, patting his shoulder bag. "Please tell. These texts talk about why everyone does not have these powers. Everyone has a barrier to them, but yours is broken. The text reads that a person experiences something horrible. Something that almost kills them, and often does, and that's what breaches the barrier. What happened to you? How did this start?"

Koval said nothing for a moment. His breathing was becoming more labored. At last he gave a reply. "There are two children in Serna with red hair, but only one adult that used to have red hair in youth."

Wondered about that. They're in different families. The Blue-Eyed Man cupped his chin with his hand looking away in thought.

"Sorry to ask, friend, which one…?" Koval was asleep again.

No. Not asleep. He was not breathing. The Blue-Eyed Man bent close. He could not hear Koval's breath nor feel his exhale on his cheek.

"Surgeon! Mkaela! The Lord Serna!" the Blue-Eyed Man called in sudden panic. He heard hurried shuffling as feet hit the ground amid the other tents. The flaps nearly tore off the tent as they both burst through the entrance. They were both exhausted from treating the rampant frostbite. The march down was hard, but the march back was even worse. A few outright froze to death. They worked at him for a few moments as the Blue-Eyed Man stood back. The frantic labor of a few moments ended with Master Danfrey's arms folded in frustrated defeat and Mkaela kneeling by the bed wearing silent tears of loss.

Farewell, friend. Graffin save you. Acrist see the good in you. Kostray clean you. And Orneth take you into her everlasting bliss, the Blue-Eyed Man prayed. Koval and the Blue-Eyed Man had not been friends before the war, but they had grown to trust and respect each other. Koval had been very reliable as a field commander and a faithful subject before the war. *You will be missed. Long live the Lady Serna. Had hope to ask you and your wife about Judane.*

***

Eight Days Later
Palace of Yvel City.
Freezing rain pelting the windows.

The Blue-Eyed Man stood in front of the palace library's door. It was eight days later, after a bitterly cold march back to Yvel. The march was quicker after they passed through Serna, since the prince and his entourage had moved ahead of the main body of the army. They had left behind those that could no longer fight in Serna, and the townsfolk were glad to receive additional hands to help. Cooking, baking, sewing, and various other crafts that the too-young and too-old had been shouldering were now further enabled by those who could no longer fight, for want of a missing leg or hand.

Those refugees that could still fight were conscripted to rebuild the Keppa Regiment from the one company that remained of it. Those bloody, hollow-eyed veterans were all promoted and given the task of training the new conscripts. The Yvel Regiment soaked up more conscripts from the countryside and a few more volunteers once they arrived in Yvel. Serna could not spare anyone for building their own two regiments, the very large militia company they furnished, and the patrols with which the prince had tasked them.

The Blue-Eyed Man cursed the bitter failure at Keppa. The Toliodrans were supposed to be raising two regiments at Keppa.

They were barely finishing one, when that fool of theirs fumbled the day. Well, more fools to go around. He wasn't there in Keppa, so that blame lies with another. And she's probably dead.

Passing through Serna had been very unpleasant. The Sernans accepted Koval's survivors with a mixture of anger, sorrow, and resignation. The Blue-Eyed Man had a hard time facing Judane then. Her iron face had shattered to pieces and she cried on her mother's hem. Her mother, however, Lady Mariss, had remained impassive and stately. Neither spiteful nor welcoming. *What can you expect?*

The Blue-Eyed Man was irritated with himself. He had wanted Judane to cry on *his* shoulder. But after Serna was a day behind him, he recognized not only that he was being selfish, but that he ought to place some of the blame on himself for the disaster that had passed at Keppa. There had been signs of something like this on the horizon, whether it was a push on Keppa or something else, which he should have recognized.

Nicholas was responsible for providing intelligence on the enemy's movements, but the Blue-Eyed Man had let the ever-curious librarian dally with his other studies for too long. This lax attitude was compounded by Koval's loss of control, but it was for the foolishness of Jof, who had been forced on Koval. He wanted to blame these two men, Nicholas and Jof, as a way to excuse himself from the fault for the defeat and the loss of Koval.

But it did not matter. The people needed a prince. The prince needed to lead, needed others to lead in his stead, and needed to take care selecting those who would lead in his stead. The Blue-Eyed Man needed to manage others that led for the prince. *And thank Orneth there were no more deaths in the royal family. What would the Prince do if he lost Aered, Velthuria, or Oswald? Graffin save and keep them.*

The Blue-Eyed Man took a deep breath preparing for what would undoubtedly prove to be a difficult discussion with the first of the two men, and pushed open the library doors. Predictably, Nicholas was buried in a pile of books. The Blue-Eyed Man could identify Old Paetic lettering etched onto some of the weathered covers. Nicholas had sent ahead for servants to lay out pastries and coffee, but the Blue-Eyed Man was in no mood for them. He stood in the doorway watching Nicholas, who did not raise his gaze to acknowledge the looming figure.

"Are you going to eat?" Nicholas asked after a while.

"What are you doing?" the Blue-Eyed Man asked, ignoring the hospitality.

Nicholas turned a page and scribbled into a separate book, still not looking up. "Working on a spell to create a barrier of air to block arrows. I started looking for it after one of Zaya's reports noted that one of the sorcerers can do it."

The Blue-Eyed Man was suddenly torn. *That sounds really interesting. And useful.* But he reminded himself to remain steadfast to the decision he had made, and this was the time to act. "When did the Prince find out that Soorin had fallen?"

Nicholas paused and then put down his pen to look at the Blue-Eyed Man. "When reports arrived that Keppa was under attack."

"Yes. The Prince had assembled an army, and was actually on its way to Versingit when the messenger from the Marshal reached us. We had to turn around."

"I see," said Nicholas, lowering his gaze again.

"And what size of enemy force attacked Keppa?"

"I don't have those numbers."

"What was the composition of the enemy force?"

"Orcs and goblins, I suspect, much as it was at Borly and Serna," Nicholas said hesitantly, looking askance at the Blue-Eyed Man. "What are you driving at?"

"Ogres."

"They had ogres? Like from… ?"

"Yes. And the Prince has someone who is supposed to tell him about these things. The Prince has someone who maintains a fairly impressive network of agents, spies, saboteurs, assassins, informants, and pretty much anyone who is directly or indirectly, witting or unwitting, loyal to the Prince's Crown."

The Blue-Eyed Man stalked into the room, his voice low and baleful. "People who tell this person, or his chief agents, things that the Prince needs to know. The Prince needed to know about Soorin before the enemy reached Keppa, and the Prince needed to know that *ogres* are *real* and the enemy has them."

"I see... how did...?" Nicholas began.

"Badly," the Blue-Eyed Man said, cutting him off. "Very badly. One regiment is destroyed. The other lost more than two battalions and cannot be used as a regiment until it recruits or conscripts five more companies, picks a new regimental leader and two battalion leaders."

"Did Koval retire?" Nicholas asked.

"Koval is dead," the Blue-Eyed Man said quietly.

Nicholas steadied himself on the heavy table. "I see."

"And that considerably hurts chances of the courtship between Oswald and Judane, what with the Prince getting Judane's father killed and all," the Blue-Eyed Man added. "Do you know what Brindi said to the Prince?"

"What?" Nicholas hollowly inquired.

"She said to make better choices next time the Prince goes to Keppa," the Blue-Eyed Man said.

Nicholas squinted at the Blue-Eyed Man with a wry expression. "I hardly think that–"

"You are not in charge of the magic program anymore," the Blue-Eyed Man interrupted.

Nicholas' sheepishness transformed into outrage in a flash. "Now, see here–"

That got an authentic reaction. "No. You clearly are having trouble focusing on your primary duties–and that doesn't mean as a librarian."

"But, there are so many possibilities! Applicable ones! I have one here for changing your own appearance–all of it!–height, weight, skin color, facial features! You can impersonate someone or just generally disguise yourself as someone else."

"Interesting. Hand it off."

"What!?"

"Hand it off." The Blue-Eyed Man continued, the certainty

of his decision growing. "The Prince will appoint a minister of magic. An equal to the Minister of Information. If needed, the Minister of Magic will assign someone to assist the Ministry of Information."

"But–but… there… no one else has gotten nearly as far as I in these studies," Nicholas protested.

"In a minute. The teams. Bring two more into Yvel as reserves. Take half of what remains and focus on crushing the council's interests. One of those will be for assassinating council members. The rest go to further destabilize our unhelpful neighbors. The rulers of Heath and Vidara need to be out of the way. How did their last assignments fall out?"

"Mostly successful," Nicholas said. "Now what about–"

"What do you mean 'mostly'?"

Nicholas studied the pile of books on his desk. "The King of the Berks and the Princess of Kotara are dead. The Primarch in Clovis had a good scare…"

"But?"

"But the team I sent to scare the Tamark Queen deserted." Nicholas turned his head away sheepishly.

"Well, now." The Blue-Eyed Man squarely put his hands on his hips. "What's your remedy for that?"

"Hunt them down," Nicholas mumbled. "I was going to dispatch a team for that tomorrow."

"I wager you were. Execution on sight. No risk to this project," the Blue-Eyed Man said sternly.

"Yes. Of course," Nicholas paused. "So… who will be this minister of magic?"

"Kolus."

"Kolus!? Kolus is one of mine!"

"Not anymore. The Prince is appointing Kolus as the Minister of Magic. Kolus will be informed very soon."

"And how will you guarantee Kolus' loyalty? Hm?"

"An oath spell."

"An oath spell?" Nicholas repeated skeptically.

The Blue-Eyed Man produced a book of Old Paetic scrawlings from the shoulder bag nestled under his cape and held it out for Nicholas to see the cover.

"Erkond..." Nicholas recognized the name of the wizard who authored the book centuries ago. He gulped. "When did you find the time for all of that?"

"Sleeping spell. Only need to sleep for an hour every week now. It was the first one that I figured out. Much more time efficient now," the Blue-Eyed Man said.

Nicholas gestured towards the book. "Can I–"

"No. Remember? You are having trouble remembering what your primary duties are. No dabbling," the Blue-Eyed Man scolded.

Nicholas, accustomed to always getting his way, immaturely stamped his foot in frustration. "Anything *else* in there?"

"Commentary on natural sorcery. Apparently, everyone is a witch. Everyone with a mind, that is. Each person's abilities are different, though there are similar power types... like eye color. And there is a barrier. Deadly to overcome to gain access to the powers. Spells to detect both."

"Have you used any of that?"

"Koval Covendran, as suspected, was a witch. He could control fear," the Blue-Eyed Man continued, "and I suspect that his wife and children are similar in some way or another."

Nicholas listened with rapt attention again. "Really? I–"

"No. You've already been told," the Blue-Eyed Man said firmly.

Nicholas pounded his fist on the table in frustration, "Just because of a setback–"

"Setback!?" the Blue-Eyed Man challenged. "*Setback?* A good thing the royal family didn't accidentally get smaller. What would you call that? You call losing a major town, our primary source for cut stone, ore, our main smelteries, secure crossing over the Pelik, not to mention all of the *people* that live there, a *setback*? *Our* people? Or the *two* regiments that have to be rebuilt? We could be building two *more* regiments instead of having to rebuild destroyed ones."

This was the first time the Blue-Eyed Man had needed to seriously rebuke Nicholas, and had to ensure that it made a lasting impression. He circled the tables where Nicholas had his books laid out. "Can we not call it something more fitting? Something along the lines of 'costly defeat' or 'disaster,' the kind which the Prince has people like *you* to help prevent! Let's call it that."

The air left Nicholas as he was forced to acknowledge the depth of consequences that had stemmed from his oversight. He paced away, his back towards the Blue-Eyed Man.

The Blue-Eyed Man sighed. "Try to be reasonable. Maybe you can continue after the war. But right now, the Prince needs–"

"I *know* what the Prince needs," Nicholas hissed sullenly, spinning to face the Blue-Eyed Man before turning his back again.

"The next visit, the coffee and pastries will get the attention they deserve, and we'll have our talks like all the other times, but this has got to change." The Blue-Eyed Man looked at Nicholas' sulking back. "You understand?" The reprimanded librarian nodded sullenly. "Good. Have someone come by to start collecting the books. Until next time, friend." The Blue-Eyed Man departed, closing the doors behind him.

Nicholas stalked over to the baked goods, angrily consuming two at once, and started on a third. He poured himself a cup of coffee and violently chewed the last of the third pastry. He would have to pick which of the books he wanted to study most. Concealing more than five in his care seemed unlikely. *Still, he was right. I have responsibilities to uphold. Five or six should be manageable without neglecting the Prince's needs. Maybe seven...*

Chapter 17

A secluded manor, northwest of the town of Krogen, Yvel Principality.
By the Goblin Calendar, twelfth day of the First Moon Cycle, 3115.
By the Human Calendar, Twosday, second week of Arinochis, 794.
A brisk, late morning winter day.

"I see you, Kachem," Kolus teased. He had meant it to sound playful, but his voice had changed since he had been sick in the mountains. Now, his voice rattled in the back of his throat, and he loathed how it sounded; like he was dying of winter fever whenever he spoke. He had learned to ignore it most of the time, but any time he tried to inflect emotion into his voice it sounded like a frog choking on rocks.

"Tch! Great One. You always catch me!" Kachem was one of his goblins, the only other one that was sick in the mountains. Like Kolus, Kachem's skin had changed after the fever, losing some of its coloring. Kolus' pale complexion, indicative of a life spent largely indoors, had turned the grey of dark clouds full of rain. His blond hair had also fallen out. Kachem's blue skin had turned very dark, almost black–a cold-feeling black–but for some reason, Kachem had kept his jet black hair. *And I would like to know that reason so I can get mine back*, Kolus internally blustered. Kolus particularly regretted the loss of his eyebrows, for all of the specks of dust that assaulted his eyes on a daily basis; eyes which, like Kachem's, had turned completely black. Just like those tiny red-skinned abominations from the hidden library in the Serna Hills.

Kachem could hide himself in plain sight. He described it as hiding in the folds of light. Kolus had a hard time following his description, but there were times where Kachem could disappear completely from plain view. Disappear from everyone's view except from that of Kolus. Kolus' vision had changed and now he could see in complete darkness. It had started with being able to see clearly at night, which he had tested by walking about in the root cellar at night.

It was vision without color, and the shades of grey were

peculiar to him, but it was quite functional. Though this vision seemed to take over as a reflex in poor lighting, he had to be more deliberate and focus on it in good lighting. What Kolus also could see, sometimes, was a glow or, almost, like an aura of things, if he had to put a word to describe it. Kachem described the same thing, though the goblin had said he had already been able to see heat before. He could see Kachem's silhouette even when Kachem disappeared from view.

Kolus had named the six goblins he had brought from the mountains, of whom Kachem was one. There were also Mersik, Spara, Jerna, Panil, and Ys. All had been given to him by the Ministry as prisoners to be used for work. The goblins had given him a choice of the social constructs that were within their cultural understanding: either he was their owner and they were his slaves, or he was the leader of their tribe, their 'Great One,' and they were to be either property or members of his tribe.

Never again, he had thought when they brought it up time after time, but they were quite obstinate on their point that there was no difference between being a slave and being a prisoner. So, he had agreed to be their 'Great One,' but insisted on several conditions. First, that this 'tribe' of his would be subordinate to a greater tribe; second, that there would never, *ever* be any slaves, and lastly, that there would be no more cannibalism. They had agreed to his terms if their own counter-conditions were accepted: that they were all in a clan in this tribe, and that they would meet the leader of the greater tribe one day. Kolus was not sure how he would make that happen, but that was a problem for later.

This all seemed straightforward enough, but they then informed him that his agreement of shared clansmanship constituted entering into a marriage. To all of them. He had argued desperately, and was able to fend off Panil and Kachem's advances in order to keep them as 'brothers' instead of husbands. But… it still shocked him. He suddenly had two 'brothers'… and four wives… and his two brothers were also married to his four wives… and the brothers were married to each other… and the four wives were married to each other. Apparently, this was how Goblin families existed. Everyone in a Goblin clan was married to everyone else in the clan, except for the children, who were to be raised and exchanged with other clans to the young ones' preference when they reached breeding age. This unfamiliar dynamic was quite outlandish to Kolus.

Surprisingly, they all seemed happier–Kolus included. Each morning, after waking up, he and his goblins would go about the chores of maintaining the manor and preparing breakfast. Their manner of cooking was… interesting, but Kolus had come to enjoy it, and after the first time in the mountains, they had never tried cannibalism. Kolus forbade it. They told him it was more of a custom from the hobgoblins that goblins would sometimes mimic.

Kolus would study the piles of books that would routinely arrive, try to make sense of the writings within them (mostly in the old language), and perform an experiment every now and again, which, these days, meant twice daily. A long day of study punctuated with light meals, ending in a sumptuous one, and one or two goblins waiting for him at the end of the day to keep his bed warm. Sometimes three or more.

Many of them had given each other earrings, sometimes two or three earrings in one ear, though occasionally for the eyebrow or the nose. Sometimes in other places. Kachem had two earrings in one of his ears, and he used to have tattoos, but they seemed to have melted away when he had been sick in the mountains. Mersik had an elaborate tattoo of vines that traced from her left hip across her belly, around her waist, and ended on the back of her right shoulder. Much of Panil's chest was covered in a latticed tattoo of interlocking, symmetrical shapes. This was also new and quite bizarre. Yet… he could not turn them away, nor bring himself to spurn their kindness and affections. He could swear that he could almost hear their thoughts when he touched them.

Shipments of books or supplies would arrive weekly, delivered by a lone woman with a cart. They hardly spoke and rarely looked at one another. This was one of many standard operations practiced within the Ministry, enacted so that anyone caught in a compromising situation would have little to no information that could compromise others. All the same, he wore a deep hood and took care to cover his skin; his appearance had changed enough that it would be easy to describe him as 'the bald man with black eyes and skin like a corpse.'

263

And so, the days passed, now into winter with snow kissing the ground. Kolus found it odd that he and Kachem were not bothered by the cold in the slightest. He could dress in a light shirt and breeches, riding boots or even sandals. and walk about in the snow, the slush, or the freezing rain without any discomfort.

It was a strange day when he heard a greeting from the front of the manor. A strong voice of a man calling. "Hello?"

Kolus opened the front door, as he could not let anyone see his family. He recognized a man with striking blue eyes.

Kolus was surprised. "Oh, uh–"

"Don't mind me, Kolus, and let's skip the formalities, please."

"Uh, of course, uh, y–" Kolus stammered.

"Just 'sir,' if anything, Kolus," the man with blue eyes said.

"Uh, yes, sir." Kolus stood awkwardly in the doorway, unsure of how to deflect the unexpected visitation and get this man to leave before he saw anything he was not supposed to. Of course, he owed this man much respect, but he had not known the guest to be in the ministry, and was quite alarmed at this unexpected encounter, let alone the visitor knowing Kolus' name and not being put off by his unusual appearance.

"I'm here for a couple reasons, Kolus," the man said energetically, slightly leaning forward.

"Oh, uh, and what might those be, sir?"

"I'm here to appoint you the Minister of Magic in service to the Crown of Yvel," he answered, as if it were a normal sort of thing to do on a Twosday.

"Ah... right," Kolus answered hesitantly.

"Oh, come now, Kolus, I know enough about what goes on here and who your new friends are. You really don't need to hide it," he said. "And really it's quite tiresome that you try," he muttered.

"Very well, uh, sir," Kolus said skeptically. "You seem quite... accustomed to seeing people that look like me."

"Well... no, this was a surprise," the man said, gesturing

to Kolus. "I'm sure the goblins will be a surprise, too; I've never met any besides at Borly. But, I knew it was here and have a general idea of what you've been up to."

"Right, well… how does one go about appointing a minister?" Kolus said, looking at the ground. Kolus felt unsettled by the abruptness of it all, and of a person of such import suddenly arriving and declaring that they knew such intimate details of his life. Details that could have him burned alive in most places.

"Let's do this the quick way," the man with blue eyes said, producing a book from a shoulder bag hidden in the folds of his cape. Paging through it, he stopped at one towards the middle of the tome and showed it to Kolus.

"What does it do?" Kolus asked.

"It's an oath spell. It requires your consent and binds you to the terms of the oath," he explained. "Would you be willing to accept such a constraint?"

"I… think we're rushing into this, sir. What does being a minister entail?" Kolus paused in thought briefly before continuing. "And how did you learn about that?"

The man sighed. "I was hoping to get you into the job before telling you," he smirked. "Do you… have any coffee?"

"Coffee?"

"Yes, I haven't had any today. I'm dying for it." His azure eyes flitted about the room, seeking signs of a coffee kettle. "To answer your question, I taught myself Old Paetic, and then taught myself from the books I could keep with me."

"Uh, coffee," Kolus chanced a look at the man before turning behind him. "Mersik. It is safe. This man will be our guest. He is very important and I would like us to show him respect."

Mersik emerged from her hiding spot around the corner. Under a thick, undyed shawl, she wore a faded pink dress, contrasting with her deep blue skin. Kolus had been surprised at what avid knitters they were. Her blue hair, which she favored putting in one thick braid, had grown past her shoulders since he met them the previous autumn. "Yes, Great One?" she answered hesitantly, eyes on the visitor.

Kolus watched the man with blue eyes out of the corner of his eye and saw him offer the goblin a friendly smile.

"Coffee, please, my love. Could you make some? And an early midday meal, please."

"Yes, Great One." She disappeared.

Kolus turned back to the unexpected company. "Sorry," he said, "I don't speak Goblin yet. What's happening?" Kolus had completely forgotten. So ingrained in daily life was he, that he had forgotten the once-thick language barrier.

"Sorry, sir, I don't mean to be rude. That was my dear Mersik, my, uh… one of my, uh, uh, wives. She will make some coffee and have the others start on the midday meal."

"She's cute. Quite cute. Might be tempted to get one, as well," he said. Kolus stared in shock. "Oh, don't mind. She is quite appealing, but it's not likely. Propriety, you know. No harems. We're not Easterners like the Mardalons and it would not do to take on the customs of our enemy. Besides, there's already one…" he pursed his lips, "though, I doubt she wants to talk anytime soon, let alone be anywhere near…"

"They're not a harem, sir," Kolus said.

The man with blue eyes looked at him, stunned. "Then what…"

"I had said she is my wife. They're my wives and brothers," Kolus corrected.

"You're serious… is that how…"

"Yes. I find… I'm quite taken with them." Kolus felt his face heat in bashfulness, though he doubted his cheeks were turning red. *More like black.*

Mersik peeked around the corner to motion that the coffee was ready as the two men, blue-eyed and black-eyed, further discussed the proposition. The man with blue eyes wished for Kolus to take on multiple–*multiple!*–apprentices, each of whom would also take the oath spell, and teach them magic with particular focuses. As necessitated, the trained apprentices would be available either individually or in groups to be assigned to military, diplomatic, and constructive tasks.

"If I may be bold, sir, what's my incentive?" Kolus inquired.

"Well, you get to put your mark on all the trained sorcerers of the realm and do things of greatness that will be told of in histories for centuries to come." The visitor frowned, sat up straight, and continued, gesturing grandly. "Through your leadership of younger magic users, Yvel will become a powerful nation, able to shrug off all threats and build unrivaled prosperity for itself."

Kolus sipped his coffee before answering. "Begging your pardon, sir, but I meant more in terms of tangible and the near future."

The man with blue eyes was slightly taken aback but wryly amused. "Well, what do you want?"

"Well, there are a few things we're short on–" Kolus began.

"No," said the man with blue eyes, breaking in.

"No?" Kolus repeated disbelievingly.

"If you need something for its success or maintenance, then we need to give it to you. Don't consider that part of the incentive, just ask for it as part of what you're already doing. This is actually a rather high priority *and* it would be surprising if you asked for the same things as the army or on a comparable scale. This is a very important endeavor to the Prince, so it absolutely must succeed." The visitor finished his first cup of coffee and started to pour himself another from the kettle.

"Use the filter, sir," Kolus cautioned.

"What?"

"The goblins, they brew the coffee directly over the fire. The ground up berries are in the kettle with the coffee."

"Ah, thanks," the man said, fumbling with the wire mesh to filter the coffee out of the iron kettle and into his clay mug. He smiled, gazing at the muddy brew. "They have wonderfully strong coffee."

Kolus scrunched his hairless brow anxiously. "Can I ask later, sir?"

"About the incentives?" the man clarified. "Yes. You can

request three things. General things. If it can be done, you will have them, but no guarantees. It would be best if we could settle now, but if you're willing to take the oath, then let's get on with it."

Kolus was unsure of what to ask for from a man of such importance and responsibility. *If I ask for something too big, it could not be routine. If I ask for something too small, it will not be enough for our endeavor…* "May I have more for my tribe?"

The man with blue eyes looked at Kolus dubiously. "More? Meaning more goblins?"

"Yes. I'll take hobgoblins, orcs, too, or really anything else. Especially more people– humans, that is," Kolus added, clarifying.

"Really? By Orneth. Let's get started on others of our own kind knowing magic before we leap into educating those recently of the enemy… but, no reason not to, supposedly. There will be some added building materials in your supplies. Additional tribe members will exceed the space you have," the man noted. "That's all?"

Kolus braced himself for the next request. "I want to bind them to me."

"With the binding spell? Only on the condition that they are bound to the Prince higher than you–and that *will* be in your oath."

"I understand. And–and I want to teach them magic," Kolus knew he was reaching the limits of what he could reasonably ask regarding the needs of his family.

The visitor paused. "Very well, that's treated as one thing–but your oath and theirs is an absolute." He looked at Kolus, assessing him. "Two more."

"Thank you, sir." Kolus continued. "I want access to all of the research that everyone else in the Ministry has done."

"That will happen anyways," the man with blue eyes waved his hand in dismissal. "You will be *the* Minister of Magic, you know. Still two more things."

"I… will have to wait on those. I'm sorry, sir," Kolus admitted.

The man with blue eyes held up his hand. "No rush. We

have a whole war to win. Maybe two or three. It will take time."

Kolus furled his brow again. "Two or three?"

"Perhaps," the man smirked. "Now, after midday meal, let's go over some of these other spells," he advised, patting his laden shoulder bag.

"What do you have?" Kolus asked.

"Some items to determine your innate sorcerous powers, the strength of your barrier, and a spell that, if maintained, you won't have to sleep more than an hour a week."

"Indeed. I would like to share some of mine, too." Kolus sat up, realizing that this would take some time. "How long will you be staying?"

"Until tomorrow afternoon."

"I see." *This is quite a disruption to the quiet routine.*

"There will be someone else coming. That is the other reason I am here," the man with blue eyes said quietly, leaning back in his chair. "A disciplinary matter for him is an opportunity for us."

"If you say so." Kolus was skeptical. *I had forgotten. He said he was here for a couple of reasons.*

"Why are you so taken by them?" the man with blue eyes asked abruptly.

Kolus' monstrous, angular face fumbled for words and sheepishly half-smiled. "They're really quite sweet-natured, sir. Though, surely, they have their bizarre customs. Their strange foods."

"Cannibalism?"

"…That is something they have done since I've known them… they tell me it is a way of showing respect for the dead," Kolus explained. "I've asked them not to do that anymore."

"Ah, you're already taken with them. Not a fair question. Hm. You're sure they're up to it? That is, that they've the smarts for it?" the man with blue eyes asked.

Kolus leaned forward, full of confidence. "Yes. I am certain. They're all originally from a tribe of engineers from a city of theirs. Kogylar."

"Kogylar…" the man with blue eyes mused. "Well. Very good. Might have to ask for a detailed report on Kogylar from their knowledge… you're sure they would give that information to you?"

"I do think so, sir. They are wholly on our side. Tribe and family," Kolus answered.

The afternoon passed into the evening. Kolus took the oath spell and felt it bind around him in a very invasive yet intangible way; like his soul was being tied with rope. The man helped him perform the sleep spell, and Kolus was surprised at his wakefulness as they studied and exchanged notes late into the night. Spara came to take him to bed, her dark blue hair braided into Marin-style tails, but Kolus, torn between two things he wanted, waved her off sorrowfully, promising to make it up to her tomorrow night. She pouted balefully, her golden nose ring glinting in the candlelight, but left and said that she would make him jealous. *Probably will*, Kolus thought.

The sun rose the next morning and they broke study for the first meal. Spara was sullen after a neglectful evening spent without him, but they all ate together pleasantly. The man with blue eyes was delighted at the sweet and sour cheese they had made themselves. Kolus was glad and relieved that he did not ask what kind of milk they used. He would have had to tell them that it was the goblins' own breast milk. And then there's the whole process for *extracting* the milk. But the man with blue eyes did not ask, so he did not tell.

Ys entered the study and motioned for Kolus to lean close. Ys' skin had tanned into a shade of dark teal, which the others had told him was uncommon, even joking that she had an orc for a grandfather. She had become quite cross with them over it. Kolus could not help but wonder if there was any truth to it. Though she was the youngest, she was also the tallest. The blue-green skin of her neck peeked from underneath a thick shawl that matched the color of her violet eyes, and her shoulder-length indigo hair was tied back.

"Yes, my love?" he said, answering her in Goblin.

"Is this man joining the tribe? It is rude that we do not know him." Ys sounded cross.

"What? No. No, he is not joining. As I said, he is an important guest and I just wish to show him honor. He is going to do very helpful things for us, so I want to make sure he has the best we can offer. He will leave today," Kolus said.

She looked at him skeptically and then hugged his arm and whispered, "Good, because I made this one with Jerna and I want you to make sure that you eat some. It is my turn when you go to bed. No skipping." Kolus flushed dark as coal and she departed without a further word or glance.

"What was that?" the man with blue eyes asked.

"Uh, nothing, sir. Just... you know. Goings-on between husband and wife–wives!" Kolus stammered.

"Hm... maybe better that I watch how you fare from afar rather than plunge in myself," the man with blue eyes chuckled. "You know, Kolus, for the ones that you trust and see an intellect in, it's a good decision that you train them. So long as they are bound under the oath spell to the Prince and the Crown. Suppose through your oath is good enough."

"Thank you, sir, I..." Kolus looked down and smiled. This was something that he had wanted to do but dared not ask. He had often wished he could share the joy of his studies with the family. He had found great fulfillment in both his studies and his new familial relationships. They were his first friends in a long time–really, his only friends, as he could not return to anyone in his former life with such an altered appearance. Not with the rumors about witches and bringers of ruin and such.

"Did you just get something for free?" The man with blue eyes smiled at him. "Good. Satisfied ministers work harder." Kolus could hear him mutter under his breath, "but how to manage the unhappy ones?"

They were finishing transcriptions of the spells that they had learned from each other overnight when a knock came at the door.

"Ah, there he is. Let me try something else." The man scooped up another one of his books, flipped it about a third of the way open, and seemed to find what he was seeking. He briskly stalked to the door and pulled it open. A surprised, young Eklendan nobleman was about to knock again in front of the snowy backdrop of a winter morning. The man with blue eyes uttered an incantation and the young man was seized by an unseen hand. Unseen to most, but Kolus could clearly see the lines between the fingers of this ethereal fist that seized the man, lifted him into the air and forcefully slammed him down. The young man bounced, broken teeth scattering from his now bloody mouth.

Kolus was alarmed. "Sir!? What's–"

"I told you, Kolus, this is disciplinary. Come with me. This is a research opportunity," the man with blue eyes said.

The man used the otherworldly hand to pick up the unconscious noble and brought him to one of the outbuildings of the manor. He laid the young man on a table, holding him in place with ropes made of woven air summoned by another spell.

"Where do you come up with this?" Kolus asked incredulously.

"I told you, I sleep for about one hour per week. It's been that way for almost three months," he said.

Kolus was shocked. "You've been doing this for three months!?"

"Yes. Also, separately, we should make a distinction. There is a difference between the witches we first discovered, and the kinds that we are attempting to create. The ones that have the power in themselves, or that the power builds in them like rain water in a bowl, *those* are sorcerers. The ones that learn from books," the man with blue eyes explained, hefting a book for emphasis, "those should be called wizards."

"You know," Kolus said, anxiously eyeing the unconscious man who was probably going to die soon, "I read something similar last week."

"Really? What book? Who wrote it? Lend it out?" the man with blue eyes was paging through yet another book produced from his seemingly bottomless shoulder bag.

"Uh, Perganott. Yes, you may, sir," Kolus said. "What's this about? Why is he being disciplined?"

"He cost the Prince dearly. He committed two companies

into a fight in Keppa. They died alone, but he *somehow* managed to crawl away. Ultimately, the whole contingent fell into a trap. The regimental leader lost control of the regiment because of this one's foolishness and we lost a lot more soldiers, and the whole of Keppa that day."

"Shouldn't the regimental leader be disciplined?" Kolus suggested.

"I would agree somewhat if he had lived through that. This one's foolishness led to many deep losses, and the Prince should have known better than to force the regimental leader to take this one on as a battalion leader when he was not ready. The Prince should have seen the signs, but now the Prince has to correct mistakes and ensure they do not happen again. That is why this is happening."

"I see…" Kolus said from the side. The man with blue eyes was toiling over other books and the young man. "What are you doing now, sir?"

"Reading his aura, the magic of his blood, if you will, and measuring his barrier," the man said. He muttered several incantations over the minutes. "Ah, another Firecaster. Excellent! And… barrier intact. Very intact. Hm. Well, let's try to pry it open."

"Pry it open?" Kolus looked at the spell the man with blue eyes was tracing with his finger. "That's necromancy…"

"Pah! There's much worse in these books and you know it," the Blue-Eyed Man scoffed.

Kolus couldn't recall the last time he had been astonished this many times inside a day or two; indeed, he could not remember being this surprised ever. Even at Serna Hills, when they all almost died, they were too busy trying to stay alive to have room for surprise. Maybe it was because they expected danger there. Here, Kolus had become accustomed to a quiet life of study with his sweet and loving companions. It seemed as if that life was about to change.

The young man bled a torrent through his eyes, nose, mouth, and ears. The man with blue eyes backed away hastily.

"… Hm. That did not work. Very delicate process."

"Sir?" Kolus called after the man who had started back

towards the manor.

"He's dead, Kolus. I'm sorry to ask, please take care of the body."

"Won't somebody be looking for him?"

"No. Not here, at least. Records say that he went on a diplomatic mission to Eklenda, hoping they would be more helpful than our neighbors. Being a veteran of two battles would, at least seemingly, give him enough credibility to send him on such a mission, especially if he were to survive the journey."

"I see." *Good thing he trusts the oath spell.*

"The sorcerers will be separate from you for a while longer, but they will come to you eventually. Apprentice wizards will come to you much sooner, though. Be ready. Other slaves for you, too."

"Tribe members, sir," Kolus corrected.

The man turned to him with an arched eyebrow. "Truly?" His tone was earnest. "Even with all they've done?"

"Truly, sir. They're not so bad. Just different in their ways," Kolus said.

"But... you know... the war?"

"Yes, sir, but... the war won't last forever. At some point, we have to face each other as people."

The man looked toward the manor, where some of the goblins were bringing in more firewood. "Perhaps you're right. Haven't had the exposure you have." The man looked down for a moment. "A different exposure than most of us... but at the same time, they could have come out of the mountains asking to trade or inviting us to visit. Instead, they came as conquerors and slavers." He looked up at Kolus, "Envy you a bit. Quite a bit," he said with a wink. The man brought his own horse, mounted and rode off in the late winter morning.

Kolus stood in front of the blood spatter where the man with blue eyes' spell had smashed the young man to the ground. He slowly walked back to the outbuilding and looked at the abused body. Blood had stilled from seeping from his eyes, mouth, nose, and ears. He gazed upon him for a while. *Perhaps there is a safer way to open the barrier. That spell is incredibly invasive.*

"What troubles you, Great One?"

"Ah!" Kolus was surprised. "Kachem! Don't sneak up on me like that!"

"I am deeply sorry, Great One," he said. Kolus appreciated that when goblins said they were sorry, they meant it. There was something very direct about the Goblin language. "What troubles you?"

Kolus extended an ash grey hand towards the body. "This young man. He caused a disaster, but I still wonder if he deserved this treatment."

Kachem studied the lifeless figure, lost in thought for a few moments. "I think I know how we can show this young man a way to make up for his failings and be of use to the greater good."

"How's that?" Kolus asked.

"Well, we can use his skin to make pages in a book or a drum. His bones have many uses. Beads, fletching tools–"

"I do not think we need fletching tools," Kolus apprehended. *Oh no...*

"–pins and needles, tool handles..."

Chapter 18

East of the town of Bervale, Yvel Principality.
By the Human Calendar, Sortingday, second week of Arinochis, 794.
A cold and overcast early winter afternoon.

areum and his patrol of twenty-five picked their way through the wreckage of another caravan. This was the fifth one they had come across on the road between Yvel and Bervale, yet had encountered no trouble for themselves. Not even a hint of it.

They had passed through Garber along the way. Arynn and Eevarel briefly visited Sieraean, their dark-haired Elven companion, who had been stationed there earlier by Holbrin to aid in the formation and training of their militia company and, later, the First Garber Regiment. Sieraean barely had time to sit with them for a hasty midday meal, but nonetheless it was a pleasant respite for many in the patrol. Several of the militia–Tenleader Baryn, Conwyn, Alain, Marsen, and Lena–had not seen Sieraean since the Battle of Serna Hills and enjoyed the brief reunion. Sieraean even smiled.

Arynn, however, was concerned that some of the elves were getting too attached to some of the humans, herself included. It was a danger. Elves would live on for many human generations after their friends had died, turned to dust, and were forgotten. It could be very dangerous to become attached to such a temporary kind of creature. *Such a temporary creature...* Arynn thought.

After their visit to Garber, they had pressed on and found this abandoned caravan a few days' ride west. Seven wagons. Like the others, they were all littered with the bodies of the merchants and their guards. Not a single orc or goblin body, though plenty of Goblin arrows, and one axe, long-hafted with a curved spike on the back side, after the style of some western orcs. Garven paced nearby. He motioned to her and pointed at one of the bodies.

Arynn had been looking around at the rest of the carnage when he got her attention, "What is it?"

"Tamarks," Garven said, gesturing towards the exposed

skin of the faces and hands of the dead caravan guards.

"The guards?" she asked.

He nodded. "And most of the drivers. Can tell by the freckles. Most of them are thicker about the waist, too, as their kind tends." She looked at him, but he did not meet her gaze. "Except for these two." Garven motioned towards another pair of guards.

Arynn stepped closer to see what Garven was mulling over. "What do you mean?"

"It's odd."

"What is?" She spoke calmly, but Garven's way of speaking usually included understatement. He was as bad as Tyrnimar in his own way.

"The last few caravans–all of the guards were Tamark and most of the drivers were, too. Dunno why, but that's the way it's been. All the other guards are Tamark except these two. All the other guards have the same gambesons. These... don't fit. Their gambesons were made somewhere else. Different cotton, different weave, different dye..."

"Maybe they're drivers?" Arynn suggested.

"Maybe," he said, crouching down to examine one.

"But...?" she prodded placidly.

He looked up at her and then quickly away. "Um. None of the drivers are wearing gambesons on this one. None of the *other* drivers. I dunno."

"You should tell Dareum Covendran," she said.

"Sure." He got to his feet and walked off.

Arynn was irritated with him and his stingy words. It was always so much to pull the words from him, *almost like he wants the attention!* She continued to look around, but Garven's focus on the two out-of-place guards seemed like a good place to continue. She traced the steps around them. This had been one of the places a struggle had occurred. There were several bodies laying around besides these two. *Hm.*

Arynn noticed that the majority of the other bodies had at least one arrow planted in them. These two did not. One had a gash, maybe from an axe, and the other's skull had started to cave in. She looked closer at the axe wound. It seemed too small to have been made by the long-hafted axe, a weapon favored by more than a few orcs. *More like from a hatchet.*

She searched the area and found some tracks leading away. There were traces of footprints at the other attack sites, but they had been quickly brushed away or covered, so it was odd to find some still intact. *Maybe someone got away.* They clearly were too light for orc tracks, and too heavy for goblin tracks. Unless they were hobgoblins. Arynn had neither seen nor heard of any gnolls on this side of the mountains, nor had she heard that bugbears had joined the invaders, so it was either human or hobgoblin tracks in shod feet. The tracks went on for a few dozen paces before they were scrubbed away. *Hm. Scrubbed away in a similar way to all the other tracks.*

They lost the rest of daylight to digging graves into the frozen ground through the snow and ice for the drivers and guards. Arynn was inspecting Garven's two outlying guards when Alain and Baryn came to move one of them to his grave.

"Hey!" Baryn exclaimed.

"What?" Alain was clearly tired from excavating the frozen dirt.

"Don't you recognize him?" Baryn asked.

"Who? Him?" pointing at the dead non-Tamark guard in the differently made gambeson.

"Oh, what was his name? Remember? Five, six years ago, something like that?" Baryn continued.

"What? What happened?" Alain's patience was wearing thin. Dark would be upon them soon, and with winter's early sunset, they knew they would not make it to Bervale before nightfall. All the same, they did not want to sleep near the fresh graves and Alain was aiming to put as much distance between the carnage and their camp as they could.

"What's this?" Hearing Baryn and Alain's sharp tones, Dareum Covendran and Garven approached.

"My Lord! See? You recognize him?" Baryn pointed excitedly towards the blank-eyed corpse.

Dareum's expression changed from irritable to studious as he peered at the body. "Wasn't he the one that got lost in the drink and stabbed the peddler from Yvel? Five, maybe six years ago? Bondan, I think?"

"Bondan!" Baryn belted out. "That's it! I knew I recognized him from somewhere." He whirled to Alain excitedly. "See?"

"Piss off." Unlike the others, Alain's mood remained unchanged. He was still quite tired and irritable.

"I thought he was in prison for it," Baryn said.

"Me too," Dareum agreed. "These ones you were talking about?" he asked Garven.

Garven nodded. "Was thinking they might be mercenaries."

Dareum shook his head. "All the mercenaries have been contracted, recruited, or conscripted into militia companies or regiments, if they haven't left the area entirely. Pretty funny, if you can imagine a mercenary running from a war. I guess they prefer the quiet caravan work instead of fighting a real enemy." Dareum looked around at the deserted wagons riddled with arrows. "I suppose this enemy's real enough, though. Anyways, all the mercenaries are taken up with someone or another. That's why the guards are all Tamarks these days. The merchants are hiring on Tamarks in the west, since all of their regular guards are in fighting units or dead on the side of a road like this."

"It is a wonder that the army can still function," Arynn observed.

Dareum looked over at her. "What do you mean?"

She gestured back towards the looted wagons. "There is nothing of use left in any of these that we find. Everything is taken."

Dareum looked at her and he almost felt the sparks flying between his ears. "You're right! ... Almost nothing gets through without being hit, but the army never runs out of supplies!"

"Maybe it's coming from the north road through Borly or by boat over the Tald," she suggested.

"Maybe..." He was quickly withdrawing, consumed in

thought. Several of the militia were eyeing him expectantly. When it became apparent that he was too deep in thought to share his insights, eyes drifted towards Baryn, as the ranking tenleader of the patrol.

Noticing everyone was looking at him, Baryn started. "What? Oh, right then. Finish up with these four," he ordered, indicating towards the remaining bodies, "and then we move off a mile down the road. Best to quit this place before settling for the night. Don't want to be around or the Lady of Seven take us." He walked a ways towards the graves before turning back towards the party. "Come on, then! Get moving or you'll catch a chill," he scolded a few of the militia, cajoling them into motion. "You, too, Amryst. Don't give me that look!"

The sun set before they were done with the graves, but found their eagerness to travel in order to make distance from the wreck. Hastily assembled shelters of pine boughs and oiled leather tarps were their only shelter from the wind, and several large fires kept the cold at bay. Someone would be up at all times during the night making sure the fires stayed alight. Arynn had found a log not too far taken with rot to use as a bench and sat squarely facing the fire. She brooded, thoughts consumed by the dancing flames. *How will this all end?*

Garven sat down on the log next to her, surprising her. She hated when he did that. He always seemed to know when she was lost in thought and jerked her out of it. He handed her a stick with a roasted squirrel on it, pressing the grip end into her hand before minding his own roasted squirrel.

"Thank you..." she said irritably.

"Don't thank me yet. Try the inside," he mumbled while chewing.

Exhaling vexedly, she took a bite. She expected the slightly tangy taste of animal meat that came from a creature living off the land. She was not expecting it to be juicy with oils, or the bittersweet, nutty flavor with a soft crunch. "Where did you find the acorns?"

"Same place I found the squirrels this time of year. They heard we were coming and spent the autumn preparing." His manner was quietly smug. "You like acorns, right?" He looked at her sidelong with a mouthful of squirrel meat.

"They are passable," she fibbed. She finished her squirrel before he did. "How do you think this ends?" she asked him.

"This? What? You mean the patrol? The year? The war? What do you mean?"

"The war."

He looked back and forth between the fire and the roasted meat he was finishing off. Grabbing some snow to melt with the heat of the fire, he washed the grease from his hands before answering. "I think that some of my friends will die and others will leave. Maybe I live, maybe I die. Maybe I have a place to go back to at the end, maybe I don't. Doubt I'll be happy with the end, but... do what I can, you know?"

"I see," she said.

***

The next two weeks passed with little incident. There were other wrecked caravans, but no useful tracks. They had all been scrubbed. Most of the fresher markings could be followed up to a point, but they usually crossed a small stream, where Arynn and the other trackers would lose the trail. The three of them: Eevarel, Garven, and herself, agreed that there were twenty to thirty people in the raiding parties, and that the tracks were too heavy to have been made by goblins and too light to have come from orcs. They passed through Bervale, spending one blessed night in an actual bed with an actual roof, before moving on towards Krogen. They reached Krogen at the end of two of the human ten-day weeks, early in what the humans called the month of Halinochis, the coldest month of the year, or what the elves would simply consider to be deep winter.

The patrol walked and rode in through the city gate. Krogen, like Borly, was surrounded by a stone wall. Not being from Krogen nor widely studied in local history, no one in the patrol knew the exact reason why, but Arynn suspected that like Borly, it had been erected in response to raids from border nobles of decades and centuries past.

They arrived in front of an inn, the Ten Wagons, apparently named so for its size–a huge, red-painted building standing five stories with balconies on the fourth floor and the fifth being an attic. It was large enough to accommodate several caravans of merchants, though it was probably tighter living with more guards these days. A very large stable constructed in a barn-like style stood next to it to accommodate horses and wagons.

Another caravan of seven covered wagons had recently pulled in as they arrived. The guards were still unpacking. They looked tired. Curious, Arynn approached them. The lead driver stood at the seat of the wagon, packing things into a bag. He eyed her suspiciously as she approached.

"Good day, master driver," Arynn called.

"Good day," he had paused his packing, but he was still bent over, looking at her sidelong.

"Did you have any trouble on the road?" she asked.

"The cold is all," he replied, guardedly.

She looked at him sidelong. "No trouble from orcs?"

"No. No orcs. I hear the trouble about that is bad, though."

Arynn glanced at his wagon and the other ones behind him. "Where are you coming from?"

"Why are you asking, fair lady?" the driver huffed, agitated. "An awful lot of questions about my troubles from someone I don't know."

"Oh. Your pardon, master driver. I am with Lord Dareum Covendran. He has been taken to task by Prince Arnold to eliminate the Orcish and Goblin raiders on the caravans and the villages."

"The villages!?" The master driver was surprised.

"Yes… have you not heard?"

"Uh, well, being bound to the road, we hear about the things that make us worry the most. So, of course, we hear about troubles on the road. I wasn't… I hadn't heard that the villages were getting raided, too." The master driver squinted off to the side in thought.

She studied him. "Indeed. So, master driver, have you seen anything that might be helpful? Where are you coming from?

Knowing your safe route might help us focus our search along other routes."

"Uh, right," he mumbled, his eyes darting nervously.

Another driver called from further back. "Bisin? Where should I put this?"

"In your own filthy wagon, ya turd courier!" he shouted back irritably before turning back to Arynn. "Sorry, fair lady. Um, we're here from Ivria, by way of Vidara. We kept to the main roads, traveled by day, avoided places with higher ground near the road where we could. Simple matters."

"Thank you, master driver. Good day." Arynn departed, considering the brief interview. *He was peculiar and likely had told everything he knew for his answers… still… he was hiding something.*

"Fair lady?" he called after her. There was a hesitant tremor in his voice.

"Yes?" She turned to look at him.

"You… you smell very nice," he said quietly, his head cast down, looking at her from under his brow.

"Good day, master driver," Arynn left.

***

Jak's crew stood in a circle surrounding him. He was clad in his wrappings to cover his greenish skin, though on this occasion was playing the part of a regular person bundled against the cold, rather than that of a leper.

"Alright, you know the normal. What's expected. Enjoy yourselves. Stay out of trouble. We've got two days here before we move on. Maybe three. No fights. No debts. None of that. You've got your pay, stay within it. You go somewhere, let someone know." Jak put his hands on his hips and cast his gaze about the crew. "I come looking for you tomorrow night. I better find you here in the common room. If I don't, I think that's going to mean something and I will come looking for you. Got it?" Twenty-three quiet nods and grunts answered him. "Right. If you're paying for it, don't eat it. Can't have you catching a pox." More nods and grunts, peppered with a few chuckles, answered him.

They followed him inside and he booked rooms for each of them. He allowed them to pair off if they wanted, and every now and then he was surprised at who wanted to share a room with whom. He was mildly interested in seeing which pairings remained steady and which changed. It was a balance between morale and discipline. Every now and again he had to step in and resolve a dispute, but most kept to themselves and went to the locals for those kinds of needs. When the room assignments were given out, he took a meal up to the third-floor room that he would share with Tansher.

An urgent knock at the door jarred Jak and Tansher from their recreation.

"A minute," Jak buckled his belt in annoyance. He cracked the door. It was Bisin. "What?"

"We've got a problem," Bisin fretted.

"What's that?" Jak asked irritably. "Is this a little problem that can wait or a big problem?"

"Big problem. Can I come in?" Bisin practically pranced, poorly containing his nervous energy. Bisin never asked to come in. He tended to stay away from Jak when he was with Tansher. Jak had asked him about it a while ago and he had gone on another one of his bizarre rants about smells. Jak motioned for Tansher to cover up the rest of the way. "In a minute." Jak closed the door, found the rest of Tansher's clothes, and put a shirt on before letting Bisin enter.

It was one of the larger rooms–they had the money. Jak had been careful to manage and ration it so that the crew would have enough for a good time at the end of the job. *And that was a bad job.* The room had a large bed, already disheveled, a small round table, some chairs, a dresser, and a cupboard. Jak pulled a kettle of water from the fire while Tansher retrieved some cups from the cupboard. Bisin paced nervously as Tansher sprinkled in tea leaves and Jak poured the steaming water. Jak also set out a bottle of plum brandy.

"What's the problem, Bisin?" Jak said as he brought a third chair over to the table and sat down, joining an already seated

Tansher.

Bisin continued to pace. "Someone's looking for us," he blurted out nervously.

Jak curled his lips wryly. "Can you give me a little more than that?"

"Someone talked to me outside before you sent the crew off asking about how we did on the road," Bisin said.

"Who?" Tansher asked.

"A girl–no, a *woman!* She smelled wonderful..." Bisin trailed off dreamily.

"I wager she did, Bisin. Again, give me a little more to work with," Jak said patiently.

"She had a strange look and a strange voice. She had pointy ears like I've never seen before. Must be some kind of deformity... but the smell–" Bisin continued distractedly.

"Yes, Bisin, the smell. I heard the first time. So, a woman with mangled ears was asking if we had problems on the road? Why? Did she say?"

"She said that she was part of a patrol sent by that rotten prince of these parts, sent to find the Orcish and Goblin raiders. She was asking if we had trouble like that on the road."

"And what did you tell her?"

"What we agreed on," Bisin said defensively. "That we came from Ivria, through Vidara. No trouble on the road."

"Fine, then. What else? What about this patrol?"

"She said the prince of these parts told them to do it."

"She say who's leading the patrol?"

"Uh, Covendran or something like that, I think," Bisin answered.

"Fine, then. Don't worry about it anymore," Jak replied.

"Don't worry about it?" Bisin repeated incredulously.

"Yeah. Don't worry about it. They're looking for orcs and goblins. That's how it's supposed to be. I'll bring it up at my next meet. Go on, now. Get."

"Alright, fine." Bisin put his hands up, peaceably. "One

more thing, though."

"What?"

"She said that orcs are raiding the villages, too."

"Huh," Jak said. "Didn't know someone was doing that. Fine. Off with you. Out."

Jak shooed Bisin out of the room and closed the door. He turned to Tansher, who was still sitting at the table. "Get on the bed."

"Aren't you worried about this?" she asked.

"No. I'm not worried about a group of people that are looking for someone that's not us. That's what's supposed to happen. Now get on the bed."

***

The Next Day
A lightning-struck tree, several miles outside of Krogen.
A cold and overcast late morning.

"It's not your problem," Darent said. Jak gave him a flat-mouthed, blank stare, punctuated by the gritting of his small tusks, and waited for Darent to elaborate. "Meaning, I'm pushing you out of here. You're getting reassigned elsewhere."

They were standing out by a lightning-struck tree a few miles outside of Krogen the following afternoon. The air was crisp and scentless. Snow from the previous week blanketed the countryside. Normally, merchant traffic and travelers would have trampled the road to muddy slush by now, but traffic was a bit sparser since the rumors of orc raids had spread. Darent's horse waited on the side of the road as they spoke.

"Ok, wait," Jak started. "First thing's first. The last job–"

"Your crew did a good job on that one," Darent casually interrupted.

Jak pressed on with what he knew he needed to say. What he needed to make absolutely clear to Darent. "We can't do another job like that."

Darent regarded him for a moment, suddenly cold. "That's not up to you."

Jak shook his head and pressed on firmly. "Look. It wasn't the cold, it wasn't the climb, it wasn't all of the people we had to befriend only to cut their throats later. It was the kid."

"It's still not up to you," Darent replied high-handedly, frowning.

Jak knew that Darent would be intent on keeping his balance of power in this relationship. Jak was mostly content with this arrangement as long as the coin kept flowing and Jak had relative freedom to run his team. But, still… the line had to be drawn somewhere. "Kill anyone. Sure." He looked at Darent. "Anyone but kids. I mean, you had to be there. Ripping a kid to pieces like that. I don't know if you believe my story or not, I don't care." He put his hands on his hips and looked at the ground ruefully. "It doesn't matter if I was a killer before 'cause I am now. And I don't mind. No one had a problem throwing me in the hole, so I don't mind ending them… but not a kid, okay? A kid hasn't hurt anyone yet."

"That *kid* would throw someone like you into the deepest pit they could find," Darent warned.

"Maybe."

"Listen, if you can't run this crew, perhaps I need to find someone who can," Darent suggested.

"I really don't think you can find someone to replace me," Jak said wryly. "Not from *inside* the crew, at least. Bisin would be fine if he didn't kill people because of how they smell. Tansher wants to be a string puller. She doesn't want to be *in charge* of anything. Sirid also wants to be a string puller and hates Tansher. Those are the strongest in this crew besides me." Jak leaned on one leg and pointed at Darent. "If you've got someone else hanging in your coat, send 'em my way and we'll see who wins in a knife fight. Oh, and by the way, if you *do* replace me, send an additional fighter too."

"Why?" Darent asked.

"Because Tansher and Sirid are gonna try to kill each other to be the next guy's girl… or the next girl's girl. They both really like controlling things without being responsible. I wouldn't put anything past 'em. The only reason I took a girl is because they were gonna take someone that could challenge me if I didn't," Jak explained. He looked at Darent, "So, I don't know what this bandit baron of yours or whatever they wanna call it is trying to do. Being bandits is fine. Killing a few specific people. Fine. But I'd take a guess that getting people for this kind of work isn't easy. From what I'm hearing *all* up and down the road, you and your bedfellows have a whole lot of us sprung out of prisons for this kind of work. I don't think you've got much to spare that can actually run a crew. But maybe I'm wrong."

"You do the job I give you," Darent said.

Jak sighed. "You're not listening. Look, if you've got a kid to kill, get someone else to do it. You and your bandit king or whatever. You need a hard job done, harder than this one, we can do it."

Darent looked at Jak for a bit. "How much harder?"

Jak returned Darent's gaze. "I'm guessing there's no paper with orders waiting in the hollow of that tree."

"No, things have changed. That's why I'm reassigning you. But, depending on what you tell me, it'll change where you get reassigned. How hard of a job can you handle?"

Jak shrugged. "Whaddya got?"

Darent fished in his saddlebags, checking different labels. He pulled out a large leather purse, heavy with coins. Darent handed it to Jak. Jak looked at the label, silently moving his lips.

Darent observed patiently. "Learning your letters?"

"Tryin'. Slow goin,'" Jak answered.

"The instructions are inside."

"One more thing," Jak had almost forgotten about Bisin's report.

"What?" Darent frowned, concerned that Jak would bring challenge something else.

"One of my guys heard in town that another group is raiding villages and killing everyone." Jak fussed with the drawstring on the purse. "That's not the kind of job we can handle.

Send a weak team to do that."

Darent stiffened. "Noted."

Jak peeked into the purse and pulled out a coin. He turned it over, recognizing the face on one side. "Going to Vidara?"

"Read the instructions. Take a boat back and wait in Ralang. Don't come back this way. It's in the instructions."

Jak put the coin back, pulled the drawstrings closed and tucked it inside his coat. Covering his face back up, he turned to walk back to Krogen. "See you."

"Good hunting," Darent murmured.

***

The Next Day
At the stableyard by the Ten Wagons Inn, Krogen.

Garven tucked the leather bag of hot water into the front-most saddle bag, where he would be able to reach it. Garven looked over and saw some twenty-odd people readying their wagons to depart. Looking back to Arynn, he called her in greeting. She looked up from her own preparations. "Isn't that the caravan you talked to a couple of days ago? The one with the smelly guy or something?" She nodded. "Huh…" Garven finished loading a box and walked over to one of the wagons.

"Good morrow," he called.

A brown-haired woman with a remarkable amount of freckles turned from bucking her horse's reins.

"I see you're leaving," Garven started, trying for a conversation.

"Ah, a clever one," she retorted, cheekily winking at him.

"Uh, my friend said that your caravan just got here two days ago–" Garven tried to begin again.

"Oh. Watching me now?" she teased.

"–and we were wondering which way you're headed," he continued, "cause my friend and I are with Lord Covendran."

"Are you? I think I heard of your friend asking around. Yeah, we're leaving."

"Which way are you headed? I hear there's still trouble east of here," Garven prodded.

"I'm Sirid." She ignored his question.

"Garven," he answered. *She's got the look of Tamark, maybe half Tamark. The rest of them look... local...*

She looked at him expectantly, but he returned it with a blank stare. She sighed when he did not take her bait. "Well, we're headed west. Hauling some cargo out and picking up more supplies for your folks' war for the haul back." Boredom and apathy seeped into her eyes and voice.

"*My folks' war!?*" Garven exclaimed disbelievingly.

"That's what I said. Don't like it? Whatcha gonna do 'bout it?" she taunted him.

"Safe journeys..." Garven walked away, shaking his head. *'Your folks' war!' Like it's not their problem. Honestly.* Garven entered the common room of the inn to answer Lord Dareum's question. A cluster of his patrol mates, including Dareum, were seated at a large wooden table.

Garven approached them. "Lord Dareum? They're headed west."

"Ah, good. They should be safer that way," Dareum acknowledged, nodding through a sip of drink and putting it down on the table. "Small change of plans."

The others seemed to know what he was talking about. He sighed internally. *And I am the last to know.* "My Lord?"

"The innkeeper told Tenman Baryn about a farmer that sells her crops here. She stayed the night a few months ago and was talking about some Tamark girl that had crawled onto her farm with an arrow stuck in her leg," Dareum said.

Garven looked over at Baryn. Baryn shrugged. "Best chance at getting any answers."

Arynn nodded grimly.

***

At a farmstead, one days' march from Krogen.
By the Human Calendar, Fryday, first week of Halinochis (eleventh month
of the year), 794.
Cold with blustering winds that cut like ice.

"Good day, Madam," Dareum said to one of the handful of people working the field. "You the owner of this farm?" This farmer and the others working the field were spreading manure in preparation for the approaching planting season or pruning fruit trees in a frozen orchard on the other side of the acreage.

"No, sir," the farmhand responded. "Try the barn." She pointed to a round, unpainted, building made of clay and timber with a thatched roof capped in snow. The farmhand was old, quite old. Looking around, Garven noticed that they were almost all elderly or very young.

He followed Baryn, Arynn, and Dareum to the barn. A few more farmhands were tending animals or bringing down baskets of crops for use in the farmhouse. One farmer seemed to be at the center of the action, a weather-worn woman with a thick wool coat over a brown dress. A shawl capped her head against the cold.

"Good day, madam," Dareum began.

"Good day, sir. Can I help you?" she said.

"I hope so, Madam. I'm Dareum of House Covendran. We're here looking into the orc raids, by order of Prince Arnold. One of the keepers at the Ten Wagons in town told my man here," he explained, gesturing to Baryn, "that a wounded woman came on to your farm a few months ago, maybe a survivor of one of their raids. If you're amenable and she is willing, we'd like to talk to her about it."

"Oh, I'm amenable. More than amenable. In fact, you're just the set o' people I've been hopin' to come along!" she said. She strode briskly through them, Dareum and Arynn quickly standing aside from the surety of her gait. Garven frowned internally at her presumption. *She may be the master of these parts, but Lord Dareum has been nothing but nice to her.*

Dareum looked at Baryn, who shrugged and gestured to follow her.

"Could I trouble you for your name, Madam?" Dareum called as they hastened to catch up to her brisk stride.

"Carolyn Andavan. This is Andavan Farm," she said over her shoulder.

"Andavan?" Arynn whispered to Garven.

"That's her name," he said to her.

She elbowed him. Garven was certain that no one else saw it–that was the only time she would do something like that informal. It was her style of rebuke that, apparently, she saved only for Garven.

"What?" he whispered.

"Her name is different from the other ones around here!"

"It's less common, but it's an Eklendan kind of name. Some of them end in 'dran,' some of them end with 'van.' Don't know why. Just the way it is. Probably made sense a long time ago," he said.

She nodded and they continued after Carolyn, entering the large farmhouse. She whirled and snapped at them. "Your feet! Wipe 'em off! Just 'cause I have two handfuls a nieces and nephews runnin' around here doesn't mean I put one of them to sweep up after you!"

They sheepishly paused before vigorously scrubbing their shoes on bristly mats placed by the door. Carolyn had continued around the corner. Garven guessed that all the farmhands were related to Carolyn and all stayed in the farmhouse. From both the outside and the inside, it was a patchwork; probably a hundred or two hundred years old, showing the signs of repairs and expansions as the farm grew and the seasons and years wore on it. It winded and rambled, but fit all of them; more than twenty hands, he guessed. Maybe thirty.

They had followed her cranky voice into what seemed to be a second kitchen. Carolyn pulled a timid, jumpy woman away from potato peeling and sat her at the table.

"Right now," Carolyn barked at the younger woman, "this here's your new family. You go with them now. They talk to you, then you pack your things and be off!"

"Whoa, that's a bit sudden," Baryn said, startled.

"It was a bit sudden when she showed up, all limpy-gimpy with the damn arrow stuck in her. She can barely work, so all she does is take up a bed we don't have and eat food she doesn't grow," Carolyn said briskly. "So, have your talk with her, if ya can, then have your walk with her."

Dareum didn't understand. "What do you mean, 'if we can'?"

"Try yourself! She don't talk," Carolyn started to leave.

"She doesn't talk? At *all*?" Baryn asked.

"She did at first. She was all screaming and delirium. She caught sick with the arrow. We cured that of her, but she didn't say anything since. Been more than a month."

"What did she say at first?" Garven said to Carolyn, but he was looking at the fearful woman sitting silently at the kitchen table.

"Don't know. It was probably Marin-speak. We don't got any Marin-speakers here," Carolyn said. She stopped in the doorway, her shoulders slumped and she turned. "Look, I don' mean ta be rude, but I got a lot o' problems running a farm during a war when every lord and lady turns up holding a levy paper that most of us can' read, takin' my able bodies, takin' my horses, takin' what I would normally be selling to pay for repairs and things we can' make here, like pots and hinges and barrel rims. This one," she pointed at the woman at the table, "hasn' been too bad, but things are tight and we don' have the room for feedin' one that can' do all the work, needs mindin', and can' even speak on her own."

"Does she have a name?" Dareum asked.

"We got one out o' her before she froze up. Kudre, I think," Carolyn said.

Dareum scratched his head, glancing at the floor. "I understand, Madam," he said looking up at her. He loosened a purse of coins from his belt and laid it on the stone mantle over the kitchen fireplace. "It's not much, but I hope it makes the winter and spring a bit easier. I will only take the young lady away if she is willing, though," he said pointedly. Carolyn paused and then nodded.

Dareum sat down with the younger woman. She nervously looked at the table, eyes darting over its surface, her forehead wrinkled. "Madam, I heard that you survived an attack a while ago, maybe two months ago."She shrank away from him in her seat, trembling, her side pressed against the wall.

"I'm asking because we're trying to find the orcs that did this," he said. "Prince Arnold commanded us to find them and stop the raids."

She relaxed slightly, but her eyebrows came down. With her wrinkled forehead, it made her seem confused.

"Is it true? You survived one of those raids?" he asked.

Tentatively, she nodded.

"Did you see something that, maybe, can help us find who did it?"

Again, tentative nodding.

"Do you remember anything about the orcs?"

There was that confused look on her face again. She shook her head.

"Hm. Well, maybe you'll remember. Do you think you can come with us? You'll be safe."

***

Common room of the Ten Wagons Inn, Krogen.
One Day Later

"Well, ideas would be good," Dareum Covendran muttered.

Arynn watched him nurse his hot ale. Some humans stuck with ale all year. The entire patrol, plus their new companion, sat around five tables in the common room. It was a large inn with a spacious common room, so even the entirety of their company only populated a small portion of it.

The young woman from the farm would not speak. Arynn was convinced that something in her mind broke from the fear. She and Eevarel had checked the scar on her leg. It could be from a Goblin arrow, but it could also have been from any other kind of arrow. It was beyond belief that either orcs were working with goblins, or using Goblin arrows. Of course, there *were* orcs that used bows or crossbows to shoot arrows and bolts. Their style of smithing arrow heads was different from most goblins. Really, different tribes among both orcs or goblins might make different arrow heads. It happened that the Prince's Army had not fought many Orcish units with archers, but it was odd that Orcish archers appeared here with different arrowheads...

"How about it, scoutmaster?" Dareum Covendran tossed a chicken bone towards Garven. It landed on his plate. Garven looked up from his tea. *That one is salvageable, though, even if he is a bit short,* Arynn thought, consoling herself regarding the company she had to keep. Arynn also noted that Garven had taken to tea right after meeting her, though he said he already made his tea from roots and it was just a different style that they taught him.

"Scoutmaster, sir?" Garven repeated. "Surely Arynn or Eevarel are much more practiced–"

"Be that as it may, they are not in the militia. *You* are. Korane's gone on some other thing for someone in Yvel. That makes you the senior scout *in* the Serna Militia Company," Dareum Covendran said.

"Also makes me the *only* scout in the company, sir."

"Pah," Dareum waved his hand. "We'll fix that next time we pass through home."

Garven pursed his lips. "As you said, My Lord."

"Right. So. Ideas?" Dareum Covendran prodded.

Sipping his tea and grimacing, Garven thought aloud. "Hunter always checks his snares. Want to catch the hunter? Be the bait."

Baryn was curious about what Garven meant. "What do you mean?"

"Sign onto the next caravan going east as their guard. Buy the guard contract, if we need to."

***

On the road to Garber, east of the town of Bervale.
By the Human Calendar, Restday, first week of Halinochis, 794.
Coldly crisp under the clear, winter sky.

Yonn waited for the second signal. The two members of his crew that he had put on the west-facing lookout had given the first signal nearly ten minutes ago. The second signal was late. Yonn was the leader of this crew, though he was sure there were others. He would meet a woman calling herself Ersali, though he was sure this was not actually her name, to receive orders once or twice a month in Garber.

This week's orders were to catch two caravans–this was supposed to be the second one. He had chosen to set up the ambush on a ridgeline that hugged the road to the south and had put a pair on the west side and a pair on the east side to spot caravans and any highway patrols that might rescue them. They had never encountered a highway patrol… but it was better to be ready for the first time than not. After waiting for two days in the frigid outdoors for a caravan to come through, Yonn was ready to get this one done and make off with the goods for Ersali's pickup, probably by another crew, so that they could get back to Garber and get out of the cold.

Irritated, Yonn rose to his feet and stalked towards the south side of the ridgeline, out of view of the road, to see what the problem was with his two dimwits who must have forgotten to send the next signal. The caravan ought to be right at the edge of the corner by now.

Creeping over a rock, he easily rolled down the hill five or six paces and tumbled to his feet in the position where he put his two lookouts.He was about to kick some discipline into them when he realized they were not alone. One of his lookouts was dead on the ground with her throat cut open, the other bound, his mouth stuffed with dry winter grass from under the snow. He saw the culprits –three people, a man and two women, who had made quick work of his westward lookouts. The man hissed at the interruption of being caught.

Yonn opened his mouth to shout in alarm, but the man threw his hunting knife, its tip planting firmly into the roof of

Yonn's mouth. Yonn's vision was suddenly a blur of squares, triangles, and stars of many colors as his sight quickly shrank to a pinpick.

**

Twenty Minutes Later

Baryn nudged one of the prisoners with his foot. They had captured five, killed nineteen. Some had escaped, but none of his patrol members had a firm idea of how many. Roughly five–but maybe more–had gotten away.

"Strange turn of events, huh?" Amryst said, walking up.

"Yeah… who would have thought. Our own people," Baryn said, the numbness he felt internally creeping into his voice. It was the same kind of numbness as when Bonwyn died. Six months ago seemed like yesterday. He still remembered looking into her eyes at the moment the axe split her skull. *And here these people are. No, these* animals, *using the same weapons as orcs. Killing other people. They're not human. They gave that up.*

Amryst eyed one that was glaring at her with particular venom. He was sitting on the cold ground with his hands tied behind his back and one of his own gloves stuffed in his mouth. She kicked him in the side of the head hard enough to knock him over. A muffled yelp of pain was cut short when she kicked him in the face. Tears and blood streamed down the face lying on its side.

Baryn chuckled. "I don't think he heard you."

Amryst kicked him again. "They say anything?" Amryst asked.

"Lord Dareum got a little out of them, but it seems they don't have much. Said that their leader meets someone in Garber a few times a month. Apparently we killed their leader in the scuffle on the hill." Baryn snickered before continuing. "Seems like Garven did when he donated his knife to that guy's mouth. Now *that* was a throw!" Baryn had another chuckle over that. "Anyways. Looks like he never let them go with him, so no one else saw this person."

"You think maybe that it's just bandits taking advantage of the situation?" Dareum asked, walking up. He frowned at the freshly bleeding prisoner on the ground and looked at Baryn. Baryn looked down, as did Amryst, who quickly found a reason to walk away without being too obvious. She disliked Dareum, and if she tried to hide it, which was doubtful, she did a terrible job at it.

Amryst had been in Orn's crowd–before he died–and Dareum had put Orn in his place regarding Kora and Mkaela and their witchery. Same day that Mkaela had saved Baryn from bleeding to death. Amryst still held a grudge against almost anyone that had sided against Orn, as if blaming them for his death. For some reason, though, she never took issue with Baryn. Baryn fingered the visor of his helmet, hanging by a strap from his belt. The steel visor had an orc's face, skinned from the skull, cured and stretched over it. Many in the Serna Militia had the same visor with an orc's skinned face stretched over it. Same as Amryst. Maybe they had a thing or two in common. Maybe.

"Don't know, sir. Still, they've got all the Orcish weapons and the same arrows. Don't think it's these same ones doing all of this stuff. There's too much. Have to wonder… if it's just these ones being bandits, where'd they get the weapons from?" Baryn said.

"Yeah. Good point," Dareum said.

***

Several Hours Later

The two elves returned with Garven.

"We tracked them to a cave, My Lord. We got two more of them. Good count that five more got away. They were in too much of a rush to cover their tracks. They're headed to Bervale."

"Ah." Dareum stepped away from the prisoners and motioned for Baryn to come along.

"Amryst," Baryn called, motioning to the prisoners. "Watch the garbage."

"So what do you think?" Dareum asked, moving out of

earshot.

"It's all like this," Garven said flatly.

"You think so?"

"I agree, sir," Baryn offered. "Too much fits. The weapons. No one ever sees any orcs around, either."

Dareum considered his companions' advice. "So what now? Ideas?"

"Maybe some of the prisoners were in prison, too. We could take them to Garber and see if anyone recognizes them," Arynn suggested.

"Good idea," Dareum said. "That's the next step. We'll see if we can find the rest of this bunch in Garber, and come back and look at the cave later. It's not going anywhere. Once we're satisfied with all of that, I want to go back to Krogen and see if we can get the mute girl to talk. Makes sense why she was shaking her head about the orcs if there weren't any."

Chapter 19

Council Chamber at the Palace of Yvel.
By the Human Calendar, Weddingday (third day of the week), second week of Halinochis, 794.
Cold wind rattles the shutters and seeps through the cracks around the glass windows.

Prince Arnold paced the room, exasperation rolling off of him in waves. Holbrin had been around humans for fleeting times, a year or a decade at a time, over many centuries and seen how poor they were at hiding their emotions, save for a few exceptions. Humans had not changed. *Though, neither have elves*, he supposed with a wry smile. This young prince in particular was quite adept at wearing a mask of emotion in order to achieve momentary goals. While that was a skill that every ruler must learn in order to succeed, it also bred the impression to anyone that recognized it, that one could never know what the ruler was truly thinking.

"The Prince–and the *people*–could really use your support here." The young prince stormed towards them.

Some murmured amongst each other, but Erbasil Halifar, a powerful merchant and the most influential member of the council, spoke. "The guilt you lay on us, Your Grace, does not make prices for us go down." His voice was loud but measured. "It does not lower the cost of labor–which is going up since your army has conscripted most anyone that can walk, breathe, and has use of both hands now. And you can't even keep the roads safe for the wagons to get here! You have no idea how much that costs. We have to bring in drivers and guards from Tamarkand! I haven't even mentioned insurance costs!"

"You exaggerate the conscription rates, sir," the young prince retorted coldly. "And what's more, what happens when the army fails? The enemy comes here? You speak like you have no interest in this, like your own enterprises–let alone your *lives*–aren't at stake."

"Surely, Your Grace," said another council member, "that

the regiments you've raised of brave men and women can defend us." It was Garl Est'ail, head of the carpenter and mason combined guild.

"Tell it to Keppa," he said.

That is strong guilt he is laying at their feet, though it is hard to blame the defeat on supply issues rather than surprise or overmatch. Holbrin grimaced at mental scenes of the flight from Keppa and thanked fortune and the Ways that Bierien happened to have come north for more tools and materials. *Still, four of the newly arrived elves from Abrasian's band died there.* Holbrin had told Bierien to stop at Serna and help there, as Serna was likely the next target for the enemy and desperately needed more help.

"Surely, good lords and ladies, masters and madams, we can see the common good and the common need for the army to be supplied. This is no time to be thinking of profits," said yet another councilman. Trinien had whispered into Holbrin's ear, naming the speaker as Minderl Radidran. Minderl owned shops for making pottery, tanneries, tailors, and the like. Holbrin noted that his enterprises all rested inside protected areas with walls and his income depended on materials being delivered to or from his businesses.

"He has been the most conciliatory in favor of the Prince, too," Trinien whispered.

"Was he always?" Holbrin whispered back.

"Here now," Erbasil Halifar objected loudly, ignoring Minderl. "That was surely a failure of information about the enemy and competence on the ground!"

"Surely?" the young prince challenged. "So, if they had clothing warm enough for the march and the fight to keep the frostbite off that would not make a single bit of difference? Wouldn't have saved the thirty-one more from the Yvel Regiment that died in the cold or lost bits from frostbite on the march back, either. Hm? If there were more horse-mounted scouts that could've provided early warning of the situation, that wouldn't have changed anything?"

"Well, what about–" Erbasil Halifar began.

"Well, what about put some boots on and go fight before you talk about anything besides your fat belly?" the young prince spat. It was a good performance today.

"Still, Your Grace," Garl Est'ail interjected, "this is *Yvel*.

Surely the walls are great enough here."

"Tell it to Versingit," the young prince said dejectedly to the floor. A knock came at the door. "Come!" he called.

A liveried servant entered and knelt before the prince, offering a message scroll.

"Thank you," he told the servant, unrolling the scroll.

"Clearly, this is not–" Erbasil Halifar began again.

"Important enough to interrupt a council meeting?" the young prince snapped, completing the sentence as a question while scanning the unfurled letter. "Perhaps. Though someone thought it important enough." He cast the scroll at the portly council member as he stalked past him. "Why don't you read it to the assemblage here and decide whether or not the council needs to know this."

Erbasil Halifar read the note quickly, visibly shaken. When he spoke, his voice was hushed. "The Princess of Kotara has been assassinated by orcs. She was in her chambers in her palace. She and her guards were torn limb from limb. Kotara is in upheaval with no clear successor, as the Princess was so young." The chamber was in rapt silence, so his quiet words bounced hollowly around the room.

"Read the other side, cretin," the young prince said, in a tone just as soft.

Flipping the scroll, Erbasil continued. "The King of the Berks is dead. Shot with fifteen arrows while out for a morning ride in the snow, then skinned." The merchant paled.

"So! What say the council now?" the young prince taunted.

***

Several Hours Later
The Palace Library, Palace of Yvel City.

"I saw the Prince's performance today," Nicholas said.

The Blue-Eyed Man reclined with a cup of steaming coffee brewed in goat's milk, his feet up on another chair. "Did you like that?"

"Especially the timed message on the Princess of Kotara."

Nicholas chuckled. "What theatrics! You could start a troupe."

"Sure, with time," the Blue-Eyed Man agreed. The message had come in that morning, but the Blue-Eyed Man had saved the announcement for the council meeting.

"With time…" Nicholas nodded. "Did you ever meet her?"

"The Kotaran princess? Once, a few years ago. Her parents were still around then," the Blue-Eyed Man said.

"It ever bother you?"

The Blue-Eyed Man sipped his coffee. "What do you mean?"

Nicholas sighed. "I worry about you, my friend. We've been playing with people's lives in this game for a few months."

"Planning, not playing," the Blue-Eyed Man corrected.

"Planning, fine, but nonetheless, we move people about the game board," Nicholas continued.

"To accomplish a purpose," the Blue-Eyed Man said firmly.

"We're playing with people you know, my friend. Not people you've never met, never seen. Didn't your father have some idea about you and the Kotaran getting married?" Nicholas asked.

"Oh, my. That… it's been a long time since any talk of that. Kind of hard to develop urges and feelings for a child, you know. Not with other preferences for actual women and such. If there's going to be the trouble taken to arrange a marriage, it would be nice to be able to get on with certain things, you know."

"Ah, it's always about that with you." Nicholas shook his head in mild exasperation at the Blue-Eyed Man's appetite. "But I'm trying to be serious here."

"Understand, friend," the Blue-Eyed Man said, "of course, it's hard. It's hard setting criminals to have their way with the highways. It's hard asking you to send someone to kill others, but you know what? It's hard sending people into a fight." The Blue-Eyed Man anxiously scrubbed his hair from his face. "Harder when they lose and you don't have anyone else to blame. Imagine how the Prince feels. Imagine how the Prince felt when Koval died because the Prince himself forced him to take that fool Jof. But this is all necessary. Understand?"

"I understand, friend. It's just–" Nicholas began.

"Just nothing," the Blue-Eyed Man interrupted. "Was she a nice girl? Probably. Don't know. That's not the point. The point is that when Yvel got attacked by an outsider, all the other seats did nothing–just as we knew they would. And when Ardara and Versingit fell to the orcs, that hag in Clovis decided to leap at witch scares and called up the Kotarans and the Berks and the Tamarks! So, yes, the Princess had to die."

"Alright–" Nicolas began to speak, but the Blue-Eyed Man was not done.

"And the only reason I told you to give that hag a scare instead of kill her is that, as much of a scat preacher as she is, she can organize people to do something. She just needed to be steered in a helpful direction."

"And the Berks?"

"The Berks can't see past their own succession. This was really the best time for that old man to die," the Blue-Eyed Man spat bitterly.

"What do you mean?" Nicholas asked.

"The King of the Berks hadn't chosen a successor between his two sons and daughter. They all hate each other, so they'll fight before they agree. They won't be helpful, but at least they're out of the way for now."

"I hadn't heard that," Nicholas said pensively.

"Indeed? Well, what can you tell me that's new, then?"

Nicholas frowned, flipping open a ledger of reports. "The orcs are raiding other villages."

"What?" The Blue-Eyed Man sat up in a cold rage.

"Small ones. Very small. Killing most and taking the rest."

The Blue-Eyed Man put his cup on the table, sat forward, and chewed on his fist in thought. "Have to pull Dareum and his team off of the highways."

"Can you afford that with the council?"

"Bah!" The Blue-Eyed Man rose and stalked around the

table laden with books and coffee. "You're right. We don't have the patrols to deal with that. Boiled piss pastry!" he cursed.

"We could send one of the teams we have in reserve," Nicholas suggested.

"Good idea. Send two. The best. Send the best," the Blue-Eyed Man insisted.

"The best has already been sent on the Vidara mission," Nicholas spread his arms.

"Ooh," the Blue-Eyed Man hissed his breath in. *That job needs the best. But...* "How do you take them to be the best?"

"They did the Kotara mission." Nicholas glanced between his ledger and the Blue-Eyed Man. "They're the team with the half-orc."

"Oh, they're the ones with the half-orc?" The Blue-Eyed Man stood up straight, leaning back slightly on his heels. "Ironic. Huh. Right, what else?"

"I have someone inside Keppa. The enemy looks like they're making preparations for a push north." Nicholas scrutinized the notes in the ledger for additional details.

"Hah! There's the man! Welcome back, friend." The Blue-Eyed Man grinned, before pausing in thought. "What are the conditions there?"

"They've put most of the population to work or taken them off somewhere in the mountains. Mostly orcs moved into the city. Some goblins, very few hobgoblins. Some wolf riders. Handful of these ogres, as you call them," Nicholas read off.

"How many ogres?" the Blue-Eyed Man asked quietly.

Nicholas looked up from the meticulous notes scrawled in a tiny script. "Maybe thirty, according to my man there."

"Hm." The Blue-Eyed Man strolled over to the map of the surrounding lands set up on the central table. "Well, they would have an advantage. Two regiments crushed and they have our main supply of stone, so the wall at Serna can't go much further, even if they had time. Only things Serna has is their own regiment and a palisade. Same things that Keppa had." He furrowed his brow in worry. "Don't know if we'll be ready. Kolus probably won't have anything useful on a large enough scale. Hopefully, the farm will have something…"

"What is it?" Nicholas asked.

The Blue-Eyed Man had pushed away from the table and wandered off in thought. "The Prince is concerned very much about his younger siblings. Oswald and Velthuria are coming along fine and rising to every task. Aered is learning much as Oswald's side, though he's a bit too unseen." He paced around the map table. Nicholas had to turn to keep him in view. "But, the Prince is concerned about the twins and Larz. Larz is a gentle soul. The sisters… They want to do something. They feel awful languishing about simply because of their sickliness. The Prince is tempted to send them to Kolus to study, but they'll take sick, especially on that farm, and we can't have Kolus and his thirty-eight, or however many, wives running about."

"Truly, but… maybe Kolus can work on something for that?" Nicholas suggested.

"Maybe he can," the Blue-Eyed Man said bleakly. "The Prince is tempted to ask you to introduce them to the topics in all your spare time. He would do it himself, but he's an army to lead."

"The point from then is sustained. For the Prince's will, I will try to make some time to begin the education of the sisters and Larz on these things. Perhaps as a primer before something more dedicated with Kolus. But, to pull you back, one more thing on Keppa," Nicholas said, changing the subject. "There were humans walking around with the orcs and goblins."

The Blue-Eyed Man slowly looked over with an eyebrow raised. "Start with the introductory tutoring, but about Keppa, go on."

"They seemed to be… on their side," Nicholas said. "My man is still learning the new languages; he's getting there, but it's developing slowly."

The Blue-Eyed Man turned and stared intently at Nicholas.

After an awkward moment, Nicholas spoke. "What?"

"Just as you have a man in Keppa, they'll have someone in Serna and someone in Yvel." It was a statement made by the Blue-Eyed Man, not a question.

Nicholas nodded. "You're probably right."

"If you have someone to spare, put them on it," the Blue-Eyed Man instructed.

"The only one I could spare is the new recruit, but I have him working on translating Elvish for Kolus," Nicholas grimaced.

"No, that's more important." The Blue-Eyed Man sighed. "Still, impressed that you got him to sign on."

"It's tenuous. He doesn't like doing it. He has a pretty good idea where it came from and they all know each other." Nicholas looked to the side anxiously.

"Well, keep your eye on him. I trust your judgement, friend."

Nicholas forced a small smile. "Thank you, my friend." His companion nodded, resuming drinking his coffee. Nicholas continued. "The orcs in Versingit seem to be biding their time. They've moved more orcs and goblins into the city. I have a few contacts there."

The Blue-Eyed Man raised his eyebrows. "Like that Smeld fellow, the rat-man?"

"Yes, him and a few others."

"What's your feel of it? Will they come south from Versingit?" the Blue-Eyed Man asked.

"Hard to say. The feel, for now, is that they're trying to turn Versingit into a larger logistical base."

"Hm," the Blue-Eyed Man grunted, a thoughtful expression on his face. "Well, they're deliberate, can give them that. Imagine that Smeld is cross that we're not in Versingit right now. When we get a chance, Kolus will have to do a study on what exactly they are. Never heard of rat people."

"He's a chimera," Nicholas noted.

"A chimera?" the Blue-Eyed Man repeated quizzically. "Aren't chimeras supposed to be with a lion–"

Nicholas shook his head. "Yes, yes, not a *true* chimera. A *created* one. It was in Lian's writing. Don't worry. I've handed all of that over to Kolus."

"Friend, fairly sure you kept a few books. Knowing you… as many as… seven. That's probably what you thought you could hide."

Nicholas smiled ruefully, collapsing in his chair helplessly. "You know me well, friend."

"Really, it's fine, as long as you can keep this up," the Blue-Eyed Man assured. "So. What else?"

"I don't have anyone in Clovis. Tight knit group, you see, but I would be worried that, with all of the knights arriving here due to the schism, one of them might be sending messages back."

"Understand." The Blue-Eyed Man nodded. "Do your best to keep track of what that hag does. She'll have to pick between whether to save herself from the orcs or save the Berks from themselves. If she sees through the deception and abandons the Berks, she's still dangerous, but less so without the Berks and the Kotarans. Also, let me know about chasing down that team of deserters and how you're going to put a scare of orcs into the Tamarks. What else?"

Nicholas pursed his lips. "In a few weeks, I should have someone back from Kogylar."

"You got someone into Kogylar?" The Blue-Eyed Man frowned in approval. *Impressive*. "No small task."

"It's not permanent, but it will be enough for a picture of what goes on there."

"Very good." The Blue-Eyed Man reclined again after helping himself to another coffee and pastry.

Nicholas took a deep breath before speaking. "It's something worth considering."

"What is?" the Blue-Eyed Man looked over, not comprehending. "What do you mean?"

"The orcs have humans living among them. How does this end?" Nicholas asked.

"This ends with us winning and being more secure," the Blue-Eyed Man said, squinting at Nicholas as if he was puzzled at having to state something so obvious.

"Yes, but… what about all of the Orcish and Goblin

prisoners? Knowing you, you're going to want to take something of theirs. Are you just going to hold them as prisoners forever? What about Kolus'... family?" Nicholas spread his arms and shrugged plaintively.

"Don't ask that," the Blue-Eyed Man retorted, turning away.

"Friend, you need to start thinking about these things. We've got a half-orc on one of the teams. Your Mkaela witch has two Orcish women with her, and two other women that are going to soon birth half-orcs. What does this all look like after the war?" Nicholas insisted.

"Don't ask that. Not now. Can't think about that now. *They* killed *our* people. They *killed* Prince Gerald." The Blue-Eyed Man was on his feet, ranting.

"Fine, friend. But think about it sometime, please. These people are here now and there will be more later."

"Heard one of the Orcish women joined the Serna Militia and the other stayed with Mkaela," the Blue-Eyed Man said.

"And...?" Nicholas asked, as if it made some kind of point.

"And we don't have enough people to be picky. We'll use them 'til they're dead. Maybe they can pay back some of the blood their filthy brood spilt."

***

Infirmary, Palace of Yvel City.

"Almost there! Keep pushing!" Kerzin coached. Kerzin, the elderly chief surgeon for the prince, coached Aphra on one table, while Danfreys, who usually went to the field with the army, coached Marlar on another table. Behind a curtain were rows of wounded from Keppa, either from battle or frostbite.

"ARGH! You can ROT!" Marlar screamed at Danfreys.

"It's alright, Marlar. We'll be through this soon," Mkaela soothed, though internally, worry gripped her.

Marlar swatted at Mkaela. "What would you know!? 'Cause you already squeezed out a thing or two?"

"Mkaela, get out of the way!" Danfreys scolded, shooing her away.

Mkaela felt powerless to help her friends. All she could do was stand to the side with Buel. She busied herself by checking on the wounded behind the curtain. Most of them had gone through the worst and were recovering after treatments from Danfreys, Kerzin, and herself, and just needed to rest. Some still lost a finger or two to frostbite, or part of an arm or a leg to battle, but they could still perform other jobs. *And some will go back to fight, whether they want to or not*, Mkaela thought bleakly. *And because they have seen the most, they will be given new positions training recruits and conscripts.*

"Mkaela! Help Aphra!" Kerzin's urgent call propelled Mkaela back around the curtain. Marlar came into view first, panting for breath on her bed, her face strained from the pain. But she was attended by only a nurse. Kerzin, Danfreys, and another nurse were crowded around Aphra. The nurse was patting Aphra's forehead with a damp cloth. Aphra was unconscious and pale. Kerzin and Danfreys were both crouched between Aphra's legs. A trail of dark wetness soaked from Aphra's bed and trickled onto the floor.

Mkaela's eyes went wide. "So much blood!"

"The baby's too big inside her!" Danfreys growled.

Kerzin cast a glance over her shoulder at Mkaela. "Get over here! The womb burst. Can't you close it up or something?"

Mkaela nearly slipped on the blood-slick floor as she rushed to Aphra's side. Marlar spared her a pained, angry gaze. Mkaela took the meaning; *I won't let her die.*

Mkaela placed her hands on either side of Aphra's exposed, distended belly. Closing her eyes, she delved, feeling for injury. It was not hard to find the gaping tear under the skin, deep inside Aphra. Blood and other fluids were intermixing where they should not have been. *This is really bad!* Mkaela started to close up the tear, but realized that it would squeeze the baby. *Scat!*

"You're right. The womb tore, but if I close it, it will suffocate the baby," Mkaela fretted. Glancing up at Aphra, whose breath was shallow, she realized it was bleeding, not pain, that had caused Aphra to lose consciousness.

Danfreys' tone was calm but laced with urgency. "Is the baby too big? Do we need to cut it out of her?"

Kerzin grimaced as she inspected Aphra's canal. "No... I can see the baby. It'll fit... It's going to suffocate soon if we don't do something." She looked at Danfreys. "Push it."

"No, we can't. It'll break the womb... oh," Danfreys scurried to the other side of the bed and looked at Mkaela. "I'm going to push from the top here. How bad is it inside?"

"Bad." Mkaela did her best to hold the tremble from her voice.

"Well... do what you can." Danfreys felt around Aphra's belly until he felt the baby's struggling legs and started to press.

Mkaela felt the baby shift in the Delving. More fluids rushed and pressed into places they were not supposed to be, but the baby's out of the way, now! She closed the tear in the womb, leaving a small hole for her to urge fluids back to their proper places before sealing it. Closing the wound helped Danfreys push the baby out.

"I have it!" Kerzin panted. Seconds later, Mkaela heard the weak cry of the half-human newborn. Mkaela caught a brief glimpse of the baby. Its skin tone was halfway between that of Aphra's fair skin and the mottled green of its nameless orc father. Mkaela brought her attention back to the Delving and healed the rest of the tears. *She's lost a lot of blood...* a glance up at Aphra offered Mkaela a small relief. Her breathing was easier, and some color had come back to her face, though she remained unconscious.

The surgery staff had shuffled positions. The nurse at Aphra's head took the baby while the other nurse cut the cord and handled Aphra's afterbirth. Kerzin and Danfreys were huddled around Marlar now. Mkaela came around to the other bed.

"Well?" Mkaela almost cringed as she asked. Marlar looked irritably between Mkaela and the two surgeons.

"I see the baby. It'll fit." The tone of Kerzin's voice sent another tacit message beneath his words: but it will be tight, and this will hurt.

"It's ready," Danfreys added. "Hold her hands," he directed Mkaela. Mkaela gripped Marlar's hands.

"Mkaela?" Marlar pleaded, her anger transforming to fear.

"Push!" Kerzin commanded.

Mkaela felt Marlar's fingernails dig into her hand as she clenched her entire body.

"Breath! Push!" Kerzin beat on with a steady stream of instructions. Marlar screamed in pain, over and over again. Mkaela's hands had started to bleed where Marlar's nails had punctured her skin.

"Mkaela! Please! Can't you do something? Make it stop hurting! Ah! It hurts! It hurts!"

"PUSH! Curse it!"

"AH! MKAELA! PLEASE!"

"PUSH!"

Another crying voice weakly joined the cacophony as Marlar pushed out her baby into Danfreys' arms. Kerzin coaxed Marlar to keep pushing.

"Why?" Marlar pleaded weakly.

"The afterbirth, girl, push it out or it'll fall out of you later and make a mess." Kerzin was calmer now.

The worst is over, Mkaela comforted herself.

"It still hurts," Marlar feebly whined.

Mkaela went to work, finding the tears and bleeding through Delving and mending them inside Marlar's body. Marlar breathed easy as she accepted her large, green child from Danfreys, swaddled in one of the few clean linens remaining. Aphra still lay unconscious.

Kerzin shooed Mkaela off as she ordered the nurses to fetch a dense beef broth for the two new mothers.

Mkaela went back to tending the wounded but quickly reached a point where her fussing was more of a bother than any real help, so she waited with Merik and Risit in their guest apartment in the Palace. Hours later, Danfreys knocked at their door before entering the chambers.

"Did it...? How...?" Mkaela practically clawed at him for information.

"They're fine," Danfreys calmed her. "Everyone's fine."

Mkaela exhaled and sat back down. Merik and Risit looked at the visitor expectantly.

"But...?" Risit prodded.

Danfreys sighed. "Aphra does not want to mother her child."

"What?" Mkaela asked, dumbfounded.

"She and her sister argued about it before sleep took them, but Aphra has relinquished her child," Danfreys said.

"But... what will happen to it?" Mkaela said. "How can she—"

"Lady Mkaela," Merik said quietly, "put yourself in their shoes. Remember how those children came to be. Can you imagine going through that? Having your life destroyed like that on top of what you went through?" Merik paused, gathering his thoughts. "You told me that some of the people you found had been partially eaten alive. Can you imagine going through that? Watching that?" Mkaela squirmed uncomfortably through Merik's point. "That is what Aphra sees when she looks at that child. She can only see all of that. Marlar can see her child, but Aphra can only see the evil that came before. Can you blame her?"

"Yes, but, well, no, but what fault does the *child* have?" Mkaela pleaded.

"The child has no fault, so we do what we can for the child," Merik said. He looked to his wife, Risit, and nodded to her.

Risit spoke to Danfreys. "We would take the child into our household and raise it as a ward, if Marlar accepts. We will respect Marlar's rights as an aunt and can offer her a place for herself and her own child as well, if she accepts."

Mkaela looked at them, wiping her eyes. "This doesn't make any sense," she said softly.

"We thought this might happen," Risit said, "and we discussed and agreed. This is what the Way of Orneth is supposed to be about. Helping the weak and helping them be strong so they may help others. Fighting wrong to make right. Mercy. Forgiveness."

"It seems so far from what Dum'ail would preach about," Mkaela muttered, gazing off into an unseen distance.

Chapter 20

The militia archery range just outside the town of Serna.
By the Human Calendar, Breathday, second week of Halinochis, 794.
By the Elven Calendar, forty-fifth day of Winter, 18031.
By the Goblin Calendar, sometime in the Second Moon Cycle.
A crisp, late winter morning, with wet snow in the fields and slush in the streets.

The bow's spine cracked as Karsi pulled on it.

"That's it! That's the second one! No more! You're too dumb!" Dyram Torin'ail bellowed, snatching the splintering bow from her and throwing it onto the snowy ground. "Grab a spear or an axe and swing it hard, 'cause that's all your kind is good for!"

"You say pull to chest," Karsi defensively snapped, sweat beading on her green skin.

"Well, maybe you're too big and too dumb!" Dyram yelled.

"Maybe you–" Karsi began to spit back before someone interrupted them.

"A moment, Tenman Dyram Torin'ail," Bierien said.

Dyram scowled at Bierien. "Stay here," he curtly ordered the Orcish woman before stalking towards Bierien. Bierien noted Karsi's smoldering frustration fuming in Dyram's wake. .

"You have a problem with how I train my soldiers?" Dyram accused.

"Yes, I do," Bierien answered plainly.

"What's the problem?" he said. He was confrontational in his tone.

"You need to adjust your training methods when your soldier has a significantly different ability, and recognize when they are trying," she said.

"The piss, I do! She just–" he went on.

"Look," she said, silencing him. "Look at her. Go on. Turn

315

and look at her."

Grudgingly, he turned and looked at Karsi.

"What do you see?" she asked.

"I see a big, dumb orc," he said. She gave him a healthy knock on the helmet with her fist.

"Ah! What was that for?" he accused.

"I am adjusting my training methods for the trainee's ability," she said. "Is she wearing a gambeson?"

"Yes," he said impatiently, "a big one." Eyeing Bierien balefully.

"And a helmet?" she continued.

"Yeah," he said irritably, "a *big* one."

"Bigger than any others?"

"Yeah! They had to be made to fit her!"

"So, why are you surprised that she breaks these bows when they are too small for her?"

He turned towards Bierien, fuming. "What do you mean? What am I supposed to do with that? These are the bows we've got."

"You have bows that are a bit more than a pace long. I have asked before why you do not use the Markian tall bow."

"Because we make the Eklendan bow with horn and bone, so that it is smaller, but just as strong."

"Fine, but what if you made the tall bow with horn and bone in the same way?" Bierien asked.

"*Because* then no one would be strong enough…" He scowled at her, starting to understand the direction this was going.

"Permit me a demonstration?" Bierien asked.

Dyram sighed. "Fine."

"Is she wearing her gambeson and helmet properly?" she asked.

He glanced at Bierien sidelong. "Yeah."

"Is that how you told her to do it?" Bierien asked.

"Yeah," he said.

"So, is she dumb?" Bierien asked.

Dyram curled his mouth in defeat. "No more than the rest of us, I guess."

"Karsi?" Bierien called. "Please come here."

"What's this?" Dyram asked.

"Part of the demonstration," Bierien said, as Karsi stepped up.

"What?" Karsi asked. It was not a rude tone. Bierien knew that it was the language she had picked up from absorbing how other people spoke. The Orcish woman spoke in a confusing mix of Eklendan and Marin words, and sometimes she would structure her sentences following Marin structure, but using Eklendan words. It could be confusing for Bierien, who had learned both languages, and a few others, fairly recently.

"Could you please pick up Dyram Torin'ail?" Bierien asked.

"What?" Dyram said incredulously.

"Pick please up?" Karsi was confused.

"Lift. Gentle." Bierien said.

"Ung," Karsi agreed, which Bierien thought was her approximation of 'oh.' Towering over Dyram, Karsi reached out with one hand and grasped him by the armor through the shoulder opening, her fingers reaching the collar.

"Whoa! Wait!" Dyram protested as she lifted him off of his feet, flailing his legs and grasping her arms.

"This way?" Karsi asked Bierien uncertainly over Dyram's panicked objections.

"Yes. You can put him down now," Bierien said. "Thank you." Karsi placed Dyram back on the ground.

"So, what do you have in mind? A stronger bow?" Dyram made a show of demanding the question, but it was apparent to Bierien and Karsi that he conceded the point.

"Yes. Too strong for me to make alone. I will need her strength to help bend the wood and horn."

"How long?" Dyram asked.

"Six days of work and a moon for the bow to be done, with all the materials. I assume there are some spare pork bones and sheep or deer horn laying about."

"You mean a month? That takes it half of the way into Talinochis, if not the end of the year." He sighed, resigned. "Fine. Hope it works. Probably for the materials. See the quartermaster," Dyram waved. Bierien asked Karsi to leave with her. Bierien noticed the two of them exchange a look; Karsi's expression placid and Dyram with his face downcast but looking directly at her. It was as close to an apology and a forgiveness as they would be ready to make.

Bierien and Karsi quit the training field, saw the quartermaster for materials, and gathered them in Bierien's workshop near the smithy. They set about making three custom bows for the formidably framed soldier.

"Why this many?" Karsi asked.

"It will take time for the glue to dry properly. When we are done, I want you to use only these two. We wait half of a year to finish this one." Bierien pointed to the spine of the third bow.

"Will these two... break?"

"They should be good enough, but this one will be the best," Bierien explained, again indicating towards the third. "Use either of the first two until we finish the best one. Once we finish this best one, use that and we will try to finish these other two."

As they were making three bows, the crafting took the better part of seven days of labor. They cut and carved the wood, horn, and bones, and cut ox sinews to length. A bow of this size had to be made of strips of wood laminated together–Karsi was too tall and her arms too long for a segmented bow made of the available horns. Gluing the pieces together, they clamped them to rectangular wooden frames, leaving them to heat near the forge fire at the smith during the day for three days, and to cool during the nights.

Each time they came to the smith or the carpenter's shop, Bierien noticed the suspicious looks that Karsi received from the townsfolk. Bierien could not blame them, considering what they had been through. What they had seen. *By the Ways, never in my three hundred summers did I think that an elf would be helping an orc and humans cooperate*, she thought to herself wryly.

With the construction of the bows completed, they still required time for the glue to dry. In the meantime, Karsi had drawn a stock weapon from the quartermaster's stores to continue training while waiting for the bows to be ready. The quartermaster had issued her a captured Orcish axe, long-handled with a crude, heavy blade, taking the opportunity to jeer at her.

Rejoining Dyram and the other militia at the training fields, she wore a wry look of her own.

"Suits you just fine, does it not?" a few voices had jeered at her.

Bierien bristled at them internally, but Karsi took it without complaint.

Dyram shrugged. "I don't really have much anyone that can train you on an axe that big. Not with those arms. Here." He brought her to a practice target of straw. "Big things. Use the weight, when you can. Downward stroke at the head and shoulders." He showed her some downward and diagonal strikes. "If you cut from the shoulder to the other hip, it's harder for them to block. You try."

Karsi took the axe and raised it high. She compressed her core and arms sharply, cleaving the target dummy, wood core and all, in two. "This?" she asked.

"Uh, yeah," Dyram stammered, wide-eyed, "like that… here, let's put you on a large stump so that we still have dummies left at the end of the day."

Bierien watched from afar. Karsi was largely left to develop her own style. It was not suited to fighting in a line; she left too much of a swath around her with powerful axe swings. Her style, though still developing and clumsy, was still mainly offensive, Bierien noted. *And an offensive style needs protection.*

Bierien paid another visit to the smith. "Have you spare mail?" she asked.

"Yeah." One of the forge workers pointed to a pile of mail shirts and patches off to the side in the smithy. Her name was Arbera Rollodran; before the war, she and her husband were millers, but when the orcs came, her mill was destroyed and her husband killed. "What for? That thing you've been with?"

Like pushing a boulder up a hill. "For Karsi."

"We need it for the militia," Arbera Rollodran objected.

"Excellent," Bierien smiled placidly. "Karsi is in the militia. Thank you." Most of the other forge workers seemed indifferent—one even helped her get the mail; two unfinished shirts would do. Arbera Rollodran scowled, but said nothing.

"What's this for?" the forge worker, a man named Danick asked. Danick was part of the large Rollodran family in Serna. Bierien had worked with him for a few months before she moved down to Keppa and he seemed much more work-oriented than Arbera. Or perhaps, he simply complained less.

"I am making a shirt for Karsi. None of the shirts are big enough," Bierien explained.

Danick Rollodran shrugged. "Want help?" She looked up from her metalworking skeptically. "I can help in the evenings after my main work is done," he continued.

"That would be nice. Thank you."

He tilted his head and spoke plainly. "Fine. I have someone that badly needs employment during the day time, if you don't mind the unwilling help."

"Who do you mean?" Bierien asked.

"I'll be back," he said, and left without offering further explanation. Bierien returned to breaking and rejoining rings of mail to sufficiently enlarge the arm holes. Danick returned some time later, roughly dragging Ziek Miykodran alongside him, his mouth and jacket riddled with crumbs from a stolen pie.

"I didn't take it. She told me I could have it!" the boy protested.

"I'm sure. Well, nothing's for free. You're to help Madam Bierien with these rings until I'm happy."

At first, the boy was defiant and unhelpful. After three days of patient vigilance, in which Bierien corrected him time and again, he sullenly worked without complaint, albeit slowly. Danick joined them in the evenings, and by their combined labors, the shirt was completed within a week.

Bierien laid the piece aside in her room at the Moradran

Inn and drew on a large, rectangular piece of pork leather. She cut the skin into a stomach and chest piece, leaving a wide berth around the neck and shoulders, boiled it in wax, and set it on a round mold. Once it had cured, she affixed buckles and straps with a punch and studs. It would fit over the mail shirt and offer additional protection. Laying that aside, she released Ziek from his repayment of procured sweets and thanked Danick. She presented it to Karsi the next day.

"Thank you," Dyram said quietly as he watched Karsi train. "I was thinking the same thing."

Bierien turned her head to look at him curiously. "Then why did you not ask?"

Dyram hissed in irritation. "I mean that the way she swings the axe, she can't have anyone around to protect her. She would be all alone."

"I see." Bierien turned back towards her view of the militia training. Karsi had been appreciative, too. She even smiled, which was a rare occasion, though an occasion still marred by scowls of onlookers around at the training field or around town. Dyram looked away when Karsi smiled.

The end of the next moon approached, and the adhesive of the two bows had finished curing to Bierien's satisfaction. Well over two full paces long when strung, nearly three paces unstrung, the bows were made of laminated wood with horn on the back side, ox sinews on the front side, arms of the bow wrapped in leather, and tips reinforced with bone where the string mounted. Bierien took Karsi to the archery range. Dyram and a small crowd of militia watched. A few in the crowd jeered.

"Shut up!" Dyram silenced them.

"So, when you draw this bow, hold this arm straight, like with the other bows. Draw the string toward your face. Use these arrows." Bierien indicated towards a pile of arrows she had provided. She had to cannibalize the heads from other arrows and source longer shafts before refletching them, in order to account for the considerably longer draw of this bow.

Karsi, standing the same thirty paces from the target that other archers stood, nocked an arrow and drew it to her face. Bierien heard the wood and horn creak and cringed internally, hoping that the glue would hold.

"Now, let go," Bierien coached.

Karsi loosed the arrow. It streaked through the air in a straight line, leaving a puff of hay where it passed through the hay bale they used for a target, searing forty paces beyond, striking a tree stump and breaking off a segment of old bark.

"Whoa!" Dyram shouted amid murmurs and shouts of surprise. "You could kill a bear with that! With one shot!"

"If she can hit it," Bierien commented. "She missed the target circle on the hay bale. She'll need to work on accuracy, but she can probably hit a target with a straight shot at about one hundred paces."

"A hundred paces…?" Dyram said, "without arcing?"

"Yes, a straight shot. I will teach her how to fletch her own arrow shafts. Hers are almost twice as long as the other arrows. Perhaps something the young Ziek Miykodran can help with."

"Oh, I'm sure he'll love that," Dyram chuckled.

Bierien looked around. There were mixed reactions to Karsi's display with the bow. Many remained suspicious or afraid. Some were indifferent. Others welcomed her. It would be a long road for Karsi. A long road for any orc or goblin or hobgoblin.

***

At the edge of cut-back forest, outside Serna's walls.

By the Goblin Calendar, twenty-eighth day of the Third Moon Cycle, 3115.

By the Human Calendar, Fryday, third week of Talinochis (twelfth month of the year), 794.

Korane and the wolf rider walked at the front of their crowd of shivering humans, goblins, and orcs, nearing the end of their pilgrimage out of the mountains. "What is this place, Great One?" the wolf rider asked.

"It is the place where I am from," Korane said.

The wolf rider chuckled bitterly.

"Problem?" Korane arched an eyebrow and pierced the wolf rider with a sidelong glare.

"No, Great One," the wolf rider replied. "I thought that you were from further left along the Mountains, even if in the human lands."

"You made that impression yourself from my appearance," Korane said forcefully.

"Uh, yes, Great One. As you say." The wolf rider deferentially looked away.

Korane could see the guards on the palisade gather in response to the cluster of nearly a hundred figures walking out of the woods. When they reached a quarter mile distance from the palisade, Korane bade them to wait.

Korane walked alone to the gate.

YOU WILL THANK YOURSELF LATER.

So you say. I can't believe I let you talk me into this! Korane thought back.

I DECIDED NOTHING FOR YOU. I ASKED YOU WHAT YOU REALLY BELIEVE AND YOU CHOSE FOR YOURSELF. NEED I REMIND YOU ONCE MORE?

No. Thank you.

YET YOU SEEM DISSATISFIED.

Of course, I'm dissatisfied! They took my life from me! My son. My husband.

YOUR SON AND YOUR HUSBAND ARE AT PEACE.

How would you know!?

I AM A SPIRIT. I HAVE TOLD YOU THIS. I WAS ABLE TO SEE THEIR SOULS PASS BEYOND. THEY CHOSE A PATH OF PEACE.

So you say.

I DO.

Korane broiled on the inside. *I hate them.*

THIS WILL PASS.

I don't see how.

IT DOES NOT MATTER IF YOU CAN SEE IT OR NOT. YOU HAVE CHOSEN A PATH AND OBLIGED YOURSELF TO THESE PEOPLE. THESE ARE *YOUR* PEOPLE NOW.

My *people.*

YES. *YOUR* PEOPLE. YOU HAVE MADE A CONTRACT OF WORDS WITH THEM AND THEY HAVE FAITH IN YOUR ABLENESS TO UPHOLD THAT WORD.

But they slaughtered my actual *people.*

THE ONES HERE DID NOT. IF YOU ARE REFERRING TO THE ONES THAT MADE OFFENSE ONE-HALF YEAR AGO, ALL BUT THREE OF THEM ARE ALREADY DEAD. IF YOU SEEK TO PLACE FURTHER BLAME, THEN SEEK THAT GRIEVANCE WITH THEIR LEADERS. BUT NONE OF THEM ARE AMONG YOUR PEOPLE. MOST OF THESE HAVE NEVER KILLED BEFORE, OR IF THEY HAVE, KILLED IN DEFENSE OR WHEN THEY WERE FORCED TO FIGHT FOR THE GLEE OF OTHERS. DOES ANY OF THIS SOUND FAMILIAR?

Korane grumbled. It was hard to argue with a booming voice in your head. *And where do I find these leaders, oh wise Saint Acrist?*

NO ONE CALLED ME THAT WHEN I LIVED. I DO NOT MUCH CARE FOR THE TITLE NOW, EITHER. I UNDERSTAND WHAT SOME HAVE ASKED YOU TO DO. KEEP FULFILLING YOUR MISSION AND IT WILL LEAD TO THEIR END. OR, AT LEAST, IT HAS A DIRECT WAY TO THEIR END.

What's that supposed to mean?

I CANNOT TELL THE FUTURE, BUT I CAN UNDERSTAND WHY YOUR LEADERS WANT THAT INFORMATION AND HOW THEY CAN USE IT. DO YOUR JOB WELL AND YOU WILL GET YOUR JUSTICE.

I want revenge!

YOU MUST FORSAKE REVENGE.

But why?

IT WILL ONLY LEAD TO MORE GRIEVANCES. FOR YOU AND FOR OTHERS. SEEK JUSTICE AND LET THE GRIEVANCE DIE THERE.

How am I supposed to do that!?

"Korane?? Korane!" Korane had been in a daze, and had not realized that she was ten paces from the palisade gate.

"Uh, yeah."

"It *is* you, by Orneth!" The archers on the wall were easing the tension out of their bowstrings now that Liri Venodran had recognized Korane. "Where have you been? Who are all those people?"

"I can't go into details, but I brought back some of our missing people," Korane said.

"You what? What about all those others? Are those orcs?" Liri demanded.

"You heard me. I have some of our people. Yeah, there are orcs. And goblins. And three kobolds. And a hobgoblin riding a warg," Korane said irritably. "Can you open the gate?"

"A warg? What are you talking about?" Liri shouted from the wall.

Korane sighed. *This is going nowhere.* "Sorry, that's their word for it. A giant wolf. Who's in charge of the town right now?"

"Lady Mariss," Liri answered.

"Fine. I'm going to tell these people what's going on and then I want to see Lady Mariss," Korane said.

"You can't just go telling me–"

"I just did, Liri. Now make it happen. I'll go pay the proper respects to Lady Mariss, but I'm done arguing with you." Korane waved to signal the wolf rider forward. A short moment later, she and her steed approached. Korane spoke to her in Goblin, "I have to go tell the leader of this place who we all are and ask to enter. Let the others know and tell them I will return soon."

"Yes, Great One," the wolf rider said, wheeling her mount about, and loping off.

Liri grudgingly admitted Korane through the gates and she

walked the streets. There were eyes on her the whole way to the manor. Korane could not blame them. She had never been one to impress with her looks, but she must have seemed to be half-animal after several months walking around the mountains, sleeping under pine boughs, hunting and foraging every day. Her clothing was torn and patched with cured hide or replaced with furs, and she had only had snow for washing. It had been very cold. They had lost a few to the winter and buried them in the mountains along their way. A few times, they had to find a cave and ride out a blizzard, hunt for furs and meat, and rest.

Korane passed a stone block, roughly two paces on each side, seeming almost like the beginning of a monument of some type, and approached the manor hill. She witnessed a sight she never thought she would. Lady Mariss was mounted on horseback and riding down, wearing a loose tunic in the Covendran colors of blue and white, a suit of mail underneath, with a sword belted to her hip.

"My Lady." Korane bowed.

"Korane! By Haverst, it *is* you!" Lady Mariss seemed surprised it actually was Korane.

"Please, I have a private request." A crowd had gathered for Korane's return and she spoke as quietly as she could with Mariss mounted on horseback. Mariss drew close and dismounted.

Mariss obliged. "Certainly, come near and we will talk quietly." Korane drew near. "Now what is this all about?"

"I can't really give many details, My Lady," Korane whispered.

"Surely, just tell me," Lady Mariss cocked her head and offered an easy smile.

"I took a task for a different lot of folk that work for Prince Arnold and they sent me to scout what we thought would be an Orcish city called Kogylar." *Why am I saying all this? I'm not supposed to say all this!*

"Keep going. Did you find what you were looking for?" Lady Mariss urged gently.

"It turned out to be mostly a Goblin city. It's a city built into the walls of a great sinkhole or maybe a topless cavern. I found most of the information I was asked for. They needed an idea of how many and what types of enemy soldiers were there." Korane wiped sweat from her brow. *Why am I sweating when I'm outside in the winter!?* "What they mainly do and make there. How to get there and the surrounding land." *I am definitely not supposed to be saying this!* Yet Korane felt compelled. Urged. A pulsing in her chest made her extremely nervous at the idea of *not* saying it.

"So, why did you come here instead of Yvel?" the lady asked.

"I could figure my way out of the mountains to get here better than Yvel. I don't know the land near Yvel hardly at all. It was from here that I left for this task. Also, I found a slave trader there and broke slaves out. I found thirteen of our missing people, but have almost a hundred people needing shelter," Korane answered, again compelled.

"A hundred people? Surely bring them in! Why have you not already? It is nearly the new year's feast and it will be merrier."

Korane did not feel compelled and was surprised, but felt her own urge to caution. "My Lady, only about thirty of them are humans. The others are orcs, goblins, kobolds, and a hobgoblin riding a wolf."

That gave the lady pause. "I see. And why would I allow things such as those in here?"

Korane felt an overwhelming urge to answer. "My Lady, please know that I would never bring danger into this place. These are all rescued slaves, save the hobgoblin and her wolf. They are all loyal and pose no threat of malice at all. At most, they do not know the language or customs. Please, I seek refuge for their safety. They are sworn to me and it is now my responsibility."

"And how, by Haverst, did that come to be?" Mariss wondered out loud.

"It is a long story, My Lady, but, in short, it reflects how they understand leadership structures. Some insisted, and it was the best way to get them all organized and away from Kogylar. I didn't know anyone to ask this kind of thing anywhere else."

Mariss looked at Korane for a few breaths. "I suppose you did not. Very well. They may enter freely, but there is no housing left. They can build their own. We can spare some materials, but not that many. They can cut more wood and use our tools to mill it and build. I would like them to help where they can." Mariss looked at Dyram, Liri, and some of the other militia assembled in the crowd. "Some help with the militia will go a long way, but it must be like a separate company."

Korane hastily and gratefully agreed. "Yes, of course, My Lady."

"To make sure that the guards recognize these... other people... as friendly, they should be accompanied by some of the other humans. Where did the other ones come from?" Lady Mariss asked.

"My Lady, that's actually not a good measure. The enemy has human allies among their number," Korane cautioned.

"Surely, they do not!" Mariss exclaimed.

Korane nodded, recalling the shock she had herself felt upon learning this information. "They do. The other humans that I took from Kogylar are from Ardara and mountain villages near there. They tell me that some of the humans captured with them agreed to work for the invaders."

"What could have ever convinced them to...?"

"Promises were made, I'm told," Korane muttered, her cast down but eyes looking up at Mariss from under her brow.

"Promises? Of what character?"

"Honor and fortune, I hear, which really meant a chance to fight and own things–mostly slaves." Korane looked over her shoulder, as if she could feel some of the Ardaran spies watching her.

"... Indeed." Mariss, still unsettled from the shocking development, was reluctant to deliver unwelcome news of her own. "There are other things you should know. Things that have happened since you've been gone."

"My Lady?" Korane felt the grip of anxiety in her chest.

Mariss spoke with measured dignity. "Keppa has fallen. My husband died there."

"Lord Koval..." Korane felt a pang of loss. She had

never liked Koval. Most people were at least a little afraid of him. But Lady Mariss was an outsider, by comparison. Korane and her family had been selling meat and furs to Koval and his parents for generations. Korane had been, herself, since she was Ziek's age. "I'm sorry."

"Thank you, Korane. I want you to see the quartermaster and the sheriff about building materials and land inside the palisade... we still need a way to identify them," Lady Mariss said.

"We can make them colors to wear," Korane suggested.

"Serna colors?" Lady Mariss asked.

"No, My Lady. They did not swear to Serna or your House... we'll dye some. We'll gather berries and make dye."

"That will be a great lot of berries, Korane." The lady almost seemed as if she was joking. "Will that be your color?"

"Uh, *their* color, My Lady," Korane corrected.

"A color you picked for them," Lady Mariss pointed out.

Korane's eyes darted about. *What do I need a color for?* "That's what's at hand, My Lady."

"So, you picked it. That is your color now," Lady Mariss explained with a matter-of-fact smile. "Regardless, bring your people inside. I will send the sheriff to meet you. A good number of people from Keppa fled here, but we cannot know if they really came from Ardara in bad faith. Make a plan and come to me with a way to find any of the enemy hiding within."

"Yes, My Lady." Korane sensed her dismissal and took a half step away before Mariss spoke again.

"Oh, one more thing," Mariss added, stopping Korane with her pleasant words. "How will you tell your people in Yvel?"

Again, the irresistible urge to answer. "I think they have someone here that will find me."

"Who?"

"I don't know, My Lady."

"Very well. Go make preparations and bring your people in. I will inform the people here." Mariss smiled and actually let Korane go.

YOU DO WELL, Acrist said in her head.

Don't tell me about it! Korane mentally spat back.

YOU RIGHT WRONGS AND BRING FORGIVENESS.

Why did I tell her those things?

SHE MADE YOU.

How?

SHE USED THE MAGIC OF HER SOUL.

Lady Mariss used magic!?

SHE DID. IT SEEMS SHE DOES SO MUCH, AND OFTEN. SHE IS VERY PRACTICED.

How can it...?

DOES SHE ALWAYS GET WHAT SHE WANTS?

I don't want to talk about it. I have much to do. Why are you still in my head? You got what you wanted, right?

THERE ARE STILL OTHER THINGS THAT WILL COME UPON YOU SOON.

I thought you couldn't tell the future.

I CANNOT, BUT I CAN SEE THE PRESENT WELL AND LOOK AT A STRAIGHT LINE TO SEE WHERE IT LEADS.

Korane brought her tribe of liberated slaves inside the palisade and faced a mixed reception. The human slaves were welcomed warmly enough, but many Sernans scowled pointedly at the orcs and goblins, though just as many others made way for them, helped them in the lumber yard, or helped clear the field for their camp inside the wall. The quartermaster allotted them a sizable field that was turning poor crops as their space to camp.

The next two days blurred together. There was a happy, tearful reunion of the thirteen Sernans that had been missing for half of a year with their families. The foundations of shelters were built and supplemented with the pine boughs and hide tarps that the wanderers had made over the journey in the mountains. Basketfuls upon basketfuls of dark berries lay in an ever-growing mound as a loose camaraderie of orcs, goblins, humans, and the kobolds crushed them. Cauldrons of dark dye were already being put to use, turning out shirts of mild to deep lavender.

"Great One," the wolf rider at Kovane's side said in Goblin. Her wolf, tied so that it did not wander or eat something, or someone, it was not supposed to, gnawed on some bones a short distance off. "That color," she continued, "has a special meaning. It almost makes me think you are getting ready for celebration. Like a great sport."

"Sport? What? We do not have time for games! There is too much to do," Korane said absently, her mind on a hundred things. She had barely slept for those two days.

"Perhaps, when the day's work is done, there can be sport? It has been a long time, Great One, and we spent Longnight on the march, and all," the wolf rider proposed.

"Maybe. For whoever wants, I guess. What kind of games?" Korane asked without really paying attention.

"Well, I was thinking–"

"Great One? There is someone here to see you," her Talzborn goblin called. The quartermaster, the portly former merchant Beren Enkr'ail delicately picked his steps through the camp. The wolf rider looked down in disappointment and quickly found somewhere else to be.

"Over here," Korane called, gesturing towards her shelter. She pulled over a small table, a stool, and a box to accommodate their small conference and offered the stool to the portly fellow and sat down on the box. "Sorry, I do not have much to offer to drink."

"Pardon?" Beren said.

Korane forgot herself and had spoken to Goblin. She apologetically switched back to Marin. "I forget myself. Most everyone speaks Goblin here, even the Ardarans. I was trying to say sorry that I cannot offer any tea or proper shelter against the cold. What can I do, Master Beren?"

"Well, now that we have a minute, our friends in Yvel will be quite concerned about this development."

"… It's you. You're their person here," Korane guessed.

Beren looked down and smiled as he leaned forward on the table, "One of them. Don't mind it. I'm more on the mundane side.

No one really cares about how many nails get made, bought or sold, except for a very small group of people. The main reason that I'm here is to finish the report, since you're indisposed." He rested his chin on a fist.

"… Right," Korane said cautiously, leaning back and crossing one leg over another.

"Here are the things that I will need to know, in addition to any specific instructions from your mission." He produced a paper filled with neat script and pushed it towards Korane. She picked it up and looked at it for an uncomfortable pause.

"Can't read it?" he asked after a minute as he produced a small, blank sheet of paper.

"I have others that can help me with it," Korane said.

"You should learn your letters," Beren responded, mildly scolding her.

Korane chuckled bitterly. "Oh, I've been learning plenty of letters."

Beren was slightly taken aback by her comment. "I see." His unease at her seething resentment was poorly disguised. "At any rate, I don't know exactly what your mission was, but I can help with the report. You should know, questions and instructions will come back."

"I understand. I have obligations now, though. Allegiances." Korane sat up straight and spoke earnestly.

"You have one allegiance, to the Crown Prince. Surely, you understand that another mission will come and you will have to leave," Beren said, leaning on the table with his elbows and pointing to emphasize his words.

"I swore that oath, good and fine, but these people are sworn to me," Korane sighed. "Look, most of them lived in enemy territory for a long time and they can provide information. New reports can be written. I can send more scouting missions out from here, once they get settled." She placed a hand flat on the table and leaned over, contemplating the grains of the wood surface. She started to speak before she looked up. "I think… the situation has changed, but it's for the better. We can do more. They can serve the Crown, but I am responsible for their well-being. It best serves the

Crown that we stay here."

Beren looked at her, seemingly uncertain of what to say or do. "So be it. They'll say if they agree or not, whoever *they* are." He shrugged and scrawled down a hasty note with a pen that seemingly appeared from nowhere.

"I was supposed to be there for about a month. At least several weeks, but some of the ones that I brought back have been there for months, even years, and would know more than I would've been able to learn."

"The Ardarans that you brought back. Do you think any of them are with the enemy?"

"No. Putting them in slave pens doesn't seem like a workable way to get spies into a place that doesn't buy their slaves."

"Fair point," Beren noted, scrawling more. "Your plan to catch spies for the Lady Mariss is going well, I hear."

"Caught two yesterday. My people recognized them. Can't say there aren't more, though," Korane quipped, crossing her arms.

"They'll hang tomorrow, you know." He nodded approvingly.

RIGHTING WRONGS. PREVENTING FURTHER INJUSTICE.

Shut up.

"Good," she calmly said aloud.

"On a separate note, the Lady Mariss would like to learn the Goblin and Orcish languages. Can you send some people to help her learn them?"

"Is this part of...?" Korane asked.

"No. This is from and for the Lady Mariss," Beren said.

"Yeah, I'll pick a couple and send them that way in the morning."

"What will you do when orders come for you to leave?" he asked.

"You mean with these people?"

"Yes."

"I don't think it's going to work like that anymore. The

shelter that Serna provides–that Lady Mariss gives–is not without cost. These people are obliged... I'm obliged–to help Serna. That means we stay here. That's what the tribe–"

"The tribe?" he repeated, incredulously.

"That's how they seem to understand things. Not by towns or princes or queens," she explained. "If they want to leave the tribe, they can, but I need to make sure they have a place to go."

"You meant even the non-humans?" he asked.

"Any of them, but yeah," she said. "They trust me. I owe them that much."

"What about your oath?" Beren asked.

"I am still inside the oath. Protecting Serna does that. Bringing these people to make a home here does that. Finding those spies does that," Korane retorted, fervently enough to surprise herself.

"This tribe have a name?" Beren asked.

"No, but it needs one, I guess." Korane pondered for a moment. "Akalai."

"Akalai?"

"It's the Goblin word for 'free.' I suppose everyone in there needs a name, too."

Epilogue

A farm, west of Yvel City, Crown Sorcerers' Proving Grounds.
By the Human Calendar, Restday, third week of Talinochis, 794.
By the Elven Calendar, ninetieth day of Winter, 18031.
By the Goblin Calendar, late in the Third Moon Cycle, 3115.
Noon on a cold and windy late winter day.

Tyrnimar set down the iron kettle on the fencepost and hurriedly walked to the other side of the field, getting well and safely behind Ayza. She looked back at him and he nodded. He could see her aura's focus as she bent the air around her into a semisphere. She compressed it into a shell and lost track of her movements in the intricacies of how she manipulated the inner and outer shell. Sparks and arcs of light started to course over the semi-sphere for a few seconds. The arcs intensified an instant before a jagged bolt tore through the air.

Tyrnimar was mostly prepared for the blinding light and the sound. He had closed his eyes against the brightness, but even though his fingers were in his ears, it sounded like the world cracked.

He opened his eyes and unplugged his ears, though they were still ringing. The air smelled strange, though vaguely familiar. The iron kettle had vanished and the fence post was smashed to ashy bits, smoldering and lit with small flames. The ground around the post was etched with steaming, jagged lines in a two-pace ring. The dirt of the field had been mostly churned up and heated in a variety of ways during their training, so despite the cold, no snow remained in the vicinity. Raw, blustery wind whipped them, cutting through their clothes.

"It is where?" he asked. "Was it destroyed by you?"

Ayza was breathing heavily. "I don't think so. I think I can feel its path through the air," she said. Searching the field, they located the iron kettle, scorched and partially melted along the line where the lightning had struck it. The kettle faintly glowed with lingering heat. They waited for it to cool before Ayza picked it up by its handle, using a spare scarf to pad her hands. Passing by where the fence post had been, they heard a dull ping. Turning around to investigate, they saw nothing but the churned dirt and splinters. Then they heard another ping. And another.

"Look." Tyrnimar pointed towards the kettle. Nails were clinging to its side.

"Are they alive?" Ayza asked.

"No. It is a thing done sometimes between some metals when lightning is involved," Tyrnimar said.

"Really? How do you know?" Ayza was suddenly excited.

"Uh. It is not remembered by me. It must have been in a book that I read a long time ago. Yes, many years. Maybe a hundred."

"Oh." His answer seemed to disappoint her.

"Will the kettle be used by you again, or will other things be tried?" Tyrnimar looked for other objects to use as targets.

"What do we have?"

Less than an hour, and a collection of six clay and metal vessels later, Ayza leaned over, holding herself up with her hands pressed above her knees. "I think," she gasped, her chest heaving, "I think that's all… for today…"

"Very good work was done by you. It is thought by me that more efficient methods for making the lightning will be thought of by you with more practice."

"Sure," she heaved. "Thank… you."

Ayza went inside the farmhouse to rest as Tyrnimar rolled two short logs out of a shed, placing them forty paces away from where Ayza had stood and twenty paces apart. Kora strolled out to take Ayza's place as Tyrnimar returned safely behind the testing position.

"And so please remember that distance was what was decided on for being worked on," Tyrnimar reminded Kora.

"Right. I want to try something. I was thinking about it last night," Kora grinned.

Tyrnimar smiled back warmly. "It is pleasantly anticipated

by me. A target should be picked by you."

"Hm. That tree," she said, tilting her head to motion with her nose.

"Where?" Tyrnimar looked towards where Ayza had nodded.

"Right there." She pointed to a tree well beyond the edge of the field, further than she had ever been able to reach with her magic.

"Wh–out there!?" Tyrnimar was surprised. "Well, that would be some distance… ah, but first, the beginner exercise."

"Yeah," she agreed and readied to gather the nearby energies. Tyrnimar watched her magical energies swirl about her frame as she pulled the heat from the air and ground, converting it into heat in front of her hands. She pointed her left arm at one log and shot a thick pillar of fire towards it, engulfing it in flames. With her right arm, she pointed at the other log, sending a thin beam streaking towards it, snapping a patch of bark and wood open and incinerating it from the inside. Sap and moisture began to bubble out of the top.

"Excellent control!" Tyrnimar said. *I hope this much fun can be had by Eevarel. Her doings are wondered about by me.* "Now for it." She was starting to steam and smoke. The air around her shimmered with heat in the late winter afternoon. The edges of the fabric of her simple dress blackened and singed, yet the mud around her feet began to freeze.

Kora summoned more energy from her surroundings. Tyrnimar could see her pulling it and shaping it into a tight, orange ball glowing in front of her. When she began to strain to contain it, she sealed off the energy and 'threw' it, though 'throwing' was an imprecise term for her action. She did not use her arms to throw the flaming ball–it was more as if she had unseen limbs made of energy that… 'threw' it. This was one of those frustrating things that Tyrnimar understood in concept, but words failed to describe. The kind of thing that Eevarel would ask him to explain just to watch him struggle.

The orange ball arced high and plunged two, then three hundred paces away. He saw the blast. Roaring flames expanded in a globe of inferno. A few seconds later, he heard the blast, but he already knew the problem. *Well… if it is* considered *a problem…* The bottom of the globe collapsed inwards and its bright halo turned to a mushroom-shaped cloud of smoke.

He approached Kora, wheezing from the exertion as her sister had been. Her dress started to catch fire, but Tyrnimar kept a large towel soaking in a bucket of water nearby for such occasions. He hastened to the bucket, seized the towel and swatted out the flames.

"Ow!" Kora yelped in surprise, her midsection stinging from the wet towel on a cold day.

"The dress would be burnt!" Tyrnimar protested.

"Thanks," she said, not bothering to hide the sarcasm in her voice. Tyrnimar was unphased by her tone and continued to offer her additional direction.

"For the next one, the ball should be constructed by you so that the heat is released in the shortest amount of time." He cast the towel back in the bucket.

"What will that do?"

"It is the difference like this. The energy was released like this by the first ball," he explained, slowly pushing her arm. "If the second ball is made by you, for the energy to be released in shorter time, it would be more like this." He flicked his wrist and slapped her forearm.

"Ow!" she objected again.

Remaining on topic despite her protestations, he continued. "Same amount of energy. Less time."

"You sure know a lot about this for a book reader. Are you sure that you don't know about all this magic stuff? Maybe I should ask Ayza what she thinks," Kora said.

"Kora, a promise was made by you," Tyrnimar reminded her urgently.

"Hm?"

"Kora! Hey!"

***

A secluded manor, northwest of the Gershan city of Krogen.
By the Human Calendar, Fryday, third week of Talinochis, 794.
By the Goblin Calendar, late in the Third Moon Cycle, 3115.
Lightly snowing.

Kolus leaned forward, squinting at another bound book full of intricate handwriting. He sat in what was supposed to be a cozy sitting room with a couple of bookshelves built into the walls, but it had been overtaken by piles of more books on the floor and tables; some from the bookshelves in this room and others that had migrated from the library. A tray of cold tea and breadcrumbs on a plate occupied a space on the floor by Kolus' chair. Jerna reclined on a couch, reading amidst a stack of books that had overflowed from the floor. Jerna reached for her cup of tea, tipping it with a finger to peek inside and frowning that it was empty before going back to her marked place on the page. Mersik entered the room, holding something behind her. Kolus did not notice at first and Jerna was content to not move.

"These notes from the farm are very helpful! I wish I could meet this Tyrnimar," Kolus said aloud. He sat on a round, mid-height stool at a small table, reviewing a sheaf of pages containing tidily scrawled notes and diagrams.

"Do you know him, Great One?" Mersik turned her head and looked at him sideways.

He shook his head, "No, no. I only know of him through these reports and translations of his notes."

"Ah. So, were they taken without his knowledge?" Mersik turned her head to look at him directly again. Jerna briefly glanced over from her book, but continued reading after a breath.

"Yes, I believe so." Kolus turned the page and his eyes crawled over another page of tasty script. "That kind of thing happens a lot in the things that I do."

"It would happen where we are from, too," she remarked while casting her gaze down.

"Really?" Kolus spun around on his stool to look at her.

"What about? What kinds of notes and such are we talking about?"

Jerna ignored the conversation, turning a page in her own book, held her place with the thumb of the hand holding up the book while she flipped open another book and paged through it to cross reference some curiosity.

"Usually plans and designs, Great One," Mersik explained, glancing over at Jerna in brief, unspoken question before returning her gaze to Kolus.

"For what?" He was interested.

"Different machines, usually. Bridges. Complicated buildings. Different designs of siege crossbows or for pulleys and levers for mine workers." Jerna sensed that the conversation was going to drag on. She closed both books and dismounted the book-laden couch. Mersik frowned at her as she left. "A lot of those went around when Oygariyet's speakers came to our tribe–our tribe back then, Great One–when they asked that tribe to join their war. Things like that."

"Huh." Kolus considered Mersik's input and was quite impressed. *Industrial espionage amongst goblins. What a world of wonders...* "And that happens often?"

"Eh. Sometimes. It *is* rude, Great One. People get very angry about it, but it does happen."

"Hm. I supposed Tyrnimar might agree and be angry that we are reading his notes. You can read them, too, but we have to get *you* on your Eklendan letters." His last visitor, or rather, his last *living* visitor, had granted him that he could teach his goblins magic as long as they took a binding oath. They had all wanted to, and so he swore each of them to an oath. One by one, each of them bound their souls to his. He was, in turn, further oathbound by his last living visitor. Day by day, he felt a deeper connection with each of them. *So, this is family.* He sighed contentedly. *What a change. Before I looked mild, but a monster lived within. The things I had to do... now, I look like a monster, but I have gone soft for all of them.*

"Oh, but that is not what I came to ask you about, Great One." Mersik twisted about, slyly holding her hands behind her back. He had not noticed until just then that she held her hands behind her back since she entered the room.

340

"What is it, then?" he hesitantly asked.

She bounced as she happily produced a short wooden cylinder with leather stretched over its top. "It's done! The drum!" she beamed.

Kolus glued his smile in place before speaking. "Mersik, is that the young man's face?"

"Argh! No, Great One," she confessed. "The face was too damaged and did not come out of the curing well. It cracked and broke apart. We must have over-dried it. This is the skin from his leg."

"Ah, what a shame," Kolus muttered. *Thank Orneth!* He had been nervous about eventually having a visitor that recognized the face on the drum. "What are these symbols painted on?"

"Oh, those are for joy and prosperity. They are Goblin runes," Mersik explained.

"Runes? I never saw any of those in all the letters I learned from you. Have you been keeping secrets from me?" he scolded playfully.

"No, Great One," she laughed, "these are runes. The stories of many goblins tell about times when we had our own magick and painted runes on things to make them have qualities. Like joy or prosperity." Mersik, being the eldest of the goblins, was normally the most reserved, but she twisted like a petted cat in this conversation. "So, by the stories, someone that uses this drum would have joy and be more prosperous. We saw how you felt sorry for that man. Since he could not have joy when he died and dying is not very prosperous, we wanted him to be useful to others, so he can share the joy and prosperity he did not get to use when he was alive."

That is really sweet if you do not consider that we are talking about a drum made out of a person's skin, Kolus thought. "It is very kind of you to help him like that."

"I never believed any of those stories, Great One. I thought they were just stories to tell children to put a smile on their face," she said. "Not until you brought us here, Great One."

Kolus smirked, looking at her sidelong. "Are you being nice to me to get something later?"

"No, Great One!" she protested, "I just wanted to show you the drum…"

Kolus looked at the runes on the drum more closely. "They remind me of something." He rose from his seat and placed the sheaf of notes on the table before walking into the next room. "Something I saw…" He rifled through some books on a shelf. "Erkond… Perganott, Lian… Ranus…" Kolus wandered into the next room, parsing through another pile of books on one of the tables. "Ivriel, Agonich… Girslig. Girslig!" He pulled a book from the pile, others collapsing over the table, two spilling onto the floor.

Kolus was too lost in excitement flipping through the chapters and pages to be aware of the mess he was creating, or note Mersik restacking the books as neatly as she could manage, wearing the patient face of someone who had cleaned up the same mess many times before and knew she would time and again. Muttering to himself, he found the target of his search.

"Here. 'Appropriate runes and symbols can impart properties to the object or person, based on the material, the ink, knife, or marking medium, the rune, the writer's intent, and the below incantations…" Reading on, he was unaware of the grin he wore.

"What is this?" Shaven-headed Panil carried in a tray of fresh, hot milk, a rump of porcupine meat, and a crust of bread for Kolus' late afternoon meal.

"The Great One found something that sounds like the magick rune stories," Mersik said.

"Ah, has he?" Panil set down the tray and rubbed her hand affectionately. She kissed his cheek in return and wrapped her arm around his waist and squeezed him.

"No, truly," Mersik protested.

"Oh, be true with yourself. Those are just stories for children," Panil dismissed. She scowled at him, hands on her hips, in response to his skeptical smirk. Kolus was too immersed in this new idea to notice the friction between them. Mersik continued glowering at Panil and he looked away after a moment. He scratched his head abashedly. "I did not mean to make sorrow."

She scowled a moment longer before sighing and walking

off with him, arms around each other's waists. Jerna silently rejoined Kolus a few minutes later with a fresh, steaming cup of tea. She resumed her place on the couch and they read together as the afternoon crept into the evening.

A few days later, Kolus was making the last arrangements for the experiment.

Ys watched thoughtfully. "Strange luck that you saved some of those flowers in a pot."

"I really like how they look. We never had anything like that when we were home," Spara said.

"The Great One provides our home now," Panil mumbled. Kolus heard him, but the others did not.

Kolus had arranged sunflowers into the same rune patterns as the symbol painted on the drum skin designated, and was burning the daisies like incense after a drizzling of oil. He then began reciting the incantation, an act which would continue for hours. In simplified terms, the intent was to introduce the symbol to its intended purpose, giving it a true meaning, and then introducing the drum to the symbol. This would help the symbol and its purpose agree that the drum would give a home to the symbol, and that the symbol would give the power of its true meaning to the drum. Kolus would, effectively, be serving as the intermediary between the objects.

The sun set and rose during the recitation. The goblins began to get excited. They had not asked how long it would take, and he had not thought to tell them, but he could not stop without spoiling the incantation. Understanding how the magical energy would flow, he was aware that interrupting the chant might be dangerous both to the incanter, or others within the vicinity. The goblins watched, snacked, dozed, wandered off, and did chores while he recited. He was jealous of their snacks and naps, but he shrugged it off with promises to himself of sweets later.

Finally finished, he sat back and let out a hearty sigh. He leaned against the wall and was just dozing off when Spara walked in carrying a plate of light brown, glossy cubes.

"What is that?" he mumbled.

"Caramel, Great One," she said. "It is something we would

make where we are from." She put the plate down on the table, smirking. "Used my own milk for the butter."

"Uh, I do not question," Kolus said before immediately frowning in question. "How is it that you all produce milk?"

"We do not, Great One," Spara corrected.

Kolus clarified his comment with a playful eyeroll. "I do not mean Panil."

"I understand, Great One. Ys does not. She never bore a child. She came of bearing age after we left our home. Our former home."

"You have all borne children?" Kolus was quietly surprised.

"Yes, Great One," Spara matter-of-factly stated, as if she were commenting on chores she did yesterday.

"What happened to them? How will they survive without their mother? Did the father also go to war?"

"The children stay with the breed family, Great One. The whole family does not go! Only half of the women can bear children at a time–well–only half are allowed by custom." She shrugged and spread her hands in explanation. "How would we have children and how would our people continue to survive if *everyone* went off to war? And what do you mean 'mother,' like there is only one? Is it not this way among your people, Great One?"

Very different in yet another way. "Among my people, children have only one mother and one father. The mother and father are only with one another, and, most of the time, they have as many children as they can to ensure that enough of them survive to be adults."

"Oh…" Spara said, considering. "Well, we keep aware of who the *birth* mother and *birth* father are to prevent inbreeding, but they are all children of the family. Your people with their family of one man and one woman… do they not get bored?"

"I… would not know," Kolus admitted. "I have never been 'married' before I met you." He used the Eklendan word for 'married,' as the word did not exist in Goblin–its meaning was lost within the broader concept of 'family.'.

"'Married'?" she puzzled, popping into his lap and hugging him around the waist. She nestled her head into the crook of his shoulder.

"That is what my people would call it. You call it 'family,' but for my kind, 'family' means the mates and the children. A man and a woman are married to one another," he explained. "The man is called the 'husband' and the woman is called the 'wife', just as you and the other women are my wives. Just as Panil and Kachem are your husbands."

"Oh… and only one with one? And always a man and a woman? Never a man and a man or a woman and a woman?" Spara asked. "And the children are part of the family, too!" she added, surprised.

"Uh, it is difficult to have children that way. Many children do not live to reach adulthood and are lost to disease, starvation, accidents… *wars*, things like that. And, yes, I know the children are part of the family among your kind, but it is different than between the mates."

"Well, of course, it is different! It does not even need to be stated! But, the same with our people and many dying, Great One," she explained, making a chore of it. "That is why we have very big families."

"Most people feel the urge to have children, and our people, all of *our* tribes, need to continue," Kolus continued.

"Yes, I *understand*, Great One." She was mildly irritated. Her nose ring shifted as she briefly crinkled her face. She pushed away from him and sat up.

Kolus considered these new insights. "So, wait, are you all from the same breed family?"

"We are now, Great One," she replied, smiling.

"What do you mean?"

"Great One," she laughed, "did you not know? We are in *your* breed family. What is a family for but to breed children?"

Breeding… Kolus had blundered into this sort of marriage, but he had never thought of having children. "…I had no idea.

That is to say, I never thought of…" This fresh revelation certainly helped to explain the expected activities every night since they had arrived at the manor. "How… would we… breed? Will this even work?"

"We will find out," she grinned slyly at him, leaning into him again, her braided tails of blue hair dangling. "What did you think the Longnight celebration was about? But if you have doubts, we could even try again right now. We keep talking about your kind and my kind, but how would our children be? I am really quite eager for that answer, you know."

"Uh, well now," he stammered, flustered, "do you not want to try the drum first?" The Longnight celebration. Kolus had not forgotten the night almost four months ago. They had all told him it was a tradition to celebrate the hardest on Longnight, *and that foul-smelling, awful herbal tea that they brewed every day and had me drink for a week.* Kolus wondered where they got the energy for such vigor. *Wait! Spara? Bearing my child!? How…?*

"Oh, is it done?" She yipped excitedly and leapt out of his lap. He retrieved the drum from a shelf and held it out for her to take. She sat down, folding her legs and holding the drum on her lap. She began to strike an aggressive, three-beat rhythm. Kolus closed his eyes, returning to the moment. *I will have to return to that later. But, wait, if Spara has my child, then… Panil and Ys? Or was it Kachem and Ys?* Coming back to the present, again, the sound of the drum was incomplete–he could tell that it was a beat meant to played with other players and other drums. Nonetheless, it had a calming effect.

Spara suddenly stopped and Kolus opened his eyes. Her eyes were squeezed shut, holding back tears.

"What is wrong?"

"Nothing," she sobbed, "nothing at all, Great One. The runes glowed and I felt so happy playing it." She rose and stumbled to embrace him around his thighs and continued weeping. He picked her up and tried to offer comfort, stroking her thick, blue hair.

"It will be alright," he said. "We are having a new year begin in a few days, according to my people's calendar. We would have a feast. Let us make a grand one, yes?"

"No, Great One, it is good," she sniffled. "You make our dreams come true. We need to make two more drums, a set of prongs, and a strummer for the whole set."

"Strummer?" Kolus queried. Through her sniffles, Spara tried her best to describe a long-necked instrument with a hollow base at one end and metal wires strung along its length. By the time she could speak more clearly, Mersik arrived to check on the scene.

"What is all this and the noise?" Mersik was mildly alarmed at Spara's tears after music had stopped.

"Play the drum," Spara managed. Mersik began to play, striking the same three-beat rhythm. Panil came to watch, then Ys, and then the rest.

One by one, all of the others played the drum with similar reactions. It was sometime later that Kolus managed to try the caramel. The candy was very sweet, but not too sweet. It was chewy and buttery at the same time. It melted in his mouth. *Bliss*.

***

By the Human Calendar, Restday, third week of Talinochis, 794.
Two Days Later (last day of the year).

A man rode his horse alongside a woman driving a mule-drawn cart. Both were bundled in layers to protect themselves against the cold and wind on the overcast day.

"And he looks very strange," she went on.

"Strange how?" he asked.

"His skin is grey like fireplace ash, and his eyes are all black," she looked at him sidelong.

"That sounds strange," he agreed.

"He lives with others here, but I never see them. Just movement in the windows. Makes the hair on my neck stand up." She shrugged her shoulders in the memory of a shiver.

"Well, it's got to be better than where I was," he consoled

himself.

She gave him a sidelong glance. "If you say so…"

Her mule pulled the cart the last bit up the road to rest in front of the manor.

"Here. Help me unload," she coaxed.

The man dismounted his horse and helped stack the boxes and the bottles on the ground behind the cart. "Doesn't he normally help?"

She grunted as she heaved a box onto the pile. "Yeah, but this way I get to leave sooner."

"Alright, fine," he said. They worked quietly and finished quickly.

She knocked on the door. Moments later, it opened. Out stepped a man, strange beyond description. He wore a thick house coat over a grey shirt with faded red breeches. Undyed leather shoes peeked out below the hem. He was bald, with skin grey as storm clouds and eyes as black as the darkest night. He had a symbol painted on his forehead; a vertical line with three diagonal lines coming off of it in a sharp, downward stroke.

The newly arrived man was stunned enough by the grey man's appearance that his mouth dropped open.

The grey man looked between him and the woman. "Who is this?" he asked in Eklendan.

"Don't know. I was told to bring him here and give you this." She handed him an envelope. He took it hesitantly.

"Here are your supplies, so I'll see you in a week," she said, mounting the cart and gently snapping the mule's reins.

"Uh, alright," the grey man called. Eyeing the newly arrived man, he opened the letter, quickly reading its contents.

"Have a good feast," the man called after the woman driving the wagon.

"Yeah," she replied gruffly.

"Have you read this?" The grey man now spoke in Marin.

"No, I never saw it. Didn't even know she had it. Listen, I've been waiting for a while in Krogen for this, but no one's told me what this is about," the newly arrived man confessed.

"Fine," the grey man said, clasping his hands in front of him, the letter still gripped in one of them. "My name is Kolus. What is yours?"

"Julian. Julian Panr'ail," the newly arrived man offered tentatively. "How did you know I prefer Marin?"

"I didn't. You have the Marin look and a Marin name. I guessed." Kolus studied him.

"Oh." Julian looked at him askance. "So what does it say? The letter?"

"It says that I am authorized to take you as an apprentice and gives me a few other requirements that I must fulfill. I may pierce two beasts with the same arrow on this one." Kolus' dark eyes glittered in the sunlight.

"What do you mean? And could we go inside?" Julian was eager to get out of the cold and still considered the presence of this sinister fellow preferable to the hate and resentment that followed him everywhere in Serna.

"There are things you need to know first. Before you cross a point over which there is no return," Kolus cautioned. Julian could not be certain, as the eyes of the grey man were entirely black, but it seemed that his gaze bore directly into him.

"Like what?" His curiosity won against his cautiousness. "And what kind of apprenticeship? What do you do here?"

"You have heard of the witches from a small town called Serna that the Prince has appointed as his 'sorcerers'–I believe that is the term he used?"

"Oh, I'm from Serna," Julian remarked.

"Ah!" Kolus smiled. That smile gave Julian the feeling that Kolus had an intense thirst for something, and it was quite discomforting. "I should like to hear about what you saw!"

"Um, fine, but you were asking for a reason?" Julian reminded.

"Ah, yes, we here endeavor to make other witches, in simple terms," Kolus explained. "Though, if I am understanding the translations properly, those who make magic from formulae,

349

incantations, and similar things would be called 'wizards.'"

Julian shifted hesitantly. "Um, fine. So, I am to be a wizard?"

"Well, I'm thinking you might be a witchfinder for me. But first, there is the matter of an oath."

"An oath?" Julian squinted.

"This endeavor is for the Prince and the security of his rule against all enemies. I cannot go teaching anyone that will just run off with the knowledge and use it against Yvel, the Crown, or the people."

Julian nodded, hesitantly. "That makes sense."

"So, there is an oath-binding spell," Kolus began to explain.

"What does it do?" Julian asked.

"It ensures that you cannot act against the Prince." Kolus' gravelly voice made the words a bit more ominous.

Julian shrugged. "I've seen the Prince fight. He fought for us in the hills." Julian nodded, considering. "I'd fight for him again. I'll take this oath."

"It is no light matter, Julian. It will bind your soul. Are you sure?" Kolus cautioned.

Julian's brow tightened in contemplation before answering, his lips pressed into a thin line. "I have nothing else."

***

Holbrin entered his chamber in the apartments that the prince had provided for the elves' stay in Yvel. It had been another long day working with the prince's adjutant, Gunst Ver'ail, and his marshal, Mot Gundr'ail. A very long day, but the Yvel Regiment was well on its way to being rebuilt, and nothing was going to burn down or fall apart while new life entered the regiment. Hopefully.

Holbrin was fussing with his boot when he noticed a plain, unsealed envelope placed on his bed pillow. He gingerly opened it and unfolded a simple note. The script was Elvish, but the handwriting itself was executed at the skill level of a child; clumsy and difficult to make out all of the letters, but Elvish, nonetheless.

> *I am translating manuscripts, notes, and letters from Elvish to Eklendan. Some of them seem like old texts, but some of them seem recent. I suspect that at least some of the notes and letters were written by Tyrnimar. Thought you should know.*

End of Book 2. Unseen Wrath

Appendix I: Glossary of Terms

age of selection: Period of time in which a young elf reaches adulthood and they embark upon journeys and apprenticeships to select and petition for a vocation or occupation within one of the orders of Elven society. See *The Witches of Serna (Book I)*, Appendix XI: Elves: Culture and Economy.

Aiz (*iez*): Third month of the Human Calendar, and the third month of spring. See Table 1: Comparison of Yearly Calendars Between the Races of Paeta.

Anz (*ahnz*): Second month of the Human Calendar, and the second month of spring. See Table 1.

Arinochis (a-*rin-oe*-chiss): Tenth month of the Human Calendar, and the first month of winter. See Table 1.

Banreni (bahn-*ren*-ee): Seventh month of the Human Calendar, and the first month of autumn. See Table 1.

battalion: Among western human armies, a military organization consisting of two or more companies (usually three) totalling to roughly three hundred soldiers. A battalion is led by a battalion leader. See *The Witches of Serna,* Appendix X: Humans: Organization for War.

Berenk (*behr-enk*): Sixth month of the Human Calendar, and the third month of summer. See Table 1.

Black Order: See Order of Trade.

Blue Order: See Order of the Book.

blueskin: Derogatory term used to refer to goblins and hobgoblins, stemming from the fact that western goblinkind are predominantly blue-skinned.

Breathday (*breth-dae*): Fifth day of the human week. See Appendix VI: Calendar Systems of Paeta, Revised.

Brother Knight: Address used between knights of the Orders Militant of the Church of Orneth. See Table 4: Rankings with the Religious Orders of the Church of Orneth.

cast-out: Term for the peoples driven out of the lowlands and into the unforgiving climes of the Kaskev Mountains. Most often it refers to orcs, goblinkind, gnolls, and similar groups, but has broadened to include other mountain-dwelling peoples such as ogres, who have rarely had positive relations with humans and elves.

Charmer: Sorcerer who imposes their will on others through an influence that appears benevolent. See *The Witches of Serna*, Appendix IX: Magic: Blood Magic.

Chosen: From Ornethian scripture, an individual selected by the saints or by Orneth herself to receive a blessing or a special task. See Appendix VII: The Western Reformed Church of Orneth.

Church of Orneth (*oer*-neth): Primary religion of humans on the continent of Paeta, founded over a millennia ago by a woman of the same name. Its primary tenets of belief are mercy, justice, peace, humility, and hard work. Nearly eight centuries ago, the Church of Orneth split into an Eastern and Western Church. See Appendix VII.

company: Among western human armies, a military organization consisting of approximately one hundred soldiers, organized into groups of ten (called 'tens'), led by a company leader. See *The Witches of Serna,* Appendix X: Organization for War.

Darri (*dar-ee*): Fifth month of the Human Calendar, and the second month of summer. See Table 1.

Elder: Relatively senior clergy rank for a member of a clerical order of the Church of Orneth. See Table 4.

Ers (*ers*): First month of the Human Calendar, and the first month of spring. See Table 1.

Fearmonger: Sorcerer who imposes fear on others. See *The Witches of Serna*, Appendix IX: Blood Magic.

Firebrand: Sorcerer who controls the flow of heat, usually expressed by the ability to create and control fire. See *The Witches of Serna*, Appendix IX: Magic: Blood Magic.

Firecaster: See Firebrand.

First: Highest-ranking subordinate to the great one of a hobgoblin tribe. See *The Witches of Serna*, Appendix XIII: Hobgoblins: Cultural Attributes, Tribal and Clan Construct.

fist: Among hobgoblin and goblin militaries, a military organization. Generally, four to six hundred hobgoblin soldiers or two hundred to one thousand goblin fighters. See *The Witches of Serna,* Appendix XIII: Organization for War.

foot: Using the benchmark of the average of a foot of an adult Vostindin male human, roughly analogous to twelve inches or 30.5 centimeters in the real world. See *The Witches of Serna*, Appendix VII: Units of Measurement and Navigation.

Fourth: Fourth and most junior-ranked subordinate to the great one of a hobgoblin tribe. See *The Witches of Serna*, Appendix XIII: Cultural Attributes, Tribal and Clan Construct.

Fryday (*frie*-dae): Eighth day of the human week. See Appendix VI.

Garad'Dai (*gar*-ad *die*): Term among orcs that loosely translates to 'subleader,' and is awarded to orcs that have proven loyalty (most importantly) and strength or skill to their Great One. A great one may appoint any number of Garad'Dai for any number of tasks. Garad'Dai may even be appointed over other Garad'Dai. Appointments may be either temporary or permanent, though most temporary appointments end in death through some form of betrayal or assignment of an impossible task. Such situations are sometimes used as clever ways for a great one to eliminate political threats within their tribe.

Great One: Title for the leader of a tribe of orcs, goblins, or hobgoblins, though the actual word and nuance will differ between the Orcish and Goblin languages. See *The Witches of Serna*, Appendix XII: Orcs: Culture and Tribal Construct; *The Witches of Serna*, Appendix XIII: Culture and Tribal Construct; *The Witches of Serna*, Appendix XV: Goblins: Culture and Tribal Construct.

Green Order: See Order of the Harvest.

greenskin: Derogatory term used to refer to orcs, stemming from their green skin.

Guardian Council: One of the governing bodies of the Elven people. See *The Witches of Serna*, Appendix XI: Governing Bodies and Societal Organization.

Halinochis (hall-i-*noe*-chiss): Eleventh month of the Human Calendar, and the second month of winter. See Table 1.

hand: Informal measurement, which is simply the spread of a person's hand, thumb-tip to pinky-tip. It is highly subjective. See *The Witches of Serna*, Appendix VII.

headman: Lowborn community leader based on seniority among western human societies.

Healer: Sorcerer whose power is to heal wounds on and within a person's body. This is a rare type of sorcerer. See *The Witches of Serna*, Appendix IX: Blood Magic.

Invader: Term for the sun used by goblinkind, orcs, and other races that live on the slopes or heights of the Kaskev Mountains.

Invisible Hand: Sorcerer who can control objects and master invisible forces with their thoughts. See *The Witches of Serna*, Appendix IX: Blood Magic.

Iron Crown: Institution of kingship in the Dwarven realm of Drenia. See Appendix VIII: Dwarves.

Laborday: Seventh day of the human week. See Appendix VI.

lay lord: Non-clerical nobles that are part of the flock of the Church of Orneth. See Appendix VII.

Liberator: Term for the moon used by goblinkind, orcs, and other races that live on the slopes or heights of the Kaskev Mountains.

Longnight: A holy day among orcs and goblinkind (goblins, hobgoblins, and bugbears). See Appendix VI.

magus (may-*gus*): Trained and sanctioned user of book magic among the elves of the Blue Order.

Marshal of the Crown: Title among several human militaries for the senior military official in service to a ruler.

Merchant Council of Yvel (*wie*-vel): One of the governing bodies of the Principality of Yvel which represents the interests of laborers, craftspeople, and so forth, represented in the prince's court. In practice, it functions as a council of oligarchs.

mile: Measurement of length which is two thousand paces (280 feet shorter than a mile in the real world). See *The Witches of Serna*, Appendix VII.

Ministry of Information: Cabinet-level organization within the government of Yvel that collects, researches, and reports information to the Crown to aid in decision-making and governance.

Morningday: First day of the human week. See Appendix VI.

Nansima (nan-*see*-ma): Ninth month of the Human Calendar, and the third month of autumn. See Table 1.

Old Paetic (*pae*-tik): Ancient, now-dead language dating back to the days of the Ornethian Empire.

Ongkanir (ong-kha-*neer*): Eighth month of the Human Calendar, and the second month of autumn. See Table 1.

Order: 1. Division of Elven society by practice, such as agriculture, knowledge, martial studies, and so forth. See *The Witches of Serna*, Appendix XI: The Orders.

2. Clerical or militant organization of clergy of the Church of Orneth. See Appendix VII.

Order of the Book: Order of Elven society devoted to scholastic pursuits, primarily focused on magic. Also known as the Blue Order. See *The Witches of Serna*, Appendix XI: The Orders.

Order of the Harvest: Order of Elven society focusing on agriculture. Also known as the Green Order. See *The Witches of Serna*, Appendix XI: The Orders.

Order of Peace: Order of Elven society comprised of diplomats and ambassadors, often informing the decisions made by members of other orders. Also known as the White Order. See *The Witches of Serna*, Appendix XI: The Orders.

Order of the People: Order of the governing bodies of the elves. Membership is based upon appointments, nominations, and petitions and is reserved for those most esteemed within their previous order. Also known as the Order of the People's Will, the Order of the Will, the Will, and the Purple Order. See *The Witches of Serna*, Appendix XI: The Orders.

Order of the People's Will: See Order of the People.

Order of the Sword: Militaristic-based order of Elven society. As well as providing soldiers, generals, and weapon masters, members are also often scouts, spies, or logisticians. Also known as the Order of the Sword or the Red Order. See *The Witches of Serna*, Appendix XI: The Orders.

Order of the Sun and Moon: Order of Elven society comprised of artists and craftspeople. See *The Witches of Serna*, Appendix XI: The Orders.

Order of War: See Order of the Sword.

Order of the Will: See Order of the People.

Order of Trade: Order of Elven society concerned with mercantilism, trade, travel, and commerce. Also known as the Black Order. See *The Witches of Serna*, Appendix XI: The Orders.

pace: Measurement term for the average stride of the same one hundred adult Vostindin males, which is two and a half feet. See *The Witches of Serna*, Appendix VII.

Pev'Baki-Norn (*pev-bock*-ee *norn*): Term to refer to orcs who are no longer part of the Baki-Norn tribe–in this case, because the tribe no longer exists. See Appendix III: Tribes and Peoples; entry for "Baki-Norn."

Place: Definite article used for locations in the Goblin language, adopted into Orcish (e.g., *Place-called-Kogylar*).

Playday: Ninth day of the human week. See Appendix VI.

Primarch (*pry*-mark): Senior official of the Church of Orneth. There is a Primarch of the Western Church of Orneth, as well as the Eastern Church of Orneth. See Table 4.

principality: Realm governed by a prince or princess.

Purple Order: See Order of the People.

Red Order: See Order of War.

regiment: Among western human militaries, a collection of two or more battalions, usually three, generally comprising roughly a thousand soldiers and commanded by a regimental leader. See *Witches of Serna*, Appendix X: Organization for War.

Restday: Tenth day of the human week. See Appendix VI.

Reverend Knight: Rank of all knights of the Orders Militant of the Church of Orneth that are junior to the Chapter Master and Master of the Order. Among Reverend Knights, there is an informal rank structure, largely based on age and accomplishments. See Table 4.

ridin (*rih*-din): Liquor made from mashed, fermented, and distilled roots or tubers.

sapper: Soldier trained in siege warfare, specializing in the construction of fortifications, siege engines, and related works.

Second: Second-highest ranking subordinate to the great one of a hobgoblin tribe. See *The Witches of Serna*, Appendix XIII: Cultural Attributes, Tribal and Clan Construct.

Seer: Sorcerer capable of perceiving phenomena beyond the ordinary ability to perceive reality and surroundings. One such manifestation is to see the auras of people. See *The Witches of Serna*, Appendix IX: Blood Magic.

Seer Council: One of the governing bodies of the Elven people. See *The Witches of Serna*, Appendix XI: Governing Bodies and Societal Organization.

Serna Militia Company: Auxiliary fighting unit serving under the banner of the Lord Serna to protect the town of Serna and its immediate surroundings. This company was formed at the onset of the war, in the immediate

356

aftermath of the first orc raid on Serna in Talinochis, 793. It occasionally reinforces Yvel's regular army formations. It is also the first unit to accept non-human soldiers into its rank and file.

Sister Knight: Address between knights of the Orders Militant of the Church of Orneth. See Table 4.

Sortingday: Sixth day of the human week. See Appendix VI.

Soulblade: 1. An enchanted weapon, usually a sword, which draws power from a living soul that has been sacrificed and imbued into the weapon.

2. In goblinkind legend, a weapon in which the respective gods of goblinkind imbue the soul of one of their own into a weapon and gift the weapon to a chosen champion.

spawner: Goblins of breeding age in a clan that participate in breeding. See *The Witches of Serna*, Appendix XV: Family, Fertility, and Property.

Stone: Definite article for locations in Goblin languages that are particular to castles, fortresses, and fortifications that stand apart from towns or cities (e.g., *Stone of Rykooth*).

Stormbearer: Sorcerer capable of controlling the air around them and, to some extent, the weather. Colloquially termed 'Stormwitch' by some. See *The Witches of Serna*, Appendix IX: Magic: Blood Magic.

Stormwitch: See Stormbearer.

Talinochis (*tah*-li-noe-chiss): Twelfth and last month of the Human Calendar, and the third month of winter. See Table 1.

ten: Among western human militaries, the basic fighting unit of ten soldiers, led by a tenleader (included in the ten). See *The Witches of Serna*, Appendix X: Organization for War.

tenday: Term referencing the week of ten days, by the Human Calendar. See Appendix VI.

tenleader: Title for a supervisor of ten soldiers (including the tenleader). The title is prevalent in most human armies west of the Kaskev Mountains. Colloquially, the term 'tenman' is often used. See *The Witches of Serna*, Appendix X: Organization for War.

tenman: See tenleader.

Third: Third-highest ranking subordinate to the great one of a hobgoblin tribe. See *The Witches of Serna*, Appendix XIII: Culture and Tribal Construct.

Thirstday: Fourth day of the human week. See Appendix VI.

Traveler: Elf journeying beyond the Elven Lands to explore foreign lands, peoples, and cultures, collecting information on behalf of the ruling bodies of the Elven Lands. See *The Witches of Serna*, Appendix XI: Governing Bodies and Societal Organization.

Twosday: Second day of the human week. Folklore amongst humans links this day to meeting a person that one will eventually marry. See Appendix VI.

Unbreakable: Sorcerer who can grow a very hard layer of outer skin, often metallic, that protects them, while remaining as flexible to their movements and actions as their own skin. See *The Witches of Serna*, Appendix IX: Magic: Blood Magic.

Under-Provost: Rank of seniority within the Order of the Book.

underworld: Realm beneath the sunlit lands, home to cities, communities, and various livelihoods.

Warmonger: Sorcerer who can induce strong feelings of anger in others. See *The Witches of Serna*, Appendix IX: Magic: Blood Magic.

The Ways: Religion of the Elven people. See *The Witches of Serna*, Appendix XI: Culture and Economy.

Weddingday: Third day of the human week. Folklore links it to a fortunate day to marry. See Appendix VI.

White Order: See Order of Peace.

The Will: See Order of the People.

Woodwarper: Vocation among elves to magically shape wood, not only for furniture, tools, and art, but also for dwellings, including those shaped from the interior of living trees.

Youri (*yoe*-ree): Fourth month of the Human Calendar, and the first month of summer. See Table 4.

Appendix II: Index of Characters

Abiah Zug'ail (ah-*by*-uh *zug*-ai-yil): Female ethnic-Marin human. Townswoman from Serna. Died while on a militia patrol near Serna, Talinochis, 793.

Abrasian Darkmoon (a-*brae*-see-un *dark-moon*): Male High Elf of the Order of the Sword. Appointed as lead sword to a contingent of elves to reinforce the Yvel Army.

Aered Torg'ail (*ae*-red *torg*-ai-yil): Male mixed-ethnic Marin-Eklendan human. Prince-Heir to the throne of Yvel. Son of Gerald; third eldest sibling of Arnold, Larz, Oswald, Pantaria, Praxia, and Velthuria. See also: Torg'ail, House of.

Akriun Ydren (ak-*ri*-un *ee*-dren): Male High Elf. Has red hair and a long face, often wearing an expression of impatience. Member of the Order of Peace. Councilor of the Guardian Council.

Alain Tun'ail (*a*-lane *tun*-ai-yil): Male ethnic-Marin human from the town of Serna. Militiaman in the Serna Militia Company. Veteran of the Battle of Serna Hills.

Aleksan Odr'ail (a-*lek*-sun *ode*-drai-yil): Male ethnic-Marin human. Knight in the Crown Guard.

Alis Benidran (*al-iss ben*-e-dran): Female ethnic-Eklendan human, from the town of Serna. Works at the local tannery.

Allana Hunr'ail (al-*an*-a *hun*-rai-yil): Female Marin human. Carpenter from the town of Serna.

Amryst Veradran (*am*-rist *ver*-a-dran): Female mixed-ethnic Marin-Eklendan human from the town of Serna. Sour-faced and blunt. One of the people initially saved by Mkaela Ran'ail in her awakening as a healer.

Andavan: See Carolyn Andavan.

Anrior: See Lierialuth Anrior.

Aphra Lin'ail (*af*-ra *lin*-ai-yil): Female ethnic-Marin human from the town of Serna. Brown hair, blue eyes, with a deferential demeanor. Twin sister of Marlar. Abducted during the first orc raid of Serna and thereafter bore a half-orc child.

Arami (ah-*ram*-ee): Male ethnic-Berk human. Reverend Knight of the Order of Saint Kostray the Pure. Supported Sir Merik and Mkaela after Sir Merik won the trial by combat in the aftermath of the Battle of Serna Hills.

Arbera Rollodran (*ar*-ber-uh *roe*-loe-dran): Female ethnic-Eklendan human, from the town of Serna. Tends towards superstition. Married to a miller; relation of Danick and Imick.

Arcaezhia Moonwhisper (ar-*kay*-jha *moon*-whis-per): Female High Elf of the Order of the Sword. Second to Abrasian Darkmoon; part of the contingency of elves arriving to assist the Yvel Army.

Arkiban the Great (*ark*-a-ban): Male purple-skinned (Eastern) hobgoblin. Great One of the Okaramine tribe until losing a duel to Oygariyet the Great of the Zirn. Died during the Sixth Moon Cycle, 3113 by the Hobgoblin Calendar (Aiz, 792, by the Western Church of Orneth calendar).

Arladran, House of (*ar*-la-dran): A clan of nobility, loyal to the Crown of Yvel. The banner is eight vertical stripes, alternating between red and white. The House Arladran provided a battalion of soldiers to Prince Gerald at the Battle of Serna Hills. See Dorvin Arladran, Kovarre Arladran.

Arnold Torg'ail (*ar*-nold *torg*-ai-yil): Male mixed-ethnic Marin-Eklendan human. Particularly tall for a Marin, with icy blue eyes, a narrow nose, backswept brown hair, and a distinctive mole on his neck. Clever and hard-working. Crown Prince of Yvel. Son of the late Prince Gerald; eldest sibling to Aered, Larz, Oswald, Praxia, Pantaria, and Velthuria. Veteran of the Battle of Serna Hills and the Battle of Borly. See also: Torg'ail, House of.

Arozrien: See Holbrin Arozrien.

Arvr'ail: See Jaro Arvr'ail, Sora Arvr'ail.

Arynn (*ah*-rin): Female High Elf of the Order of the Sword. Exceptionally skilled at tracking, as well as possessing staunch emotional self control. Reserved and dutiful, even by Elven standards. One of the travelers appointed by the Guardian Council. Veteran of the Battle of Serna Hills.

Aselifar: See Merik Aselifar, Risit Aselifar.

Ayza Orint'ail (*ai*-za or-*in*-tai-yil): Female ethnic-Marin woman with black hair, blue eyes, and pale skin, and medium build and height. She is level-headed and protective of her sister, Kora. Former glazier from the town of Serna. Crown Sorceress of Yvel (Stormbearer). Veteran of the Battle of Serna Hills.

Bandal Okla'ifar (*ban*-dahl oek-*lae*-far): Male ethnic-Berk human. Noble of the Kingdom of Berkmar and emissary of Berkmar to the Primarch of the Western Reformed Church of Orneth.

Baryn Kevr'ail (*baer*-in *kev*-rai-yil): Male ethnic-Marin human, from the town of Serna. Tenleader in the Serna Militia Company. Veteran of the Battle of Serna Hills.

Baswyn Gerndran (bass-*win gern-dran*): Female ethnic-Eklendan human, from the town of Serna. One of the people initially saved by Mkaela Ran'ail in her awakening as a healer.

Baydran: See Garen Baydran, Jorn Baydran.

Belifar: See Melz Belifar.

Ben'ail: See Erest Ben'ail.

Benidran: See Alis Benidran.

Beredran: See Idris Beredran.

Beren Enkr'ail (*beh*-ren *en*-krai-yil): Male ethnic-Eklendan human. Reserved, meticulous, and pragmatic, but carries a pot belly with him. Formerly a traveling merchant based in the town of Serna. Quartermaster of the Serna Militia Company and Garrison.

Bers Der'ail (*burz der*-ai-yil): Male ethnic-Marin human; short and pudgy of stature with blond hair. Bold and opportunistic public speaker, though not often convincing. Yvelian nobleman and Agent of the Ministry of Information of Yvel.

Bierien (bi-*ehr*-i-en): Female High Elf of the Order of Industry. Wavy brown hair and green eyes. Almost always wears belted trousers with a tucked shirt, frequently also wears the leather apron of a smith. Empathetic and perfectionist, and a skilled blacksmith. One of the travelers appointed by the Guardian Council. Veteran of the Battle of Serna Hills.

Bindeyet (bind-*ie*-yet): Blue-skinned (Western) goblin leading multiple tribes of goblins operating in Kogylar.

Bisin (*biss*-in): Male ethnic-Marin/Eklendan human. Short, sweaty, and scruffy, with brown eyes and short brown hair (frequently cut by himself). Member of Jak's team of raiders. Nervous, paranoid, and neurotic, with an uncanny sense of smell.

Blar'ail: See Orn Blar'ail.

Bonwyn Kevr'ail (*bon*-win *kev*-rai-yil): Female ethnic-Marin human. Wife of Baryn Kevr'ail. Died while on a militia patrol near Serna, Talinochis, 793.

Brindi Wrin'ail (*brin*-dee rin-*ai*-yil): Female ethnic-Marin human. Has blonde hair, blue eyes, and a narrow nose. Fiery and ambitious. Sister of Prince Eron of Versingit.

Buel (boo-*el*): Female orc. Is of average height for an orc woman (significantly taller than human men), with small black eyes and black hair tied in simple braids. Quiet, thoughtful, and loyal. Formerly enslaved to the late Dariyet the Great and captured at the Battle of Serna Hills. Saved from execution by Mkaela Ran'ail, to whom she has remained a companion.

Buin (*boo*-win): Male ethnic-Eklendan human child from the town of Serna.

Carolyn Andavan (*car*-oe-lin *and*-uh-van): Middle-aged female ethnic-Eklendan human. Does not suffer fools. Owns Andavan Farm near Krogen.

Cavalry Leader, the: See the Messenger.

Chariss Ordavan (*char*-iss *oer*-da-van): Female ethnic-Eklendan human, squire to Sir Harl. Veteran of the Battles of Serna Hills and Borly.

Clay: Male ethnic-Marin human. Barkeep at the Valley Spring Inn in Serna.

Conwyn Extardran (*con*-win ex-*tar*-dran): Male ethnic-Eklendan human, from the town of Serna. Shieldbearer in the Serna Militia Company. Veteran of the Battle of Serna Hills.

Covendran, House of (*kov*-en-dran): A small noble family in the principality of Yvel that holds lordship over the town of Serna. The banner of House

Covendran is checkered blue and white. See also: Dareum Covendran, Judane Covendran, Koval Covendran, Mariss Covendran.

Creasan (*cree*-sen): Dareum Covendran's horse.

Damarus Olid'ail (dam-ar-*us* o-*lid*-ai-yil): Male ethnic-Marin human from Serna. Worked as a stablehand at the Valley Spring Inn. Abducted during the first orc raid of Serna.

Damerwyn Perndran (*dam*-mer-win *pern*-dran): Male ethnic-Eklendan human from the town of Serna. One of the people initially saved by Mkaela Ran'ail in her awakening as a Healer.

Dandran: See Garn Dandran.

Danfreys (*dan*-frees): Male ethnic-Marin human. A surgeon in service of the Crown of Yvel. Veteran of the Battle of Serna Hills.

Danick Isrdran (*dan-ik* is-*er*-dran): Male ethnic-Eklendan human. Townsman from Serna. Died during the first orc raid on Serna, Talinochis, 793.

Danick Rollodran (*dan-ik roe*-loe-dran): Male ethnic-Eklendan human. Works at a forge in the town of Serna. Relation of Arbera and Imick Rollodran. Shares no relation to Danick Isrdran.

Darent (*dhar*-ent): Male human. Meets with Jak to provide instructions, funding, replacements, and resources from his organization.

Dareum Covendran (*daer*-ree-um *kov*-en-dran): Male ethnic-Eklendan human; red-haired with a temper to match. Tends towards idealism and fast action. Nobleman and son of Koval and Mariss; brother to Judane. Known by his family as 'Darups.' Company Leader in the Serna Militia Company. Veteran of the Battle of Serna Hills. See also: Covendran, House of.

Dariyet (*dar*-ie-yet): Male blue-skinned (Western) hobgoblin of the Zirn. Aquamarine-eyed and muscular, with two gold earrings and a cape made of human faces. Raised from numbered status by Oygariyet to command a portion of the Borys-Karang orcs in the forest and hills east of Serna. Killed by Prince Arnold Torg'ail at the Battle of Serna Hills, Fifth Moon Cycle, 3114, by the Hobgoblin calendar (Anz, 794, by the Western Church of Orneth Calendar).

Darkmoon: See Abrasian Darkmoon.

Deni Oilaravan (*den*-nee oy-*lar*-uh-van): Male ethnic-Eklendan human, squire to Sir Harl. Veteran of the Battles of Serna Hills and Borly.

Der'ail: See Bers Der'ail.

Dorrels Joledran (*do*-rels *jol*-a-dran): Male ethnic-Eklendan human. Chamberlain under the Prince of Yvel.

Dorvin Arladran (*dor*-vin *ar*-la-dran): Male ethnic-Eklendan human. Nobleman and head of House Arladran; battalion leader in the Crown Army of Yvel. Died in a night raid during the prelude to the Battle of Serna Hills, Anz, 794; survived by his wife, Kovarre. See also: Arladran, House of.

Dryalos: See Erensed Dryalos.

Dum'ail: See Ereman Dum'ail.

Dyiriyet (d-*yer*-ee-yet): Female blue-skinned (Western) hobgoblin. Formerly Oygariyet's Fourth. Elevated and named during the expedition to Ikria.

Dyram Torin'ail (*die*-rum tor-*in*-ai-yil): Male ethnic-Marin human, from the town of Serna. Blond and blue-eyed, with an expression that invites challenge and a propensity to act and speak brashly. Relation of Sedra and Seedar. Tenleader in the Serna Militia Company. Veteran of the Battle of Serna Hills.

Eevarel Mazurnine (*ee*-var-el *maz*-ur-nine): Female Wood Elf with green eyes, auburn hair, a fair complexion, and a slender but muscular physique. Partially descended from High Elf lineage. Notably independent and enjoys playfully teasing those of whom she is fond. Prefers modest, practical garments and coiffing. Member of the Order of the Sword. One of the travelers appointed by the Guardian Council. Veteran of the Battle of Serna Hills.

Enardran: See Iblar Enardran.

Elbin (*el*-bin): Male ethnic-Eklendan human from Ardara. A collaborator of Maglaban and the Barituul hobgoblins.

Enkr'ail: See Beren Enkr'ail.

Erbasil Halifar (*er*-bae-sil *hal*-i-far): Male ethnic-Berk human. Member of the Yvelian council. Powerful merchant with equities in grain, tobacco, and livestock.

Ereman Dum'ail (*ehr*-e-man *doom*-ai-yil): Male ethnic-Marin human. White-haired and long-bearded. Elder Reverend in the Church of Orneth, Order of Saint Kostray the Pure. Sole and senior religious figure in the town of Serna. Presided over religious services from the chapel in Serna until the confrontation with Koval Covendran over the existence and tolerance of 'witches' in their midst. Rallies and leads Western Church of Orneth efforts to exterminate witches and all who support them.

Erensed Dryalos (*eh*-ren-sed *drie*-a-los): Male High Elf at the age of selection. Blond hair and green eyes. One of the Travelers appointed by the Guardian Council. Under the tutelage of Irduin Usrani. Veteran of the Battle of Serna Hills and the Battle of Borly.

Erest Ben'ail (eh-*rist ben*-ai-yil): Female ethnic-Marin human. Has a face that has made many hard bargains. Member of the Merchant Council of Yvel.

Erion Feradran (*eh*-ri-on *fer*-a-dran): Male ethnic-Eklendan human. Squire to Arnold Torg'ail. Veteran of the Battle of Serna Hills and the Battle of Borly.

Erisa of Urrissio (*eh*-riss-a, *er*-iss-ee-oe): Female Dark Elf. Very black skin, like charcoal, with white hair. Beautiful, playful eyes, and a mischievous smile. Graceful in her movements. Princess of the subterranean Dark Elven city of Urrissio.

Eron Wrin'ail (*er*-on rin-*ai*-yil): Male ethnic-Marin human. Has blond hair, blue eyes, and a narrow nose. Prince of Versingit. Brother of Brindi; husband of Fyon. Veteran of the Battle of Versingit.

Ersali (ehr-*sa*-lee): Female ethnic-Marin human. Meets with Yonn to provide instructions, funding, replacements, and resources from Ersali's organization, comparable to Darent's relationship with Jak.

Erseyet (*ehrs*-a-yet): Female blue-skinned (Western) goblin. Newly raised as the Great One of the Venjeer tribe of goblins of Kogylar. Shares leadership with Kogleyet. Veteran of the Battle of Versingit.

Ervan Panr'ail (*ur*-van pan-*rai*-yil): Male ethnic-Marin human. Known to be jovial and bold, bordering on foolhardy. Livestock farmer from near the town of Serna. Younger cousin of Julian Panr'ail. Engaged to Terah Miykodran. Died in a night raid during the prelude to the Battle of Serna Hills, Anz, 794.

Est'ail: See Garl Est'ail.

Evren Jundran (*ev*-ren *joon*-dran): Male ethnic-Eklendan human. Blacksmith hand supporting the Serna Militia.

Extardran: See Conwyn Extardan.

Feradran: See Erion Feradran.

Fndeyet (fin-de-*yet*): Powerful clan leader of the Talz tribe of goblins from the goblin city of Berkasliriyig.

Fris'ail: See Marsen Fris'ail.

Fyon Wrin'ail (*fyon* rin-*ai*-yil): Female ethnic-Marin human. Has blonde hair, blue eyes, and a narrow nose. Skilled with the arming sword. Wife of Prince Eron of Versingit.

Garen Baydran (*gehr*-en *bay*-dran): Male ethnic-Eklendan human. Farmer in the Serna township. Son of Jorn Baydran. Died while on a militia patrol near Serna, Talinochis, 793.

Garl Est'ail (*garl* es-*tai*-yil): Male ethnic-Marin human. Member of the Yvelian Council. Head of the Carpenter and Mason Combined Guild.

Garn Dandran (*garn dan*-dran), Male mixed-ethnic Marin-Eklendan human. Knight of the Crown Guard of Yvel. Veteran of the Battles of Serna Hills and Borly.

Garitan of Drenia (*gaer*-a-tan, *dren*-ee-a): Male dwarf of the deep clans. Emissary of King Nerim of Drenia to the city of Urrissio.

Garrick (ga-*rik*): See Turin.

Garsiyet (*gar*-see-yet): A blue-skinned (Western) hobgoblin overseeing logistics at Kogylar.

Garven (*gar*-ven): Male ethnic-Marin human. Medium height and scruffy, with shaggy brown hair and brown eyes. Curious and perceptive with an easy manner. Scout and tracker in the Serna Militia Company, trained by senior scout Korane Lowdran. Close friend of Arynn. Veteran of the Battle of Serna Hills.

Gerald Torg'ail (*jer*-ald *torg*-ai-yil): Male mixed-ethnic Marin-Eklendan human. Tall and handsome, with grey (formerly brown) hair and blue eyes. Late Prince of Yvel. Father to Arnold, Aered, Larz, Oswald, Pantaria, Praxia, and Velthuria. Killed by Dariyet in a night raid during the prelude to the Battle of Serna Hills, Anz, 794. See also: Torg'ail, House of.

Gerndran: See Baswyn Gerndran.

Goss (*goss*): Male ethnic-Berk human. Kozain's huntsman.

Grotis the Loner (*gro*-tiss): Male Orcish mercenary from the hills of the Western Kaskevs; literally translated to "alone." Atypically short for an orc (standing roughly the same height as a tall human male), with closely cut black hair. Wears reinforced leather armor dotted with a myriad of pouches, pockets, knives, and other tools. Characterized by an unusually curious and scholastic nature.

Gudreka (gud-*rek*-a): Male dwarf of Drenia. Member of Clan Gulrull. Serving as a major captain in the Drenian Army under the command of General Therog.

Gundr'ail: See Mot Gundr'ail.

Gunst Ver'ail (*gunzt* ver-*ai*-yil): Male ethnic-Marin human. Aged in his forties, with a careworn face and receding hairline. Nobleman and head of House Ver'ail, and former battalion leader in the Crown Army of Yvel. Adjutant of the Army of Yvel. Veteran of the Battle of Serna Hills. See also: Ver'ail, House of.

Halifar: See Erbasil Halifar.

Harl Oleandran (*harl* oe-*lee*-an-*dran*): Male ethnic-Eklendan human. Knight and former co-leader of the Yvelian Crown Guard and Baron of Borly. Veteran of the Battles of Serna Hills and Borly.

Hifen (*hih*-fen): Male ethnic-Marin human. Apprentice smith from Serna and member of the Serna Militia Company. Died on patrol in the Serna Hills following the orc raid in Talinochis, 793.

Holbrin Arozrien (*hoel*-brin *uh*-roz-*ree*-en): Icy-eyed, brown-haired male High Elf of the Order of the Sword. Known by his placid demeanor and unshakeable self-possession. Holder of a wing-engraved blade. Appointed as lead traveler by the Guardian Council. Veteran of the Battle of Serna Hills.

Hrene (*hreen*): Female dwarf of Aedon. Serving as a captain in King Naurom's legion, Hrene is one of the few surviving and free dwarves of Aedon that were at the fall of Adyrnaarn and leads a small caravan of survivors. Veteran of the Battle of Adyrnaarn.

Hunr'ail: See Allana Hunr'ail.

Iblar Enardran (*ib*-lar *en*-ar-dran): Male ethnic-Eklendan human farmer from the town of Serna. Taken prisoner in the orc raid in Talinochis, 793.

Idris Beredran (*id*-riss *ber*-e-dran): Male ethnic-Eklendan human. Third company leader of Battalion One of the Yvel Regiment.

Ig'Pon (*igg*-pon): See Kogleyet.

Imick Rollodran (*im*-ik *roe-loe*-dran): Female ethnic-Eklendan human from Serna. Relation of Arbera and Danick.

Indariyet the Great (in-*dar*-ee-yet): Female purple-skinned (Eastern) hobgoblin. Keeps her black hair tied into a tail. Often wears a gambeson or brigandine with a curved cavalry sword at her belt. Meticulous, shrewd, and impatient. Raised from second status and named by Oygariyet the Great to be the Great One of Okaramine tribe after Oygariyet's duel with Arkiban. Manages planning and logistics of the war on behalf of Oygariyet.

Iquarren: See Tyrnimar Iquarren.

Irduin Usrani (*ir*-doo-in *us*-rhan-ee): Female Grey Elf of the Order of the Sword and holder of a wing-engraved blade. Snow-white skin, silver hair, and violet eyes. Author of several books regarding swordcraft and military history. One of the Travelers appointed by the Guardian Council. Mentor to Lazura, Lierialuth Anrior, and Erensed Dryalos. Captured a great wolf as a replacement for her lost steed in the aftermath of the Battle of Borly. Veteran of the Battles of Serna Hills and Borly.

Iriaden Olari (ir-ee-a-*den* oe-*lar*-ee): Female Grey Elf with light blue hair and a pleasant and easy smile. Member of the Order of the Book. Councilor of the Guardian Council.

Isrdran: See Danick Isrdran.

Isriaden Kasriel (is-ree-a-*den kas*-ree-el): Female Grey Elf. Under-Provost of the Tower of Ebariel.

Ja'Kend (jah-*kend*): Female ethnic-Berk human. Dame Reverend Knight of the Order of Saint Kostray the Pure. Ja'Kend was one of the three knights of Saint Kostray, along with Sir Arami and Dame Kozain that sided with Sir Merik Aselifar after standing accused of heresy and winning the trial by combat.

Jak "Greenskin" (*jak*): Male half-human, half-orc, and taller than most humans. Released prisoner from a jail somewhere in Yvel Principality, after which he preferred to remove his formerly unkempt beard trimmed to no more than a few days' scruff. Originally from the Yvelian town of Keppa. Leader of a team of former prisoners that conduct raids against caravans originating from west of Yvel.

Jana (*jah*-na): Female ethnic-Eklendan human. From a village west of Keppa that had been raided.

Jaro Arvr'ail (*jah*-ro arv-*rai*-yil): Male ethnic-Marin human. Knight of the Crown Guard of Yvel. Husband to Sora. Veteran of the Battles of Serna Hills and Borly.

Jawn (*jon*): Male human and member of Jak's team of raiders.

Jerna (*jur*-na): Female blue-skinned (Western) goblin. Wears her hair loose and has heavily pierced ears: three earrings in one ear, five in the other. Lazy and shirks chores when she can; enjoys cozy days. Formerly of the Talz goblins of Kogylar. Member of Kolus' clan along with Kachem, Mersik, Panil, Spara, and Ys.

Jireyet (jir-*ey*-yet): Male blue-skinned (Western) goblin. Great One of the Venjeer tribe of goblins of Kogylar.

Jo'Kaul (*jo*-kawl): Male ethnic-Berk human. Reverend Knight of the Order of Saint Graffin the Defender. One of the Church Knights that opposed and was bested by Sir Merik during the trial by combat in Serna after the Battle of Serna Hills.

Jof Toliodran (*jof to*-le-oe-dran): Male ethnic-Eklendan human. Tall, slender, blond, blue-eyed, and dashing. Young member of House Toliodran of Keppa. Served as a company leader in the Arladran Battalion at the Battle of Serna Hills and as a member of the Prince of Yvel's Crown Guard at the Battle of Borly. Relation of Kirstan Toliodran. Veteran of the Battle of Serna Hills and the Battle of Borly.

Jolaban (*joe*-la-ban): A purple-skinned (Eastern) hobgoblin overseeing logistics at Kogylar.

Joledran: See Dorrels Joledran.

Jorn Baydran (*jorn bae*-dran): Male ethnic-Eklendan human. Farmer in the Serna township. Father of Garen Baydran. Died while on a militia patrol around Serna, Talinochis, 793.

Jovaela Varion (jo-*vale*-uh va-*rie*-un): Black-haired, black-eyed female High Elf of the Order of the Sword. Wears her hair in a single thick braid. Adheres strictly to rules, instructions, and social normatives. One of the Travelers appointed by the Guardian Council. Chosen by Holbrin Arozrien to report to the Guardian Council regarding the opening stages of the war in the west.

Judane Covendran (joo-*dane*-kov-en-dran): Female ethnic-Eklendan human. Dark of hair and eyes, with an angular, narrow jaw. Resentful of those that look down upon her; otherwise remains conciliatory and level-headed. Noblewoman and daughter of Koval and Mariss; sister to Dareum. Company Leader in the Serna Militia Company. Veteran of the Battle of Serna Hills. See also: Covendran, House of.

Julian Panr'ail (*joo*-lee-an pan-*rai*-yil): Male ethnic-Marin human. Lanky and lithe former livestock farmer with a mop of sandy brown hair from outside the town of Serna. Defined by his reliability and stoicism. Elder cousin of Ervan Panr'ail. Tenleader in the Serna Militia Company. Veteran of the Battle of Serna Hills.

Jundran: See Evren Jundran.

Juray (ju-*ray*): Male ethnic-Tamark human. Guard at the Palace of Kotara.

Jutzdran: See Yamis Jutzdran.

Kachem (*ka*-chem): Male blue-skinned (Western) goblin. Survivor of the demon blood fever, which changed his skin tone to its current dark blue-grey and his eyes to solid black. Black-haired with one earring in each ear. Cheerful, gentle, and slightly effeminate. Formerly of the Talz goblins of Kogylar. Member of Kolus' clan along with Jerna, Mersik, Panil, Spara, and Ys.

Karas (*ka*-ras): A minor demon kept in captivity by Valnos the wizard.

Karidran: See Taram Karidran.

Karsi (*kar*-see): Female orc. Average height for an orc woman (significantly taller than human men), with shoulder-length black hair that she keeps tied in a simple tail and black eyes. Hard-working and stoic. Formerly slave to the late Dariyet the Great and captured at the Battle of Serna Hills. Saved from execution by Mkaela Ran'ail. Member of Serna Militia Company.

Kasriel: See Isriaden Kasriel.

Kersis, House of: Ethnic-Vostindin house of nobles that sided with the west during the Great Shattering and settled into the lands around Yvel.

Kerzin (*ker*-zin): Female ethnic-Eklendan human. Chief Surgeon in the service to the Crown of Yvel.

Kevr'ail: See Baryn Kevr'ail, Bonwyn Kev'rail.

Kirstan Toliodran (*kir*-stan to-*lee*-oh-dran): Female ethnic-Eklendan human. Baroness of Keppa and head of House Toliodran. Relation of Jof Toliodran.

Kogleyet (*kog*-ley-yet): Male blue-skinned (Western) goblin. Newly raised as the Great One of the Venjeer tribe of goblins of Kogylar, sharing leadership with Erseyet. Also called Ig'Pon ("No-nose") due to his nose being shot off by an arrow during the Battle of Versingit.

Kolus (*ko*-luss): Male ethnic-Eklendan human. A survivor of a demon blood fever, his appearance has significantly changed. Skin is now grey, eyes are solid black, and all of his hair has fallen out. Ruthless and practical when needed, though has 'gone soft' for his new family. Friendly and studious. An operative of Lord Nicholas investigating the possibilities of magic on behalf of the Ministry of Information.

Korane Lowdran (kor-*ain loe*-dran): Middle-aged female mixed-ethnic Marin-Eklendan human from Serna. Jet black hair, save for a silver lock in the front that appeared after the attacks on the town of Serna. Scarred on her cheek and leg from an altercation with a hobgoblin. Tends towards brooding and vindictive behavior. Former senior scout and tracker of the Serna Militia Company. Recruited into the Ministry of Information after the Battle of Serna Hills. Veteran of the Battle of Serna Hills.

Kora Orint'ail (*kor*-a or-int-*ai*-yil): Red-haired, brown-eyed ethnic-Marin female human of medium build and height. Immature, and prone to feeling strong emotions. Often acts out of anger or panic. Former apprentice glazier at her family's workshop in the town of Serna. Sister of Ayza. Crown Sorceress of Yvel (Stormbearer). Veteran of the Battle of Serna

Hills.

Koval Covendran (*koe*-vahl *koe*-ven-dran): Male ethnic-Eklendan middle-aged human. Black hair with silver wings, and a trimmed salt and pepper beard. Proud, and does not like his authority or competence questioned. Quick to rely on intimidation in order to get his way. Lord of the town of Serna and surrounding villages and farms. Father of Dareum and Judane, husband to Mariss. Regimental Leader of the First Yvel Regiment. Veteran of the Battles of Serna Hills and Borly. See also: Covendran, House of.

Kovarre Arladran (*kov*-air ar-la-dran): Female ethnic-Eklendan human in her mid-thirties. Pale olive skin, black hair, and dark, brooding eyes. Bitter, coldly vengeful, and committed to defeating orcs and goblinkind. Noblewoman and widow of the late Dorvin, head of House Arladran. Battalion leader of the Arladran Battalion, an auxiliary battalion in the Army of Yvel. See also: Arladran, House of.

Kozain (*ko*-zaen): Female ethnic-Berk human. Reverend Knight of the Order of Saint Kostray the Pure. One of the Church Knights that supported Sir Merik, along with Sir Arami and Dame Ja'Kend, after the trial by combat in Serna after the Battle of Serna Hills.

Koziathin (koe-*zie*-a-thin): Female ethnic-Berk human. A cook in the Palace of Yvel's kitchens treasured for her skill in brewing coffee.

Kudre (*koo*-dra): Female ethnic-Tamark human. Caravan driver that survived an ambush by Jak's team of raiders.

Kurelig (ker-*el*-ig): General in the army of Drenia.

Larz Torg'ail (*larz* torg-*ai*-yil): Male mixed-ethnic Marin-Eklendan human. Sandy brown hair and blue eyes. Prince-Heir to the throne of Yvel. Son of Gerald; sixth oldest sibling of Aered, Arnold, Oswald, Pantaria, Praxia, and Velthuria. See also: Torg'ail, House of.

Lazura (*la*-zur-a) Autumnleaf: Female Sylvan Elf at the age of selection. Blond hair and blue eyes. One of the Travelers appointed by the Guardian Council. Under the tutelage of Irduin Usrani. Veteran of the Battles of Serna Hills and Borly.

Lena Pardran (*len*-uh *par*-dran): Female ethnic-Eklendan human, from the town of Serna. Spearbearer in the Serna Militia Company. Veteran of the Battle of Serna Hills.

Lierialuth Anrior (leer-*ie*-a-*looth* ahn-ree-or): Female High Elf at the age of selection. One of the Travelers appointed by the Guardian Council. Under the tutelage of Irduin Usrani. Veteran of the Battle of Serna Hills. Died at the Battle of Borly, Sixth Day of Summer, 18031, by the Elven Calendar (Youri, 794, by the Western Church of Orneth calendar).

Lin'ail: See Aphra Lin'ail, Marlar Lin'ail.

Liri Venodran (*lee*-ree *ven*-oe-dran): Female ethnic-Eklendan human from the town of Serna. Rider in the Serna Militia Company.

369

Lowdran: See Korane Lowdran.

Machidran: See Nicholas Machidran.

Maglaban (*mag*-la-ban): Male purple-skinned (Eastern) hobgoblin. Shaven bald with a grim face. Wears armor for all occasions, and carries a glaive used to direct people as much as it is used in combat. Practical, honor-bound, and loyal, with no patience for petty conflicts, selfishness, or cowardice. Great One of the Barituul, hailing from the hobgoblin city of Golardeg.

Marchag (*mar-chag*): Male dwarf of the realm of Aedon. Sergeant in the King's Legion, under Captain Hrene, as King Naurom of Aedon reinforced the city of Adyrnaarn against the Drenian invasion. Veteran of the Battle of Adyrnaarn.

Mariss Covendran (*ma*-riss *kov*-en-dran): Female ethnic-Eklendan human. Dark hair and dark eyes. Introverted, sweet, and exceedingly persuasive. Lady of the town of Serna. Wife of Koval, mother of Dareum and Judane. Manages the construction of fortifications around Serna and the mustering of additional forces for the Yvel Army near Serna. See also: Covendran, House of.

Marlar Lin'ail (*mar-lar lin*-ai-yil): Female ethnic-Marin human from Serna. Has brown hair, blue eyes, and an argumentative streak. Twin sister of Aphra. Abducted during the first orc raid of Serna and bore a half-orc child.

Marsen Fris'ail (*mar*-sin friz-*ai*-yil): Female ethnic-Marin human from Serna. Militiaman in the Serna Militia Company. Veteran of the Battle of Serna Hills.

Mazurnine: See Eevarel Mazurnine.

Melz Belifar (*melz bel*-i-far): Male ethnic-Berk human. Elderly, bald, and slow-moving. Ornethian Bishop of Yvel.

Merik Aselifar (*mer*-ik *ae*-sel-i-far): Male ethnic-Berk human. In his mid-thirties; taller (and broader) than average, with a muscular build. Has brown hair and hazel eyes. Is loyal and idealistic. Reverend Knight of the Military Order of Saint Graffin the Defender. Husband of Dame Risit. Champion of Mkaela Ran'ail. Veteran of the Battle of Serna Hills.

Mersik (*mer*-sik): Female (Western) blue-skinned goblin. Vine tattoo that starts on her left waist, crosses her abdomen, curls around the right waist and ends on the back of her right shoulder. Pragmatic, studious, and thorough; dominant in a matronly manner. Formerly of the Talz goblins of Kogylar. Member of Kolus' clan along with Kachem, Jerna, Panil, Spara, and Ys.

Messenger, the: Female blue-skinned (Western) hobgoblin. Dark eyes and deep black hair reaching mid-back tied into a tight tail and tucked inside her helmet. Uses berries when available to stain her hair purple. Jagged scar runs across her jaw and onto her neck (from a knife fight with Korane Lowdran). Scars for an entry and exit wound on her left knee from an arrow wound (also from Korane Lowdran). Former cavalry subleader of the Wiridil tribe. Veteran of the prelude to the Battle of Serna Hills (but not present for the pitched battle).

Minderl Radidran (*min*-dur-ul *rad*-i-dran): Male ethnic-Eklendan human. Member of the Merchant and Guild Council of Yvel. He owns stores, workshops, and warehouses for industrial purposes in Yvel City.

Miykodran: See Terah Miykodran, Ziek Miykodran.

Mkaela Ran'ail (*mik*-ae-la ran-*ai*-yil): Female ethnic-Marin human. Wavy brown hair and brown eyes; petite with a soft build. Kind and humble, but often blunt of manner. Former baker and apprentice apothecary of the town of Serna. Divisive figure among Sernans, Yvelians, and clergy of the Western Church of Orneth; regarded as a saint by some and a heretic by others due to her awakened healing powers. Veteran of the Battles of Serna Hills and Borly.

Mollog (moh-*log*): A highborn Drenian clan; banner is red with three golden medallions embroidered into the center of a triangle. See also: Therog, Gazetteer: Drenia.

Molok (*moh*-luk): Male ethnic-Eklendan human. From a nameless village west of Keppa that had been raided. Knows Jana and Sontrin.

Moonwhisper: See Arcaezhia Moonwhisper.

Mot Gundr'ail (*mot* gund-*rai*-yil): Male ethnic-Marin human. Heavy set, with a large, hard belly hanging over his belt. Clean-shaven and mostly bald with wisps of white hair combed over. Walks with a cane, on a peg leg. Marshal (formerly a general) of the Crown Army of Yvel. Veteran of the Battle of Borly.

Murchian (*merch*-ee-yan): Male gnoll. Tribal leader on the Slopes of the Invader (Eastern) of the Kaskev Mountains. Part of Oygariyet's coalition.

Muydiyet (*moy*-dee-et): Female blue-skinned (Western) hobgoblin. Great One of the Wiridil tribe of hobgoblins, a small tribe that specializes in raising great wolves as battle steeds and fielding wolf cavalry. Veteran of the Battle of Versingit.

Naurom of Aedon (*naw*-rohm, *ae*-don): Male dwarf of the middle clans. King of Aedon and head of the royal clan of Uirull. See also: Uirull.

Nerim of Drenia (*nehr*-im, *dren*-ee-a): Male dwarf of the deep clans. King of Drenia and head of the royal clan of Noian. See also: Noian.

Nicholas Machidran (*nik*-oe-las *mah*-chi-dran): Male ethnic-Marin human. Sports neatly-combed black hair and an intelligent expression. Is studious, thorough, and urbane. Guarded to most, friendly to a selected few. Chief Librarian and Minister of Information in service of the Crown of Yvel.

Noian (*noy*-an): Royal clan of Drenia. See also: Nerim of Drenia; Gazetteer: Drenia.

Odr'ail: See Aleksan Odr'ail.

Olari: See Iriaden Olari.

Ogrekin (*oh*-gher-kin): Male blue-skinned (Western) hobgoblin. Formerly Oygariyet's First and of the Zirn tribe until earning a name by successfully recruiting Urazor's tribe of ogres.

Oilaravan: See Deni Oilaravan.

Oklaifar: See Bandal Oklaifar.

Olavy (oe-*lah*-vee): Female ethnic-Berk human. Dame Reverend Knight of the
    Order of Saint Acrist the Judge. Olavy was one of the Ornethian knights
    that fought Sir Merik in the trial by combat when Sir Merik stood accused
    of heresy for supporting Mkaela Ran'ail. Dame Olavy lost the trial in
    addition to two fingers, but rejected the verdict.

Oleandran: See Harl Oleandran.

Olid'ail: See Damarus Olid'ail.

Ordavan: See Chariss Ordavan.

Orint'ail: See Ayza Orint'ail, Kora Orint'ail.

Oris (*oer*-iss): Male ethnic-Eklendan human. Headman of a small village or hamlet
    somewhere between Keppa, Garber, and Serna.

Orn Blar'ail (*orn* blar-*ai*-yil): Male ethnic-Marin human. Shingler and thatcher from
    the town of Serna. Murdered by the Blue-Eyed Man in a night raid during
    the prelude to the Battle of Serna Hills, Anz, 794.

Orsir, Trinien: See Trinien Orsir.

Oswald Torg'ail (*oz*-wald tor-*gai*-yil): Male mixed-ethnic Marin-Eklendan human.
    Similar in appearance to his older brother, Prince Arnold. Clever, laconic,
    often with an amused expression. Prince-Heir to the throne of Yvel. Son
    of Gerald, brother to Aered, Arnold, Larz, Pantaria, Praxia, and Velthuria.
    Veteran of the Battle of Serna Hills. See also: Torg'ail, House of.

Oygariyet the Great (*oi*-gar-ee-*yet*): Male blue-skinned (Western) hobgoblin. Bald,
    muscular, and agile; prefers to fight with a sword and mace. Ruthless
    yet kind; visionary and bold; clever and scheming. Respectful of his
    possessions. Great One of the Zirn tribe. Oygariyet forged an alliance
    between most of the hobgoblin and goblin tribes of the mountains, as well
    as the majority of the orcs and groups of ogres, gnolls and kobolds.

Panil (*pa-nil*): Male blue-skinned (Western) goblin. Bald and muscular with a lattice
    of symmetrical shapes tattooed over his chest. Stoic, gruff, protective,
    loyal, and upright. Formerly of the Talz goblins of Kogylar. Member of
    Kolus' clan along with Kachem, Jerna, Mersik, Spara, and Ys.

Panr'ail: See Ervan Panr'ail, Julian Panr'ail.

Pantaria Torg'ail (pan-*tar*-ee-a *torg*-ai-yil): Female mixed-ethnic Marin-Eklendan
    human with black hair, blue eyes, and a sickly constitution. Princess-Heir
    to the throne of Yvel. Daughter of Gerald, fifth eldest sibling of Aered,
    Arnold, Larz, Oswald, Praxia (her older twin), and Velthuria. See also:
    Torg'ail, House of.

Pardran: See Lena Pardran.

Parendien (pa-*ren*-dee-en): Male High Elf of the Order of Peace. One of the
    Travelers appointed by the Guardian Council. Black hair and blue eyes.

Enjoys trying different alcohols. Wounded in a night raid during the prelude to the Battle of Serna Hills. Veteran of the Battle of Serna Hills.

Peregan (*per*-i-gahn): Male ethnic-Marin human. Recently arrived in Versingit and joined the Versingit Regiment to defend the city.

Perndran: See Damerwyn Perndran.

Persis (*per*-sis): Kozain's warhorse.

Pine (pien): Julian Panr'ail's horse.

Praxia Torg'ail (*prax*-ee-a *torg*-ai-yil): Female mixed-ethnic Marin-Eklendan human with black hair, blue eyes, and a sickly constitution. Princess-Heir to the throne of Yvel. Daughter of Gerald; fourth eldest sibling of Aered, Arnold, Larz, Oswald, Pantaria (her younger twin), and Velthuria. See also: Torg'ail, House of.

The Primarch (*pri*-mark): Female ethnic-Berk human. Matronly woman in her fifties with a face that has judged many people. Shrewd and calculating; jealously guards the Church's (her) power and position. Has a taste for fine foods, robes, and other fine trappings of the office. Highest ranking clergy member of the (Western) Reformed Church of Orneth.

Radidran: See Minderl Radidran.

Ran'ail: See Mkaela Ran'ail.

Rangli (*rang*-lee): Male dwarf of Drenia. Serving as a scout under the command of Major Captain Gudreka.

Reskladran: See Yander Reskladran.

Rielan Yidr'ail (*ree*-lun yih-*drai*-yil): Male ethnic-Eklendan human. Townsman from the town of Serna. One of the people initially saved by Mkaela Ran'ail in her awakening as a healer.

Risiar of Urrissio (*riss*-ee-ar, *er*-iss-ee-oe): Male Dark Elf. Dashing and handsome, with white hair and black eyes. Eloquent, diplomatic, quietly charismatic. Nobleman of Urrissio. Friend and ally of Princess Erisa.

Risit Aselifar (*ris*-it ae-*sel*-i-far): Female ethnic-Berk human in her thirties with red hair, freckles, blue eyes, and a muscular build. Dame Reverend of the Military Order of Saint Graffin the Defender. Merik Aselifar's wife.

Rollodran, Arbera: See Arbera Rollodran, Danick Rollodran, Imick Rollodran.

Ryn (*rin*): A minor demon who serves as the familiar for the Dwarven wizard, Aemzon.

Sarl (*sarl*): Male ethnic-Berk human. Kozain's servant.

Sedra Torin'ail (*sed*-ra tor-in-*ai*-yil): Female ethnic-Marin human. From Serna; cousin of Seedar Torin'ail, relation of Dyram Torin'ail.

Seedar Torin'ail (*see*-dar tor-in-*ai*-yil): Female ethnic-Marin human from Serna. Cousin to Sedra and Dyram Torin'ail. One of the people initially saved by Mkaela Ran'ail in her awakening as a healer.

Selonikah (*sel*-on-*ik*-ah): Female ethnic-Marin human. Is blonde with brown eyes, and quite lean from time spent in captivity. Is independent, trusting, and hard-working. Former barmaid and housekeep at the Valley Spring Inn in the town of Serna. Abducted during the first orc raid of Serna and given as a slave to Oygariyet the Great.

Seros of Urrissio (*ser*-roes, *er*-iss-ee-oe): Male Dark Elf. Is nearly always dressed in laboratory clothes, showing the stains of alchemical agents or other materials. Keeps his white hair cut short. Lean, but not muscular. Is cautious, methodical, and mercenary. Under contract as a magus to Princess Erisa and Lord Risiar of Urrissio, to perform various types of magic and alchemy, as well as the crafting of drugs and poisons.

Sieraean (see-*rae*-en): Female High Elf of the Order of the Sword. Wears her black hair in a thick waist-length braid; highly proficient with the shortbow. One of the Travelers appointed by the Guardian Council. Wounded in a night raid during the prelude to the Battle of Serna Hills. Veteran of the Battle of Serna Hills.

Sirid (*syir*-id): Female ethnic-Eklendan human. Slender but athletic; offers a smile made of knives. Often wears long skirts. Bitter and resentful of affluent persons; sarcastic, scheming, and sometimes flirtatious. Member of Jak's team of raiders.

Smeld (*smeld*): Half-human, half-rat bipedal creature from the catacombs of Versingit.

Sontrin (*son*-trin): Female Eklendan human. From a village west of Keppa that had been raided. Knows Jana and Molok.

Sora Arvr'ail (*soe*-ra arv-*rai*-yil): Female ethnic-Marin human. Knight of the Crown Guard of Yvel. Wife of Jaro. Veteran of the Battles of Serna Hills and Borly.

Spara (*spar*-a): Female blue-skinned (Western) goblin. Wears her hair in Marin-style braids and wears a nose ring. Playful, mischievous, and physically affectionate with her family members. Formerly of the Talz goblins of Kogylar. Member of Kolus' clan along with Kachem, Jerna, Mersik, Panil, and Ys.

Stanis Tw'ail (*stan*-is *twai*-yil): Male ethnic-Marin human. Clerk on Prince Arnold's staff. Served Prince Gerald and Prince Arnold during the Battles of Serna Hills and Borly.

Tansher (*tan*-sher): Female ethnic-Tamark human. Brown-haired and freckled with green eyes, rosy cheeks, and a pleasantly soft figure. Manipulative, jealous, and self-serving. Member of Jak's team of raiders.

Taram Karidran (tar-*am kar*-i-dran): Male mixed-ethnic Eklendan-Daearan human; elder resident of the town of Serna. Aged but virile appearance, with scraggly, greyed hair and deep wrinkles offset by well-defined musculature and posture. Is also known by the names Bellarden and Joriss. Tenleader in the Serna Militia Company. Veteran of the Battle of Serna Hills.

Terah Miykodran (*ter*-ah *meek*-oe-dran): Female ethnic-Eklendan human. Medium complexion, auburn hair, and dark brown eyes. Seamstress from the town of Serna, where she produces livery for the militia. Formerly engaged to the deceased Ervan Panr'ail.

Therog *(ther-*og*)*: Male dwarf. Head of the highborn Drenian clan Mollog; general in the army of Drenia. See also: Mollog.

Toliodran: See Jof Toliodran, Kirstan Toliodran.

Torg'ail, House of: The ruling family of Yvel Principality. The House of Torg'ail banner has a red, upward-pointing chevron on a gray background. See Aered Torg'ail, Arnold Torg'ail, Gerald Torg'ail, Lars Torg'ail, Oswald Torg'ail, Pantaria Torg'ail, Praxia Torg'ail, Velthuria Torg'ail.

Torin'ail: See Dyram Torin'ail, Sedra Torin'ail, Seedar Torin'ail.

Trinien Orsir (*trin*-ee-an or-*seer*): Male High Elf of the Order of Peace. Wears an amused expression and, when circumstances allow, pink hair (though it is naturally blond, and worn as such in the presence of humans). One of the travelers appointed by the Guardian Council. Wounded in a night raid during the prelude to the Battle of Serna Hills. Veteran of the Battle of Serna Hills.

Tun'ail: See Alain, Tun'ail.

Turaean (tur-*ae*-an): Male Wood Elf of the Order of the Sword. One of the Travelers appointed by the Guardian Council. Died in a night raid during the prelude to the Battle of Serna Hills, 46th day of Spring, 18030 (Anz, 794 by the Western Church of Orneth Calendar).

Turin (*turr*-in): Male ethnic-Marin human. One of Lord Nicholas' operatives in the Ministry of Information. Also known as Garrick (*Gar*-ik).

Tw'ail: See Stanis Tw'ail.

Tyrnimar Iquarren (*teer*-ni-mar *ik*-war-en): Silver-haired, violet-eyed male Grey Elf of the Order of the Book (the Blue Order). Very tall and thin, with an air of uncomfortability about him. One of the Travelers appointed by the Guardian Council. Observing the development of blood sorcery in Kora and Ayza Orint'ail, at the Crown Sorcerers' Proving Grounds. Veteran of the Battle of Serna Hills.

Uirull (oo-ee-*rull*): The royal clan of Aedon. The banner is a downward-facing axe. See also: Naurom of Aedon, Gazetteer: Aedon.

Urasen (*ur*-a-sen): Tyrnimar Iquarren's horse.

Urazor (*yur*-a-zor): Female ogre. Priestess and leader of an ogre tribe that joins Oygariyet's coalition.

Usrani: See Irduin Usrani.

Vanre (*vah*-ner): Female ethnic-Tamark human maid at the Palace of Kotara.

Varion: See Jovaela Varion.

Velthuria Torg'ail (vel-*thur*-ee-a *torg*-ai-yil): Female mixed-ethnic Marin-Eklendan human. Tall, like her older brothers, with red hair and dark eyes. Is eager, daring, and calculating. Princess-Heir to the throne of Yvel. Daughter of Gerald; second eldest sibling of Aered, Arnold, Larz, Oswald, Pantaria, and Praxia. Veteran of the Battle of Borly. See also: Torg'ail, House of.

Venodran: See Liri Venodran.

Veradran: See Amryst, Veradran.

Ver'ail, House of: Noble house in the Principality of Yvel. Banner is blue and gold in a checkered pattern. Fielded a battalion to accompany Prince Gerald of Yvel at the Battle of Serna Hills. See Gunst Ver'ail.

Virek (*vir*-ek): Male ethnic-Marin human. Knight and co-leader of the Yvelian Crown Guard. Died in a night raid during the prelude to the Battle of Serna Hills, Anz, 794.

Wrin'ail: See Brindi Wrin'ail, Eron Wrin'ail, Fyon Wrin'ail.

Yamis Jutzdran (*ya*-mis *juts*-dran): Male ethnic-Eklendan human. Townsman from Serna. Died while on a militia patrol near Serna, Talinochis, 793.

Yand'ail: See Zaya, Yand'ail.

Yander Reskladran (*yan*-der *resk*-la-dran): Female ethnic-Eklendan human. Squire to Sir Harl. Veteran of the Battle of Serna Hills. Died at the Battle of Borly, Youri, 794.

Ydren: See Akriun, Ydren.

Yidr'ail: See Rielan Yidr'ail.

Yonn (yon): Male ethnic-Marin human. Leader of another team of bandits, similar to Jak's.

Ys (*ees*): Female blue-skinned (Western) goblin. Has violet eyes and dark blue hair. Skin has a blue-green tinge, and she is taller than most goblins, implying Orcish lineage in her bloodline. Hot-tempered. Formerly of the Talz goblins of Kogylar. Member of Kolus' clan along with Kachem, Jerna, Mersik, Panil, and Spara.

Zaya Yand'ail (*zai*-ya yan-*dai*-yil): Female mixed-ethnic Marin-Tamark human. Has wavy dark hair, a narrow jaw, and a fair, freckled complexion. Talkative, enthusiastic, and determined. One of Lord Nicholas' operatives within the Ministry of Information.

Ziek Miykodran (zee-*ek mik*-oe-dran): Young male ethnic-Eklendan human. Has olive skin, medium brown hair, and is prone to finding himself in troublesome situations despite his best intentions. Resident of the town of Serna. Saved from a mortal wound by Tyrnimar Iquarren and a summoned dryad during the orc raid on Serna in Talinochis, 793. No other members of his family survived, and he is now under the care of multiple families in Serna.

Zug'ail: See Abiah Zug'ail.

Appendix III: Index of Tribes and Peoples

Ablar (*a*-blar): Hobgoblin vassal tribe to the Zirn.

Ahng-Gorah (*aun-go*-rah): Tribe of orcs from the eastern slopes of the Kaskevs. They favor swords with forward-curving blades, as is more common on the eastern side of the mountains. The Ahng-Gorah falls under the broader umbrella of tribes that are vassals to the Borys-Karang. Contributed warriors to fight at the Battle of Versingit.

Baki-Norn (*ba-ki norn*): Orcish vassal tribe to the Borys-Karang; literally translated to "The Thrill of Blood." Perpetrated the original raid on Serna in the winter of 793. The tribe was destroyed (administratively disbanded, by Orcish custom) and consumed by the Borys-Karang.

Barituul (*bar*-i-*tool*): Tribe of purple-skinned (Eastern) hobgoblins from the hobgoblin city of Golardeg. Led by Maglaban the Great.

Berk (*burk*): Human ethnicity predominantly populating Berkmar and northwestern Gersh; majority representation of clergy in the Western Reformed Church of Orneth. Physically tend towards lighter complexions and stocky builds. See *The Witches of Serna*, Appendix X: Humans; *The Witches of Serna*, fig. 13: Humans by Ethnicity: Berks and Tamarks.

Bren-Derz (*bren-durz*): Orcish tribe; literally translated, "the Crushing Fist of Very, Very Hard Stone."

Borys-Karang (bo-*reez ka*-rang): Orcish tribe; literally translated, "The All-Consuming Flame." Vassal tribes include the Bren-Derz, the Derz, the Gardek, the Gezierad, the Talz (the tribe which destroyed and absorbed the Ahng-Gorah), and the Tiralk, among others. The Borys-Karang has destroyed and absorbed the Baki-Norn.

bugbear: Physically largest race of goblinkind. See Appendix IX: Ratfolk, Gnolls, Bugbears, and Ogres.

Daearan (day-*ar*-an): Ethnicity of humans predominantly from the Kingdom of Daeara.

Dark Elf: Elves that were banished from the surface long ago after a conflict between the Elven peoples. See *The Witches of Serna*, Appendix XI: Elves: Physiology, Appearance, and Ethnicity.

demon: Creature from the Pit.

Derz (*durs*): Orcish vassal tribe to the Borys-Karang. Literally translates to, "the Fist Made of Hard Stone."

Donbat-Karang (*don*-bat ka-*rang*): Orcish tribe. Literally translates to, "Flaming Sword." Vassal to the Borys-Karang.

Drauchi (*draw*-chee): Goblin tribe.

Drell: Tribe of kobolds.

dryad (*dri*-ad): Race of tree fairy with minor powers.

dwarf: Short, stocky humanoid, standing halfway between a goblin and a short human. Dwarves primarily live in subterranean environs. See Appendix VIII: Dwarves.

Eklendan (ek-*len*-den): Ethnicity of humans that are the predominant population of the Kingdom of Eklenda and southern Gersh. Compared to most western humans, they tend to be tall and slender, with narrow jaws, olive complexions, dark eyes, and black, brown, or red hair. See *The Witches of Serna*, Appendix X: Physiology, Appearance, and Ethnicity; *The Witches of Serna*, fig. 14: Humans by Ethnicity: Eklendans and Marins.

elf: Tall and graceful sentient humanoid, blessed with beauty and long life. Elves are roughly the height of medium to tall humans, but more agile, and slighter in frame. See *The Witches of Serna*: Appendix XI; *The Witches of Serna*, fig. 15: Elves Arguing with a Human.

Gardek (*gar*-dek): Orcish tribe.

Gezierad (gez-*eer*-ad): Orcish tribe. Despite being powerful in their own right, are reportedly deferential to the Borys-Karang.

gnoll (*noel*): Odd mix of a bipedal creature and a canine with spotted fur, as tall as orcs. See Appendix IX.

gnome (*noem*): Diminutive humanoid with proportions between that of a human and a dwarf, but scaled small enough for two or three to comfortably stand on the palm of a human hand.

goblin: Physically smallest race of goblinkind. See *The Witches of Serna*, Appendix XV: Goblins; *The Witches of Serna*, fig. 20: Goblins Arguing with a Human.

goblinkind: Collective term for humanoid creatures comprising goblins, hobgoblins, and bugbears.

Grey Elf: Ethnic minority of elves, largely concentrated around the city of Ebariel. See *The Witches of Serna*, Appendix XI: Physiology, Appearance, and Ethnicity.

halfling: Humanoid race resembling that of humans, but reaching full height at approximately one pace, or half of a human's average height.

High Elf: Majority ethnic group of elves, primarily centered in Elven cities. See *The Witches of Serna*, Appendix XI: Physiology, Appearance, and Ethnicity.

hobgoblin: Middle-sized race of goblinkind, standing the same height as a tall human. See *The Witches of Serna*, Appendix XIII: Hobgoblins; *The Witches of Serna*, fig. 18: Hobgoblins Planning an Attack.

human: Most populous people of Paeta, but fractured across many ethnicities, cultures, and realms. See *The Witches of Serna*, Appendix X; *The Witches of Serna*, fig. 13, 14.

Kad Rang (*khad rang*): Gang of thieves from Verdunsk.

Kilindiban (kil-*in*-di-ban): Hobgoblin vassal tribe to the Zirn.

kobold (*ko*-boeld): Race of small, bipedal horned lizards, roughly half the height of humans (similar in stature to goblins, halflings, and dwarves). Typically dwell in caves and mountainous climes.

Marin (*mah*-rin): Ethnicity of humans, predominantly from the Kingdom of Markia. Marins tend to be short in stature with light complexions, narrow noses, blue or brown eyes, and blond to medium brown hair. See *The Witches of Serna*, Appendix X: Physiology, Appearance, and Ethnicity; *The Witches of Serna*, fig. 14.

Mindosh (*min*-dosh): Goblin tribe.

lizardfolk: Race of bipedal lizards; unlike kobolds, are taller than humans (on par with hobgoblins) and lacking horns. Prefer warm, humid regions, generally along the southern Paetan coast east of the Kaskevs.

Okaramine (oe-*kar*-a-*meen*): Hobgoblin tribe. Led by the Great One Indariyet.

orc: Race of tall and physically powerful, green-skinned people. See *The Witches of Serna*, Appendix XII: Orcs; *The Witches of Serna*, fig. 16: Portraits of Orcs, fig. 17: Orc Warrior and Orc Slave.

Peradek (*per*-a-dek): Goblin tribe, literally translated to "the Stone-Breakers."

ratfolk (*rat*-foek): Humanoids living beneath the streets of Versingit. They are roughly the same height and build as humans, though their faces, ears, hands, and feet are decidedly more like mice or rats. See Appendix IX.

Surent (sur-*ent*): Hobgoblin vassal tribe to the Zirn.

Sylvan Elf: See Wood Elf.

Talz (*talz*): Tribe of goblins renowned for their engineering and technical prowess. They have a wide scattering of clans between Kogylar and Berkasliriyig.

Talz (*talz*): Tribe of orcs that is resentful about being mistaken for the tribe of goblins of the same name. The Talz are a vassal tribe of the Borys-Karang and fought at the Battle of Versingit.

Tamark (*ta*-mark): Ethnicity of humans primarily from Tamark and western Gersh. See *The Witches of Serna (Book I)*, Appendix X: Physiology, Appearance, and Ethnicity, fig. 13.

Tiralk (*teer*-alk): Orcish tribe, literally translated to "the Smell of Foot Treads in the Night."

Venjeer (ven-*jeer*): Goblin tribe from the city of Kogylar that fought at the Battle of Versingit.

Vostindin (voe-*stind*-in): Ethnicity of humans that populate the human realm of Vostind, east of the Kaskev Mountains.

Wiridil (*whir*-i-dil): Hobgoblin tribe. Led by the Great One Muydiyet.

Wood Elf: Reference to an ethnicity of elves, though over the centuries, the term has also come to include non-ethnic Wood Elves who opt for a rugged lifestyle or path. See *The Witches of Serna*, Appendix XI: Physiology, Appearance, and Ethnicity.

Zirn (*zern*): Hobgoblin tribe. Led by the Great One Oygariyet. Its vassal tribes include the Ablar, Kilindiban, Okaramine, Surent, Barituul, Wiridil, and others.

Appendix IV: Gazetteer

Adyrnaarn (ad-*er*-narn): City in the Dwarven realm of Aedon. Districts and landmarks of note include Junction Cavern, Korlaeith, New Adyrnaarn, and Old Adyrnaarn. See fig. 4: Map of the Dwarven City of Adyrnaarn.

Aedon (*ae*-don): One of four large Dwarven kingdoms beneath the Kaskev Mountains, alongside Dranomar, Drenia, and Medria. Until recently, the kingdom was ruled by King Naurom. Some of its major cities include Adyrnaarn, Ashgar-Isriol, Ezkaarn, Kandaneria, Verenaz, and Zol. The dwarves of Aedon are called Aedons.

Aezel (*ae*-zel): Island northwest of Tamarkand, across from the Boznin Sea. See fig. 1: Map of Paeta.

Agnesia (ag-*nee*-see-a): Island off of the southwest coast of Eklenda, in the Agnesian Sea. See fig. 1.

Agnesian Sea (ag-*nee*-jee-un): Sea off of the southern coast of Eklenda. See fig. 1.

Ardara (ar-*dar*-ah): One of the princely cities of the Gershan Lands. Nestled at the foot of the central-western Kaskev Mountains, Ardara is a major exporter of ores and minerals to eastern Gersh and northern Eklenda. Ardarans are primarily a mix of Eklendan and Daearan humans. See fig. 3: Map of Yvel Principality and Nearby Vassal Towns.

Ashgar-Isriol (*ash*-gar *is*-ree-oel): City in the Dwarven realm of Aedon.

Atlayan Mountains (at-*lae*-un): North-south range of mountains that separates Vostind and Gilliam from Mardalon. See fig. 1.

Baan (*bahn*): City further north of Kogylar and Rykooth, primarily populated by orcs and located in the Kaskev Mountains.

Ballic Marshes (*bahl*-ick): Wetlands formed by the River Ballic entering Lake Tald. See fig. 3.

Balta (*bahl*-tuh): Capital city of Gilliam, sitting on the southern coast. See fig. 1.

Berkasliriyig (ber-*kas*-le-er-ee-*yig*): Subterranean city built by goblins in the northern Kaskev Mountains. Like Kogylar, it is a hub of trade. While primarily populated by goblins, many other races come to conduct trade.

Berkmar (*burk*-mar): Kingdom of humans northwest of the Gershan Lands, west of Markia, and northeast of Tamarkand, populated almost exclusively by ethnic-Berk humans. Berkmar has a territorial dispute with Markia, holding the view that Markia has taken Berk lands. Berks from Berkmar and northwest Gersh comprise the vast majority of the clergy, both clerical and militant orders. See fig 1.

Bervale (ber-*vale*): Vassal town of Yvel Principality, on the road between Yvel City and Vidara; west of the town of Garber. See fig. 3.

Bissen (*bis*-in): Capital city of Eklenda, sitting on the southern coast. See fig. 1.

Boaz (*boez*): Princely city in the Gershan Lands on the western shore of Lake Tald. Populated by ethnic Berk and Tamark humans. See fig. 2: Map of the Gershan Lands, fig. 3.

Borly (*bor*-lee): Walled vassal town of Yvel Principality, sitting between Yvel City and Versingit. Home of Borly Keep. See fig. 3.

Boznin Sea (*boz*-nin): Sea off the coast of northern Tamarkand, northwest Gersh, and west Berkmar. Transitions into the Korozian Ocean. See fig. 1, 2.

Clovis (*kloe*-viss): One of the princely cities of the Gershan Lands, chiefly populated by ethnic-Berk humans. Clovis is the location of the Cathedral-Palace of the Western Reformed Church of Orneth and seat of the Primarch of the Western Reformed Church of Orneth. The Prince of Clovis has nominal power and is largely (and unofficially) subordinate to the Primarch. See fig. 1, 2.

Cogril (cog-*rill*): Vassal town of Soorin on the road between Keppa and Soorin. See fig. 3.

Daeara (*dae*-ar-a): Human realm at the southern tip of the Kaskev Mountains, nestled in a large valley at the southern end of the Kaskev Mountains where the range splits. Inhabitants of Daeara are called Daearans (dae-*ar*-ans). See fig. 1.

Dotinhinin (*doet*-in-hin-*in*): Capital city of Daeara. See fig. 1.

Dranomar (*dran*-oe-mar): One of four large Dwarven kingdoms beneath the surface of the Kaskev Mountains, alongside Aedon, Drenia, and Medria. Dranomar is roughly the depth of the Kingdom of Drenia and deeper than most of Aedon and Medria. Like Aedon and Medria, Dranomar profited from Drenia's decline through a combination of border skirmishes, mining, and industry where Drenia only saw loss. The dwarves of Dranomar are called Dranomars.

Drenia (*dren*-ee-a): One of four large Dwarven kingdoms deep beneath the Kaskev Mountains, alongside Aedon, Dranomar, and Medria. Roughly the same depth as the realm of Dranomar. Drenia fell into decline over the past century, having lost territory to wars against its neighbors, as well as to underground flooding which made several very productive mines untenable and forced the Drenians to abandon the cities of Mezar-Rin and Rael Dol-Buen. The crown to Drenia's humiliation was the loss of its city, Ikria, to a horde of orcs which now occupy it. Other major cities include its capital, Grednir, as well as Veres-Dyra, Kerolus, Goroboln, and Toen-Kosh. The dwarves of Drenia are called Drenians.

Ebariel (ee-*bar*-ee-el): Elven city in the western Elven Lands, in the low mountains on the eastern side of the middle of the Kaskev Range.

Eklenda (ek-*len*-da): Human realm on the western side of the Kaskev Mountains, towards the southern end of the range; west of Daeara and south of the Gershan Lands. See fig. 1, 2.

Elven Lands: Homeland of all Elven peoples on Paeta. A rich land of fertile fields and vibrant forests in the center and the east and the foothills of the Kaskev Mountains in the west. Lakes and rivers divide the landscape and a small number of cities concentrate a portion of the population, mainly Juin, the capital city, and Ebariel in the west. The Elven Lands are ruled by a series of councils of experts, notably the Guardian Council and the Seer Council. Only elves are permitted in the Elven Lands. No humans, orcs, or any other kind has successfully entered the Elven Lands in recent memory. See fig. 1.

Ezkaarn (*ez*-karn): City of the subterranean Dwarven kingdom of Aedon.

Garber (*gar*-ber): Vassal town of Yvel Principality, between Yvel City and Vidara; east of Bervale. See fig. 3.

Gavant (*guh*-vant) Vassal town of Versingit. Sits on the shore of the River Ballic, near the entrance of the marshes. See fig. 3.

Gersh (*gursh*): Region in western Paeta, landlocked between the Kaskev Mountains in the east, Eklenda to the south, Tamarkand in the west, and Berkmar and Markia to the north. Gersh is populated largely by a mixture of the Eklendan, Tamark, Berk, and Marin ethnicities of humans, with a small population of Daearan humans in the south. Gershan terrain is plains, forests, rolling hills and river valleys. Several rivers drain from the mountains and cross Gersh in a generally westward current. Lake Tald is the dominant terrain feature in Gersh, where several rivers meet and other rivers begin their flow out to the western seas. People from Gersh are collectively called Gershans, though there is no particular unity between Gershans. The Gershan Lands are a collection of thirteen city-states ruled by princes or princesses, which include Ardara, Boaz, Clovis, Heath, Ivria, Kangad, Keata, Kotara, Soorin, Versingit, Versinth, Vidara, and Yvel. See fig. 1, 2.

Ghetrak (*geh*-truk): Only known Orcish-built city. Primarily populated by orcs.

Gilliam (*gil*-ee-um): Human realm east of the Kaskev Mountains, on the southern end of the range. Daeara and the southern Kaskev Mountains are to the west, the Kingdom of Vostind is to the northeast, and the Koroz Ocean to the south. See fig. 1.

Ginrisian Sea (*gin*-riss-*ee*-un): Sea off of the northern Markian coast on the northern end of the Kaskev range. See fig. 1.

Golardeg (*goe-lar-deg*): City of hobgoblins on the eastern slopes of the Kaskev Mountains; home to Maglaban and the Barituul tribe of hobgoblins.

Goroboln (goe-ro-*boeln*): Dwarven city in the realm of Drenia.

Grednir (*gred*-neer): Capital city of the Dwarven realm of Drenia.

Gulf of Atlan (*at*-lan): Deep inlet at the southern end of the Atlayan Mountains. See fig. 1.

Gulf of Kuzore (koo-*zor*-eh): Body of water linked to the Korozian Ocean that separates Eklenda and Tamarkand. Provides the only seafaring port (Ivria) among the Gershan Lands. See fig. 1.

Gulf of Tazaria (ta-*zahr*-ee-a): Body of water forming an inlet between southeastern Eklenda, Daeara, and southwestern Gilliam. See fig. 1.

Heath (*heeth*): One of the princely cities in the Gershan Lands. The city overlooks the northern shore of Lake Tald. Roven is one of its vassal towns. Populated by ethnic-Marin and ethnic-Berk humans. See fig. 2.

Ikkal (ik-*kal*): Island on the far side of the Sea of Szolobad, southeast of Mardalon. See fig. 1.

Ikria (*ik*-ree-ah): Dwarven-built city; former territory of the Kingdom of Drenia. Currently occupied by orcs.

Iliarzin (*ill*-ee-*ar*-zin): City in the mountains frequented and traded in by goblins, hobgoblins, orcs, kobolds, gnolls, and the like.

Invader Side of the Mountains: Eastern slopes of the Kaskev Mountains and the lands that lie further to the east. The peoples of the Kaskev Mountains view the mountains as the center of the world and directions are given in reference to the mountains. See Glossary of Terms: Invader.

Ivria (*iv*-ree-a): Princely city in the Gershan Lands at the mouth of the River Chessa, on the shore of the Gulf of Kuzore. It is the only salt water port in the Gershan Lands. Populated by ethnic-Tamark and Eklendan humans. See fig. 2.

Juin (*joo*-in): Capital city of the Elven Lands, situated on the River Beros in the eastern portion of the Elven Lands. See fig. 1.

Kaitur (*kie*-tur): Capital of Berkmar, situated on the northwestern coast. See fig. 1.

Kandaneria (*kan*-dan-*ehr*-ee-a): City in the Dwarven realm of Aedon.

Kangad (*kan*-gahd): Princely city on the border of the Gershan Lands across from the Kingdom of Markia. The northern forests of Markia stretch down into Kangad's lands. Kangad is an agrarian-based territory. See fig. 2.

Kaskev Mountains (*kass*-kev): Long, generally north-south mountain chain bifurcating the continent of Paeta. See fig. 1, 2, 3.

Keata (*kae*-et-a): Princely city on the southern border of the Gershan Lands, abutting the border of the Kingdom of Eklenda. Keata is mostly populated by ethnic-Eklendans, with a strong presence of Tamarks. There is a small population of Marins who generally reside in unfavorable areas of the city. See fig. 2.

Keppa (*kep*-ah): Vassal town of Yvel City, located between Yvel and Soorin on the River Pelik. South of Serna, the town serves as an access point to several mines and quarries vital to industry and construction for Yvel Principality and elsewhere. Notable districts are Old Town, New Town, and South Village. See fig. 3, fig. 11: Map of the Town of Keppa.

Kerolus (ker-*oe*-lus): City in the Dwarven realm of Drenia.

Kogylar (*kog*-il-ar): Goblin city in the central western slopes of the Kaskev Mountains, built into the walls and floor of a vast sinkhole. Kogylar is a major trade hub for the various peoples of the mountains, with markets on every level of this vertical city offering goods from food and crafts to industry and slavery. The city also supports agriculture through diverted mountain streams and underground rivers to provide running water, sewage, and irrigation to the city and surrounding area. While predominantly goblin, its population also includes hobgoblins, orcs, kobolds, humans, and various half-breeds. Many of the goblin tribes of Kogylar answered Oygariyet the Great's call to muster. See fig. 2.

Koroz Ocean (koe-*roez*): Ocean south of the continent of Paeta. Named from a Gill-culture folktale after a sailor, Koroz, who explored the southern coast of Paeta. The same explorer appears in Tamark-culture tales, associated instead with the Korozian Ocean. See fig. 1.

Korozian Ocean (koe-*roez*-ee-an): Ocean east of the continent of Paeta. Named from a Tamark-culture folktale after a sailor, Korozi, who explored the western coast of Paeta. The same explorer appears in Gill-culture tales, associated instead with the Koroz Ocean. See fig. 1.

Kotara (koe-*tar*-a): Princely city in the Gershan Lands, nestled in the eastern side of the Samzik Mountains. Populated by ethnic-Tamark humans. See fig. 2.

Koult (*koolt*): Island off of the eastern coast of Thabia. See fig. 1.

Krogen (*kro*-ghen): Vassal town of Yvel City, sitting on the road between Yvel and Vidara, west of Garber and Bervale. Home of the Ten Wagons Inn. See fig. 3.

Ladern (la-*dern*): Vassal town of Yvel Principality, sitting on the northeastern shore of Lake Tald on the mouth of the Ballic River and at the edge of the Ballic Marshes. Ladern is a fishing town that also has transloading docks for transferring cargo between river boats, lake ships, and road transportation. See fig. 1, fig. 3.

Lake Tald (*tahld*): Large lake in the Gershan region on the western side of the Kaskev Mountains. See fig. 2, 3.

Lake Volosk (voh-*loesk*): Small lake nestled in the Samzik Mountains in the valley below the city of Kotara. See fig. 2.

Left Side of the Mountains: Region of the Kaskev Mountains, named from the perspective of those who live there and view the range as the center of the world (the cast-out races). On the eastern slopes it refers to the northern end of the mountains (or further north along the eastern slopes); on the western slopes it refers to the southern end (or further south along the western slopes).

Liberator Side of the Mountains: Western slopes of the Kaskev Mountains and the lands that lie further to the west. The peoples of the (Kaskev) Mountains view the Mountains as the center of the world and directions are given in reference to the mountains. See Glossary of Terms: Liberator.

Mardalon (*mar*-da-*lon*): Human realm at the eastern end of Paeta, beyond the wall of the Atlayan Mountains. See fig. 1.

Markia (mar-*kee*-a): Human realm at the northern tip of the Paetan land mass, northwest of the Kaskev Mountains and northeast of Berkmar. See fig. 1, 2.

Mastania (mahs-*tan*-ee-a): Continent to the east of Paeta, across the Red Ocean.

Medria (*med*-ree-a): Dwarven kingdom beneath the surface of the Kaskev Mountains, bordering Aedon and Drenia. Medria is located at a higher depth than Drenia or Dranomar, and roughly at the same depth as Aedon, even possessing some cities, outposts, strongholds, or other settlements with surface contact. Like Aedon and Dranomar, Medria profited from Drenia's decline by creating opportunities where Drenia saw loss.

Mernan (*mer*-nan): Vassal town to Yvel Principality, deeper within Yvel's territory. See fig. 3.

Mezar Rin (*meh*-zar *rin*): Lost Dwarven city of Drenia. Mezar Rin was lost to subterranean flooding.

Nustavian Sea (noo-*stav*-ee-an): Sea off of the Thabian coast, on the northern end of the Kaskev Mountains. See fig. 1.

Paeta (*pae*-ta): Large continent, centrally divided by the Kaskev Mountains. Many races live on Paeta, though it is predominantly inhabited by humans. See fig. 1.

Rael Dol-Buen (*rayl* dol *boo*-wen): Lost Dwarven city of Drenia. Mezar Rin was lost to subterranean flooding.

Ralang (rah-*lang*): Vassal town of Yvel City that sits on the eastern shores of Tald Lake. Ralang is predominantly a fishing town with a transloading dock for transferring cargo between lake-faring vessels, river barges from the River Guth, and wagons. See fig. 3.

Red Ocean: Ocean to the east of the continent of Paeta. See fig. 1.

Ren-Gol (*ren* gole): Recently-built Dwarven town, founded by Medrians in former Drenian territory.

Right Side of the Mountains: Region of the Kaskev Mountains, named from the perspective of those who live there and view the range as the center of the world (the cast-out races). On the eastern slopes it refers to the southern end of the mountains (or further north along the eastern slopes); on the western slopes it refers to the northern end (or further south along the western slopes).

River Ballic (*bahl*-ik): River which serves as the border between the principalities of Yvel and Versingit, originating in the foothills of the Kaskev Mountains. See fig. 2.

River Beros (*beh*-ros): River that runs off of the eastern slopes of the Kaskev Mountains, flowing through the Elven Lands, past the city of Juin before joining a larger network of rivers and lakes.

River Chessa (*cheh*-sa): River that runs from its source in the Kaskev Mountains to the Gulf of Kuzore in the west. Joined by the River Eron and the River Pelik at the city of Soorin. See fig. 3.

River Eron (*eh*-ron): River that originates deep in the Kaskev Mountains, joining the River Chessa and the River Pelik at the Gershan city of Soorin. The River Eron terminates at its joining with the River Chessa. See fig. 3.

River Guth *(guth)*: River that originates in the Kaskev Mountains and splits with the River Pelik. The River Guth flows by the princely city of Yvel and empties into Lake Tald. See fig. 3.

River Pelik (*pel*-ik): River originating in the Kaskev Mountains. It flows generally westward, splitting with the River Guth and joining the River Eron and the River Chessa at the city of Soorin, where it terminates. See fig. 3.

Roven (*roe*-venn): Vassal town of the Heath, one of the princely cities of Gersh. Just north of Heath, it lies on the road to Clovis. See fig. 2.

Samzik Mountains (*sam*-zik): Small range of mountains that separate Tamarkand from the Gershan Lands. See fig. 1, fig. 2.

Sea of Polonikin (poe-*lohn*-ik-in): Sea east of the Thabian coast and north of the Atlayan Mountains. See fig. 1.

Sea of Szolobad (*zoel*-uh-bad): Sea south of the Mardalon coast. See fig. 1.

Serna (*ser*-na): Vassal town of Yvel City, sitting on the road between Yvel and Soorin. Places of note include the Valley Spring Inn (burned down), Moradran Inn and Soup Shop, Mkaela's bakery, and Serna (Covendran) Manor. See fig. 3; *The Witches of Serna*, fig. 3: Map of the Town of Serna, *The Witches of Serna*, fig. 4: Map of the Town of Serna After the Fire.

Soorin (*soo*-rin): One of the princely cities of the Gershan Lands. Soorin controls the intersection of a major north-south road intersection with the River Pelik, the River Chessa, and the River Eron, and boasts a robust network of bridges. Soorin is an important Gershan city in trading and transloading ore from mines and quarries in the Kaskev foothills, as well as other cargo and curbing the historical threat of the Eklendans to the south. Sooriners are primarily ethnic-Eklendan humans, though despite this, possess a historical animosity towards the Eklendans of Eklenda. See fig. 2, 3.

Srkyavna (sir-*kyav*-na): Continent west of Paeta, across the Korozian Ocean.

Stone of Rykooth (*rie*-kooth): Dwarven-built fortress high in the Kaskev Mountain. Oygariyet the Great conquered Rykooth years prior to embarking upon his endeavor to reclaim the lowlands. See fig. 2.

Tamarkand (tam-ar-*kand*): Human realm at the western tip of the Paetan land mass. See fig. 1, 2.

Tawruk (taw-*ruk*): Capital of Tamarkand, sitting at the inner reaches of the Gulf of Kuzore. See fig. 1, fig. 2.

Tazarian Sea (ta-*zahr*-ee-an): Sea forming an inlet between southeastern Eklenda, Daeara, and southwestern Gilliam. See fig. 1.

Thabia (*thay*-bee-a): Human realm at the northeastern tip of Paeta. Thabia lies east of the Kaskev Mountains and north of the Elven Lands, Vostind, and Mardalon. See fig. 1.

Thabian Mountains: Mountain range extending east from the Kaskev Mountains into Thabia. See fig. 1.

Thabian Channel (*thay*-bee-an): Body of water separating Thabia from Koult; joins the Nustavian Sea and the Sea of Polonikin. See fig. 1.

Thafanmir (*thaf*-an-meer): Capital of Vostind and former capital of the ancient Ornethian Empire. See fig. 1.

Toen-Kosh (*toe*-in *kosh*): City of the Dwarven realm of Drenia.

Trukan (*troo*-kun): Town immediately across the River Guth from Yvel City. Trukan, for all intents and purposes, is part of Yvel City. The town grew around the ferry landing that carries all passengers and freight over the River Guth. It has some transloading docks to transfer cargo between barges that come from upstream, river boats, and transport over land.

Ungat (*oon*-gaht): Continent south of Paeta, across the Korozian Ocean.

Urrissio (*er*-iss-ee-oe): City of Dark Elves. Urrissio is built in a series of large caverns, far beneath the surface at the depth of the Dwarven Kingdoms.

Verenaz (ver-eh-*naz*): Dwarven city in the realm of Aedon.

Veres-Dyra (*ver*-iss *die*-ruh): City of the Dwarven realm of Drenia.

Verdunsk (vur-*dunsk*): Capital of the Kingdom of Markia, the northern-most realm of the western human lands of Paeta. See fig. 1.

Versingit (ver-*sing*-et): One of the princely cities of the Gershan Lands. Versingiters are primarily ethnic-Marin humans. Controlling the intersection of a major north-south road intersection with the River Ballic, Versingit trades ore and stone that come from mines and quarries in the foothills of the Kaskev Mountains, transloading them from barge to river boats out to the Tald Lake or on to land transports. Districts and landmarks of note are Back Town, East Gate Village, Little Berk Town, and North Gate Town. See fig. 2, fig. 3, fig. 5: Map of the City of Versingit.

Versinth (ver-*sinth*): One of the princely cities of the Gershan Lands, located between Gersh and the Kingdom of Markia. Its territory spans hills, forests, plains, and rivershore, with roads connecting south and west to the rest of Gersh. Versinth serves as a gateway for Markia and eastern regions coming through the northern passes of the Kaskev Mountains. See fig. 2.

Vidara (vih-*dar*-a): One of the princely cities of the Gershan Lands. The city overlooks the southern shore of Lake Tald. Populated by ethnic-Eklendans and ethnic-Tamark humans. See fig. 2, 3.

Vostind (voe-*stind*): Largest human kingdom in the eastern lands and largest remnant of the Ornethian Empire. Vostind is populated by ethnic-Vostindin humans. See fig. 1.

Yvel City (*wie*-vel): Capital of the Yvel Principality in eastern Gersh. Districts and landmarks of note include Baldinet ("New Markia"), Banik Square, Barkton, the Marin Quarter, Mikal's Hill, the Palace of Yvel, Roentown, Trent Abbey, and Trukan. See fig. 2, 3, and *The Witches of Serna*, fig. 9: Map of the City of Yvel.

Yvel Principality (*wie*-vel): One of the thirteen city-states of the Gershan Lands, Yvel is located in Eastern Gersh, between the foothills of the central Kaskev Mountains and the Tald Lake. Yvel has the following vassal towns: Borly, Serna, Keppa, Garber, Bervale, Krogen, Ralang, Ladern, and Mernan. See fig. 2, 3.

Zol (*zoel*): Dwarven city in the realm of Aedon.

Appendix V: Index of Figures, Artifacts, and Events of Lore and History

Achadar (*ak*-a-dar): First human ruler of Eklenda.

Agonich (ag-*on*-itch): Wizard who lived centuries ago; contributor to writings on the science of wizardry.

Arranel (*ar*-run-el): Elven author and member of the Blue Order, known for writings on blood magic awakenings among primarily elves, both recent and historic.

Battle of Borly (*bor*-lee): Siege of the town of Borly from winter of 793 to summer of 794 led by orcs of the Borys-Karang and goblins of the Talz. The siege ended as the First Yvel Regiment and the Crown Guard of Yvel arrived. See *The Witches of Serna*, fig. 10: Battle of Borly.

Battle of Serna Hills (*ser*-na): Series of skirmishes leading to a decisive engagement in the Spring of 794 in which the Prince of Yvel led the Arladran Battalion, the Ver'ail Battalion, and the Crown Guard of Yvel to destroy most of the horde of the Baki-Norn orcs, led by Dariyet the Great. See *The Witches of Serna*, fig. 5: Map of the Prelude to the Battle of Serna Hills; *The Witches of Serna*, fig. 6: Map of the Battle of Serna Hills.

Battle of Versingit (ver-*sing*-et): Endeavor of Oygariyet the Great's forces to seize the human city of Versingit in eastern Gersh during the summer of 794. Under Oygariyet's command, the assault was led by the Donbat-Karang orcs, reinforced by Talz, Borys-Karang, and Ahnh-Gorah orcs, Venjeer and Talz goblins, and Wiridil and Barituul hobgoblins, against the the Versingit Regiment and the city guard under Prince Eron Wrin'ail. See fig. 6: Map of the Battle of Versingit, First Assault; fig. 7: Map of the Battle of Versingit, Second Assault, Phase One; fig. 8: Map of the Battle of Versingit, Second Assault, Phase Two; fig. 10: Map of the Battle of Versingit, Second Assault, Phase Three.

Beren the Great: See Berin the Great.

Beres Wars (*beh*-rez): Series of minor conflicts over the past three centuries between Gilliam and its neighbors, with shifting alliances across the different wars.

Berin the Great (*beh*-ren): General in the Eastern Ornethian Empire in the late imperial period, who fought to preserve the cohesion of the empire and attempted to conquer the Elven Lands. Widely renowned as an effective leader and tactician. In the west, he is referred to as Beren the Great.

Bog Knight: According to folktales, a wandering or dying knight who was taken to or became lost in the realm of fairies long enough to transform into a fairy himself. Also called the "Knight of the Bog."

Book of Graffin (*graf*-in): Sacred text within the Book of Orneth, extolling the virtues of mercy and protection of the weak.

Book of Kostray: See Five Holy Books.

Book of Orneth (*oer*-neth): The holy scripture and authoritative record of the teachings of Orneth.

Church of Orneth: See Appendix I: Glossary of Terms: Church of Orneth; Appendix VII: The Western Reformed Church of Orneth.

Deweter's Chronicle of the Broken Lands (*doo*-ett-ur): Multi-volumed history books regarding the formation of Gersh and its neighbors after their secession from the Ornethian Empire.

Erkond (ehr-*kond*): Wizard who lived centuries ago; a contributor to writings on the science of wizardry, with a focus on magic controlling the air.

Erseyet/Ersiyet (ers-*ay*-yet/ers-*ee*-yet): Folktale among goblins and hobgoblins, in which a powerful warrior woman led her tribe and led them to victory and safety from humans and elves, beginning life anew. Among goblins she is called Erseyet and was known to be a goblin; among hobgoblins, she was a hobgoblin named Ersiyet (reflecting the spelling and pronunciation differences). The tale is a very old story among these peoples and possibly the foundation of their egalitarian societies.

Five Holy Books: Sacred portion of Ornethian scripture, also called the Book of Kostray, teaching the purities of spirit, intent, and purpose.

Girslig (*ger*-slig): Wizard who lived centuries ago; contributor to writings on the science of wizardry, with a focus on the magic of runes and their meanings.

God of Stuff: See Jirmishik.

Great Shattering: See Western Secession Wars.

Holy Rules: Guide to the ideal life and practice of a hobgoblin. The Holy Rules are viewed as a religious text and are adhered to devoutly by most tribes.

Imperial Secession Wars: Series of conflicts, fought eight centuries past, in which the western territories of the Ornethian Empire sought independence.

Ivriel (*iv*-ree-*el*): Wizard who lived centuries ago; contributor to writings on the science of wizardry, particularly about extending or sharpening the senses and viewing or perceiving places from a far distance.

Jirmishik (*jur*-mish-ik): Formal name of the chief deity in the Orcish pantheon, presiding over material possessions; commonly referred to as the God of Stuff.

Karap (ka-*rap*): Local legend among the Ikrian orcs. Karap codified customs and laws for conduct of the Orcish tribes of Ikria to reach a modicum of coexistence.

Knight of the Bog: See Bog Knight.

Lady of Grace: Formal title for a holy person; colloquially, a saint walking in the flesh.

Lady of Seven: Fairy from a folktale, said to have seven eyes, seven arms, and seven very skinny legs. Tales describe rituals to summon her, such as uttering 'seven' seven times, seven minutes after sunset. She is often depicted wearing a long skirt, seated on a lilypad, and drinking tea.

Lian (*lee*-un): Wizard who lived centuries ago; contributor to writings on the science of wizardry, with a focus on merging two or more existing creatures to create a whole new being (known as a chimera).

Leriyet (*lehr*-ee-yet): Legendary hobgoblin who briefly united all hobgoblins under one banner and authored the Holy Rules.

Ornethian Empire (*oer*-neth-ee-an): Human-ruled empire that controlled all lands on Paeta except for Mardalon and the severe climes of the Kaskev Mountains and surrounding ranges. Dominance ended with the Imperial Secession Wars eight centuries ago, followed by gradual collapse over the next five centuries.

Perganott (*per*-gan-ott): Wizard who lived centuries ago; contributor to writings on the science of wizardry, the art of sorcery, their differences, and how the two could complement one another.

Pit: Religious concept predating Ornethian belief, denoting a place in the afterlife for evil souls.

Ranus (*ran*-us): Wizard who lived centuries ago; contributor to writings on the science of wizardry, particularly on the barrier between life, death, and the space in between.

Saint Acrist the Judge (*ak*-rist): Disciple of Orneth during life, embodying justice, law, and mercy. Patron saint of victims, constables, jailers, executioners, convicted and released criminals, as well as repentance, redemption, and forgiveness. See Table 4: Saints and Values of the Western Reformed Church of Orneth.

Saint Aldira (al-*dee*-ra): Patron saint of peace and compromise. See Table 4.

Saint Andren the Builder (*an*-dren): Patron saint of carpenters, masons, coopers, wagonwrights, drivers, and architects. Writer and exemplar of construction, community, and productivity. See Table 4.

Saint Arenox the Smith (*aer*-in-*ocks*): Patron saint of crafters, particularly metalsmiths; scripture elevates pride derived from labor. See Table 4.

Saint Berikin (*behr*-i-kin): Patron saint of manual laborers and sailors; scripture promotes responsibility, obligation, community, and group consequence for individual indulgences. See Table 4.

Saint Eolanos (*ee*-oe-*lan*-oes): Patron saint of knowledge, students, teachers, librarians, scribes, books, mathematics, and the studies of science and history. See Table 4.

Saint Graffin the Defender (*graf*-in): Patron saint of the weak and oppressed. See Table 4.

Saint Haverst the Bold (*hav*-irst): Patron saint of boldness, audacity, and risk. Commonly prayed to by gamblers, businesspeople, soldiers, and military commanders. See Table 4.

Saint Inse the Hunter (*intz*): Patron saint of hunters, trackers, furriers, trappers, tanners, and cooks, as well as nature, cleverness, patience, and puzzles. See Table 4.

Saint Karbor the Farmer (kar-*bur*): Patron saint of farmers, ranchers, millers, butchers, herbalists, and cooks, as well as patience, resilience, anticipation, and timing. See Table 4.

Saint Kostray the Pure (*kos*-trae): Patron saint of causes, purity of intention, innocence, kindness, self-sacrifice, and martyrs. See Table 4.

Saint Nilas (*nie*-lus): Patron saint of platonic, familial, and romantic love, as well as fertility. See Table 4.

Saint Orlon the Thinker (*oer*-lon): Patron saint of patience, prudence, pragmatism, and forethought. See Table 4.

Valnos (*val*-noes): Long dead male ethnic-Daearan human wizard; studies focused on the exploration of the barriers between life and death.

War Among the Elven Peoples: Civil war fought among the elves approximately three thousand years ago.

Western Secession Wars: Conflict preceding the Imperial Secession Wars during which the newly seceded Western Ornethian Empire disintegrated. Also called the Western Shattering or the Great Shattering.

Western Shattering: See Western Secession Wars.

Appendix VI: Calendar Systems of Paeta, Revised

Within this world, upon which the continent of Paeta and the other nearby continents (Srkyavna, Mastania, and Ungat) exist, the solar day is twenty-four hours, the solar year is 360 days, and the lunar cycle is thirty days.

For humans, the year is divided into twelve months of thirty days, each organized into three ten-day weeks. The days, in order, are the following:

1) Morningday	6) Sortingday
2) Twosday	7) Laborday
3) Weddingday	8) Fryday
4) Thirstday	9) Playday
5) Breathday	10) Restday

The Western Human calendar treats the year 0 as the break between the East and West Churches of Orneth. The humans east of the Kaskev Mountains have an older date of their calendar's origin, 2634 years ahead of the western counterpart.

The human new year begins in the first month that plants noticeably bud, according to where the calendar was originally set. They celebrate the seasons placing a large emphasis on the new year in the spring.

Coincidentally, dwarves begin the new year on the same day, on average, as it is when the thaw on the surface has flooded the underground waterways the greatest, coinciding with the spring season's thaw and rains on the surface. Their calendar, developed over centuries, marked the most frequent day (measured by the amount of surface days, which they had to send an expedition to measure) when the floods began as the first day of the year and measured the number of days, on average, until the next first flood. The whole year is considered one 360-day month. The idea of 'days,' a different concept to most dwarves, came from trade with surface dwellers and the very few dwarves that ventured to the surface or Dwarven settlements that have surface exposure. To most dwarves, it is simply a measurement of time on their mechanical clocks that coincides with their preferences for sleeping and waking. Few know or understand that it has to do with the passing of the sun and moon.

Goblins, hobgoblins, and bugbears mark the new year by the winter solstice and celebrate the occasion which they call Longnight, the longest night of the year. Longnight celebrations take place on the winter solstice, the longest night of the year. It symbolizes a time of greatest safety and advantage against their historical enemies, the humans and elves as well as the mark of a new year. Customs differ by region, race, and tribe, but there is generally some sort of celebration involved.

Elves organize their calendar by the season, each of which is ninety days of the season. The end of the year is marked by summer's end. Elves have no set work or rest days, assuming that each elf will make the best choice for their livelihood and the needs of the many when work is needed.

Orcs, with their shorter and (generally) more violent lives, tend to have little use for marking the years. As orcs reach adulthood quicker than the other races (thirteen years is a mature adult orc analogous to a human of twenty years). They mark the time of day by the position of the moon or sun, and the time of the lunar cycle by the phase of the moon. City-dwelling orcs, whether in an orc city or another race's city, usually goblins or hobgoblins, usually use the calendar system utilized by the rest of the city. This is generally the Goblin Calendar, though there are cases where orcs use the Dwarven Calendar, such as the orcs that conquered the Dwarven city of Ikria.

Table 1: Comparison of Yearly Calendars Between the Races of Paeta

Season	Human Month	Goblin/ Hobgoblin Lunar Cycle	Elven Season	Dwarven Calendar
Spring	Ers (New Year)	Fourth Moon	Spring	New year begins with spring, when underground rivers flood. Dwarves mark 360 days individually until the next flood
	Anz	Fifth Moon		
	Aiz	Sixth Moon		
Summer	Youri	Seventh Moon	Summer (New Year)	
	Darri	Eighth Moon		
	Berenk	Ninth Moon		
Autumn	Banreni	Tenth Moon	Autumn	
	Ongkanir	Eleventh Moon		
	Nansima	Twelfth Moon		
Winter	Arinochis	First Moon (New Year)	Winter	
	Halinochis	Second Moon		
	Talinochis	Third Moon		

Table 2: Formulae for Calculating Year Differentials by Calendar

Western Human Year (benchmark)	Western Human Year + 0.
Eastern Humanw Year	Western Human Year + 2634.
Dwarven Year	Western Human Year + 9690.
Elven Year (spring)	Western Human Year + 17236.
Elven Year (summer, autumn, and winter)	Western Human Year + 17237.
Goblin Year (spring, summer, and autumn)	Western Human Year + 2320.
Goblin Year (winter)	Western Human Year + 2321.

Figure 12: Clerical and militant clergy of the Western Reformed Church of Orneth

Appendix VII: The Western Reformed Church of Orneth

Administered from the Cathedral-Palace in Clovis, the church is divided into core leadership and twenty-six orders; thirteen clerical and thirteen militant. The Primarch offers or gives guidance and influences political leaders through bishoprics (usually one per large city, such as the city-states of Gersh and the large, non-capital cities of other realms), and archbishoprics (usually one per capital city of a major realm). The bishops administer religious services and teachings to their cities, significantly through their subordinate clergy, but also manage the enterprise of clergy in the smaller towns and villages to ensure the Church's will and influence is felt amongst the commonfolk.

All clergypersons are members of one of the clerical orders with the exception of the Primarch. Primarchs are chosen from among the clerical orders and elected by the heads of each order, both clerical and militant (Table 3). The newly chosen Primarch leaves the order from which he or she originated. The heads of each order are elected from within each order, with a strong emphasis on seniority, and validated by the seated Primarch.

Each order is named after one of Orneth's saints and endeavors, at least in their charter, to study and embody the teachings of their patron saint. The orders militant mirror the clerical orders in the name, an overlap of some studies, and a shared mentality. However, the orders militant are, by their conception, a force of well-trained and well-equipped soldiers and leaders of lay soldiers.

There are comparatively fewer members of the militant orders, and thus there are few chapters assigned outside of Clovis. Unlike members of the clerical orders, most Reverend Knights maintain estates around Clovis or southern Berkmar, where they train themselves and any soldiers whom they retain. In this way, the Knights Militant are largely the same population as the nobility of Clovis. The vast majority of all clergy members are ethnic-Berks, to the point of discrimination against non-Berks and those of impure Berk heritage.

Clergy members are permitted to marry, sire, birth, and raise children, and own property. Reverend Knights often marry other Reverend Knights. It is highly frowned upon for clerical members to take up arms. Most would suffer reprimand or disciplinary action of some, dictated by other members of their order, if they were found to be involved with any violent incident, though the first members of the orders militant were clerical members, so there is existing precedent in certain circumstances.

Table 3: Saints and Values of the Western Reformed Church of Orneth

Saint Name	Moniker/Patrony/Matony	Themes
Graffin	"The Defender"	Mercy and protection (especially of the weak)
Andren	"The Builder"	Productivity and helpfulness
Kostray	"The Pure/The Healer"	Purity of heart, intent and purpose, and honor
Berikin	Workers	Responsibility, obligation, consequence, and
Orlon	"The Thinker"	Forethought and planning
Haverst	"The Bold"	Boldness, luck and audacity
Nilas	Love	Platonic, familial, and romantic love, and fertility
Eolanos	Learning/Knowledge	Study, learning, literacy, and teaching
Arenox	"The Smith"	Quality of work and craftsmanship
Karbor	"The Farmer/The Fisher"	Work to reward, farming, fishing, harvest, feast, pragmatism, and conservation
Inse	"The Hunter"	Patience, wisdom, and self-sufficiency
Aldira	Peace and Compromise	Compromise, negotiation, diplomacy, and peace

Table 4: Rankings within the Religious Orders of the Church of Orneth	
Primarch*	
Clerical	*Militant*
Chancellor of the Order	Master of the Order
Archbishop	Chapter Master
Bishop	
Abbot	Reverend Knight
Prior	
Elder	
Reverend	
Deacon	
Senior Brother/Sister	
Brother/Sister	
Younger Brother/Sister	
*The Primarch is the highest rank, but is not of any order.	
**Compared to any members of a clerical order, Reverend Knights are all ranked slightly inferiorly. Informally, seniority amongst the Reverend Knights creates a hierarchical system which allows the most senior of the group to interact with members of clerical orders.	

Figure 13: Dwarves and gnomes meeting humans and elves

Appendix VIII: Dwarves

Overview

Dwarves are a long-lived, reclusive people that largely live beneath the surface in vast underground cities. Their distinctive appearance of approximately one and a half paces in height, but stocky and muscular and, especially, the long beards worn by the males mark them among other humanoids. They are known for efficiency, industry, and exquisite craftsmanship. There are four powerful Dwarven monarchies: Aedon, Dranomar, Medria, and Drenia. While there are other Dwarven political powers, they are small clusters of settlements or isolated city-states.

There is a small diaspora of dwarves that become separated from their home and their people for various reasons. Knowing they will not be accepted by other dwarves, even their own countrymen, they choose to forge a new existence among other civilizations.

Physiology, appearance, and ethnicity

Dwarves generally stand to four feet tall; taller than goblins, but squatter than short humans. They have broad bone frames and tend to be muscular and stocky. This race generally have ruddy skin, especially those who live closer to the surface, though some communities deep underground tend towards paler complexions. Most have brown eyes, with hair color ranging from blond through red to brown, black, or grey. The male dwarves grow long beards, often reaching down to their bellies or long enough to braid, which some do. Men and women both style their hair as they prefer, long or short, shaved or braided.

Dwarves show signs of their aging in manners similar to humans, but on scales longer by decades. While they reach cultural adulthood at twenty years, aging slows significantly thereafter. A fifty-year-old dwarf will appear to still be in their twenties by human standards. Roughly, ten years of aging for a human appears as one year for a dwarf.

Dwarves seem to be roughly of the same ethnicity across Paeta, separated more by language and geographic barriers rather than any notable physical features.

Culture

Dwarves are an industrious, materialistic, and clannish society. They tend towards xenophobic views, allowing few or no non-dwarves into their cities and settlements. The ownership and production of fine goods is a considerable driver of culture and trade. Most dwarves hold the secrets of their trade very closely–even more so, when non-dwarves are concerned.

The ownership and production, and the ability to produce fine goods is a major driver of culture and trade for hard and soft power. Among their trade secrets are two definitive factors. Firstly, is their alliance with gnomes. Gnomes are humanoids wearing conical hats, small enough to fit several on the palm of a human or Dwarven hand. Gnomes, every bit as sentient as dwarves, are able to help with very precise measurements to aid Dwarven craftsmanship and finishing.

The secondary asset available to craftspeople is Dwarven magic, which largely focuses on a deeper, more agile interaction with crafted materials. Dwarves can achieve higher levels of precision and ask more of the materials they use than most craftspeople of other peoples. Note that though most Dwarven magic is oriented around industry and craft, they also study and practice magic for other purposes, including militaristic.

Society is focused around families and clans (as described in the following section), and align their interests around the clan, sometimes even before immediate family, then to their own governing bodies, then to Dwarvenkind at large. Clans tend to focus on a specific set of crafts and trades, master them, and dominate the local market.

Each city is ruled by a lord or lady, though some realms, such as Drenia, restrict the political power of their women. The more powerful clans represent their interests (such as rights for business ventures, defense, official positions and titles, contract arbitration, etc.) to their lord and fill the role of oligarchs. Smaller settlements are usually governed by a single clan and/or minor lord, but generally jurisdiction falls under the scope of power of a nearby city. Realms are ruled by a king or queen, but have to balance the interests of the influential clans, lords and ladies, and must frequently forge a consensus for successful rule.

Some dwarves leave their communities, whether exiled for crimes, war, or other problems; these dwarves sometimes form their own enclaves, typically underground but occasionally on the surface. Such dwarves are viewed as 'broken dwarves' by their fellow dwarves, to which a negative stigma is attached.

Governing Bodies and Societal Organization

Like humans, dwarves are born into highborn and lowborn families. Families that share multiple relations frequently form clans. Clans generally specialize in a particular vocation or several related crafts. Generally, the most powerful highborn clan will hold the title for the city or settlement, but the other powerful clans are represented with seats on a council to which the lord must pay respect. Though there is no official leverage that the other clans have over the lord, each clan has a business and all of the businesses are interrelated.

The ruling clan of each city typically possesses a seat on their monarch's council. The sovereign of each realm tends to be from the wealthiest, most powerful clan of the realm, and has the power to pass laws and decrees, declare war, make peace, establish and break diplomatic relations, set state policy, and so forth.

Titles tend to be hereditary within clans. Lowborn clans are limited from offices that they may hold. While guildmasters, and even in rare cases generals, may be lowborn, lords and ladies of Dwarven cities and realms must be highborn.

402

However, there is historical precedent for lowborn clans being raised to highborn status, thus providing a not impossible path to higher rankings.

Aedon, Medria, and many of the separate Dwarven city-states hold the rights of men and women to be equal. However, Drenia and Dranomar both limit the power of women in their societies.

Language

Dwarves speak separate languages by realm. The different dialects arose from geographic separation and other influences, but as the realms formed and controlled territory, each chose their mother dialect as an official state language.

Cities and Architecture

Most Dwarven cities are subterranean, built into the walls of both natural and created caverns. They favor larger caverns, for the benefits of air circulation, near underground sources of water, though it is also common for cities and settlements to be located near mineral veins, as the mining trade supplies key industries and exports. Extensive bridging is erected to ease transportation about the cavern, and aqueducts are positioned to supply water throughout. Cities are predominantly made of stone, though some structures are formed of metal; steel, for example, in cases where the structural integrity of stone is unsuitable. These settlements are feats of design and engineering, as well as showcasing the dwarves' remarkable ability to impose their will on the rock, clay, metals, and soil.

Cities are predominantly composed of residences, most of which are clan halls in which related families dwell, with craft industries and workshops built directly into them. Most cities have several markets. Walkways, bridges, and stairs connect the city's various zones. The cavern of the city will usually have hand-cranked pulleys attached to cargo elevators to more efficiently transport large amounts of goods and materials over vertical distances.

Most underground roads are cut and maintained by Dwarven settlements, though they have also served as a boon to civilizations that are hostile to dwarves, such as the orcs that conquered and occupied the Drenian city of Ikria. Dwarven roads are generally wide and tall enough for at least two wagons to travel side by side so as to accommodate travelers and caravans to safely pass each other from opposite directions.

Arms and Armor

Dwarven goods are of exquisite quality, surpassing most human-made goods. Even day-to-day wares are crafted, with the assistance of gnomes, Dwarven magic, or simply the Dwarven pride and obsession with quality, to exacting precision. Additionally, the most common application of Dwarven magic focuses on their crafts with the focus of more intimately interacting with the materials, such as altering material strength, heat dispersion, etc.

As it applies to the production of arms and armor, dwarves produce fine mail and resilient plate armor. Most of their warriors wear a combination of mail and plate. Their plate is harder and more durable than even Daearan water steel, yet lighter at the same time, even when crafted by only mundane methods.

Dwarves favor one- and two-handed axes, hammers, and all-steel crossbows. They sometimes carry spears and other polearms and, less commonly, swords. Wood being scarce in the underground realms, most items made from this material are polished wooden sculptures possessed by wealthy clans. Therefore, axe and hammer hafts, spear shafts, and so forth, are frequently manufactured of iron, steel, or other tough metals. They often carry medium-sized steel shields, though larger ones are sometimes carried as part of sieges.

Crossbows are entirely made of steel, as well as the bolts. The limbs generally require magical crafting techniques in order to allow the steel to bend in ways not natural to mined ores. The bowstring and crank cables in the crossbow are steel wire or cable.

Siege weapons for dwarves are primarily great siege crossbows: a large, crew-served crossbow with all steel construction and all steel bolts the size of spears, and battering rams with protective enclosures. These items, too, are generally constructed entirely of steel. The siege crossbows are highly accurate with fine sights and the ability to adjust them precisely with the aid of gnomish crew members.

Organization for war

Dwarven fighting forces across most of the realms organize into legions, though the size and composition of most legions varies by realm and the city in which they are garrisoned. Nearly uniformly, they are well-equipped with heavy armor and melee weapons. Many legions have specialized siege troops and crossbow units. In rare instances, dwarves employ wizards or sorcerers for military purposes. Sorcerers are exceptionally rare and, often, their gifts do not coincide with a military purpose or the craft which their clan holds dear. For more information about sorcery, see *The Witches of Serna*, Appendix IX: Blood Magic.

Soldier is the lowest rank amongst the Dwarven troops. Sergeants are the most common leader, and the scope of their responsibilities can differ significantly. Some sergeants are in charge of only a few soldiers or occupy some form of staff position, while others have great influence or direct supervision over dozens of soldiers and other junior sergeants. The officer ranks begin with minor captain, major captain, high captain, and general. In most cases, officers in legions are highborn, though there is fairly common precedent for lowborn sergeants that excel and show great valor or cunning to be raised to low captain and progress their career from that point.

Appendix IX: Ratfolk, Gnolls, Bugbears, and Ogres

Ratfolk: Overview

Beneath the streets of the Gershan city-state of Versingit lies a vast network of catacombs, cisterns, sewer tunnels, and forgotten places. Within those dark places are disparate enclaves and underground villages of bizarre-looking rodent or rat people. They speak the same Marin language as their surface-dwelling neighbors, albeit with some differences in accent and slang that have arisen over centuries of vertical separation and isolation. They are roughly the same height and build as humans, though their faces, ears, hands, and feet are decidedly more like mice or rats. The ratfolk are reviled by the surface-dwelling Marins, considering them to be thieves and bad luck.

Gnolls: Overview

As tall as orcs, but some odd mix of a bipedal creature and a canine. They frequently have canine heads of various types and canine hind legs but with broader feet for upright walking. Their arms and hands are more human-like, though their fingers are clawed. Their bodies are furred like canines. Their society is highly tribal, similar to orcs, but that have nuanced social standing and martial sense about their culture that is a bit more akin to hobgoblins.

Bugbears: Overview

Bugbears are the third and largest member of the family of goblinkind. They are roughly the same height as orcs and gnolls, though they are relatively hairless, like hobgoblins and goblins, though they tend to be hairier than their goblinkind cousins (and humans). Their skin tones match those of their goblinkind brethren, primarily blue, purple, red, and grey. They grow their hair long and the males grow their facial hair long, as well. Their frames are broad, lean, and muscular, in general. Their eyes and ears are as large as those of a goblin. Bugbears have powerful jaws and sharp teeth.

Ogres: Overview

Standing as tall as a well-built house or three (human) men standing on top of each other's shoulders. Ogres are muscular and powerful, but also fatty and carry much extra flesh on their bodies. Despite their size, they are quick and relatively agile at scale. Their long legs and powerful bodies allow them to overtake horses at a gallop, tumble buildings, or pick up humans with one hand and throw them. They have fair to tanned skin and sloping foreheads. Ogre society is loosely organized into small, matriarchal tribes led by a priestess.

Credits

Cover design by Sam Kipp and Morgan Spring-Glace.

All maps by Luke Bauer.

All illustrations by Morgan Spring-Glace.

Calligraphy by Esther Wong

About the Author

Morgan Spring-Glace grew up in Massachusetts, went to college, joined the United States Army in 2004 and served for twenty years (and one day), and has settled in the Midwest United States. He thinks too much and excels at losing arguments. He is a nerd and a gamer. This continues to be a very fulfilling progression from when he first drew a map of the town of Serna for a campaign setting in 2011. For more information, updates and previews of future content, visit www.morganspringglace. com.

Note from the Author

I hope you enjoyed this installment of *The War of the Mountains*.
Please consider leaving me a review on the Amazon page, with
what you did or did not enjoy. The more reviews we get, the more
the books sell and the more I know to keep writing more for you.
Rest assured that I read every review. Feedback is always a gift.
https://www.amazon.com/gp/product/B0FS9N752H

Thanks. I do hope you enjoyed this installment and I'll have the
next book, Winter Fever out by Autumn 2026.